Ruckus Royale

The Bedlam Boys

Ruby Vincent

Published by Ruby Vincent, 2021.

Author's Note:

This book is much darker than my usual fare. Do not use previous
Ruby Vincent books as a guide. Ruckus Royale features consensual
non-consent, violence, and gore.
Read with this in mind.

Prologue

Branches snatched and tore at me, ripping red seams on my arms, cheeks, and exposed legs.

Legs? Why were my legs bare?

I jumped off a landing, splashing down in a puddle of mud that clung to cover my pale skin, and I still running, running, running.

Why were my legs bare?

Because I ran.

They came and I ran so far and fast, I had no time to put on pants. The kettle left screaming on the stove. My phone charging by my bedside. My sister soundly asleep in her bed. All left behind.

Why? Why am I running?

The thought passed and I picked up speed. Muscles burning, lungs aching, my feet dotted barely there imprints on the soft earth. I was flying. Flying away from the monsters.

Who?!

Who was chasing me? Why was I running?

I snapped my neck around, searching the endless dark for shifting shadows. Who was coming for me?

Cold bit into my skin, freezing the mud that was my only cover. No owls to chant my way. No creatures to skitter from my presence. I ran too far into the forest—farther than the animals dared to tread, and where the trees drew closer together as if to share warmth.

I had to be safe. No one would come this far. No one was chasing me.

I slowed, stumbling out into a clearing, the release from the pressing trees that open their arms to the edge of the cliff.

I stepped to the rim, peering down to the gawping abyss below.

This cliff has a name. A funny one that always made me laugh.

I laughed then. Huge, racking guffaws that stole the little air left in my aching chest.

I was fine. I was safe. Whatever was chasing me was gone now. I could go home.

I turned, and walked into their arms.

A hand clamped on my mouth, penning in the cry before it could leave my lips.

"Does the kookaburra laugh or does it scream?" Their mouth pressed to my ear, pouring their words directly into my soul. "Does the mighty kingfisher cry or does it dream? Where are you, kookaburra?"

"Please, stop," I rasped. "I didn't mean to. I never wanted this."

They couldn't hear me. Their hand swallowed my plea as the rest of them took everything else.

"Tell me, oh, tell me," they whispered. "Why is nothing as it seems?"

Hands cradled my back and shoved. I soared over the edge. For a short, glorious moment, I was flying.

Then I fell. Fell to the bottom of the cliff with the funny name.

And I laughed.

Chapter One

"This way, everyone. Follow me." The small, triangular flag whipped high overhead, boasting its crest for all to see. "Did you all bring your lunch?"

A few people murmured yes.

"Perfect." Zoey's cheery voice gathered us around her like bees to the queen. "This is Homer Green, as we call it. At any time you'll find students hanging out, studying, or running around here."

I scanned the sprawling campus, taking in the rising spires, stone facades, sprawling waves of green, and countless coeds walking among them. Bedlam University looked impressive in the brochures, the glances out the window as I drove past, and the single time I gathered a trace of courage and came here for a frat party. None of that compared to seeing this campus up close and personal under the beaming sun.

"Sit down and let's get to know each other."

I slid my backpack off my shoulder and tugged out the blanket. The orientation packet said to bring it and I was nothing if not a sucker for lists and instructions. I was among the few.

Most of my group pulled faces sitting on the dew-covered grass. I dropped on my blanket and pulled out my lunch.

"How smart were you bringing a blanket."

A shadow fell over me. I glanced up into shining green eyes and a wide smile.

"Mind if I sit with you?"

"Course not. Go for it."

She plopped next to me, wiggling her shoulder against mine like we shared a cool secret. Up close, she was even more beautiful.

A light dusting of freckles covered her round nose, and soft blonde strands flowed past her shoulders and mine. She was so close they were blowing in my face.

"How old are you?" she whispered, and then it made sense why she was sitting so close. People saved the intrusive questions for under their breath. "You don't look like a freshman."

"I'm a junior, technically. I did two years getting my associate's and then transferred to Bedlam."

She gasped. "Really? Me too. I—"

"Excuse me, ladies." Zoey pinned on us. "If I could have your attention, we're going to play an introduction game to get to know each other."

"Sure thing, Zoey," said my new nameless friend. "Sorry about that."

"All right, this is an easy one. We'll go around and either replace or add our name into the title of our favorite movie or show," Zoey explained. "For example, I'm Zoey and my favorite show is *Doctor Who*. So I'd say I'm Zoey Who. You guys have three guesses to name my show from Zoey Who. Got it?"

"Got it," we chorused.

"Okay." She passed to the guy next to her. "You first."

My blanket mate tapped me. "Hey, mind if we share? I forgot to pack a lunch."

"Didn't you read the information packet?"

She shrugged. "Lost it."

I gaped like she said she lost her kid in a shopping mall and couldn't be bothered to go back and get them.

"Uh, yeah." I slid over half my sandwich. "Hope you like caprese sandwiches."

She took a bite and moaned. "I do now."

I passed over the kettle chips and my spare water bottle too. It was ingrained a long time ago to make more food than I'd eat. Older sisters were forever stealing food off your plate.

"Your turn," chirped Zoey.

It took me a second to realize she was looking at me.

"Oh, sorry. Mine is Rainey Day Afternoon."

"Rainey?" A guy in glasses and suspenders slurped a beer I assumed he was old enough to drink. "Is Rainey your name?"

"Yep, Rainey's my name, so what's the movie?"

"Ooh, ooh," cried a girl across from me. "I got it. It's dog. *Dog Day Afternoon*!"

"Got it in one."

Suspenders Guy laughed. "Is that really your favorite movie, or could you just not resist the symmetry of Rainey Day Afternoon?"

"Both."

We shared a smile, and I was forced to notice how cute he was when he smiled.

I ducked my head, cheeks warming. First day of university after years of home and virtual school. The last thing I should be doing is flirting with a cute guy who dressed like characters from my favorite old movies.

None of this is why I'm here.

I drew my backpack closer, hand falling over the zipped pocket on the side. There would never be time for cute boys with cuter smiles.

Never again.

"Next."

I glanced up at my blanket mate and found her staring at me. I flung my hand off the pocket, stiffening as her eyes narrowed. Did she know what I had been thinking? She was certainly boring into me, like she wanted to peer inside my head.

"Rainey?" she asked. "As in... Rainey de Souza?"

"Yes. How did you know that?"

"It's me! Paris," she cried. "Paris Keller."

She turned to the group. "We got our associate's degrees from Bedlam Community College's online classes. We were all a bunch of names and pictures on the screen, but I remember you," she said, whirling on me. "I thought your name was so pretty."

"Awesome," Zoey said. "You made your first friend here before you even met."

Zoey and the others clapped for us like we performed a magic trick.

"Cool to meet you in person, Paris. Now that I think of it, I remember your name popping up too."

"My turn," she said. "Paris Park."

The game continued on around me as I shifted my bag behind my back. Paris didn't know. No one knew. No one could help.

Eventually, we wrapped up our lunchtime detour and resumed orientation.

Paris stuck close to me, chattering away in my ear about how cool it was to go to an actual college, and that she couldn't wait for the parties, late-night sessions, and the guys guaranteed as part of the package. It seemed I had made a new friend despite my resolution to avoid anything with friend in the title for the foreseeable future.

"—though my brother goes here." Paris dropped her voice as we went into the library. "He's been at Bedlam since freshman year. A senior, though. You'll meet him tonight."

"I will?"

"Yeah. He and his friends are throwing a party. I'm going, so you're going."

"Thanks," I said simply. I'd make an excuse to get out of it later. "Sounds fun."

"So, don't be shy. Tell me about yourself."

Her beaming smile drew it out of me. "There isn't much to tell, really. I'm a major geek. I'm into all things sci-fi, love anime, and my idea of a fun night is playing Catan while passing around a bucket of fried chicken—and yes, that's how I spend most of my Saturday nights."

She flapped a hand. "Be still my heart, you've found your soul mate."

"You're kidding."

"You're looking at the girl who has every single Catan expansion pack, and watched Ouran High School Host Club four times."

"Are you single? Because...?"

Paris smacked my arm, cracking up.

"The only cool thing about me, according to Ivy, is that I'm into archery. Been doing it since I was six."

"That is cool. You have to teach me."

I smiled in place of answering.

The tour continued with Paris keeping up the conversation and Suspenders Guy, whose name was Alfie, tossing me one-sided smiles over his shoulder. It was almost a relief when my group was separated to choose our classes, and those two ended up walking down a different hall.

Paris was nice, but she was distracting me. I couldn't afford to be distracted. This time, I would see everything. Hear everything. Notice everyone. This time would be different.

Zoey waved us into a small computer lab. I chose a seat at the back, opened my pack, and fished out my notebook. I chose my classes two weeks ago, though they didn't let new students register without going through the song and dance of orientation. Even if those students were transfers who already did two years of this.

Ten minutes later, I was signed up for Bankruptcy Fundamentals, Civil Rights Law, Ethical Issues in Law, and Land Transfer.

Not the most exciting course schedule, but I left the fun, philosophical law classes in my freshman and sophomore years. Now it was time to learn the things that would launch me into law school. If I would still be able to go after—

I shut the door on that thought. Breathing slowly, I peeled my fingers off the mouse, releasing the death grip.

I was going to Harvard Law. That was the plan, and I never veer from the plan.

"Done?"

I jumped. Zoey had some soft footsteps.

"Yes, I'm done."

"You can head out. It's too nice a day and too nice a campus to be shut inside."

"Okay, yeah. Thanks, Zoey, you're..." I smiled at her. "You're a really lovely person."

She beamed. "Ah, Rainey. Thank you. You are too."

No, I'm not. I brushed past her. *That's why I'm here.*

Paris was chilling on the stone steps, messing with her phone when I came out. Of course she was. She'd have had her course schedule chosen in advance as well.

"Hey, Rainey."

"Hey." I dropped next to her.

"Ugh. My brother is the literal worst. I know all siblings say that about each other, but only I'm telling the truth. Look at this." She flashed the screen at me.

Assface: You better not show up tonight. If you do, the first impression everyone on campus gets of you is being thrown out on your ass.

Paris: I'd like to see you try. I'm coming, and fuck you for not inviting me. I had to hear about the party from Roan.

Assface: Roan's out on his ass now too. You both have fun making other plans for tonight.

"Charming, isn't he?" She shook her head. "One year between us and he treats me like a baby."

I seized on my chance. "But if he doesn't want you there, isn't that a no for your plus-one too? I'd rather not piss off the Great and Terrible Assface."

She laughed. "You're funny. Why didn't you tell me you were funny? My brother is all bark, no bite. Besides, tonight's the night Dante announces the Kings of Ruckus. Assface and his friends are so sure it'll be them, they already arranged the *coronation*."

The words blurred on the screen. "The Kings?" I rasped. "D-Dante?"

"Oh, sorry, I should explain," she chattered on in a tone too bright for the thoughts going through my head. "Dante hosts an online secret radio show. He—"

"I know who he is," I cut in. "I grew up in Bedlam."

"You did?" Paris cocked her head. "Then how are we just meeting today?"

"I was homeschooled. We had a farm. Grandma needed help running it, so we did chores all morning, and school in the afternoon. Even way out with the chickens, I heard of Dante's show, and the Kings of Ruckus." I found myself taking the phone from her grasp. "You're saying your brother is going to be named a King?"

"That's what he thinks," she scoffed. "Probably right too. He and his friends do whatever, and get whatever they want around here."

"Why?"

Paris heaved a sigh. "The whole story is going to come out soon enough. I'm not skipping to the end because right now you like me, and I want to be friends a little longer." Paris got to her feet, slipping her phone from my grasp. "See you tonight. Right here at ten o'clock, yeah?"

"Yes," I said before she ended her sentence. "I'll meet you here. Can't wait for my first college party."

She waved goodbye, running off to meet a group of girls idling on the sidewalk. Orientation was over for the day. We returned tomorrow for the tour of our individual colleges, then I was officially set loose on Bedlam University.

I lifted my pack on my shoulder, brushing the pocket as I did so.

Transferring to this campus was the easy part. Tonight, and all there was ahead of me, that was impossible. Not hard. I wished for hard. Fucking prayed for it. I did and survived hard things my whole life.

What I had to do was impossible, and as surely as Paris foresaw the end of our friendship, this was going to break me.

TEN O'CLOCK ON THE dot, I was sitting on the same steps in the same red boots I wore to orientation. I traded everything else out for a clutch bag, slinky black top, and striped skirt. Ivy would be pissed if she found out I raided her closet, but I didn't have anything remotely party-worthy in mine.

"Rainey!" Paris arrived with her girl band in tow. "Come and meet everyone."

I ran up, waving to all the new faces. Paris was gorgeous in a hot-pink dress and high white boots. It was very seventies go-go dancer, but somehow looked incredible on her. Paris's crew didn't bend the fashion rules quite as much. They were dressed similar to me in miniskirts and thin, swishy tops.

"This is Elise, Presley, Zara, and Amy. We went to high school together," Paris said.

Elise had a lithe, dancer-type thing going on. She was pretty in all the obvious ways. Presley, though, had small features. A small nose, small mouth, and eyes close together. Still, when she smiled at me, it transformed her whole face.

I shook Zara's hand, marveling that her unblemished tan skin was as soft as it looked. Long, dark hair ran down her back, and curled tighter the closer you got to the end. As for Amy, she had the same girl-next-door vibe that Paris gave off. Naturally, she fit right in with this gorgeous group.

"Guys, this is Rainey. She's Bedlam-born, but homeschooled."

"Ahh." They all nodded like that explained everything.

To be fair, it did explain a lot. Bedlam had two elementary schools, two middle schools, and one high school. It was hard not to know everyone around here.

"Let's go," Presley whined. "Gunner should be doing Jell-O shots off me right now."

"Gunner should be doing Jell-O shots off the dumpster lid that'll protect his new home." Paris hooked an arm through mine and marched me off with the group. "That guy's the worst."

"You say everyone's the worst."

"You're right, I'm sorry. Assface is the reigning champion of jerks, but Gunner takes a close second."

"You say that because you're biologically programmed to be blind to how hot your big bro is," Zara returned.

"I say that because he used to put his boogers in my hair."

I stifled a snort, then marveled that Paris had made me do that.

I laughed? Two months, four days, and six hours, and it's a snappy comment about boogers that finally makes me laugh.

I eyed Paris Keller out of the corner of my eye. Yes, she was definitely a dangerous distraction if she got me for one second to believe I was just another normal college girl.

I was silent on the walk across the shadowed campus, letting their inside jokes and unknown names wash over me. I was going to this party for one reason, and one reason only.

Pounding music reached our ears, leading the way as we rounded a building and arrived on scene with the dozens of people dressed like us. Blue, red, purple, and orange light bled through the blinds, casting its glow on those privileged enough to enter.

The people, the lights, the noise, the music—it rushed inside my head, filling to bursting.

I stopped dead, holding my pounding head as my heart raced to match.

I was here for one reason, and I couldn't do it. *What the hell was I thinking? I can't do this. I can't do any of it! I have to go now.*

Spinning on my heels, I set off blindly, clutching my heaving stomach.

A hand grabbed my wrist. "Rainey, where are you going? It's this way."

"Rainey." Suddenly Zara and Amy were in front of me. "We talked about ourselves the whole time. Narcissists. Tell us about yourself." They threw their arms around me. Penning me in. Cutting off escape. "We'll grab some drinks, find a spot inside, and grill you without mercy."

"I... I..."

They led me up the steps and inside, closing the pine double doors shut behind me.

Taking a deep breath, I exhaled slow. It did nothing to calm my heart, head, or stomach. I had to get out of here. Out of this house, this school, this town, then—

Then what? a voice whispered. *Drive to Chaney Bridge and jump off? Because there's no way you'd be able to live with yourself.*

Tears filled my eyes. It's not fair.

"I didn't ask for this."

"Damn," said Zara. "It's only ten and this place is packed. Let's go out on the porch. Paris, Rainey, get the beers."

Orders given, Paris reclaimed my arm and tugged me after her. I stumbled behind, dizzy and fighting to breathe.

"Hey, you okay?" Paris leaned me against the kitchen counter. "You don't look well. Want me to get you some water?"

I just nodded.

"Whoo! Yeah!"

My fingers dug into my temples. How were they getting even louder? I could barely think for the headache splitting my skull.

Paris returned, pulled away my hand, and pressed the cool bottle to my forehead. "I know what made you sick."

I snapped up, eyes popping. "What? What are you talking about?"

She drifted over my shoulder. "That's enough to turn anyone's stomach."

I followed her line of sight, eyes growing wider. Standing in the middle of the living room was a half-naked bronze god being doused with honey by the hooting crowd. A strange enough sight. Add to it the three girls rubbing and licking his pecs clean, I had a wild moment where I wondered if I was really stuck at some awful party and not tossing in my bed at home, tormented by endless nightmares.

The girls were really going to town—tonguing him all over like there was a prize at the end of the all-you-can-eat buffet.

He slipped his fingers through the lining of his boxers and whipped them down. The girls descended on his cock like piranhas.

"Fucking hell!"

Paris seized my shoulder and spun us both around. Why me too?

"Dammit, Cairo! Someone bleach my eyes."

"Do you know him?" I asked.

"Course I do. That's General Assface himself."

"That's Ass— That's your brother?" I twisted, tearing from the moaning girls and sticky abs, and traveled up his face as he raised his head. Our eyes locked across the room.

"I've had enough of this, de Souza. Go home. Now."

"Please, just listen." My scuffed shoes squeaked on the linoleum, growing louder and more piercing as I chased him. "Listen! I'm telling you something isn't right. I—"

A wall of black appeared before me. I slammed into a hard body and bounced off, falling flat on my back. Brilliant pools of green captured me, holding my reflection in their depths, and flicking away before I could capture him.

Stepping over me, his dirty boot came down on my hair, and he walked off.

"Asshole!"

He didn't bother to turn or slow his stride. I was dismissed as quickly as I crashed into his life.

I straightened—headache fading, pulse slowing. "Cairo."

He frowned, as if hearing his name. As if sharing the memory.

"You know my brother?"

I almost forgot Paris was there.

"You can't live in Bedlam and not have heard of the Bedlam Boys," I said, too soft for her to hear me.

He shook the girls off. Yanking up his clothes, he barreled straight toward us.

"Here it comes," Paris muttered.

Five foot ten worth of muscles, ink, and sharp cheekbones stormed into the kitchen. Our second meeting, and his beauty struck me numb—even as anger rose to burn it out.

"What the fuck are you doing here, Evie?"

"I told you I was coming, but I guess now I know why you didn't want me here. You're not happy unless you're mentally scarring me for life."

Seeing the two of them together, it wasn't surprising I didn't immediately peg them as brother and sister. Cairo was bronze, where she was porcelain. They were both gifted with green eyes, but hers set in wide, round orbs while Cairo's were hooded. And angry.

"Get out."

Flipping her hair, Paris rolled her eyes. "Make me."

Cairo hefted her screeching over his shoulder.

Bluff called immediately.

"Put me down! Put me down right now, Cairo."

He turned to go and paused, locking on to me. I backed up on instinct.

"Hello, who is this?" Cairo dumped his sister on her feet, then came for me.

I scooted away fast.

Bang!

His fist slammed on the counter, rattling the vodka bottles, and blocking my retreat. I swallowed hard as he molded to me, gluing our bodies together with honey, closer than the day I slammed into him.

"Evie, you know where the door is," he tossed over his shoulder.

"Where did you come from?" Cairo's nose skimmed my cheek, stealing the breath needed to answer. "I know, and tasted, every woman in this town between the ages of eighteen and twenty-six. How did you slip away?"

He doesn't remember me. Again, rage and awe battled for dominance. Rage pulling ahead. *Asshole steps on me like trash on a sidewalk, and can't be bothered to remember.*

"Rainey transferred in today," Paris said. "She got her associate's online like me."

"That explains it."

"Can— Can you give me some space, please?" I shoved on his chest.

Cairo held my wrists fast. "Don't tack *please* at the end of a demand. It weakens the command and cheapens your fake politeness. But since you asked so nicely, no." A smirk stretched across his lips, revealing long, gleaming canines. He dropped my hands down to his waist, nudging his thigh between my legs. "I won't give you space."

I gaped at him. Was this guy real?

"Back off, perv." Paris elbowed between us. She didn't need tips on making demands of him. "Your queen bee has arrived. She'll be wanting your honey."

Paris whisked me away. I scraped up enough dignity not to glance back for one more look.

Amy and the girls were staked out on the patio chairs, flirting with a group of guys trying to appear aloof and unaffected by standing six feet away.

It wasn't much quieter out here. Speakers were rigged to pump Years and Years throughout the whole town.

"I'm sorry about him." Paris ignored the interest flashing her way and sat us in an armchair. "I tried to warn you."

"I didn't realize he was Cairo Sharpe."

"So you do know him."

"It's better to say I know of him," I explained. "I do know your dad though."

"Ah." Paris dropped her eyes. "His dad, not mine. Sharpe and Keller. He's my half brother."

I read her expression. "I won't ask if you don't want me to."

She smiled a smile that wasn't one at all. "It's okay, I don't mind talking about it. Mom was married to his dad when she cheated on him with mine. We were eight and nine years old, and Mom packed me up in the middle of the night and rushed out to meet my new dad idling at the end of the street. The divorce was, to put it kindly, messy."

"Ouch. I'm sorry, I can't imagine how hard it was for you."

Her gaze drifted off. "Harder for Cairo, I think. He woke up one morning and his family was ripped in half."

"So did you," I said, squeezing her hand.

"Yeah, but... my mother didn't leave me behind."

My heart panged painfully in my chest. "Yeah," I whispered—another one unheard. "That'll mess you up." I shook my head. "Damn, we're getting deep right out the gate. Now I'm going to start thinking of your brother as a wounded bird who needs someone to fix his broken heart. I've always been a sucker for those."

"Don't fall for it," she said, bumping my shoulder. "Cairo Sharpe is many things, but a wounded bird is not one of them. I'd say he's closer to a wounded wolf."

Twice as deadly when he bleeds. "Good to know."

Elise stuck herself between us. "Is she telling you all about the Bedlam Boys, our infamous hosts? Wow. What I wouldn't do to be the sixth in that orgy."

"I know about the Bedlam Boys," I said. "Cairo Sharpe, Arsenio Creed, Roan Banks, Jacques Stone, and Legend St. James. We weren't that sheltered out in the muck. My sister had a run-in with the Bedlam Boys a few years ago."

The girls huddled in. "What happened?"

"They were hanging lifelike corpses off the top of Chaney Bridge as a Halloween prank. The driver in front of her slammed the brakes and Ivy rear-ended her. Ivy got out and chased them off with a tire iron. That's my sister."

"Um, she's awesome," Paris said. "Where is she? Invite her to join us."

I shook my head. "Ivy moved out two years ago. After our grandma died."

"Oh, I'm sorry."

"Let's not bum ourselves out," Amy said, though she rubbed my shoulder in sympathy. "Back to the lawless hotness. Your sister went after the Bedlam Boys with a tire iron. How did she survive?"

"She said they thought it was funny. They skipped away laughing their heads off, and said they'd run into each other real soon."

"Did they?"

I shrugged. "Don't know. She never said. But over the years, I'd come into town and hear their name mentioned, like passing stories of the boogeyman. 'Lisa Nash's house burned down. Maybe it was the Bedlam Boys,' or 'I was coming out of a bar and the Bedlam Boys cornered me.' Bedlam Boys. Bedlam Boys."

I looked to Paris. "I never really understood what their deal was other than they were dangerous and I should stay away. Are they in a gang? Are they *the* gang?"

She pinked. "It's not a gang. They're just friends."

"The most lethal combination of friends," Presley said. "You know who they are, Rainey, so you know who their parents are. Cairo's father is the sheriff. Jacques's mother is Judge Stone. Legend's family owns the distillery that employs half the town. Roan is the son of Dean Banks. Arsenio is the mayor's son.

"The children of every single person in this town you'd be a fool to piss off, and they go and become best buddies. Their parents own Bedlam. That's why—"

"—they call themselves the Bedlam Boys," I finished. "Goodness, why didn't I see that? I guess out on the farm we didn't have to worry about who's who. The only ones who had control over our lives were the cows and the loan officer."

"They're not that bad," Paris spoke up. Assface or not, it seemed the family loyalty ran deep. "They messed around in high school, acting like they were kings of the school, but every teenage guy is like that."

Amy raised a brow. "P, you haven't been on campus the last three years. Believe me, they are still very much the kings. They rule."

A shiver crawled up my spine.

It wasn't that she said it with menace. It was that she stated it like a simple fact of life. Rain fell from the sky. The sun's heat hazed the air. The Bedlam Boys were our lords and masters.

As the silence stretched, I waited for someone to contradict her.

No one did.

"Here's what I really want to know," I said. "Paris and Cairo? Are you hiding a twin sister named London?"

Paris laughed, breaking the tension. "Our parents first met and fell in love on a trip to Cairo. They honeymooned in Paris. Thus, our names were chosen."

"Well, it could've been worse. Imagine if they honeymooned in Bangkok."

"Bangkok Keller? Hmm. I think I could pull it off."

Zara clapped. "Settled. That's your new stripper name."

Amy jumped to her feet, working and grinding her hips. "Bangkok on the stage, ladies and gentlemen! Get those dolla bills ready!" She thrust like a wild woman, sending us all to the floor, howling.

For a minute, I forgot what brought me here. I forgot I had to keep my distance from everything and everyone. I forgot friends, parties, and happy memories weren't something I could have. I forgot for a minute.

Just a minute.

"Yo, guys!" A dude stuck his head out the porch door. "Dante's about to announce the Ruckus Kings."

The backyard emptied out, everyone piling inside. Amy and Zara helped me up and tugged me in after them. They were not concerned that I mentally excluded myself from their gang.

As they led me through the house, I took a proper look around. Did Cairo and his friends live here, or did they take over a frat house? Passing by on the street, I noticed the black Greek letters hanging over the doors. Walking through the hall, instinct nudged me toward believing this was their domain.

A regular frat house—going by years of movies and television—was filled with cheap, worn furniture and decorated with vomit stains. This place boasted gleaming hardwood floors and an expensive runner rug to cover them. Fully outfitted gamer chairs tucked between the leather couches. I recalled the kitchen gleamed like it had been torn out and replaced with the high-end finishes. Gram certainly couldn't afford a fridge with an interactive screen.

It's not a surprise they have money to throw around. Legend St. James of St. James Whiskey had to be flush.

Our group pushed through the crush of people to get in the living room. The music cut off with a screech that jolted us. We broke free of the crowd in time to see Suspenders Guy, Alfie, disconnect the speaker cords and hook them into a laptop. He set them on the coffee table before Cairo.

"Here you are, Cairo."

He waved him off by way of thank you.

Seeing him sitting there, taking up an entire five-person couch while everyone else pushed and huddled around him, it was hard not to picture Cairo the King.

He opted for ripped jeans, but left his shirt wherever he dropped it. Gleaming, sticky trails of honey spiderwebbed his chest, similar to the network of ink covering his body. My feet carried me of their own accord, bringing me closer for a look.

There was a collection of tattoos stamped across his pecs in Sanskrit. Tucked between the V leading down to his impressive length was a variation of the yin-yang symbol remade in the image of snarling black and white wolves—forever at war.

My view was blocked by a new addition to his lap. A drop-dead gorgeous, stepped-out-of-the-pages-of-a-magazine girl straddled him and attacked Cairo's lips to suck the breath of life from him.

Long, black locks swayed above her lower-back tattoo—also something written in Sanskrit. The brief glimpse of her face revealed an upturned nose, full pouty lips, and a dusting of glitter blush on her cheeks. Cairo stuck his hand up her skirt in plain view of us watching.

"You know about Ruckus Royale, right?" Paris asked.

I tore away like I'd be punished for staring. "Yes, but I've never joined. Gram practically barricaded the doors when the Royale blew through town. She'd have killed us if we went out on Ruckus night."

"Sensible woman."

I nodded. All Gram ever wanted to do was keep us safe, and when our parents died, that's what she did. Protected us from what existed beneath the shiny image of Bedlam. It was only after she was gone did I see the truth of the hell I lived in.

"Ruckus is fun." Presley stuck her head between us. "A town-wide booze-fest in the streets. Music, drinking, and of course, the sacrifices. As long as you're not one of them, you'll be having fun, and getting some dick. Or pussy," she added, smacking my ass. "Whatever you're into."

My nails pierced my palm. *As long as you're not one of them. A sacrifice.*

A bee to honey, my eyes found Cairo. "And your brother is going to be a King this year."

"That's what he thinks," Paris said. "Don't know why since no one knows who Dante will pick until he announces them."

Cairo broke away from the girl and snapped to me. I bit off a gasp.

I couldn't help it. Something in those bright, glinting eyes unsettled me. The most brilliant, beautiful green should invoke images of raindrops clinging to delicate leaves. Fields of rolling grass. A soft, mossy riverbed beneath rushing water. Scenes of life.

Cairo's held no such things. In his eyes were icy winters that withered the leaves on their branches. Dark, crushing depths where even the sun couldn't reach. An endless abyss dragging me down, down, down.

He was wrong. Fuck it to hell, there was something inside Cairo Sharpe that was very, very wrong. If his model girlfriend could see it, the last place she'd be was within ten feet of him.

As it was, she was tugging and nipping on his chin, trying to draw him back into the kiss.

"You." Cairo snapped his fingers at Alfie. "And you, you, and whatever the fuck your name is." Three more guys were pointed out of the crowd, then his finger turned on us. "Escort my sister and her friends out of here. They're crashing."

"Wha— Hey!"

They were on us in a flash, hooking our waists, shoving us back, and tossing her over a shoulder in Amy's case.

Alfie flashed a shy smile as he gripped my wrist in iron. "Sorry about this, Rainey Day."

"Cairo!" Paris pelted her brother with curses that would make a grown man blush. "You fucking wait."

Cairo cupped his ear. "What's that? I'm not fluent in empty threats. Explains why you're out on your ass as promised. Fonsie!"

Alfie jerked. "Me, sir?"

Sir?

"Not that one." Cairo dumped the girl off him and patted his lap. "She sits here."

"I sit— Wait, get off!" Alfie half wrenched my arm out of the socket dragging me to Cairo.

"Hello, hello, hello, Bedlam." The unmistakable voice of Dante poured out of the speakers, covering my shouts.

"What are you doing?!" Alfie swept me up and dumped me as ordered on Cairo's lap. He secured me around the chest and under the knees. I wasn't going anywhere.

I shoved against his shoulder. "Let me go! Let go!"

"Hush, Rain. You and I are going to fuck eventually, might as well be tonight. We'll go upstairs as soon as my win is announced."

I gaped at him. I had my answer. This guy was not real. I must've stumbled to the motel after orientation and passed out on the bed. This was one of my many vivid nightmares.

"It's Rainey, and you and I will fuck when America slips into the sea and we begin worshiping King Neptune."

His grin sharpened on a razor edge, filling me with the same strange feeling. "You can call me King. Everyone else does."

The previous occupant of his lap raked me up and down, her poisonous glare flaying me.

"Stop looking at me like that," I snapped. "You want me off, help me."

"Don't talk to me, bitch." She stalked off, shoving people out of her way.

"—all been waiting for: this year's Kings of Ruckus."

I bent my nails back digging them in his arm. "Let me go n—"

"Stop," Cairo said. "Or you'll regret it."

The sentence stuck me through, releasing my grip from his arm and stilling me.

A hardness existed in his voice. A sound like the crack of a whip. Merciless and unforgiving.

I believed him. He would make me regret it.

"—you all know how it works," Dante continued. We were a silent, obedient crowd hanging on his words. "The Ruckus Kings host the Royale. They choose the venue. They supply the sacrifices. You leave your inhibitions in the sock drawer where they belong."

Dante Last-Name-Unknown was something of a staple in Bedlam. Today, he was a digitally altered voice over the airwaves, passing news no one dared talk about in public, blasting underground bands, and once a year, heralding the start of Ruckus.

Decades ago, before the internet, Dante was a byline in the newspaper that showed up on people's doorsteps during the night. Obviously, the person back then couldn't be the same man now, but somehow and someway, the torch was passed on, and Ruckus Royale reigned.

His docile captive, Cairo tucked my head under his chin. His touch was almost loving, skating his fingers up and down my arm. If it wasn't for the notes of possession in the firm grip on my knee. Cairo barely knew my name, and already he thought he owned me.

"We've got six Kings of Ruckus this—"

Bang!

"Hey! How— How did you get in here?"

I lifted my head, brows snapping together. The panic in his voice was not fake.

"Stop! You can't do that!"

Feedback ripped through the speakers, making me cry out.

"Hello, hello, hello, Bedlam." An entirely new voice filled my ears.

"Get away from there! You can't do this!" Dante's shouts faded to nothing.

"It's your friendly neighborhood Bedlam Boys, here to announce the Kings of Ruckus. Bow down, peasants. I'm serious." A chill crackled his speech. "Bow."

The order no sooner left his lips than everyone dropped to their knees. Stiffly I turned to Cairo, heart yammering to fill this silent room with noise. The smile on his face was terrible to see.

"Your Kings this year are who they have always been: Arsenio Creed, Cairo Sharpe, Roan Banks, Jacques Stone, and Legend St. James. You're all invited to our celebration, if you can find it. Nigri colles viduae."

The broadcast ended.

"There you have it," Cairo said. "One week. See you there." He hefted me up.

"Where?" someone asked. "Negri what what?"

"Was that the clue?"

"What's it mean?"

"What language is it?"

Cairo carried me through the parting crowd, ignoring their requests for information. They were dismissed as easily as the girl on his lap.

My mind spun while he ascended the stairs. At the back of my mind, I wondered why Cairo was sitting on his throne alone, now I knew. The other boys were out ambushing and unseating Dante. A man the cops have fought to root out for decades, each new captain taking on the mantle of catching the rebel no one has ever seen. And they found him just in time to end a hundred-year tradition.

"Why did you do that?" I rasped. "He might have chosen you anyway."

"I don't wait to be given what's mine. I take it."

"Spoken like the random sociopath who's bringing me upstairs after I've clearly stated he doesn't have a chance." I twisted, reaching for the banister. "Put me down now, or I'll scream."

Cairo jerked me up and my grasp went wide. "Scream to who? You think anyone down there is going to help you?"

Real, soul-deep fear curdled my stomach. "What kind of creep-ass thing was that to say?" I hissed, praying he couldn't hear that fear. "Let me go or that pretty face is getting fucked up."

Cairo laughed. "I like you, new girl. You've got spirit. We broke that out of everyone else so long ago, I could unzip my pants in the middle of a party and girls will fight to suck my dick without even asking."

We passed down a long corridor. No one else was up here. Nothing else either. Other than the hardwood floors beneath, the twinkling chandeliers above, and the five closed doors behind, not a picture frame or credenza broke up the trail.

"I was starting to get bored." Cairo raised my head and kissed me full on the lips. "Now there's you."

I punched him dead in the face. He laughed so hard the sound rumbled in his chest and shook me. I sensed my mistake almost immediately.

Blood dripped in his mouth, tingeing his grin. Cairo was enjoying every minute of this. Frightening me, exercising his power, claiming me in a roomful of witnesses who resumed their party the minute we left the room. My wild punch was a cornered animal lashing out. An act that would enrage a bully, but turn on a psychopath.

I glanced down.

Now I knew with certainty which one described Cairo Sharpe, and the door was closing behind us.

The room blurred. He dropped me on my feet and slammed me against the door. I gasped as his hand closed around my throat.

Cairo bore over me, his crushingly handsome face filling my vision. My mind cast for someone to compare him to, and came up empty. He was a beauty of his own creation. The soft lips, the sharp angles, the once-dead eyes coming to with my fear lighting the match.

"You punched me." It almost sounded like a question. "I'm bleeding."

"You deserved it," I spat.

"Did I? I haven't hurt you. Haven't punched you, hit you, or spilled your sweet blood. Why did I deserve it?"

Trembling lips pressed tight together.

Cairo constricted on my throat. "Answer."

"You... know why."

"Because I made you afraid," he whispered. "No one likes to be afraid, but you, Rainey..." Cairo licked my cheek. "You've experienced true, helpless terror. You've been reduced to a cowering, sniveling lump in soaked jeans, and you couldn't hit that person. You couldn't take your hands off your face to do anything at all."

My whole body shook, throat bobbing against his grasp. *How do you know?*

What are you seeing in my eyes?

"So, now you lash out at everything that returns you to that place, hoping that one day you'll have the courage to strike back at the person who matters." He kissed me again—harder, forceful, punishing me for tainting our first. "How'd I do?"

I gripped his wrist, pulling him back to let me speak. "Wrong." I met those eyes head-on, even as everything in me screamed to look away. "I punched you because you're an asshole who humiliated and threw his own sister out, then kissed me while his girlfriend was downstairs."

He chuckled. "That reason works too." My throat was given relief only for my wrists to take their turn. Cairo crossed them over my head, secure in his hold.

I strained and thrashed against him. Cairo just gazed at me like I was a curious thing. Goose bumps popped along my skin to trail his fingers skimming my collarbone. Such a gentle touch for an iron man.

It enraged and suffused my skin with heat in equal measure. He looked at me like he wanted to hurt me, but touched me like a precious, delicate thing.

"Where were you hiding from me, Rain?"

He continued down, tracing a line to my cleavage, and kept going, dragging the fabric over and off my breasts. The black lace bra I chose for the night was on full display.

Arching my back, I flattened against his chest. I think I did so to force him away, then he slipped around my waist, palm warm on the small of my back, and my mouth went dry at his cock hard and unyielding against my thigh.

"Let me go."

"I might," he said, loosening my top button. "If you really wanted me to."

"I do."

"Then why aren't you trying to get away?"

"What the fuck have I been doing since you ordered your hench-man to hand me over?" Even as I said it, my face burned, knowing ex-actly what he meant. Why hadn't I kneed him in the groin? Smashed my skull on his nose? Screamed like I promised to?

Why wasn't I trying to get away from this beautiful, terrifying man?

"Stop me, Rain." He nibbled on my bottom lip, and drew it into his mouth. I moaned as he scraped me between his lips. "I'm the true terror. I'm the beast everyone is too afraid to fight. Defeat me, and that shadow hanging over your life will be nothing at all."

"Cairo..."

He slipped beneath my band and struck my clit dead center. Heat-seeking missile—target found.

Cairo pinched it between calloused fingers, setting my nerve endings alight in exquisite pain.

I gasped, and it was his invitation. Cairo plunged in, tangling my tongue with his, milking my moans with a farm boy's exper-tise—which made me the wanton heifer. Grinding against his hand, lifting my leg for better access, drowning in his curious scent of spicy pink peppers, honey, and oakmoss.

Why did he smell so good? Why was everything about this man from the deep, husky voice to the soft, blond hairs on his chest de-signed to draw you in like a moth to flame? Why did I suddenly de-sire to be burned? I wanted it more at that moment than I wanted to be free of the very shadow clinging to my life, tormenting me with a fear I never knew I could feel.

Then he was gone.

Hands, lips, body, Cairo ripped away and I stumbled, dropping flat on the floor.

"My mistake." Cairo wiped his glistening mouth with the back of his hand. "I thought you were different from the other sheep out there. Still refusing to be broken. I would've had so much fun doing what the other monster in your life couldn't. Oh well."

What just happened? What was he saying?

Cairo stripped off his pants and boxers. My lower belly tightened at his hardness, pointed straight at me in defiance of his owner's supposed lack of interest.

"I need a shower. See yourself out." With that, he turned his back on me and made for the bathroom.

He was angry with me. I saw it in the hard line of his shoulders. I couldn't name why that bothered me—why it made me lash out again.

"Want to know who's the shadow hanging over my life? Who's made me so helpless and afraid that your weak-ass attempt to be a bad boy doesn't even register?"

Cairo halted.

"Ask your daddy."

I ran out of the room, slamming the door to knock the picture frames off the wall, if there were any.

No one paid me any mind running downstairs and escaping outside. I didn't stop till I was across campus, free of the noise, the crowd, and Cairo.

I slowed, chest heaving, and continued to my new home at a reasonable pace.

The girls hadn't waited for me after being kicked out. A good thing. One of them might've offered to take me home. I wasn't up for explaining why I didn't have one to go to.

Thankfully, the motel was a short walk from campus that still afforded me the scenic sights of Bedlam.

Old Bedlam, to be exact. Where hundreds of years ago, they built this big, towering university that grew in size and prestige while our little town didn't. I assumed our blood-soaked history had something to do with that.

We were once called Crystal Canyon. Then the revolution. Riots raged in the streets, buildings burned, and people were ripped from their beds and slaughtered in the town square for a cheering, howling audience.

The very square I passed through, trailing my hand along the fountain's basin, and soaking in the peaceful babbling water.

A peace that our town didn't know for thirty days and thirty nights. The revolutionaries rooted out everyone who stood against them, including the militias and government forces that marched against them, fighting to return order.

They fought so savagely to repel them, relying on the stockpile of weapons in the gun factory that later became the distillery. Soon, the militias were wiped out, and the army itself was forced to retreat. They went back home and the nation's papers reported Crystal Canyon had fallen to bedlam. With that, we were given our name.

"That's the blood that runs through your veins, my Sun and Rain."

I smiled at my wavering reflection as Gran's voice calmed my mind.

"You came from the strongest of people. The fiercest. People who would give up their lives before surrendering their freedom."

I raised my chin like she used to do. I felt her kiss on the tip of my nose.

"Never forget who you are, girls. Fighters."

It's funny. The only two people to call me Rain were Gran and Cairo. It was fitting they'd be connected in this way since both changed my life. Gran raised me to be anyone I wanted to be, and Cairo sealed in stone who that person would be.

I returned to the motel, waving to the night manager, Daisy, on the way down the hall.

My room was modest. A simple twin bed, small television, wobbly TV stand, matching dresser, and bathroom that sprayed water in either hot or cold. The place was freshly vacuumed and bed made when I stepped inside. That's as far as the cleaning went around here. A thought tested and proven by the fact it had been weeks, and my little collage on the back side of the closet doors still hung undisturbed.

I opened them as I did every morning and night, then I sat down to study them as I always did.

A flurry of names, faces, phrases, and articles connected by blue string, making the connections I saw constantly in my mind.

Sliding my backpack across the floor, I unzipped the side pocket and drew out the letter.

A plain black envelope with a single white card inside. Who knew the day I plucked it off the welcome mat would change my life forever?

I slid out the note, repeated the words now seared on my soul.

"Does the kookaburra laugh or does it scream? Does the mighty kingfisher cry or does it dream? Where are you, kookaburra? Tell me, oh, tell me, why is nothing as it seems?"

I flipped it over, reading the message on the back.

Ruckus will have its sacrifice. The question is, darling Rainey, will it be her or me?

You decide.

There had been more letters since. Placed on my welcome mat every week on different days, outside of the week I stayed up seven nights in a row trying to catch him.

More letters to taunt me. Urging me to be the one to catch him where all the others failed.

I assumed it was a him, based solely on the stats saying one in six serial killers was a woman. That left the five in six for the ones with the extra appendage.

But assumptions were all I had. None of the following letters said more about him. None of them gave a clue to who he'd kill during Ruckus Royale other than *her*.

This envelope that I carried with me always was the single hint to his identity. The only information I'd been given to find him. It was less than nothing to go on, but lucky for me, he was perfectly clear in the following letters on what I was to do if I solved his riddle.

Kill him.

He promised—he threatened—that it was the only way to save the unknown innocent woman he chose for death on Ruckus night.

Turning him into the police wouldn't save her. Appealing to his better nature was laughable.

It was him or her, and finally, thanks to Cairo Sharpe, I made up my mind.

I knew what I had to do, and who had to die.

Chapter Two

Buzz. Buzz. Buzz.

I peeled my eyes open, squinting in disbelief at my phone. What the hell? Was someone... calling me?

Picking it up, *Paris* flashed on my screen.

"Hello?"

"Hey, Rainey. Hope you don't mind I put my number in your phone."

"When?" I cried. "It was in my purse all night."

"Not *all* night." She laughed. "Sorry, I'm a pretty handy pickpocket. I don't spread it around for obvious reasons."

"Who are you?"

"The girl who'll pick you up and drive you to school as soon as she gets your address. There weren't any car keys in your purse, and busing it from your farm to school must be killer."

Busing it to and from the farm would be killer, if I still lived there.

The thought panged my heart.

"You're sweet," I said, pushing myself up. "I actually booked in a motel while I'm getting a handle on things. It's a ten-minute walk, so I'm good."

"Then let's meet in the student union. They've got this yummy bagel place. My treat."

I hummed. "Why are you being so nice to me? Do you feel bad for taking off last night?"

Silence descended on the other end. "Yes, I do. I know Cairo didn't let you leave. I tried to get back in and help you, I swear. The guys blocked the door and wouldn't let me in. He didn't... do anything to you, did he?"

I knew that tone in her voice. Hesitation. Shame. Paris loved him. Wanted to see the best in him, even when the truth stared her in the face.

"If he did, I'll kill—"

"He didn't," I cut in. "Cairo was a perfect gentleman. Honestly, we talked and he helped me come to a decision over something I was struggling with."

"Really? That's great." A gush of breath crackled over the line. "I feel fractionally less of an asshole now, though I'm still a jerk for taking off. Bagels?"

"Had me at your treat."

I hung up and got dressed, lingering in front of the closet while I tugged up my jeans.

Day and night, I've worked to solve the riddle. At the start, once I realized this wasn't a horrible joke, I hoped I could solve it quickly, find the bastard, and follow him till I had proof he was a crazed maniac. Proof that no one, not even Sheriff Sharpe, could deny.

Weeks passed with me stuck on where to find kookaburras. They weren't native to our area. Bedlam had a private wildlife sanctuary, but they didn't house any kookaburras, and I called three times and visited to check.

The nearest pair was fifty miles away in Hunter's Crest—a town three times the size of ours and boasting a zoo. I took the bus out there and grilled one of the keepers. He backed up everything I read online. Kookaburras are known for laughing, and they do not cry or dream. What this was supposed to tell me about the man, or woman, who ordered their execution, I had no idea. For a long time, I was stuck. Then I received the orientation packet for Bedlam University.

I closed the closet doors, grabbing my backpack on the way out.

One interesting fact I discovered about kookaburras, when they laugh, it means rain is coming.

PARIS STOOD IN THE middle of the student union, talking to a guy with long hair, sandals, and a laugh that echoed through the room. I hung back, letting them have a minute.

The student union was three floors of restaurants, study rooms, club rooms, and meeting halls. During finals week, they stayed open late and served free meals to those still hanging around at one in the morning.

Ivy used to leave at midnight to join her friends here. They'd kick back, eating and studying, then crash in one of their dorms. She told me the best spot was on the second floor near the back staircase. There was a quiet nook up there next to the vending machine, and the stairs were closest to where they set up the food. First in line.

I had to send her a pic of me eating pizza in the nook, goofing that it's my spot now. Despite us not talking much these days, she'd get a kick out of it.

Paris and the dude kissed, then he strode off. I moved up to take his place.

"Boyfriend?" I asked.

"Playmate," she corrected. "I don't really do boyfriends."

"Why not?"

"Because I'd fall for one of them and then get it into my head that it won't be so bad to settle down and pop out a bunch of babies in good ole Bedlam. That's a fucking lie, so better not to give the idea a chance."

"You might meet someone who wants to leave as much as you do." We set off down a branching hallway, making for the heavenly smell wafting through the corridor.

"That's not what anyone seems to do around here. My parents—
I mean my mom and Jack, they used to travel all over the world, then
they moved back here to have kids and just stopped. Mom hasn't
been farther than Hunter's Crest since. Something about Bedlam,"
she said softly. "It just keeps you. Doesn't let anyone leave."

I stumbled.

*I get to keep you, Rainey. No matter what you decide, you're mine
forever.*

I swallowed through needles, quickly righting myself. Of all the
ways to phrase that, it had to be a sentence so close to the one that
psycho sent me. And they were right.

This person, whoever they were, had infected me. Every person I
passed on the street was looked at with suspicion. Everyone who said
something too similar to the notes filled me with horrible visions of
their bodies at my feet as their blood dripped from my fingers. What
I would be after Ruckus Royale, I was afraid to consider. Only one
thing was certain, no matter what I did, they would win in what I
now knew was their true desire—to make me a killer.

*But why me? Why did they choose some random girl living out on
her farm who never hurt a living soul?*

I never even raised my voice to our bobbleheaded chickens, forever wandering through the fence and getting themselves lost. No
one could hate me as much as this person surely did. If anyone was
wronged, it was me.

"Rainey?"

I slammed the door on those thoughts, smiling at Paris. "Sorry,
what you said made me think of something. You're right that most
people tend to stay in Bedlam. Probably why my sister was determined to leave."

"Where is she now?"

"Chicago."

She groaned. "I'm jealous. You have to hook us up. I want to hear about every minute of every day she gets to be away from this place."

The sign for Bagel Glory loomed ahead of us. The little café was a small, cozy corner of the union that opened out onto a terrace. Paris got a blueberry bagel and I tossed my cinnamon sugar on the pile.

I smiled at the girl counting out our change. "You have the prettiest blue eyes."

"Oh, I—" She brightened. "Thank you."

I accepted the money and followed Paris outside to a two-seater tucked under a shady spot.

"Why didn't you go to college out of state?" I asked.

"My parents talked me out of it. Bedlam offered me a great scholarship. They said it was nuts to turn that down and then take out thousands in student loans to go out of state. Mom said when I started my new life outside of Bedlam, I'd want to do it debt-free."

I inclined my head. "Sensible woman."

"She is," Paris said, even while rolling her eyes. "I couldn't fault her logic, and I know she just wants what's best for me. I've lived here for nineteen years. Two more won't kill me." She squeezed my hand. "But everything does work out for a reason, because we met."

Paris was nice. A supersweet person introducing me to her friends and taking me out for bagels, though all we knew about each other was from being names in an online class. Why was she so nice? What did she want from me?

I tugged my hand away, picking up my bagel to cover it. My stomach knotted and pushed my bite back up my throat.

This is what they've made of me. I can't hang out with a new friend without wondering if they're a killer.

It can't be her, a voice spoke up. *What do kookaburras have to do with Paris Keller, political science major, and pretty, popular girl waving to almost everyone walking by? Disturbed sociopaths tend not to fit in that category.*

"I'm glad we met," I finally said. "I don't have a lot of friends. It was always me, Gran, and Ivy growing up."

"Can I ask what happened to your parents?"

"They died in a car accident when I was three. I never really got to know them."

"I'm sorry. Gosh, I feel like I'm always saying that to you."

I flicked over her shoulder. "Anyone who knows me for more than twenty-four hours ends up apologizing for asking me about my life." I spoke to her, but I was looking at the sight that caught everyone's attention. "It's just that depressing."

"It's not depressing. You've just had— What are you looking at?" She twisted in her seat. "Oh."

Have you ever seen those movies where a group of blindly attractive people walk and not even the cameraman can resist zooming in and capturing every inch of them? I mean, that's the real reason almost every movie has a hottie slo-mo moment. All that recording and footage is expensive, and yet twenty minutes just watching people walk is a vital scene.

The thing is, you never think you'll have that moment in real life. To have such a high concentration of gorgeous people in the same place at the same time is rare. To have them all walk in while your lips are covered in cinnamon sugar and your hair is in a messy bun because you rushed out to get bagels, that's one of the many reasons people were always apologizing for my sad life.

The world slowed around them, stopping the birds in flight, silencing the cicadas singing to the trees. He swayed as he moved side to side with a walk reserved for the runway. Dressed in a jacket, white tee, and baggy jeans, Cairo took the simplest of outfits and reduced the guys loitering around the terrace to hobos in cloth sacks.

Were there other guys on the terrace? I could only see Cairo and them.

A tall guy with glasses and inky black hair strolled at his side. A long-sleeve sweater and black pants should've turned him into a library assistant. If they had angular cheeks, a broad nose, and a shadow's dusting on their chin and cheeks, changing my opinion on beards forever.

"That's Jacques," Paris said. "He and Cairo have been friends longer than the others. Judge's son and sheriff's son. They used to sit in the back and watch when they were in court. Jacques is insanely smart. Seriously, IQ off the charts. Highest GPA in the school. His mother used to enter him in national tournaments. Earned us some recognition in the big papers. Bedlam, home of the prodigy. Did you ever see the articles?"

I shook my head. "My *Doctor Who* DVD marathons didn't come with interruptions for news of local celebrities."

"Just as well," Paris said. "He's a complete douchebag."

I choked on a laugh. "Just to save myself some time, are all of your brother's friends douchebags?"

"Absolutely."

"Great." I slid back to them. No one said the beautiful had to have personalities to match, but still, they were ridiculous.

"The guy on Cairo's right is Roan."

Roan Banks. I knew the names. Now I got to put them to faces.

Roan was the son of Dean Banks, the attractive woman at the end of the orientation video, welcoming us to the best years of our life. A head of wavy red hair pointed this way and that—falling over his eyes and brushing the tip of his pointed ears. People spent an hour in the mirror trying to get the sexily tousled look this guy was born with.

He was tall and slim without looking stretched. Roan laughed at something the person said on the other side of his phone, and his lips quirked up in a wicked half grin that must've gotten him in trouble even when he was innocent. I couldn't say yet if he was a douche. I sensed all the same I should keep my distance.

"You don't have to tell me who the guy next to him is," I said. "Legend St. James. Gran used to do business with his father. I'd see him around the distillery sometimes when we made deliveries." I was struck by how unnaturally perfect he was back then too.

Legend St. James balanced on the line of hard and soft expertly. Pronounced square chin and pink top-heavy lips. Dark locks gelled into submission and Bambi brown eyes that made you feel the world revolved around you whenever he turned on the charm.

Hard, ropey muscles barely concealed by his blazer, and long tapered fingers that'd curl around mine as he brought it to his lips, welcoming me to his family distillery for the tenth time because he kept forgetting we met before.

"Last but not least, the son of our chosen leader, Arsenio Creed."

Arsenio Creed was the product of so many ethnicities, his features spanned the world. Light monolid eyes, dark freckles, wide nose, and a head of long, cork-brown curls that caught the sun as he moved, bathing them gold. I heard someone tried to pet him once and he twisted their wrist till it broke. I didn't know if it was true. We were at the point that anything that went wrong around town, the Bedlam Boys were named for it.

"I only know him from the photos and video shots of him standing off to the side from Mayor Creed," I admitted. "I've always wondered what she thought of her kid being one of the infamous Bedlam Boys."

"I can answer that for you, she is in complete denial." Paris slid my cream cheese over and slathered it on her bagel. "Arsenio puts the angels in the heavens to shame when he's around his mom. '*Yes, ma'am. No, ma'am. I'll be home in time for dinner.*'

"He graduated salutatorian and class president. How could he be fucking around when he was busy being the perfect student? Whenever they were caught, our teachers let it slide. Would you want to be the one calling the mayor in for a teacher's conference?" She heaved a sigh. "After years of the act, she refuses to believe anyone knows her son better than she does."

"There is no beating a mother's blind spot."

"Tell me about it," Paris mumbled. She wasn't looking at Arsenio.

The shift in gaze forced me to follow, and then I was looking at him too. Cairo noticed us and nodded at his sister. Just a nod to acknowledge the person who rode around in the same womb that he did. He slid off me like my seat was empty, and turned to the final person in their group—the one who shot me a look of triumph as she perched on his lap.

"Who's she?" I tried to ask casually, but being dismissed by the guy who kissed and had his hand down my pants less than twelve hours ago leaked temper in my voice. Without a doubt, I knew the rotted fruit didn't fall far from the tree.

I didn't want anything from Cairo Sharpe other than an apology, and his ass could mail it to me. But for him to throw me back, implying I was too easy for him, ten minutes after saying he dropped his pants for anyone with a vagina, stirred my unused confrontational side. I wouldn't lose my patience with the chickens, but I yelled and threatened him. It never crossed my mind to hit Ivy the many times she tackled me like an NFL player, laughing her head off while I screeched for her to let me up. That didn't stop me from punching Cairo. Something about this guy stirred all the wrong things in me, and if his friends were even worse, I'd have no trouble staying away.

"That's Quinn Cunningham. She's their latest shared toy."

"What does that—?"

The sentence wasn't out of my mouth before she tugged Legend by the collar and planted a searing kiss on him—in full view of the guy she wanted to claw my eyes out over. Cairo didn't even blink at them.

"Ah, I get it," I said. "No need to explain."

She snorted. "If you get it, explain it to me. Girls, and guys, are so desperate to be in their orbit, they're happy to put their ass on tap if it means walking beside them in the halls. I mean, no one else can use a mother's blind spot as an excuse."

I suddenly didn't want to talk about Cairo or his friends anymore. "You know what they say, there's something about a bad boy. Thanks for breakfast, Paris." I got to my feet. "I've got to take care of something before class. Meet up later?"

"Sure. See ya."

I headed inside, pointedly looking anywhere other than Quinn's shit-eating smirk. *Keep him, Cunningham. He's all yours.*

An arm snaked around my waist. I snapped up, looking up into Cairo's eerie eyes.

"What the hell do you want? Get your hands off—"

"Be quiet." The sharp order silenced me and the couple walking past us. They picked up speed getting away. "That stuff you said about my father. What did you mean?"

I stared at him, watching his expression darken.

"Did you not hear me?"

"I'm confused," I said. "I thought you wanted me to be quiet."

His hand burned an imprint on my hip. I tried to push him off and he dug in.

"Why do you have my father's name in your mouth?"

"I'm sure everyone does," I hissed. "The bastard's corrupt. They invented the term dirty cop for him."

Cairo snapped me to his chest, stopping us short in the middle of the union. "That's a serious accusation, Rain."

My stomach fluttered at my name in his mouth. I could despise him. I could hate the bits of him that reminded me of his father, but I'd never be able to control my response to the way his lips formed my nickname in that deep, throaty voice.

"It's not an accusation if it's true, Sharpe."

"Have proof to back it up?"

"Would it surprise you that I do?" My lips pulled back from my teeth—just talking about the man would do that. "But who would I give it to? Who is going to believe me?"

A grin broke out on his face, startling me. "I just might. I'd be very interested to see this proof of yours, Rain. Bring it by my place tonight."

My jaw worked. "I— I— No," I cried. "I'm not giving it to you so you can warn him—"

Cairo gripped my chin, snapping it up. My eyes popped as he swiped his tongue across my lips.

"Hmm. Cinnamon sugar. My favorite. I might've been wrong about you—something I don't say often. It's looking like I'll keep you after all."

I get to keep you.

Cairo released me and walked off. "My place. Tonight," Cairo tossed over his shoulder. "Don't make me come and find you."

I stood for a full minute, staring at the spot he disappeared. Hand shaking, I touched my lips.

He can't be. Dear Lord, it can't be him.

I ran.

Ran out of the student union, down the causeway, and out onto the lawn. Fire ants crawled beneath my skin, setting my body on fire like he did last night. The Letter Man?

No. No, no, no! My mind rebelled. His favorite bagel worked its way up my throat.

I couldn't have kissed him. Let him touch me. Perched on his lap like the queen to his king. Cairo Sharpe wasn't him, and there was nothing more important than proving it.

I raced to the other side of campus, slowing only when the stone structure broke through the trees. Stumbling to a stop, I doubled over before the memorial, sucking in ragged breaths that burned my throat.

This was it. It has to be it!

Gripping the stone plinth, I studied every inch.

In memory of Douglas Herbert.
Your smile rivaled the sun.
Your laugh touched our lives.
Gone but never forgotten.

Douglas Herbert died two years ago. One night, he skidded off the road and wrapped around a tree. The accident crushed the hood, pinning his leg under the steering wheel. Douglas was on his way to a solo camping trip, so no one knew what happened till a random motorist noticed his car off the road two days later. I didn't know Douglas personally, but everyone in town heard of the tragedy.

But how am I supposed to know—

I circled it and stopped. At the base of the plinth, so small you might've missed it, a painted kookaburra took flight.

I DID NOT GO TO SEE Cairo that night, so when I glimpsed him on campus Friday morning, I backpedaled and went the other way. The man was not versed in empty threats. He said he would track me down, and Hera help me, he was trying.

Cairo ordered his sister to give him my number and address. Thankfully, she was the single person on this planet who didn't fall at his feet. She refused, so he worked his way down the line of Amy, Presley, and finally Zara, who told him I lived on a farm. A dead end that resulted in his stealing Paris's phone and getting my number.

For the past five days, I'd been treated to a string of threatening and curiously sexual messages. At the start of the voice mail, he was promising I'd be punished for every day I made him wait, and by the end of it, he was telling me in graphic detail how he'd dip me in cinnamon sugar and lick me clean.

As fucked up as it was, my refusal to give in to him was both pissing him off and turning him on. It's obvious no one had said no to him in a long time. That didn't stop him showing me why.

By Wednesday, he had his minions tracking me down. Alfie ran up to me in the student union under the guise of apologizing for the party. He spent ten minutes waffling and stealing glances at the entrance before I caught on.

I dumped my iced mocha on his crotch on the way out the door. Another thing I wouldn't have done a lifetime ago, but everything was different now.

That morning, I walked on campus figuring Cairo and his friends would be too busy to worry about me.

"Whoo!"

A red streak shot past me, gifting me his hot breath in my face and the full X-rated view of his half-erect penis flapping in the breeze. Then five more of his buddies came running to do the same.

Frat boys, if the Greek letters painted on their bare backs were anything to go by. Couldn't resist starting the party early. Students clapped and cheered the streakers on.

Ruckus Royale officially didn't begin until that night, but for some, the party was an all-day event.

I weaved through groups blasting music and dancing on the lawn. A few had the beers going round. It was eight in the morning.

The Bedlam men and women brought the wildness, debauchery, and public orgies, and the Kings provided the venue, music, alcohol, and entertainment. If they wanted to one-up last year's Ruckus, and Cairo seemed like the kind of guy who would, they'd be much too busy today to chase me down.

Rounding the chemistry building, I entered Burnett Hall from the back. My class was two floors up and at the end of the hall. I made it without incident. Now to avoid Cairo for the next three hundred and fifty-nine days.

Faith, the teaching assistant, stood beside Professor Valdez's desk, passing us handouts.

"Thanks, Faith. You are killing it in that dress."

"Rainey, you're such a ray of sunshine. Your parents gave you the wrong name."

I thanked her and claimed a seat in the third row. I'd say my parents weren't too far off with my name. Spending most of my life as the introverted farm girl who said more to her chickens than she did anyone outside the property line didn't earn most the title of people person.

My habit of complimenting every woman I ran into was recent. Started up not too long after I received a black letter.

It was silly, and in the end, wouldn't make a difference, but I didn't know the girl he chose to be his sacrifice. The girl who would die if I failed. So, the very least I could do was make her smile. Whoever she was, wherever she was. Grant her genuine, unasked-for kindness before a monster reminded the world why it was so rare.

I bent over my desk, brushing a hand over the pocket. I gripped it tight as I gazed at Faith. I was still giving compliments because Ruckus Royale was that night, and I didn't have him.

Squeezing my eyes shut, my jaw clamped tight. What was Cairo's wrath in the face of an innocent woman's murder? If it was a woman. The letters said nothing about her age. What would I do if a child was in his sights? How long would it take me to slit my fucking wrists after they broadcasted her death?

Cairo didn't matter. All that did was finding the right name connected to Douglas Herbert, and after five days of digging up everything there was on him, I believed I did.

I thought this was the hard part, finding the name. Nothing compares to holding the name of the person you're supposed to stop in your hands, and having no way of proving their innocence or guilt. How could I?

I followed him the day before and all he did was drive home from work, kiss his girlfriend at the door, and stay inside till I finally left at two a.m.

What did the average killer do to give themselves away? Keep trophies?

Of the twenty-six unsolved murders and disappearances in Bedlam, I didn't know who his victims were to connect them to a trophy. I didn't know the first thing about breaking and entering to bust in his place and find them anyway. It left me with only one option, and if I was wrong, I wouldn't get another chance.

I opened my eyes and met Jacques's. He stood at the bottom of the stairs in all six feet of his *tall, dark, and handsome* glory, fixed on me. My skin tightened as he passed the first row, second row, and turned down the third.

What is he doing here? He's not in this class.

The backpack slung over his shoulder defied the thought. My classes were Bedlam Boy-free. They were my safe haven from Cairo and his army of foot soldiers. He couldn't seriously have sent Jacques in here after me. They couldn't be so powerful that a professor would turn a blind eye. Then, an even worse idea occurred to me.

Jacques Stone was the son of a judge. Wasn't it entirely possible he was a prelaw student too?

No, I thought as he sat down next to me. *This was not happening. I couldn't be so unlucky that of all the classes he adds and drops, he had to end up in one of mine.*

I openly studied him. I could count each muscle that flexed as he took out his notebook, pen, and water bottle. I watched his lips form a perfect "o" to take a sip. Jacques must've noticed my attention, though he didn't acknowledge it.

He doesn't have to. All he has to do is text his buddy, and Cairo will be waiting for me.

"Good morning, students."

"Good morning."

This was my cue to look away and focus on Professor Valdez. I didn't give in to it.

I bore in the side of Jacques's head—waiting for him to fish out his phone. Maybe daring him to look back.

He did neither of those things.

"Before we begin, I feel obliged to mention this along with the many who have warned every year," Valdez said. "Ruckus Royale is not a sanctioned event or holiday."

I tore away from Jacques. Valdez said the two words that would steal my attention today, and likely for the rest of my life.

"What started as a celebration of independence has devolved into drunkenness, property damage, petty antics, and in the case of those *sacrificed*, public ridicule and humiliation." Valdez paced the length of his desk, giving the stern eye to every row. "As future lawyers, you all should know that 'this is what we've always done' is not a defense. This ridiculous event needs to end, and it will."

He was a handsome man. The kind that could make an old-fashioned tweed coat with elbow patches look natural. From the first day I met him, I got the impression he was a man out of his time. Someone who believed in picking up the check, or sitting out on the porch smoking a pipe. Why I thought that made him suited to teaching ethical issues in law, I had no idea. I just had a feeling from the first class, it'd be an interesting year. Didn't think he'd prove me right so soon.

Students in the rows ahead glanced back, catching a peek at Jacques's reaction. The guy sat there sipping his water bottle and appearing lost in his head.

"I lead a group of parents, neighbors, and members of the community committed to seeing the end of Ruckus Royale. Tonight, and every night this reckless lawlessness is allowed to run rampant through our streets, we'll take action."

Valdez stopped pretending and fixed on Jacques.

"We'll call the police, photograph the people participating, bring charges against illegal activity. We'll make it so your couches and a bowl of popcorn are the most exciting thing anyone dares to do on Ruckus night.

"I heard this year's clue is too difficult. Most of you don't know where the party is. That's for the best," he said. "When it is broken up, and it will be broken up, you don't want to be rounded up. An arrest doesn't make an attractive addition to a law school application."

No one said a word. We didn't so much as cough.

Valdez straightened his back, propping against his desk. "Forgive me for starting class this way. As my students, I had to warn you before you made a mistake tonight that you can't come back from."

My vision glazed on his handsome tweed form. *What about the mistakes I can't come back from tonight? Where's your stern talking-to for me?*

"I hope the message sunk in," he said to everyone, but addressed to Jacques.

Again, nothing but a serious thirst from my seatmate.

Valdez cleared his throat. "Let's begin. First week of classes, I'm throwing you right in the deep end. As we know, there's always been a disconnect between what is legal and what is ethical. I don't need to give examples," he said. "Dozens have popped into your head already." He swept over us. "Can anyone tell me the history of how Crystal Canyon became Bedlam?"

A hand shot in the air. "Life wasn't good for women, servants, or African-Americans back then, but in Crystal Canyon, it was hell on earth," Victoria began. "The landowning men formed a club, a cult—

I don't know the word for what they were. A group that protected and favored each other, they called themselves the Men of Honor. Holding all the highest positions in town, coupled with all the rights, they did what they wanted when it suited them. And we all know what they say about absolute power.

"Colonel James Cotton saw his wife getting too familiar with a man outside the general store. He savagely beat them both right there in the street. His wife later died from the injuries, and the sheriff didn't lift a finger. Dozens of witnesses, a victim, and a body covered in bruises. Cotton spent one night in jail and was let off for lack of evidence.

"They say that was the splinter that broke the dam. From there, they knew without a doubt they had the law under their thumb. The Men of Honor descended into total savagery and cruelty and soon started the Hunt. One night a month a young girl was chosen, chased through the streets, and brought to their lodge after capture where they'd... do what they wanted to her.

"People were scared. Terrified," she said. "Those with the means to move, left town as fast as they could. Families sent their daughters to live with distant aunts and cousins. Crystal Canyon fell into bedlam long before it became our name."

I hadn't noticed till then I was nodding along with most of the people in my row. We all grew up with the history. The gentle version as children, then more of the awful truth as we aged through school. Every Bedlamite holds one thing to be true: Evil exists.

"Months of this, years of it," she continued, "Crystal Canyon entered its darkest period with the emergence of a serial killer. No one knows if the Men of Honor knew the killer and approved, but we do know they did nothing to stop him. Why would they care about the murder of poor young women?"

"The history gets a bit murky there," Valdez took over. "Some say the citizens accepted they'd have to protect themselves. They noticed the serial killer's pattern of how they chose their victims and laid a trap for him. Mayam Westchester volunteered to risk her life drawing him out. The night he attacked on her deserted walk home, the forest lit up.

"Dozens upon dozens of lamps and torches emerged from the trees, bringing Ambrose Otis into the light. The mob got their hands on him, and years of pain and oppression broke free. They half tore him apart and displayed his body in the town square. It was the first death in the massacre that followed.

"But I said that was one version," Valdez went on, all of us hooked though we knew the stories as well as him. "The other is Mayam Westchester did not plan to be bait that night, but was attacked all the same. In the struggle with Otis, she turned the knife on him and got away. Ran all the way home and warned her family. Ambrose Otis was the son of the magistrate and one of the Men of Honor. The entire town would pay for his death. As predicted, the Men rounded people up. Dragged them from their homes, and beat and tortured for a confession.

"Mayam's family wasn't spared. They circled her home, and her husband went out, confessing to killing Otis. The Men shot him on the spot. Something snapped inside Mayam. She took her husband's gun and fired from the window, killing two Men and scattering their horses. Witnesses saw and... picked up their guns too," he said. "Which of these events sparked the revolt, we don't know for sure. All we know is Mayam and Ambrose lit the match, and the resulting inferno saw the death of every Men of Honor, their spouses, their children, and their children's children. Their homes were burned. Their businesses reduced to ash. If the Battle of Bedlam could be classed as a war, it's one of the most devastating in history. Absolutely nothing and no one survived of the enemy."

Valdez nodded at Faith. His teaching assistant scurried behind the desk, clicking on the slides.

"This brings us to the discussion of the day, ladies and gentlemen. As we've said, what is legal is not always ethical. Therefore, what is ethical, may not always be legal. Can we class the massacre and revolt of Bedlam as either?"

Thick, pressing silence filled the room. Not even the eager to impress raised their hands.

Valdez grinned. "Alright, alright. Those waters are too deep for the first week. Hold that question in your head, folks, because it's the topic of your midterm paper. Comparing then and now, if you were representing members of the revolt, what would be your argument? Legal or ethical? Could you stand on either?"

He turned his back to the class, motioning to Faith. She clicked to the next slide.

"This is our actual discussion topic this morning: euthanasia. What—?"

"It's neither."

Valdez turned back. "Excuse me?"

Jacques set down his water bottle.

"We don't have to wait for a term paper. It's amusing you think you've stumped us, but of course, you would think so, having moved here only three years ago. A born and bred Bedlamite is told of the story of Mayam Westchester and the revolt as bedtime stories, and we've all thought of what we'd do if we were in their place."

Valdez bobbed his head. "Fair point. I—"

"Quiet," Jacques snapped. "I'm speaking."

My mouth fell open. Did this guy seriously say that to a professor?

"I beg your pardon! How dare—?"

"Your puffed chest and raised voice give an excellent impression of a howler monkey. Unfortunately, I've never found primates particularly threatening."

Bugged eyes swung from Jacques to Valdez—not just mine.

"Out! Out of this classroom."

Jacques's features didn't so much as twitch, let alone the rest of him. "It's too late for you to cite classroom decorum and respect. Two things I might've given you if you proved to not be an idiot, or if you didn't pretend you were something more than a never-published, failed academic who took the first school that'd hire him after those rumors came out about you and a former graduate assistant. Have you started fucking this one yet?"

Faith flushed bright red. The smile I wanted her to have today washed away and hid as it looked like she was desperate to do.

"I— I— You—" Valdez tripped over himself, swinging from Faith to Jacques. I'd never seen a person so flustered. "We've never—"

Jacques was far from done.

"Despite being barely above contempt, I sat in silence while you threatened me, my friends, and my party guests with jail and criminal records. The least you can do is listen when I'm speaking."

In front of his class and all eyes watching, Valdez shut his mouth. "Good."

That was the first time in the conversation I heard something other than boredom leak into Jacques's voice. It sounded eerily close to pleasure.

"As I was saying, the Bedlam revolt was neither illegal nor ethical. It was war," he stated. "Revolution. The laws and ethics of society do not carry in war. They never have. To kill a stranger in battle makes you a hero. To kill a stranger behind Roadhouse makes you a murderer. We could not make the same argument for these men then or now, for they would not be prosecuted by the same lawyer under the same proceedings. They would be tried as war criminals in a courtroom the majority of us are unlikely to see inside.

"The premise of this assignment is at its root pointless, but the premise isn't the objective. Your objective is the same as other teachers, professors, and outsiders who learned the bloody history of Bedlam and gasped in horror. A savage mob killed innocent people who stood in the way of the Men of Honor. Wives and families killed. Why don't we see that? How can we praise them as heroes? Erect their statues in the square? Name their fight a revolution?

"You're not the one to open our eyes, Valdez. We see the revolt for what it was, and we accepted around the time we were learning to tie our shoes and get up on training wheels, that it's not only soldiers who die in war, but it's always the enemy."

Valdez shook with thinly disguised rage and humiliation, yet he didn't speak. He didn't do anything.

"This midterm topic has no purpose in regard to educational value or as a thought exercise. Change it," Jacques said. "Come up with something better. I'll tell you if it is."

"I disagree."

Four dozen necks swiveled. Not to Valdez, but to me. Yeah, that's right. Of all the people to open their mouth, it had to be me.

Jacques slowly turned his head, fixing like he just noticed I was there. Just noticed I existed. "Excuse me?"

"I disagree. Both with your answer and that this assignment is pointless," I said, voice holding steady. "Professor Valdez asked what our defense would be then and now, and it's a thought-provoking question because if the revolters were rounded up— If the outside militias succeeded in retaking the town, the revolters would've seen the inside of the courtroom where we'd defend them."

A wrinkle was forming between Jacques's brows, cracking that impassive mask to splinters.

"You're forgetting—"

"I didn't forget a thing."

"Then, you're *ignoring* that the people who rose up against the Men of Honor were servants," I said. "Shop workers, cooks, housemaids, women, laborers, minorities, and African-Americans. They were seen as less than in the very society that allowed them to be ruled by tyrants. If they didn't recognize their right to live as equals, they certainly wouldn't have recognized their right to fight as soldiers, or lead a revolution against the very system that benefits them.

"The uprising wouldn't have been called a battle then, and it isn't called one now except by the descendants who pass on the story. They would've been tried as common killers against the elite of society. As they should be."

"What?" someone blurted. "They should be?"

"Yes." I didn't break eye contact with Stone. "They didn't take up their guns to win a battle. The revolters didn't line the town square with bodies as a tactical move. It wasn't about what was legal, or ethical. What happened that day and in the bloody days to come was no more or less revenge."

The wrinkle became a deep groove separating thick brows fighting to meet.

"Revenge for years of living in fear. Revenge for the rapes, murders, and injustice. Revenge for splitting families apart and leaving the splintered members behind without hope. Everyone had to die from the oldest man to the youngest son, because that pain and fear had to go somewhere, and when it breaks, it showers the world in red."

My throat closed, straining to choke down the truest words I ever said.

"They took up their weapons knowing their choice was to die as murderers, or live as cowards." Black letters floated through my mind. "They took them up knowing it wasn't a choice at all. A soldier enters into war with patriotism on their lips and reluctance in their hearts. A widow doesn't march to war. They march to slaughter."

I folded my arms, half to cover my thumping heart. "So, how do you defend unrepentant murderers who'd kill and kill and kill again in the name of their children's freedom? It's an interesting question and I can't wait to tackle the paper. Love to see what you come up with too, Stone."

"Who said you could use my name?" The question wasn't loud. It wasn't even contemptuous. "I don't believe we've met, so I don't believe I gave you permission to have my name in your mouth."

A hot pit boiled my stomach. "I don't need permission."

"Or common sense, awareness, or basic survival instincts." Jacques faced me, blessing—cursing—me with all six feet, shadow dusted, and shiny-eyed bit of him granting his full attention. "If you spent less time thinking of that simplistic comeback, and more time reading the room, you'd have noticed everyone is looking at you in surprise, some horror, a lot of disbelief, and more than a little disdain. Not the faces of people about to give you a standing ovation."

I glanced around. Jacques was right. There was a mix of emotions on people's faces, none were congratulatory.

"This is my school, in my town, in my classroom," Jacques said. He tipped my chin up—a touch that could only be described as gentle. "No one talks back to me. And if they're going to conjure up the courage, they at the very least have the courtesy to not be laughably wrong."

I swallowed against his fingers. "How am I wrong?"

"For one very simple reason," he replied. "If the militias and armed forces succeeded in retaking the town, the revolters would've been executed where they stood. None would've seen the inside of a courtroom, because they couldn't be seen as equals, but would be recognized as enemies. That's always the case... in war."

My lips parted. "I think—"

"Your first mistake," he sliced in. "Don't make it again. You were meant to get by on your looks."

My face flared hot. "Wow. You are a douchebag."

Jacques faced forward—my audience with him coming to an end. "Falling back on insults because you don't have anything intelligent to say. You and I are done. Be quiet."

"I would, but I can't let it pass without mentioning how pathetic it is that you need to look so tough and cool, that you're sitting there with wet pants and pretending it doesn't bother you."

A muscle in his brow ticced. "Excuse me? My pants aren't wet."

"Aren't they?" I snatched his water bottle, twisted off the top, and dumped the contents in his lap.

Jacques leaped out of his seat bellowing.

"Rainey!" Valdez barked. "Unacceptable. Leave my class this instant."

"Me? But he's the one—"

"Enough." He smashed his fist on the desk. "I will not have another argument. I won't hear another word uttered for the next hour and a half. Leave!"

More words said to the entire room, but directed at one person, and I suspected that person wasn't me.

Even so, it was me who packed her backpack and walked out under Jacques's gaze. Those burning eyes followed me out the door and on the other side of it.

Jacques was wrong about me failing to read the room. I picked up on every face I passed as I walked out the door. They said one thing in complete agreement.

I made a huge mistake.

Chapter Three

"Rainey?"

My eyes peeled open, blinking through the cloud of cherry blossoms. My next class was around noon. Afterward, I'd have to turn my decision into action. Some peace and quiet in the arboretum wasn't too much to ask for.

"Rainey? It is her," said Zara.

The girls crowded in around me, squeezing on the bench. Paris slung her arm around me.

"Is this where you hide out?" she asked. "Not a bad spot."

Putting it mildly. This was the most beautiful spot on campus. Beds of roses, daisies, and petunias split into differing shapes by the twisting walkways. The arboretum, tucked away on the edge of campus, was the only spot that hadn't yet been taken over by the Ruckus partiers. It was a little slice of peace.

Some odd miles straight ahead and I'd be on the farm again.

"I'd rather not use the word hiding," I said. "Makes it sound like I'm afraid of Cairo and Jacques."

"Jacques? What does he have to do with anything?"

"Didn't you hear what happened in their ethics class?" Amy hissed.

I sat up straight. "Apparently you have. How? I was kicked out an hour ago."

"The video of you giving Jacques Stone a cock wash was uploaded fifty-nine minutes ago. He's going to kill you."

Couldn't be certain if I was more disturbed by her lack of irony saying he'd kill me, or that she called my dumping water on him a cock wash.

"I don't think you should come to Ruckus Royale tonight, Rainey," Zara said. "They're bad enough sober. Throw in the booze, drugs, and power-tripping as the Kings of Ruckus, and they'll make an example of you."

"She's not missing out because of my brother," Paris said. "And he's not making an example of anyone. Especially if you're not walking around tonight alone. Come with us." She kissed my cheek. "We've got your back."

Like you did last time, I thought, even on the heels of another. *When your brother trussed me up and brought me so close to orgasm, a gust of wind up my skirt would've finished me off.*

"I'm not sure I'm going," I said. "There's something I have to take care of. Might run late."

"What?"

"It's personal. Can't get into it right now."

"You're so mysterious," she teased. "Text me after you wrap up your supersecret thing. I'm DD, so I'll pick you up if we haven't left yet."

"Did you figure out the clue?"

"It was pretty easy," Amy said. "Nigri colles viduae means Black Widow Hill. Party by the canyon. My kind of venue."

Black Widow Hill was not known for the spider it was named after, nor was it a hill. It was an easy, sloping incline that lifted you up, then pitched you into the canyon floor below—down a fatal drop to the crystal clear river bottom. Crystal Canyon, the namesake of the town we once were. The hill used to have another name too.

"It's not Black Widow Hill."

"Yes, it is. That's what it means."

"It's not," I repeated. "I figured it out the night of the party. Popped it into Google Translate and got Black Widow Hill in less than a millisecond. I knew right off that it had to be anywhere but there."

"You lost me," Paris said.

"They said we were all invited if we could find it. A hint it wasn't going to be as easy as a simple translation. I looked up all the possible meanings of the Latin, then I looked up all the possible meanings of the English. Another word for hill is drumlin, and a famous Black widow in our history is—"

Amy clapped, bouncing up and down in her seat. "Mayam Westchester! It's Westchester Drumlins. Fucking hell, Rainey, you're a genius."

"Nah, it's a lucky guess." *Brought on by the hours and weeks I've devoted to learning how to crack codes and clues.* "With my luck, it's another clue wrapped in a clue."

"No, this has got to be it," Paris said. "Westchester Drumlins is perfect. I can't believe I didn't see that. An old abandoned home on the edge of town. Spooky enough to give the wannabes a thrill. Secluded enough for the hardcores to fuck, drink, dance, and snort without the cops busting in."

"Would they?" I asked.

Paris fished a bowl of strawberries from her bag and offered us some. I helped myself, settling in with the sweet treat. It wasn't the solitude I was looking for, but most often, distraction was ten times better.

"One of the reasons Gran would bolt us inside is because the sheriff locks the station door and pretends no one's home on Ruckus night."

She laughed. "Yeah, just like Gran said you'd get pregnant from kissing. It's not the Wild West, Rainey. The people in charge accepted a long time ago that Ruckus Royale was going to happen. Some of them even made sure it was held year after year. But, someone is always going to complain.

"Noise complaints and most calls for vandalism are ignored," Paris explained. "Obviously, if someone is getting murdered, or a fight breaks out, the police will come. If it does get that bad, the cops shut the whole thing down. We're expected to keep ourselves in check. For the most part, we do. What happens during Ruckus, never leaves the party."

"We?" I raised a brow at her. "I didn't peg you as interested in all this stuff. Sex, booze, and drugs."

"No booze and drugs for me, I'm driving." She flashed me a lopsided smile. "But you can definitely peg me as interested in sex."

Paris patted my knee getting up. "Text me once you've dumped that supersecret thing. I cannot let you go another year missing out on Ruckus Royale." She was up, so Amy and Zara were up too. Made sense. They were still more her friends than mine.

"If I can, I'll hit you up," I said, waving them off.

My phone buzzed. I checked it and promptly forgot about them.

Dickmaster General flashed on the screen. Hard for even me to tell if I was complimenting or insulting him.

I hit accept.

"Morning, Cairo."

"Why did you answer?"

"Why did you call?"

"To remind you of what'll happen the longer you keep me waiting," he replied. "But you know that, and you answered anyway. Why? Did you want to hear my voice?" No small amount of satisfaction laced said voice.

"Maybe I have some questions for you." I leaned back on my bench, shutting my eyes to the sunlight. "I won't get them answered by listening to your psychotic voice mails. You should stop leaving those, by the way. They're all damning evidence for the restraining order."

He chuckled. "Who exactly is going to sign a restraining order against me? My father or the woman he's been fucking for the last four years?"

The sheriff and Judge Stone?

"Touché," I said. "Do you have a sense of shame or embarrassment? Would posting the voice mails for everyone to listen to work as a threat?"

"Are these your questions?" I heard a thud and voices on his end. "They're a waste of the three minutes you have till I hang up."

"Now that I want to talk to you, you don't have time for it? Yesterday you went on for twenty minutes describing how the fear in my eyes was even sweeter than my pussy."

"Yesterday the idea of you was tantalizing. Today it's boring me. I'm sure you've heard I've got plans tonight. Be more interesting or I'm hanging up."

"Are you a killer, Cairo Sharpe? Does your lust for fear and dominance ever push you over the edge?"

A long, thick silence poured out the end—unbroken by the noises I heard before. Everything had gone quiet from Cairo.

"Answer me, Cairo. Are you a killer?"

"Hm. I asked for interesting and you delivered," he said. "How about this one? Send me nudes or I'm hanging up."

I folded my legs on the bench, gripping my calf in a stranglehold that hurt. Everything hurt. My heart bruised, banging against my rib cage. My lungs screamed for air as I held my breath. My head ached with weeks of fear and stress, and nowhere for it to go.

It was all coming to a head. A ticking bomb counting down my last seconds. And through the fog, there was Cairo. In the waking nightmare since I received that letter, the only time I felt anything other than crushing dread was when I was with him.

I did have a question for Cairo. Another one. A question that was even more important, and that he'd eventually answer for me whether he wanted to or not.

"Are you?" I pressed.

"Why would I be?" There wasn't a trace of offense in his voice. Anyone else would've shouted off at that question. Not Cairo Sharpe. "Lots of stories going around town about the Bedlam Boys and what we do. Someone spreading that we're killers?"

"They don't have to. There's something in your eyes." I shut mine, seeing Cairo darkly glorious, like he stood before me. "Something burning. Uncontrolled. I've seen that look only once before."

"You haven't. You've met no one like me."

"Just answer me."

"Why? What are you looking for, Rain?"

"I want to know how," I rasped. "How someone can take a soul without losing their own?"

Voice smooth and unruffled, he replied, "Who said I didn't lose it?"

I breathed hard, the air gusting through the speakers. He sensed my anxiety while I sensed nothing. "Why do you want me? Is it really to check me off the list?"

"Stopped being about that a week ago."

"Then why?"

"Because you need me, Rain. There's something in your eyes too."

I shook so hard I rattled the bench. "Where does this leave us?"

"You'll find out."

I nodded, though he couldn't see me. Glad that he couldn't.

"Come tonight," Cairo said. "Westchester Drumlins. Say it."

"I'll be there tonight." I couldn't have stopped myself agreeing if I wanted to. "What will you do?"

"I told you. You'll find out."

The line went dead. My three minutes were up.

MY LAST CLASS OF THE day ended at three, pushing me out onto a campus almost completely taken over. Ruckus Royale had arrived to Bedlam, and no one was holding back the fun.

Westchester Drumlins was on the lips of nearly everyone I pushed past, struggling to get through the crowd dancing in the commons. The place looked like a music festival instead of a prestigious university. Half the student body was out with paint, water guns, and competing sound systems.

A blast of water hit my neck, knocking me back. Wet soaked my white tee and plastered it to my black lace bra. The naked frat boys returned for another shot at messing up my day.

"Assholes!"

They ran off hooting, spraying every girl in range.

I broke free of the party and made it off campus. The town wasn't in a better state.

Banners hung from shop windows, poles, and apartment balconies. Either welcoming this year's celebration or warning it off.

I walked through State Street on my way. The whole row was restaurants, little shops, and craft stores—each one split on how to play this.

"Official Ruckus gear," shouted the stall owner. "Get your shirts, beads, and cups here."

Venders, stalls, and people spilled out of the shops, taking over the street.

"Want to know where to find the party?" called another. "Twenty dollars for the answer to the clue. Don't be the one to miss out."

"End Ruckus Royale!"

A flyer flew in my face.

"Rampaging and trashing our streets, the Royale is an embarrassment." Frizzy brown hair and bulging eyes blocked my way. This lady had something to say, and apparently, I had to hear it.

"The Royale must end. Do you know how it makes our town look? Like a bunch of savages!" Spittle dotted my cheek. "You and your friends must think it's all just a bunch of fun. You're ruining our beautiful town with—"

"Couldn't agree with you more, ma'am."

Her rant died on her chapped lips. "Excuse me?"

"Look at me." I flapped a hand. "I can't even get home without being hit up for cheap mugs and entered into a wet T-shirt contest. Ruckus is a disgrace."

"Yes, exactly." Her frown lines smoothed out, brightening that angry face considerably. "Good to see there are some sensible young people left in this town. Be an example to your peers."

I plucked the flyer from her hands. "I will, ma'am. Thank you."

She sent me off with a pat on the back. Holding the pink paper was my hall pass through the protesters. I turned the corner, leaving State Street behind, and trashed it in the nearest bin.

His home was up ahead. I should arrive just as he turned into the driveway like I had the day before, and the day before that.

Constitution Blvd. wasn't as loud or packed as State. That didn't mean it was spared by Ruckus.

I passed neighbors hanging up signs warning trespassers they'd either be photographed and reported, or shot. I couldn't say if it was like this every year. Like I told Paris and her friends, Gran didn't let us anywhere near town when the calendar dropped us into Ruckus Royale. I did know in the hundred years since it started, no one's been shot.

Do I know that? Those crazed letters pointed to a tradition as old as Ruckus itself. There wasn't a town on this planet where everyone lived to old age and died peacefully in their sleep.

Bedlam had its share of missing people. We had domestic violence situations that ended tragically. Accidental deaths. Murders.

I dug into all of them going ten years back, looking for a connection to Ruckus Royale, or a name that continually popped up. I came up with nothing, but then, I wasn't looking for the birds.

Creeping up to number fifty-eight, I ducked behind their sugar maple tree. The Johnsons weren't back from work yet. They'd be home in five hours to arm themselves and shoot trespassers. That gave me time to watch his house, wait for him to make a move, and figure out how the hell I'm going to stop him.

A blue Volkswagen puttered down the boulevard. I crouched in the dirt, pulse picking up at the sight of the ordinary car, driven by an ordinary man, coming home from his ordinary tax-preparer job.

Everything and nothing about him screamed psychopath. Now that I knew who the kookaburra was and why nothing was as it seemed, there was only one person who could've stopped him laughing. As surely as my grandmother was right about the dangers of Ruckus, I was certain he was the man who sent me the letters. That was a nice feeling—being certain. Because I was certain of nothing else.

He killed the engine in front of number sixty-nine. A slim, tall man climbed out of the car. Attractive man if you went for the long, swoopy-haired, boy-band thing. He wasn't much older than me. Possibly two or three years. Old enough to be out of school. Young enough to count every year sitting in a prison cell.

Scott Cavendish pulled out his briefcase, popped it open, and grabbed an apple. Leaning against the hood, he turned his face to the sun, tearing off a bite.

"Are you going to hide behind that tree all day?" he called. "Again?"

I froze.

Cavendish tossed his apple from palm to palm. "You can if you want, but my neighbors are itching to see a Ruckuser in handcuffs. I bet they're calling to report a suspicious person sniffing around the Johnsons' house right now."

My nails dug into the bark, driving splinters through my nail bed. Cavendish knew I was here. He knew the whole time.

"Come on." The soft purr made my hairs stand on end. "You've been waiting a long time for this chat. Don't get shy now."

I wasn't ducked behind a tree. I was bare. Exposed. Pinned through the hands and feet, lying naked under a microscope. He's seen everything. Maybe even the moment I figured it out.

"Come."

Rising up, I stepped out from the maple and crossed the street.

Cavendish watched me come, smile widening with every step. I stopped just out of arm's reach, lifting my chin to meet his gaze. Time had made me a liar. The look in Cairo's eyes. I've seen it twice.

"Nice bra," Scott said. His grin dimpled his smooth cheek. "Did you wear it for me?"

I fisted my jeans, though I longed to clap my hands over my wet shirt. He wanted to unsettle me. A goal he's succeeded in for weeks. Today I wouldn't give him the satisfaction of scenting my fear.

"You're not going to deny it," I rasped.

The apple crunched between his teeth. "Deny what exactly?"

"You know why I'm here, so say it. Admit it."

"I won't make it that easy for you, sweet *Rain-ey*."

I bristled. My name next to those masticated apple bits churned my stomach. As vile as the way he pronounced it, drawing it out like a joke.

"You tell me why you're here. Maybe I'll tell you if you're right."

I took a step back. Cavendish didn't make a move toward me, or look like he wanted to. Still, my instincts screamed not to get close.

"Does the kookaburra laugh or does it scream? Does the mighty kingfisher cry or does it dream? Where are you, kookaburra? Tell me, oh, tell me, why is nothing as it seems?" I recited, watching those shark eyes for a hint of something.

"Cute poem. Got a bit lazy with the rhyme though." Cavendish shifted and I shot away. His chuckle burned my cheeks.

"Critiquing yourself?" I snapped. "You had the time you were stalking and watching me to come up with something better in your first note."

He said nothing. He wouldn't. Cavendish was waiting for me to tell him why we were here, and after weeks of dying to rage in his face, I was more than happy to.

"You're a murderer." The words scraped my throat raw. "A killer. A *psychopath*! You tortured me for weeks, but it's over now, you twisted fuck!"

Cavendish kept eating that damn apple. "Me? A murderer? What gave you that idea?"

"I finally figured it out. I was taking your *clues* too literally. Running to zoos and sanctuaries when you said it. Nothing is as it seems."

He smiled at me like a dog who performed a cute trick. "One of life's truths."

"You killed Douglas Herbert. That's another one."

"Did I?"

"Yes. I remembered something my sister said. A while back, she told me about a guy she went to school with. Douglas," I began. "She couldn't stand that jackass. No one could. Douglas is remembered so fondly now, but when he was alive, he tortured people with his vicious pranks. Funny to him and his friends, but not to anyone else. The laughing jackass, otherwise known as a kookaburra."

He hummed, bobbing his head. "Clever wordplay. Subtle."

"That night, Douglas ran off the road. The traffic report doesn't say why because they don't know. It wasn't raining. There was nothing wrong with his car. They figure something must've run out in front of him and he swerved to avoid it. Was that something you?" I asked. "Did you plan it, or did you just thank your good luck in the hospital room while you stood over his unconscious body?"

Keeping one eye fixed on him, I drew out my phone. The news articles shone on the screen. "*'There was nothing I could do,' says Scott Cavendish, friend of Mr. Herbert. 'All of a sudden the machines went off and nurses were rushing into the room. At least he wasn't alone when he died. I held his hand and said goodbye.'*

"Very touching," I said. "You could almost believe you cared."

Cavendish folded his arms, bending one leg on the tire. "Douglas was one of my best friends. Why would I do something so horrible?"

No shock. No horror. He truly wanted me to answer the question. Why did he do it?

"I'll tell you why," I went on. "Once I realized this was all about Douglas Herbert, I dug into his life and time before his death. A couple weeks before, Douglas hazed a freshman in a little joke that went wrong. Survive ten minutes of waterboarding and you're in the fraternity.

"The brothers were laughing and joking it up until the kid stopped struggling. He asphyxiated, and it was someone's quick thinking that saved his life. The incident scared sense into Douglas. He nearly killed some poor kid and flushed his future down the drain. After that, he went on a mission to make amends.

"He apologized to everyone he hurt, started volunteering in the soup kitchen, and confessed to the crimes he and his friends got away with. Nathan Wade—now expelled—drove the dean's car in the lake. Sam Dillion—left town—called in a bomb threat to the school, and when they evacuated, he drove by firing blanks, causing a stampede that put two girls in the hospital. Herbert gave everyone's secrets away, Cavendish, except yours. He conveniently died, alone in a room with you, before your secrets left his lips. Does the kookaburra laugh or does it dream? He does neither thanks to you."

"Wow," he drew out. "Such a dastardly plan. Sounds like I got away with it scot-free too. Begs the question, why would I drag all this up two years later? Give you a clue to find and stop me? That's a pretty stupid thing to do, and from what you're saying, I'm not a stupid guy."

"You dragged this up *because* you got away with it. The motive, the means, the opportunity, it was all there staring everyone in the face, but no one suspected you. You four always had an audience for your cruelty—people to witness what you did even if they couldn't prove it was you. You want someone to acknowledge how wickedly clever you are. And now that you've got a taste for killing, you need an audience this time around.

"This is just a game to you, Cavendish. Another prank. That's why that disgusting smile is on your face."

Cavendish clapped. Slow at first, then faster as his laughter rang through the street. "Good, Rainey. Very good. You scared me cutting it this close. I was afraid you weren't what I thought you were." He shook his head. "You never cease to impress."

"You don't know me!"

He pouted. "After all the time we've spent together these last several weeks, how can you say that?"

I advanced and slammed against the invisible barrier made of common sense. "I'm not playing, you miserable fucker. Why did you get me involved? Why me?!"

"Ah. So, this is the part where I deliver my evil villain monologue. Thanks for giving me so much time to prepare." Cavendish straightened and cleared his throat. "I did run out in front of his car that night. Douglas was going out on that camping trip to clear his head. Work up the courage to betray his best friend since kindergarten." The first trace of temper colored his voice.

"Douglas found out something about me that he shouldn't have. He was cool to keep it to himself when he understood loyalty, then that stupid kid almost drowned. Douglas gave me till he got back from his trip to confess myself. Make things right and accept the consequences. It's the only way I'd be free. The sanctimonious bastard," he spat. "I knew the route he'd take, so I went up first. Waited for his car to drive down and jumped out in front of him. That was supposed to be the end of it, but would you believe it, he survived two days in that broken-down heap."

Cavendish tossed the apple over his shoulder. "I panicked when I found out. Had to rush to the hospital to make sure he didn't get a chance to tell anyone who shone in his headlights. A syringe, air bubble in the IV, boohoo to the doctors, and it was over... until you. Because that's what you have so wrong, *Rain-ey.*"

He moved closer, making me trip over myself backing up. "I didn't get bored. We're not here because I need the thrill of almost getting caught. This is, and has always been, about you."

"You don't know me," I forced through clenched teeth.

"So you keep saying." His eyes narrowed. "As always, focused on the wrong thing and letting it take you away from the path. I never wanted any of this to come back up. Douglas fucking Herbert is dead and buried. Let him rot, and I hope that clean conscience serves him well in the afterlife."

"If you didn't want this, why are we here?!" Frustration made me scream. Anger made me rip a shoe off and fling it at his head. It struck his forehead, breaking the skin, and leaving a streak of blood and no satisfaction. I wanted to punch his smirk in. Tear out his hair. Break his fingers. I wanted to stomp his crotch and cave his skull. I wanted to ki—

I gasped, staggering farther back as I cut the thought off at the knees. What was wrong with me? What was he doing to me? I was so angry, scared, and helpless, I felt capable of anything.

"Oh," he whispered. "Now she gets mad."

"That's what you want, isn't it?" I ripped off the other shoe. Just to hold something. To know I could hurt him again if I wished. "Why? I answered your questions, you answer mine. What do you want with me?"

"It's always been about you. Even before I knew you." Cavendish paid no mind to the blood streaking down his nose. "I had to give you a reason. The catalyst to push you over the edge, and the proof that I will carry out my word. Revealing what I did to Douglas was a sacrifice. Ugh!" he bellowed, throwing up his hands.

I jumped, heart slamming into my throat.

"People don't understand sacrifice. They're not willing to do whatever needs to be done, no matter the cost to them. Weak. Pathetic! But not me, and soon, not you." Cavendish raised his hand. It took me a terrible moment to realize he wanted me to hold it. "I've given away my deepest secret to erase any doubt that I've killed before and I'll do it again," he said. "Unless you stop me."

"Stop you? You mean *kill* you."

"Yes."

"You're insane," I rasped. "You want to die?"

"I do not, but this isn't about what I want." He moved forward, hand outstretched. "This has always been about you. You are ten times the sanctimonious bastard than Douglas Herbert could ever be. You think you're above us—hiding out with your chickens and leaving the silly townspeople to their silly games. Your ancestors ran out on the fight and your coward ass did too."

"What are you talking about?!"

"I'm talking about you, me, and Jennifer Wilson. You can't run away this time. She dies tonight unless you break free of that goody-two-boots, farm-girl act and do what has to be done."

"None of this has to be done. You don't have to hurt anyone, Cavendish. You said you don't want to die, so let's end this." I dropped my voice. There was no other word for what I was doing than pleading. "Your job, your family, your girlfriend. Remember what you killed your best friend to protect. It can all be there waiting for you tomorrow morning. No one has to die tonight."

My speech stirred nothing in his eyes. "Tonight's as good a night as any other. To die is my birthright, de Souza." And then he was there, fingers caressing my cheek almost lovingly. "But to die ripping out a piece of your soul, that is my honor."

"I won't do it."

"Then, Jennifer won't make it back to her job, family, or girlfriend tomorrow morning. I'll get to see how long you can live with that, before you blow your fucking brains out."

Teeth bared, I slapped his hand away. "You're not hearing me. No one is going to die tonight. You confessed to killing Douglas and targeting Jennifer. I have more than enough to take to the sheriff."

"Go on, then. Send him speeding out here to arrest me."

I yanked out my phone to do just that, putting distance between us in case he made a grab for it.

"Although," he said. "You may have trouble getting through. Ruckus Royale's already started for half the town, so the station's getting flooded with calls. How long are you going to listen to a busy signal before you get a hold of someone?" Cavendish flashed that grin. "I'm sure you're not expecting me to stick around until you do."

I shrugged. "Fine. Go on the run." I spoke with bravado I didn't feel. "The cops will know you're after her. They'll protect her until they eventually catch up to you. At least Jennifer will be safe."

His grin widened—a nasty, terrible twist of his handsome face, and I knew before he spoke. "Will she?"

"What did you do?"

"Nothing other than what I promised to do. I've had months to plan this. Don't you think I worked in a few fail-safes in case you caught me before time? And you did," he said. "When I noticed you lurking around my house, I went with plan B."

"What's plan B? What did you do to her?!" My phone rang in my ear. And rang. And rang. And rang.

"What did you do, Rainey? Why did you take so long? Why'd you waste so much time?" He shook his head, reeking with disappointment. "She'd be safe at home getting ready for Ruckus right now if you had killed me sooner."

"Stop," I shouted. "Stop pretending this is my fault when you're the psychotic piece of garbage threatening her. You won't make me responsible for what you do."

"You are responsible!" The bellow blew me back. Rage bulged his eyes and dots of spittle sprinkled my shoe. "You did this. We are here because of you!"

"How?" The dial tone was louder than my whisper. "Why?"

"If you want to play the innocent, then go. Run to the station, report me, and wash your hands of the whole thing. It's what Great-great-grandma de Souza would have done," Cavendish said, lips curled. "Keep the family tradition going."

"My family has nothing to do with this. I have no idea why you think you know me, but you're going to start making some sense. Why did you pick me? Why is it your *honor* to force me to take your life?"

His gaze drifted over my shoulder. "Interesting. Are they your backup plan?"

"What? My backup plan?" I turned around and screamed.

Cairo and Jacques leaped out of the truck bed, hitting the ground as Roan squealed to a stop, Arsenio and Legend riding passenger beside him.

"This is a treat," Cairo said. "Couldn't wait till tonight, could you, Rain?"

"What are you—?"

"Get her," Jacques barked. "We're taking them both."

"We don't have enough," Roan said.

"She's not a sacrifice." The look on Jacques's face answered the question. It wasn't irony. "She's mine."

He was going to kill me.

Jacques and Cairo charged.

"Wait!"

A streak cut across my vision. Cavendish threw himself in their path. They slammed into him with an audible sound of bone crunching bone and went down in a heap. I turned tail and ran.

"Get after her!"

"This changes nothing," Cavendish bellowed after me. "Make your choice, de Souza. Make your choice!"

I ran. Arms swinging, feet pounding, blood pumping loud in my ears, and not loud enough to block them out.

"This one's tasty."

"Look at her ass when she runs."

I bolted around the house and faced the six-feet-high wooden fence. Leaping, I seized the posts, heaving myself up. Hands grabbed my ankles.

"Get off!"

They ripped me down, tearing me free of the fence and leaving bits of my skin behind. My feet secure, my face rushed to meet the lawn. Pain exploded in my head.

The world went black.

Chapter Four

" ... *nothing will stop me..."*

Low, persistent rumbling filled my ear, tap-tap-tapping on my consciousness. All I wanted to do was sleep. I earned sleep after what I've been through. Gran, Ivy, Andrew. I was thrown in hell and hit every flaming spire on the way down. Just let me sleep.

"Nothing will stop me. Except you."

A thump rattled my bones, jarring me awake.

Peeling my eyes open, I met with a cascade of stars. A shining, scattering nebula so beautiful, I was ten years old again, lying out on a blanket with Gran and Ivy as we made up stories for the constellations.

The happy memory faded as quickly as it came. The earth wasn't as hard on those late-night picnics. I didn't have something digging into my cheek, or a prickly numb feeling that said my arm fell asleep. On those nights, the earth didn't move.

Twisting my neck, I took stock of my surroundings.

I was in the back of a moving truck. *The Bedlam Boys' truck.*

Yeah, it was starting to come back to me. They found me with Cavendish. Chased me, caught me at the fence, and—

A spike of pain went through my forehead, forcefully claiming my attention.

They caught and tossed me in the back like a sack of manure. Actually, like a sack of sand.

I blinked at the sandbags lining the back of the bed, and tucked in the corner, a container of gasoline. It sat next to an overturned toolbox, likely upended when they hit a bump. Explained why I was lying on a wrench.

I reached to push it away and my hand didn't move. Straining, I yanked on my binds, crying out as the ropes bit tighter. Caught, tossed, and *tied* in the back of their truck.

"Shit-brained assholes!" I shrieked. "Let me out of here!"

"Quiet down, darling," an unfamiliar voice called back. "We'll get to you soon enough."

"You can't do this to me. I have to go. I have to—"

Music blasted out of the speakers, drowning out my shouts.

Calm down, Rainey. Think. Think!

Taking a deep breath, I held it till my pulse slowed. My mind cleared. *There are tools rolling all over the place. Use them to get free.*

Shifting, I twisted to put my bound hands within reach, and our eyes locked. My scream made him grimace.

"Goodness, I have to agree with your friends up there," said Cavendish. "Quiet down."

"No." I flung myself away from him. "No, no, no."

"Relax. I can hardly hurt you tied up like this."

It was true. I assumed Cavendish put up a much bigger fight because they hogtied his ass. The ropes looped around his wrists and bound his ankles. He lay on his side, bent like my bow, ready to fire.

Dirt covered his face and clothes—streaks of black to mingle with the red. Some of the blood on him was from my shoe to the head. The rest courtesy of the Bedlam Boys.

"I don't know what you did to end up on their sacrifice list, but now you can't hurt me, Jennifer, or anyone else tonight." I spit in his face. "At the end of the night, I'll drag Sheriff Sharpe out of his office and watch him put the cuffs on you. It's over."

Cavendish barely blinked at the glob running down his face. "I admit, these guys showing up were a surprise, but this is far from over. I thought I made that clear." He observed me. "No? Then, let me spell it out for you. Jennifer Wilson left campus this morning but never made it home. She's currently staying in a place she doesn't like very much, screaming and crying for help—using up the precious little oxygen she has left."

My mouth went dry. Lips parting, I tried to speak and nothing came out.

"Kill me and you'll get her location." He tsked. "You've wasted so much time. Time poor Jennifer doesn't have. How much more will you waste playing the scared little innocent? You're not for this world, Rainey. It's time to live where the wild things are."

"You c-can't do this." Dampness soaked my cheeks, stinging in the cool night air. "You won't make me do this."

"I already did."

The car began to slow. Miles and miles of secluded forest road and our trip was so painfully short. Why couldn't Westchester Drumlins be on the fucking moon?

"But you're lying," I whispered. "If you die, there's no one to tell me where she is. I won't be able to save her, and that's what you want. For me to be a killer and a failure."

"No, baby." His voice was almost soft. "I may not have the right to say these words, but you have to trust me. I haven't lied to you since we started this together. I won't lie to you now."

The truck pulled off the road, engine dying along with the music.

"Do what you were meant to do," he said as the Bedlam Boys piled out of the car. "And you'll be free."

"No— Wait!"

Cairo dropped the tailgate, hopping in to shove Cavendish out into Roan's and Legend's waiting arms. The man didn't have a strong relationship with shirts. He was bare-chested again—back rippling in the moonlight as he lifted the grown man with ease. They were all bare-chested, and I wasn't better for it. They looked like the warriors they emulated. Strong, powerful, free of society's morals.

Sometime during my concussed stupor, they lost Jacques and Arsenio. Maybe they'd gone ahead to prep the old run-down property for the hundreds of townspeople preparing to descend.

Cavendish didn't make a sound as they carted him off. The same couldn't be said for me.

"Cairo, you don't know what you're doing." I scrambled to get my feet under me, desperate to chase down the one man who knew where Jennifer Wilson was. "He's a dangerous man!"

"I'm a dangerous man." Cairo crouched beside me. His fingers trailed the edge of my jaw, enticing a rippling shiver down my body. "He's puffed-up trash who fooled himself into thinking the rules don't apply to him. He should've known better, and you're about to learn. I saw that video you and Jacques made. On top of defying me and refusing to share your little secrets, you've racked up quite a list of offenses."

"None of that matters now," I snapped.

"Doesn't it? Mattered enough to get you here."

I shook him off. "This isn't about me and you. Please, Cairo, listen. There's a girl named Jennifer Wilson. Maybe you know her. Cavendish kid—"

"Shh." Cairo stuffed an oily cloth in my mouth. "Time for the king to take his throne. I'll play court to your pleas for mercy after."

"Hmpf!"

Hopping out of the truck bed, he closed the gate and disappeared.

Tears soaked my face. Screaming, I thrashed on the unforgiving surface, picturing with crushing clarity Jennifer trapped. Feeling the ropes cutting off circulation to her fingers. Forcing her screams through a sandpaper throat, and hearing as if she yelled in my ear, "why didn't you save me? I died cold, alone, and afraid. Because of you."

"You came from the strongest of people. The fiercest. People who would give up their lives before surrendering their freedom."

I blinked, spreading tears like raindrops.

"That's the blood that runs through your veins, Rain."

"Fight."

My heaving, choking sobs slowed.

I lay there in silence, finally understanding what I had to do next.

CAIRO

"What the fuck's wrong with him?"

Roan stopped lugging sandbags. "What?"

"Him," I said, jerking my chin. "What's he smiling about?"

He followed my gaze to Scott Cavendish. Except for tripping us up to let Rain get away, he'd been a model captive all night. He didn't fight back when Jacques buried a fist in his gut—payback for getting in our way. He didn't say a word while we hogtied and threw him in the truck. And the final indignity, prepping him for a Royale sacrifice, and all he did was what he was doing then, smirking like this was all a fun game.

Scott Cavendish noticed my attention and flicked down to me. Looking me straight in the eyes, he winked.

"He's refused to pay since he took over," Roan said. "Guy thinks he doesn't have to be afraid of us. He's still thinking it. No one gets hurt on Ruckus night. It's all fun and games."

I narrowed on that smile.

"He's a dangerous man."

What were Cavendish and my new pet talking about when we rolled up? Why was she so upset?

Why was she scared?

"All fun and games," I repeated. "Some traditions are meant to be broken."

"I'm all for making an example out of him." Roan cocked his head. "It's so much sweeter making the cute ones beg."

"Did you get everything out of the truck?"

"A couple sandbags left."

"I've got it." I marched off, finding Rain right where I left her.

I hung off the tailgate, studying her as she studied me. Her soaked face and rag said she'd been crying, though she was done with that now. Those abnormally large fawn eyes blinked at me—light and clear. I wondered what shown in mine.

Too much if our phone conversation was anything to go by. This woman thought she knew something about me. I couldn't say the same about her.

Spent her entire life in my town, and I never met or heard of her before that party. Shapely legs I haven't disappeared between. Plump lips that have yet to swallow my cock. All that long, wavy hair begging to fist in my grip as I half tore it from the roots, bending her head back to take what I'd give her.

Just when I was getting bored and thinking of some fucked-up methods to handle that problem, Bedlam surprised me with a new treat.

Dropping the gate, I climbed up and tugged the gag from her mouth. I expected her to beg or plead. I'd have even taken a glare.

Rain did neither. She eyed me warily, waiting to see what I'd do.

"I'll let you in on a secret, sweetheart," I whispered. "I don't know either."

She didn't ask me what I meant. "You need to untie these ropes, Cairo. Now."

"What do you have to do with Scott Cavendish? Why were you with him?"

"What do you have to do with him?" she shot back.

I closed the distance, my nose tracing circles on her cheek. I inhaled her perfect mix of sweat and rose soap. "I asked you first."

"We were discussing poetry."

"Lying," I said without a hitch. "Why? What's that smug bastard smiling about? Why did he throw himself in front of us to help you get away?" A nasty thought occurred to me. "Are you fucking him?"

"Let me get a question in." She raised her head, swallowing me in those fawn eyes. "Why does the thought of that make you angry?"

Good question. My hands traveled down her hips, along her legs, to the tip of the red boots Roan put back on. The only farm-girl thing about her. I tore them off and flung them in the trees.

"Another question: why did those boots make me angry? The answer is I hate any and everything that kept me from finding you until now." I nipped her nose. "That answers both your questions, doesn't it?"

Her throat bobbed visibly. "Why do you care about me?"

"I answered one of yours. You answer mine." I continued my exploration, moving up her thighs. "What makes him so dangerous?"

She held my gaze—not moving, not breathing as I slipped under her shirt. Rain was impossibly soft and warm beneath my fingers.

Delicate.

It turned on something feral within me. Something she gave me the night of the party, then ripped away by pretending to be like the rest of them.

Had it really been an entire week since I touched her? A crime fit to piss me off all over again. In that time, I've threatened and teased her alike. Sometimes I got nothing in response, but every other time she gave me as good as she got.

"The same thing that makes me dangerous," she whispered. "He's not afraid of you."

My cock twitched. If that wasn't a demand to fuck her right there and then, I didn't know what was.

"We'll see."

I found the edge of her lacy bra and drew it to me, sliding it off the reasonably sized mounds. Her shirt went the other way.

Rainey's lips parted, pants picking up speed as I unveiled her inch by inch.

"Let me go."

I blew hot breath on her nipples. They hardened to rock-hard pebbles, eager to roll around in my mouth. Normally, eager bitches put me off my lunch. I was so very obviously not a good guy. Have some respect for yourself. But this little lovely—both helpless with want and shaking with anger for it. She made me want to see what's coming for the second date.

"Stop," she said, halting my mouth a millimeter from her. "I don't want you to."

I clicked my tongue. "Another lie." With that, I swallowed her, sucking hard on her nipple and earning the most satisfying hiss.

"Fucking twisted piece of shit," she cried. "Get o-off me."

I bit down hard.

Gasping, Rain arched her back, pressing against my lips.

I felt it the first time in my room. A flash that went away quickly enough I could almost ignore it. This time, I couldn't. Pulse racing. Brow sweating. Breaths coming faster. I wasn't sure what everyone else called this, but I knew one thing, I wasn't bored.

I scraped my teeth down her stomach, catching on her jeans.

"I fucking swear, Cairo!"

The jeans were ripped down her thighs in an instant. I stuck my head between her legs, losing myself in the heady scent of her arousal. I barely did anything and she was wet to drown me. The thought of that made my arm buckle, dropping me on top of her.

Rain was beautiful like this. Hands trapped beneath us, her chest rolled and heaved—topped with mounds shining with my spit and already beginning to redden. Like a helpless chick resting on my palm, all I had to do was close my fist.

"Tell me something true," I said.

"I... don't know what you mean."

I swiped a tongue past her folds, groaning at the taste of her on my tongue. She quivered beneath my lips.

"Tell me something true, Rain."

"If you let me go," she said softly. "I'll come back to you."

I didn't speak. Slipping out from between her, I drew her up and untied her wrists.

Rain caught me as I pulled away. She pressed her fingers to my temple—rubbing slow circles with her thumbs, she wove her digits in my hair. It was a strange, oddly intimate thing to do. Stranger still, the sensation moving through my veins, spreading its paralytic.

I was stiff as her hands moved down my face, chest, legs, back. Rain tugged me close, covering my mouth with hers.

I didn't react to the kiss. Didn't pull away or press.

Soon enough, it was over. I studied her as she sat back, wondering what she got out of that.

"It was either that or beating you with this wrench." She waved it to prove her point. "I'm not convinced I chose right, so you should probably go.

"I'll find you," she promised.

Saying nothing, I grabbed the last two sandbags and loped off into the trees.

RAINEY

I got to my feet and pitched forward, dropping hard on my knees. Hands shaking, I fixed my clothes and tugged my jeans up. I couldn't think about my brief encounter with Cairo. Couldn't let my mind grasp the aching pressure between my legs, or the promise I made him. I couldn't think about the fact that I meant it.

Not now, a voice screamed. *Nothing else matters right now.*

I've wasted so much time. The one thing Jennifer did not have.

I leaped off the truck and my toes sank in the dirt. "Shit!"

Cursing Cairo six ways to Sunday, I didn't bother looking for my shoes. With nowhere else to go, I disappeared into the trees, following Cairo.

The Westchester Drumlins property was five acres of bush, overgrown trees, and a dilapidated house that looked like a good strong breeze would blow it down. Many strong winds, thunderstorms, and dozens of hurricanes have tried, but the old Westchester home proved as tough as its namesake.

She stood proudly through the break in the brush, still stately though most of her windows were broken, and the back doors welcoming her guests swung on rusted hinges.

I watched the Bedlam Boys tromp inside. Roan, Legend, Jacques, and Arsenio. They arrived at some point and must've come in from the front.

Cairo dumped the last of the sand, said something to Cavendish, then gifted him a blindfold. After he went inside with the rest. I waited as long as I dared and stepped out.

"Holy shit," I breathed.

Speakers circled the outline of the lawn, ready to pump music at mind-scrambling levels. I'd never been to a Ruckus Royale, but with one look, I knew the Bedlam Boys outdid them all.

Beer cooler fountains scattered all over the place. That was the best phrase to describe their invention—three tubs of ice stacked together like a chocolate fountain. Instead, this fountain was chockfull of bottles and raining ice water.

There were more tubs and buckets. Those were filled with—

I peered inside.

—paint. Glow-in-the-dark paint, and rows of plastic guns lined behind them, leaving no doubt.

I kept going. Passing one of the candy tables, I stopped short. It wasn't rainbow Skittles in those multicolored bowls. They were pills. Of all shapes, sizes, and potency. Who the hell knew what they were or what would happen if you downed them? The sign by the bowls simply said three words. *Get Fucked Responsibly.*

All of that was impressive, but it was not the sight to see.

Five posts stretched to the sky. The Bedlam Boys were kind— Was that the word? They were generous to build a platform for the three men and two women to stand on. Hands tied around the post and secured; blindfolds heightened their helplessness. I wasn't surprised to hear a few of them crying.

I recognized all of them except one. Professor Valdez tied to a post wasn't the surprise it should have been. If I had to pay for what I did to Jacques that morning, Valdez wasn't getting off any easier for threatening him.

A vision of the hangman's noose floated in my mind. Though that wasn't what they had planned for tonight.

I kneeled before Cavendish, touching the cool sand. The well they dug circling the sacrifices, and the tubs of gasoline beside the pill-popper table, colored the lines in for me. This was a burning.

"Cavendish."

He turned his head in my direction. "Rainey. Thought that was you. Fear makes you smell like pine needles. And sweat," he said. "I'm glad it's the last thing I'll smell before we end this here and now."

"It's not over yet, Cavendish." I didn't let my voice carry. "There's still time for you and Jennifer. Tell me where she is, and no one has to die tonight."

"I told you, everyone has to die. You give me the death I've chosen or Jennifer receives the one you've chosen for her."

"Scott—"

"Here's another rhyme for you," he said, turning his face to the moonlight and smiling as though he basked in it. "Tick, ticking, tock. Rainey ran down the clock. Time ran out. No one heard Jen shout. Tick, ticking, tock."

Rage surged up in me, balling my fists. I raised them, ready to pop his guts up through his throat and see if he found that funny, then my gaze fell on the gas container.

A thought came to me. A terrible, awful idea that unfolded with picture-perfect clarity, and suddenly the way forward was blindingly obvious.

I lowered my fists—sensing the rage leak away to be replaced with a cold, numbing calm. Everywhere but in my head.

Hissing, I pressed my palm against my aching temple. My vision blurred and a shadowed figure rose above the post. A painted, skeletal face exaggerated the shadows below his eyes and cheekbones too sharp to be real.

A blink, and he was gone.

It was just me and Cavendish, and the container.

Fingers closed over the handle. They weren't mine for all that they were attached to me.

It wasn't me who approached Cavendish.

It wasn't me who unscrewed the lid.

Chapter Five

I was running.

Twigs snapped under my bare feet, opening cuts and stealing my blood. It hardly registered.

Noise spread through the forest. Ruckus Royale was beginning. Half the town surging on Westchester Drumlins, and bringing their drunkenness, libido, and the potential word of dozens of eyewitnesses with them.

I almost didn't make it out of there before the first group of people arrived.

The party that started at the university would've carried throughout the square, sweeping through town and collecting revelers as they went. In the morning, there'd be messes to clean up and apologies to make. I wondered who I'd give mine to.

Leaping over a fallen branch, I ran faster than I knew I could. The farm was only a couple of miles away, but I was racing against a clock I couldn't see. Was there an hour left, or had my time already run out?

A familiar oak tree lit in the starlight. Our tree. Ivy and I climbed and fell off this tree more times than I remembered. I was on the edge of the property line. I was close.

My phone buzzed in my pocket.

I flicked down for a second and glanced up. The towering shadow gave a shout.

"Hey!"

I smashed into it with all my weight, lifting us both off our feet. We crumpled in a tangle of limbs—both groaning.

"What the fuck?"

Hands grabbed and picked me up.

"Where you going so fast, darling? The party's that way."

Shapes came into focus. Four— No, five of them counting the one I flattened into the dirt. Cursing, he shoved up, smacking away a hand stuck out to help him.

Slowly, I backed away. The five of them came together, standing shoulder to shoulder as if they knew the impact they had in one large dose.

Various heights, shapes, sizes, hair colors, and builds, they shared two things in common: a black shape on their necks I couldn't make out, but safely assumed was a tattoo. And an air of wicked danger that every man who *knew* he was handsome possessed.

"What are you doing here?" I asked, stepping back as they moved forward. "This is private property."

"Taking a shortcut," one said.

"And, to be accurate, it's not private property," said the guy I ran into. He tousled his hair, catching the dark green locks in the light. "No one owns that broken-down farm or the patch of grass it sits on."

"Wrong," I hissed. "I do. This is my home, so find yourself a new fucking shortcut."

"Oooh." Their jeers rippled hackles down my back. "She's tough."

"She'd have to be," Green Hair agreed. "Everyone in this town will."

They filed past me, brushing so close their lapels tickled my cheek and fingers skated over mine.

"Hope we run into each other again, darling," he tossed over his shoulder. "We'll have a chat about who owns what."

They were out of mind as soon as they were out of sight.

I sprinted the last mile to the farm, bursting out of the trees to come up beside the barn. A heavy-duty lock secured the doors. Twice as big as the last one I broke into. I blew past it and rounded the corner, passing the barren pigpen for the awning that connected them.

Dropping to my knees, I pushed apart the loose wooden slats and squeezed inside. Harder to do when you're twenty-one instead of eleven. My hips caught between the wood. I left skin behind, forcing myself through.

Clambering to my feet, I looked over a part of the home that would always be mine.

Farm equipment quietly rusted in every corner. Ever breathe in the scent of old hay? Musty and pungent, it carried the essence of the animals that came to graze and sleep, or the children that came to play. That was what became of my home—the one place I was happy.

It was now old hay, stinking of rotting memories.

Throat tight, I pushed down tears and turned my head to the loft. It should still be up there—shut away behind a lock even better than the one that tried to keep me out.

My phone went off again, the chime following me up the stairs. I answered.

"Rainey? Rainey!" Music poured out of the speakers. "Where are you, girl? You are not missing this party if I have to drag you out of that geek cave myself!"

I spun the dial, feeling the faint click resound within me.

"No need, Paris."

Light peeked through the slats, shining on the gleaming curves of my bow.

"I wouldn't miss Ruckus Royale for anything."

ARSENIO

Ruckus was in full swing. Dante would be impressed.

Actually, I could tell he was. Dancing with a group of painted naked ladies, he howled as they stripped his clothes and ran their hands all over, turning him into a Jackson Pollock painting. He'd owed us a thank-you for correcting his mistake and naming the Bedlam Boys the Kings of Ruckus. I'd collect if I cared about such things.

What good were pleases and thank-yous? Those were for people who still believed this was a world where asking nicely got you what you wanted.

The five of us spread out on the porch, surveying the party.

"Did you get it?" I demanded.

"Nah," Roan replied. "She changed the password, and the security."

"Why the fuck would she do that?"

"Punishment. She says we're getting sloppy."

"She's getting soft," I corrected. "It's not sloppy if we clean up the mess."

"But we didn't quite clean this mess up." Legend slouched against the rail, taking no notice of Roan running a hand up his crotch. "Did we?"

"We'll have to deal with it later. After Ruckus." I fished my lighter from my pocket, indulging the faint click, flickering heat as I flipped it open and shut.

The porch door banged open.

"Arsenio, baby." Hands circled me from behind. "I haven't sucked your cock in three whole days." She stuck her hand down my pants. "Feed me."

I tugged her out. Holding on to Quinn's wrist, I made her face me till those wide eyes swallowed mine. "You don't ask. I give."

"Then, give it to me."

"Not interested." I foisted her off on Jacques. "I'm getting bored with your sex tricks. Past time we got a new one."

"You're such a bastard!" She tossed her beer on my back. "You guys wouldn't dare break up with me. Trust me, there's no woman on this planet willing to give you what you need."

Quinn flounced off. Good. I stopped listening after "you're."

"What's the deal with them?" I asked, jerking a chin at the sacrifices. I didn't get involved with the Ruckus planning till that day. Someone had to deal with... the mess.

"Most of them haven't paid. Two are suffering from disrespect," Jacques answered. "One Cairo lost."

"I didn't lose her," Cairo drawled. "She'll be back. If not, there isn't anywhere she can hide from us in our town."

"She?" I scanned the faces of the sacrifices and finally noticed the one we picked up with Cavendish was missing. "Who is she?"

"Some girl. Not important," he said. "How do we handle the problem if we can't get into the computer?"

"I said we didn't have the password," Roan said. "I didn't say we couldn't get into the computer."

We let that comment hang in the air and dissipate.

It's all well and good to say we're getting sloppy when you're not the one getting your hands dirty.

"Speaking of," I said. "Three didn't pay and two were disrespectful. They clearly wanted our attention, let's not keep them waiting."

"Should we do a sweep?" Legend asked. "Take all the phones."

"No," Cairo said. "They can keep their phones. Let everyone watch them burn."

I flicked my lighter closed. "Couldn't agree more."

RAINEY

I circled the tree line, observing the party.

If every Ruckus Royale was like this, I couldn't help but see the appeal. Carnival, Mardi Gras, and Burning Man all rolled into one.

The speakers blasted everyone in the circle deaf. Seriously, we were a few miles outside the main town center, and I had no doubt they were singing along to "Looking For Me" in the police station.

When I saw the paint buckets and guns, I assumed people would be chasing each other down like four-year-olds at the water park. My mistake for not seeing their obvious use.

Girls stripped off their clothes—spinning, dancing, and giggling as they were painted head to toe in their new glow-in-the-dark skinsuits. Amy and Zara were next to step off the line, their clothes already discarded somewhere.

They ground up on each other, wining and making out while hooting guys struggled with either spraying them with the paint or their cum.

The rainbow pill bowls glowed from many hands. The stacks on stacks of beer tubs ended up half full in the short time I'd been away, and among the celebration, five captives hung from their posts—blindfolds gone. Four of them screamed for help from uncaring ears.

I didn't see Paris, though I knew she was somewhere in there—looking for me. I typed out my text.

Me: It's so packed, I can't see you. Meet me by Professor Valdez. (The guy in tweed.)

I didn't expect her to get to me right away. I wasn't worried if she did.

Sticking to the shadows, I skirted the party—gaze fixed on Cavendish. He was the only one not screaming. Cavendish didn't thrash or beg. You could almost believe he was kicking back, enjoying the party same as everyone else. He certainly didn't look like he wanted to be somewhere else.

Arriving at the front of the house, I weaved through the cars, keeping low. A woman walking around carting a bow and arrow was something people remembered.

The porch creaked under my feet. The splintered wood's better days were over a hundred years ago. I pushed on the handle-less door and stepped inside, pressing the bow tight behind my back.

A long, dim hallway opened up before me, the only thing approaching light was the glowing footprints leading around the corner and disappearing.

I tiptoed in their wake. Rounding the curve, I stuck my head in the living room.

A chandelier tangled in cobwebs hung over the room. Someone draped it in fairy lights to illuminate two busted, tipped-over chairs, and an ancient sofa currently occupied by glowing blue aliens.

The girl impaled herself on his cock, cries rivaling the noise from outside.

I recognized her even in the paint. She was one of the girls helping Cairo get the honey off his dick. Public sex must've been her thing. She had no problem with the half a dozen people in the room recording them on their phones.

But I did mind.

I snapped back, heart jumping out of my chest. All it would take is one person capturing video of that farm girl, Rainey, strutting around with a bow.

A shuddering breath blew from my hiccupping lips. What was I doing? Why the hell did I think I could do this?

"*Tick, ticking, tock,*" Cavendish whispered in my ear. "*Time's running out, Rain-ey.*"

Peeling my eyes open, I backed away from their fun, searching for another way upstairs. Old homes like this tended to have them.

My search paid off in the kitchen. I passed more couples in various states of undress, going at it like this was an *end of the world* party. These guys were so wrapped up in each other, they didn't notice me slip past, and they didn't have cameras.

Two doors in the run-down kitchen—one led outside, the other revealed the back staircase. I went up, searching for the window I noticed when I stood down below with Cavendish.

Three down on the right, I found the room. Whose room, I couldn't help but think. Was this empty, desolate space where Mayam once stood with her husband? Holding each other while they watched their children play on the lawn.

I stepped around a gaping hole in the floor, picturing it covered with a rug. Seeing a dresser against the wall. A bed covered in downy sheets, and a family just like all the rest, surviving in a town ruled by evil.

Cavendish turned his head up to the stairs again and saw me. But of course, he couldn't have known I was there. It was pitch black in the room. Even so, our gazes locked across the divide.

Fixed on him as I was, I didn't notice the only person who could steal my attention until he was in front of him. Amid the partying, debauchery, chaos, Cairo raised a fist and the music shut off.

"Bedlamites, is this not the best Ruckus Royale in history?!"

The crowd went wild, hooting, hollering, and shooting paint in the air.

"We promised you a party no one would forget, and we haven't," he said. "We haven't forgotten the people who soaked this ground red so Bedlam could rise from the ashes. This is our town!"

"Yeah!"

"This is our home!"

"Yeah!"

"What do we do to people who fuck with our freedoms?"

"Sac-ri-fice! Sac-ri-fice! Sac-ri-fice!"

The chant spread through the forest, rippling over the eastern seaboard, and twisting my stomach. If I never heard that damn word again, it'd be too soon.

Someone brought out a drum and lit a fire inside. One by one, painted disciples—I couldn't think of another word for them—handed Arsenio, Cairo, Jacques, Legend, and Roan a torch. They dipped each one inside, and spread out, brandishing their flaming torches to howls that bordered on inhuman, from captives and audience alike.

"Professor Valdez." Cairo pointed out the thrashing man with a torch held too close to his rumpled clothes. "Organized the protest against us. Ordered Nana Grace and her sewing circle to photograph us in the streets. Take our names. Report us to the police."

The boos blew the man's ears back.

"What do we have to say to that?"

What else were they going to say?

Sacrifice.

"Kimball Joe over here," he said. "He's been coming up short in his monthly payments. Now, everyone knows the community fee we collect is for the good of the town. Who fronted the Dubecheks the cash when they defaulted on their loans and the bank threatened to take their house and land away?"

"Bedlam Boys," they chorused.

"Who replaced that old, busted-up generator that died three days before Hurricane Hannah rolled through town? For two weeks, the only place with power, heat, and food that wasn't rotting in the back of the fridge was the high school, thanks to..."

"The Bedlam Boys."

"We look out for this town and all of you. All we ask is a measly seven percent cut. Tell me, what kind of low-life piece of shit–covered toilet paper can't give up seven percent to the town that's given them more in return?"

"Boo!"

"Greedy pigs!"

"Assholes!"

I rested my head on the frame, slightly stunned with awe. No, unease.

Actually, both.

Gran sheltered us from so much. Protecting us from a world where a twenty-one-year-old and his friends can admit to extortion and have his victims rail against the ones who dared to say no.

Did Gran pay the community fee? The Bedlam Boys were younger then. Maybe too young to face down a sixty-year-old woman who kept a shotgun in the umbrella stand.

"—those against the community, are out of the community," Cairo bellowed.

I straightened, tensing as Cairo converged on Cavendish.

This is it. It's now.

Raising the bow, my arms were rigid sticks. I couldn't bend my elbow to pull back. Couldn't stop trembling to do the single thing I perfected at eleven years old.

Take aim.

You can do this, Rainey. You have to do this.

Mayam did what she had to do against the Men of Honor. Surely I could summon half as much courage to save an innocent girl who needed me. A girl made helpless by a soulless man who cared only about what he could take, even if it was more than she could give.

If anyone knew what it was to be a girl like that, it was me.

I notched the arrow, tears dripping down my face.

No one saved me, but I can save Jennifer.

Cairo and his torch closed the distance. I steadied my aim between his eyes, took a breath, and let go.

The arrow clattered on the rotting floor, and me beside it.

I cried great, heaving sobs as wherever she was, Jennifer suffered alone and afraid in the dark.

"I c-can't do it. I'm sorry."

"It's Bedlam now! It's Bedlam forever!" Cairo shouted below.

"I'm so sorry."

CAIRO

"It's Bedlam now. It's Bedlam forever. And if you don't get on-fucking-board, it's—"

"Fucking hell, you can go on."

I fell silent. The voice ripped through the Drumlins estate, silencing everyone.

Lowering my torch, its light fell on a tall guy with hair that glinted emerald green. He stood apart from everyone for the simple fact he sported a cawing raven on his neck, and the clothes. Long dark coat, spiked boots, pants, and silk shirt such a dark blue, they appeared black.

The guy broke from the crowd, microphone in hand, and parted the way for more of them to pour out. All dressed like Van Helsing's idiot brother, Dan.

"We came all this way to join the infamous Ruckus Royale. See the even more notorious Bedlam Boys in action, and this is all you got?" He laughed uproariously. "Tie them to a bunch of posts while the naked hicks holler and call them *mwean names*? Boo hoo."

Roan, Legend, Arsenio, and Jacques moved slow, falling in around me. I felt the air shift as it did right before I did something I wouldn't regret.

"Who the fuck are you?" I asked, voice calm.

"We'll get to that soon enough." He circled Valdez, and the edge of the well. "Stories of you five have reached the other towns. Warnings not to cross you. Warnings not to cross the line into Bedlam at all. This fuckhole is crazy, and the inmates hold the key to the city.

"Unsurprisingly, it's all a load of bullshit." He spat in the well to punctuate his point. "If we were in charge, none of these bitches would get a light show for daring to threaten me, or coming up short!"

He punched Valdez in the crotch. The professor's jaw cracked in a silent scream.

"The Bedlam Boys are going soft! You need a lesson on how to handle disrespect!"

The shout was a call to action. The other vampire hunters ran at the sacrifices—shaking their posts, pummeling them, snatching a paint gun and spraying Kimball in his open, screaming mouth. One of them pounced on the still and silent Cavendish and ripped a knife from his coat. He buried the blade in his thigh.

"Argh!" Agony contorted his features. "Filthy, worthless cunt! I'll kill you," he roared, showering him with spittle. "I'll kill you!"

Screaming, gasping, pleas, shouts of horrors, and my new green-haired friend rose above it all, laughing himself sick.

I observed the scene, and Cavendish, eyes narrowing. Neither one of us made a move.

"When we run this town," Dan said, stalking toward me. "No one will fucking dare stand against us. Least of all y—"

I punched him dead in the throat, popping his eyes out of his skull. Hands flying to his neck, he dropped, wheezing and gurgling to amuse me. Or because he couldn't breathe.

It was funny either way.

"Stupid fuck!" The vampire band rushed us.

We whipped out our torches, skidding them to a halt. Wide eyes glared through the flames.

"Drop your sticks and fight us," one shouted.

"Mmm, nope," I sang. "I'd much rather see you burn."

I jabbed, catching the torch on his chest. He howled and staggered away, arms flailing and ripping the singed coat off. The guy tripped into the arms of Fonsie—bleating as his hands were wrenched behind his back.

"Hold them," Arsenio said. A dozen guys leaped on the intruders, hauled up the one choking in the dirt, and dragged them out of our way. "After, we're gonna have a chat about his delusions of running this town and exactly where they came from. But first!"

"Sac-ri-fice! Sac-ri-fice!" The chant began anew.

We spread out, brandishing our torches over the wells we dug around each post and filled with gasoline. Around and under each sacrifice was a mound of sand that prevented the fire from spreading and turning their deaths from metaphorical to literal. The worst they'd get out of that was uncomfortably warm. The real lesson would've come from the tubs of rotted fruit waiting inside the Drumlins, and a couple riding crops. Roan had a thing for the latter.

A little pelting, some light beating, coupled with the kidnapping, fear, public humiliation, and threats of worse if they caused us more problems, was enough to get the point across.

A point I was now eager to make, get it over with, and let them limp on home. I felt something approaching sorry for the poor bastards weeping and bleeding on their stakes. Not even I went for the crotch. I fought as dirty as the next reprehensible thug, as I've been affectionately called, but there were standards.

"Bedlam now!" I roared.

"Bedlam forever!"

I dropped the torch. A ring of fire erupted around Cavendish, blowing me off my feet. I laughed.

It was Roan's idea to have a burning. *I should tune him out less often. The guy has a good idea every now and—*

Something shot across my vision. In the millisecond the information traveled from my eyes and sent the alert in my brain, a faint *pop* rose above the flames, and was engulfed in the inferno.

The fire surged out of control, grasping for Cavendish's legs and clinging tight. Hungry. Greedy. Desperate. It crawled up his body—consuming in seconds.

"Ahh!" Screams tore from him— No, that wasn't the word. The gates of hell opened beneath his feet, and the noise that came from him as Satan himself dragged him under couldn't be described with as small a word as *scream*.

Revelers ran. Shoving and trampling over each other, they took off in every direction, fleeing for no damn reason. There wasn't far enough they could run to shake loose the sight of a human being burned alive. This would haunt them in their dreams till they died.

"Holy shit!" Dan Helsing was free—the guys on him somewhere fleeing through the forest. He seized my shoulders. "I take back everything I said. You guys are ruthless," he laughed. "Inhuman! I'll remember that when we come for you."

He sprinted off, knocking me aside and spinning me toward the house. I think part of me meant to look that way. Gaze rising to the second floor to see that face in the window.

"Cairo! Why are you standing there?" Roan got in the way. "Get a fire extinguisher. Now!"

I beat it to the pill table, grabbing one of the half dozen we stashed there and joining Arsenio and Jacques, hosing the now silent sacrifice down.

The revelers emptied out the field. The other sacrifices bellowed their heads off to be freed, and promising we'd pay for this as damp soaked their pants. And the face in the window—

I looked back up to my Rain.

She was gone.

RAINEY

I burst out of the house and spotted a familiar back of the head almost immediately.

Paris ran, clutching Amy's and Zara's hands. I raced up behind them.

"Oh no, it was awful!"

Her head snapped around. "Rainey," she cried. "I was looking everywhere for you." She hugged me tight. "Did you see? Oh my gosh, that poor man."

"I saw." A heavy, crushing weight bore down on my chest. I couldn't take in a deep breath, and at the same time, couldn't stop gasping for one. "We need to get out of here."

"That's what we're doing." Amy grabbed my hand and yanked me along.

I chanced a glance upstairs where I left my bow in the floorboards' gaping hole. It'd have to stay there till I came back for it.

Our group raced to the top of the road, finding Paris's car parked on the side, and sporting a new dent in the bumper.

"Shit!"

"Someone must've sideswiped you getting the hell out of here," Amy said. "They're assholes and we will get them later, but we have to go. We cannot be here when the sheriff finds the man the Bedlam Boys burned alive!"

"Cairo didn't do this!" she shot back even as we piled in the car. "It was an accident— Something happened. I don't know, but he did not kill that man."

"That's not how it looks," Zara said. "When are you going to wake the hell up, Paris?"

Paris spun on her. "It looks like you danced naked in a field, chanting and begging for the *sacrifice* to burn. That video is probably already up on YouTube, and your ass will be screaming innocent expecting everyone to believe you. There's plenty of doubt to go around, Zara, so shut the fuck up!"

The whole car shut the fuck up. No one said a word as she peeled from the bank and tore off. It was quiet in her little convertible, but not in my mind.

The scene played on repeat.

Me dropping the arrow and turning to leave.

Green Hair's voice bringing me back to the window.

Watching the pissing contest play out. Then the moment the knife pierced his thigh, and Cavendish's true self tore the smiling, cheerful act to shreds.

His face as he threatened him—contorted with hate, and something else.

Cavendish wanted to kill him. Wanted it more than getting off that post or even staying alive.

The desire to extract his death on a knifepoint of sharpened pain rang clear across the field, and then I saw him. Standing over Jennifer with that look on his face and it being the last one she'd ever see.

The next thing I knew, the arrow was notched and the string bit into my finger.

"I'm sorry, Paris," I croaked.

"Sorry? What—"

I stuck my head out of the window and vomited.

"Fucking hell, Rainey," Amy cried. My stomach's contents splattered her window. "Keep it together."

"Leave her alone." Zara rubbed my back soothingly. "We just saw a man freaking burned alive. His screams... I almost vomited too."

Coughing and wheezing, I let Zara tow me back in. She stroked my cheek, smearing it with tears and paint. The paint hers. The tears mine.

I did it. I killed a man. Planned, plotted, and executed the brutal end of a life, and it was all for nothing.

Trust me, he said. Kill him and I'd find Jennifer. I'd be able to save her, but how could that happen?

Was Cavendish supposed to shout her location as he burned? Well, that did not happen.

I was trapped. *We* were trapped—Jennifer and I.

My palm dug in my aching chest, feeling the weight growing heavier and heavier.

And we were both dying.

I closed my eyes. On and on the loop went, ending just as the arrow struck home.

My phone chimed.

The sound dragged me back. I fished it out and cast a surface glance at *Unknown Number*.

555-9428: 18 North Westham

Another message came through before the first one sunk in.

555-9428: Better hurry.

"Paris." I tried to keep my voice even. I didn't go too far into what this meant. For all I knew, it was another trick. Another test. I'd breathe when Jennifer was safe. "Can you drop me off first? At the corner of North Westham and Brick, please. I feel awful. I just need to get home."

"That's fine." Paris swerved a pair of brake lights. She was determined to get as far away from Westchester Drumlins as possible, and she wasn't letting the speed limit stop her.

I'm almost there, Jennifer, I thought. *Hang on.*

"Where were you?"

I blinked, jarring out of the never-ending loop. "What?"

"Where were you?" Paris repeated. "You said you were by the professor guy. I looked everywhere and didn't see you."

"I looked everywhere for you too. There was so much noise, shoving, and glow-in-the-dark aliens, we must've kept passing each other."

"Yeah." She slid back to the road. "Must have."

We didn't speak for the rest of the drive. Paris dropped me off at Westham and Brick, as promised. I fell out of the car, tossing a hasty bye over my shoulder.

They honked off, leaving me on the dark, quiet street.

No lights bleeding through the curtains. No sounds of happy families watching television or eating dinner on the other side.

Westham Street was a row of empty homes, and the wrecking ball towering at the end of the street told of what was to become of them.

Cavendish brought Jennifer here?

Where no one would have a reason to look, another voice said, *till it was too late.*

Chest tight, I stepped off the sidewalk, crossing to number eighteen.

The two-story home rose from a small lot well-tended by its former owner. Rosebushes, magnolia trees, and a ring of flower beds decorated the garden, circling the home. I thought as I pushed the creaking white fence open that this must've been a beautiful place—when the flowers weren't wilting on their branches.

I climbed the sagging porch steps and closed on the door handle. It turned without resistance, beckoning me inside.

"Jennifer?" I called.

The door tipped me out into the living room. There was an old charm to the paisley upholstered couches and the doily draped over the television. This was the home of a grandmother. Other grandmothers. Mine decked her place out with signed band posters from her days as a roadie, and an ammo collection above the fireplace.

A familiar pang went through my chest, but it was only partly for the memories of Abigail de Souza. The other part—the bigger part—was for the grandmother who left this home behind, and didn't take anything with her.

A chill skittered up my spine, rippling goose bumps on my arms. What happened to her? Why would someone who tended her garden so lovingly, showing the care she had for her home, not bring any of it with her when she left?

I passed into the dining room and bit hard on my lip at the plate and utensils on the place setting, and chair drawn out for someone to sit. I wanted out of here.

Now.

"Jennifer?" I raised my voice. "Jennifer, it's okay. You're safe. I'm here to help you. Please, if you can hear me, say something."

Saloon doors led into the kitchen, and another swinging pair led the way out. I stepped into a hallway and my gaze followed the incline upstairs, then it dropped down to the door directly in front of me.

Basement.

Where would Jennifer be? What would a cold, smirking sociopath like Scott Cavendish do to coax out every drop of fear? Every ounce of helplessness?

I went into the basement.

"Jennifer?"

Feeling the wall, I searched for a light switch, brushed against something, and flipped it up. Nothing.

"Of course there's nothing," I muttered. "No one lives here. They cut off the power."

I flicked my phone flashlight on instead, directing it into the gloom. The staircase ended at the bottom of a concrete floor. I felt the temperature dropping with each step I took. It was dark and freezing down here.

A washer and dryer came into sight. Beside them, a tipped-over laundry basket. This was a regular, run-of-the-mill basement like the normal home upstairs. Where was Jennifer supposed to be among this?

Climbing off the last step, I landed on the freezer placed unnaturally in the middle of the room. Secured with a padlock.

"Jennifer!" I sprang into action, yanking and pounding on the lock. "Jennifer, can you hear me?" The stubborn metal refused to give way.

Spinning around, I searched for something, anything, to break the lock. A wall of cabinets lined the back of the room.

"Hold on!"

I ripped the doors open and met with shelves of yarn, fabric, and craft supplies. *Come on, come on, come on!* There have to be tools. Every homeowner keeps a set of—

I burst into the second cabinet. A toolbox sat on its own on the second shelf as if waiting for me.

Grabbing it, I paused, snapping my head toward the ceiling. I listened hard.

For a second, I thought I heard a thump. Movement above.

Nothing. No sounds or bumps from above, or from the freezer.

I lifted the toolbox overhead and threw it on the floor. Tools skittered out, the hammer going flying, and I snatched it up without a skip in step. Wildly, I went at the lock.

Bang! Bang! Bang!

A mangled heap of metal fell between my feet. I threw the freezer open and gasped—hands flying to my mouth.

A woman lay curled on a bed of fish sticks and peas, so peaceful she could be sleeping. A zip tie bound her wrists. Duct tape covered her mouth and stuck strands of hair to her face. Dark ebony lines on pale cheeks.

"*Dog Day Afternoon*," I whispered.

I didn't recognize the name. I wasn't really listening while we did our little greeting warm-up. This was the girl who guessed my favorite movie. Who sat across from me eating and laughing while he watched.

"Jennifer?" I gently peeled the tape from her mouth. "Please, wake up. I'm sorry. I'm so s-sorry I was late."

Crying, I bent to lift her. The least I could do was get her out of this disgusting hole of rotting food. She deserved so much more than this, and I didn't tell her. Of all the women I've complimented and thanked over the weeks, I never made it to her. All the things I'd done that night, and that fact broke something deep inside me that'd never heal.

"He didn't get away with it," I whispered. "I hope that brings you peace—"

"Hmm."

I choked, the rest of my farewell fading on my tongue.

Jennifer's fingers twitched, then her legs. Stirring, her eyelids fluttered.

"Oh my goodness, you're okay." Something half laugh, half sob escaped me. "It's okay. You're safe—"

Thump.

I whipped around. That noise I heard clearly, and it came from in the room. I fixed on the stairs, and a pair of polished black loafers appeared on the landing.

"Hey!"

The shoes turned tail and raced off, disappearing through the doors.

I didn't think, I ran.

Tearing up the stairs, I skidded into the hallway, slamming into the opposite wall. Pain zinged up my arm. The briefest flash of a black sole vanished around the corner into the kitchen.

"Hello?" a thin voice called from the basement. "Is someone there?"

It killed me to leave her behind, but Jennifer was alive and this person who— Who what? Sent me the text? Helped Cavendish? Stumbled into an unlocked house and ran out when someone shouted at them? Whoever the hell they were, they were getting away.

I ran through the kitchen and into the living room, on the trail of those thundering footsteps. I hurried onto the porch and tripped.

"Ahh!" Pitching forward, I crashed on the steps, sliding off and collapsing on the gravel path.

Everything hurt. Dazed and pained, I lay there, listening to the footfalls fade, then disappear.

I don't know how long it took me to push myself up and see the flowerpot rolling on the welcome mat where it was placed to trip me.

I don't know how long it was till Jennifer's voice grew louder, signaling her freedom from the basement.

Getting my knees under me, I pushed up onto my feet, spared one more glance at the lonely, forgotten house, and left.

Chapter Six

C*airo*

"This is serious, Cairo! You're going to tell me the truth, and you're going to do it now!"

I puffed up my chest. "Tell me the truth and do it now!" I bellowed, then burst out laughing. "Very good, old man. You've been working on your bad-cop routine."

My father, Jack Sharpe, glared at me like he wished he could change that fact.

Get in line.

"Everything's a joke, isn't it?" He threw himself down in the chair, facing me across the interrogation table. "There's a burned corpse in the morgue and a town full of witnesses that saw you set him on fire. You're looking at kidnapping, negligent homicide— possibly second-degree murder."

"Actually, I'm not." Leaning back in the chair, I folded my arms behind my head. "I'm not sure if you heard, but my father's the sheriff and he's fucking the judge," I said. "You'll make the charges go away."

"I can't do that."

"Course you can."

"A dozen camera phones recorded the incident. It had two million views on YouTube before it was taken down," he replied, jabbing his finger on the table. A folder lay closed on his side. "This is bigger than me now."

"Nothing's bigger than us in our town."

Twelve hours since the abrupt end to Ruckus Royale. The guys and I weren't in our house for ten minutes before Dad busted in, rounding us up and carting us to the station. There wasn't time for a cover story.

I peered at the wall, where either Jacques, Roan, Legend, or Arsenio sat for their own interrogation. What were they saying happened?

"Cairo."

I shifted back to the loose-jowled, flabby-bellied man that kicked in his DNA for my existence. And I checked, sending in our samples for a paternity test. The guy was my dad, though you couldn't blame me for making sure. His eyes were dark where mine were light. His hair thin, mine thick. His chin weak, and mine defined. Plus, the little detail of my mother's history of having babies during their marriage that weren't his.

"I can't protect you from everything."

My jaw clenched. "I'd take one thing, Dad. One fucking time, and this is it. I didn't turn that shit into a flaming skewer. I'm your son," I hissed. "You shouldn't have brought me here. You should know I wouldn't do this."

"You're right," he said, voice soft. "I do know my son... and he's smart enough to not get caught."

Slowly, I dropped the chair legs on the floor, locking on to those eyes so different from mine. Dad was first to look away. Everyone was.

I've been told there's something about my eyes. Personally, I had no idea what they were talking about.

"Come now, Pops, let's not dig all that up again." My smile made him flinch. "I did not kill Cavendish. We tested it out before Ruckus. Dug the wells, bought the sand. Our setup was safe, and that's obvious, seeing as none of the other sacrifices caught fire." I shrugged. "If you saw the video, you know the vamp hunters blundered in, fucking with the sacrifices. One of them even stabbed Cavendish. Why aren't you talking to him?"

"Because Scott Cavendish did not die from a stab wound," Dad gritted. "You could try to look upset about this, Cairo. A man died a horrible death in front of you."

"Testing me for normal human emotions again? Give it up, Dad. I passed all three psych evals. I'm not a sociopath." I saluted him. "Just garden variety screwed up by my parents like the rest."

"I did my best with you! I gave you everything!"

I heaved a sigh. "This is boring me now. I've only played along because you've got to make it look good for the town. Prove you investigated. We've put on a show for long enough." I made for the door. "See you the next time I'm arrested."

"He didn't die from a stab wound."

Something in his tone stopped me with my hand on the knob.

"Scott Cavendish died when the container of gas placed beneath his feet exploded. It's not surprising the other sac— victims didn't meet the same fate," said Sheriff Sharpe. "They were spared that addition."

My mind worked, filtering through every second of the night before. "There wasn't a gas container beneath his feet."

"There was." I turned as he removed a photograph from the folder and slid it across the table. "Buried in the sand."

"I didn't—"

"And we found this underneath it."

Dad tossed the evidence bag on the table. The fucker got what he was after. My eyes bugged, brows blowing up in shock.

"I lost that," I said, snatching up the charred remains of my wallet. "I tore the house and truck apart looking for it."

"It was buried in the sand under Cavendish, son. You mentioned you were the one who dug his well. Poured the sand around him."

"Yeah, but—" I snapped up, lips peeling back. "Hold the hell up. Don't try it, old man. I told you it wasn't me. I don't know how that container got in there."

He sat back, lacing his fingers on his paunch. The balance of power had shifted. And he knew it.

"Then, maybe you have a better explanation. Your wallet was found *under* the container. To a judge, it looks like you dropped your wallet and didn't notice as you placed the container on top, then packed in the sand."

Fury licked at my self-control. The man wouldn't win any *father of the year* awards—for all that he thought he deserved them. But at the very least, he should know a decent father doesn't look so smug when he accused his son of murder.

"Damn," I said. "Sheriff truly is an elected position. All about the politics, nothing to do with the brains."

"Careful."

"If I lost my wallet in the middle of carrying out a brutal murder, don't you think around the victim would be the first place I looked?" I snapped. "Here's another for you: I tied up Cavendish, then I spread the sand, dug the well, and blindfolded him. I think he would've said something if he saw me shove a gas container in there."

"There's only your word that's the order of events," Dad said.

"The guys were there. They saw."

"They could be lying to cover for you."

I cocked my head. "Now, why would they do that?"

Jack didn't say anything.

"The Bedlam Boys have built quite a reputation if even my own father thinks I'm a cold-blooded killer. We should do something about—"

"I want to know how. How someone can take a soul without losing their own?"

I snatched the folder, dumping out the crime scene photos.

"Son—"

"Shut up."

"Cairo—"

"Quiet! You've said enough, accusing your own son of murder. The least you can do is be silent while I do your work for you."

Silence filled the interrogation room. The only sound the shuffling of papers.

I pawed through them, looking for any sign of—

There.

Nestled in the sand and ash, was a slim piece of charred wood.

So that's what that was.

I sat back in my seat, head bent to the ceiling, and considered, considered...

...and decision made.

"I did not kill Scott Cavendish," I said clearly. "The four witnesses I have backing me should be enough for a jury, and for you. He did not die because of anything the Bedlam Boys did, but it's obvious someone wants the world to think otherwise.

"After we displayed the sacrifices, we kicked back in the Drumlins and left them on their own out there for an hour. The gas containers were out there too. Someone stole my wallet and then took advantage of the perfect setup. Victim tied and blindfolded. A tub of gasoline just sitting there. We were framed."

"Who would want to frame you? More to the point, who'd murder Scott Cavendish to do it? The only people in this scenario who have a motive are the Bedlam Boys. You're on video trumpeting his list of crimes against you."

I tossed the photo back on the pile. "We don't kill for coming up short on payments. Dead men don't settle bills."

Dad winced. "Stop that, Cairo. Stop talking like some two-bit gangster."

"How should I talk, Dad? We both know why I collect those payments, and why we don't need anyone digging into them as a motive. If people knew what the Bedlam Boys really do, your right friends in the right places won't be enough to save you losing this job, or ending up in the cell next to mine." I neatly tucked the evidence away and slid the folder to him.

"The police are officially looking into the shitstains that crashed Ruckus and stabbed Scott Cavendish as their main suspects in his murder, and apologies go out to the Bedlam Boys for the suffering and suspicion they've endured. Agreed?"

It took him a minute but, jaw clenched, my father nodded.

"Agreed," he said. "I'll put Davidson and Andres on the Cavendish murder. They're good, thorough cops. If someone has framed you, they'll find out who."

He rose from his seat. "I have other matters to attend to anyway. Someone abducted a girl from the university and locked her in a freezer in an abandoned house. She and her family should be coming in now to speak to me."

I was already out the door. No idea why the guy was telling me his schedule. Since when did we chat?

Sunlight crested over the trees, telling all morning came to Bedlam, ending another night of bloodshed and chaos in the streets.

Wonder if Mayam stood in the sun the morning after, cursing it for bringing an end, when it was only the beginning.

"What good is it having a mom who's a judge and Sheriff Daddy if we can't get out of a night in a jail cell?" Legend leaned on the column, stretching out a kink in his neck.

"We have a problem," I said.

"Of course, we have a fucking problem," Arsenio snapped. "We weren't comatose the last twelve hours."

I let the comment slide. "I know who killed Cavendish."

"What?" Roan turned me to face them. "Who?"

"Didn't put it together till I saw the crime scene photos. Something flew past me before the explosion, and it came from the second-floor window."

"What are you talking about?" Jacques demanded.

"I— *We* were framed by the farm girl."

"The farm girl?" Roan repeated. "Fucking hell, Jacques. When you piss a girl off, you don't half-ass the job."

"This isn't about me," Jacques said. "You don't set an innocent man on fire for getting tied up and thrown in the back of a truck."

"They were in the back of that truck together," I mentioned. "I noticed them talking on the drive. Now I'm wondering about what."

"Does it matter?" Legend asked. "You know who did it. Tell your old man and get her thrown in the cage."

"No."

Arsenio's brows rose up his forehead, then the corner of his mouth. "I assume you have something more interesting in mind."

I held my arms out. "You always did know me too well."

"What are we going to do?" Roan spoke up.

"Remember Halloween two years back?"

Now they were all smiling.

"Good," he said, filing past with the rest. "Always did love a hunt."

RAINEY

I curled up in the middle of the scratchy sheets, watching the interview on repeat. I clicked to the start of the video, watching it again.

"It was horrible."

Jennifer Wilson looked out from my screen. By her side, an older woman with her dark hair and a man with her pale skin held her tight as she gave her story from the town hall steps. A public, violent death and a pretty young woman abducted on the same night. The careers of more than a few Bedlam journalists would be made that day. These stories were going national.

"I was getting in my car when a shadow fell over me. I felt this sudden, sharp pain in my neck, then everything went black. When I—" Her lids swelled. "When I woke up, I was in the dark."

"Miss Wilson! Miss Wilson!" they called.

"How did you escape?"

"I'm not sure. When I came to, I heard this voice saying everything would be okay." She shook her head. "Part of me thinks I imagined it, but there had to be someone there. Someone busted the lock and opened the freezer for me to get out. But I didn't see anyone."

There was a reason for that.

I closed my laptop and flopped flat on my bed.

I stuck around to make sure Jennifer got home safely, of course, but after chasing that man, or woman, out of the house, my only thought was to get out before Jennifer saw me. If she did, she'd have questions.

How did you know I was here?

Who did this to me?

Some nutcase put me in a freezer to force you to kill him?

Did you do it?

How fast can the police get here?

It was as I was lying face-first in the dirt that I accepted I couldn't answer those questions.

Because it wasn't over.

No matter how much I tried to convince myself the person in the house wandered in by mistake or was some random squatter looking for a free bed, deep down I knew it wasn't true.

Someone texted me the address after Cavendish's death, then they waited for me inside.

A shudder rippled down my body. I hugged myself, holding my knees tight to my chest. It did nothing.

I was still cold. Still afraid. Still couldn't breathe.

I did what I had to do. Cavendish had a partner and Jennifer doesn't know anything about them. She didn't know anything about Cavendish, either. That ignorance would keep her safe. The partner doesn't have a reason to go after a woman who can't point the police in their direction.

The woman who can do that is still me, and they know I won't, because that means revealing my part in Cavendish's death.

Reaching out, I slipped the black letter from my pillow. I wished I could say I was surprised when I found it on my doorstep that morning. I knew it was coming. Welcomed my fate even before I stepped up to the door.

Nicely done. You kept me on the edge of my seat with the will she, won't she, then the grand finale, fireworks display. You know, you're not the first we've played this game with. The sacrifices are as old as Ruckus Royale herself, and many have accepted the challenge of denying us what is ours to take.

You will not be the last, but you are the first to create a game just for you.

This time it's personal.

You'll forgive me if I skip the shit about birds and metaphors. That was never my style.

It's our turn to play, and it's different rules from here on. I'm going to come up with something extra fun for you. Starting with choosing someone you actually care about to motivate you to not leave things to the last minute.

Where's that sister of yours, by the way?

Stay psycho, bitch.

Love ya. XOXO

I dropped my hand, letting the letter flutter to the floor.

Once again, it's between me and my stalking shadow.

No, they weren't a shadow. At least those go away in the dark.

I jumped at my phone going off. A text from Paris.

Paris: I feel bad about pushing you to go to Ruckus. I had nightmares all night.

Me: It wasn't your fault. It's that poor man I feel sorry for. Did he have family?

For someone who vomited three times the night before and twice that morning, I was lying like an expert bullshitter.

Paris: Heard on the news his parents moved out of town a few years ago and he lived with his girlfriend. I don't know what's going to happen. People think my brother's responsible for this.

My stomach contracted. I was thankful there was nothing left in there to heave. Say what you will about Cairo, and there was plenty I had to say about him, he was Paris's brother and she loved him. What she was going through right now was my fault.

This was why I didn't want friends. They were another stone on my chest, crushing me with guilt.

Me: Cairo's dad is the sheriff. He won't arrest his own son without undeniable evidence.

And likely not even then.

A flash of anger tightened my grip on the phone. Look at that, there was room for me to feel something other than guilt. One thing Jack Sharpe succeeded at during his reign, making me a lifelong enemy.

Paris: Cairo and Jack have a rough relationship, but you're right, he won't let Cairo go down for something he didn't do.

Paris: Today's a shit day to go with an awful night. How about we hang out tonight? Just me, you, a bowl of popcorn, and a stack of Doctor Who dvds. You in?

My smile didn't reach my eyes. There was nothing I wanted more than to spend a night the way I used to. With my favorite people and my favorite doctor.

I closed out the text window and called Ivy.

The dial tone sounded on repeat till Ivy's voice filled my ear.

"Hey, this is Ivy. You know what to do."

"Ivy, it's Rainey. I know you're busy living your big-city life with your own big-city demands, but— but I could really use my big sister right about now. I'm sorry for l-last time." My throat constricted around the words. "I hate that we fought. I said a lot of stupid things that I didn't mean, but I do mean this: I love you. You're my best friend and always will be.

"Please, call me back," I whispered. "I just want to talk to you. Please."

I ended the message and waited. Half an hour passed. Then one. Then two.

Ivy did not call.

Wiping my face, I typed my reply to Paris.

Me: That sounds amazing. I can't tonight, though. I'm going up to the farm to get some things. I'm running low. Doctor Who marathon tomorrow night?

Paris: Tomorrow it is. We'll do it at my place. I've got a killer theater setup in my room. Just wait until you see it. You'll never want to leave and we'll be weirdo hermit ladies together.

Me: Lol. Not sure if we qualify as hermits if we do things together. Either way, I'll bring the caramel popcorn.

Paris: Yay! Thank you so much. I need to get my mind off everything.

I tossed my phone somewhere behind me, not caring that it fell off the bed.

There's nothing to worry about, Paris. This would all be over soon.

Climbing off the bed, I went to my closet. My work to find Cavendish mocked me with every article and string. In the end, I didn't really know anything at all. I saved a life, but it wasn't mine. I became a monster to stop a monster, and a new one sprung up in his place.

I tore down a picture of a kookaburra. It was a laughing jackass. I could hear it mocking me.

"Tick ticking tock, Rainey." I ripped off a string. "Why is nothing as it seems?"

The map of Bedlam fell as confetti on my feet.

"To die is my birthright, de Souza. But to die ripping out a piece of your soul, that is my honor! Did you get what you wanted, Cavendish? Were you honored?!"

I screamed, raking my nails down the pictures, articles, and letters, losing a few in the process.

Gathering it all up, I tossed it in the wastebin, struck a match, and set it on fire.

Fire was the best way to end something. With this being the last time I'd sit in this cheap room and read another black letter, the send-off had to be appropriate.

Face soaked and eyes puffy, I packed the little I had and carried it out to the bus stop. Frankie rolled through with the 99 bus twenty minutes later.

"Rainey, love, are you okay?"

"I'm fine," I replied as I got on.

"It's all this terribleness on the news, isn't it? Uh, what is this town coming to?"

I sat close to her, resting my bags in the seats. It was just me and Frankie. No one had reasons to drive out to de Souza Farm these days. No one except me.

"An innocent man burned alive for the entertainment of naked, hooting jackals, then some sweet girl snatched off the street in broad daylight. A friend of mine is talking about sending her daughters to that boarding school a couple of hours away, Epsilon Academy. Breaks her heart to be apart from them, but it's not safe in Bedlam these days. Mind you, when was it ever safe in Bedlam?"

Frankie spent entire rides in silence. Passengers preferred to be on their phones than talk to her. The result was she talked the ear off of anyone that would listen. That ear was mine and she was welcome to it. If she was talking, I didn't have to.

"That young woman, Jennifer, I think her name is. She said someone rescued her," Frankie continued on. "No doubt about it, she didn't get out of a locked freezer bound and gagged on her own, but you have to ask why they didn't stick around? They're a hero. Why not receive your deserved praise?"

"What's your theory?" I asked, wiping my face on my sleeve.

"I think the person who put her in there had a change of heart. Couldn't go through with it, so he let her out and ran. The coward couldn't face her when he attacked. He couldn't face releasing her either."

"Do ruthless psychopaths change their minds? Suddenly grow a conscience?"

She snorted. "My cheating bastard of an ex-husband didn't when he emptied our bank account and ran off with my yoga instructor, so I'm betting not."

I almost cracked a smile. I'd been hearing about that cheating bastard since the day he skipped out. Three months and he still managed to come up with new ways to torture Frankie. The latest was dodging child support while at the same time sobbing to their friends and family he had to leave because Frankie stopped loving him years ago. I guess we all have a monster in our lives.

"I'm going to miss this, Frankie," I admitted. "There's not a lot of people you can have a good bitch session with."

"Any time, love, but what do you mean you'll miss it? You going somewhere?"

I nodded. "I decided to move back to the farm."

"Move back? Why? You got the motel in town so you'd be closer to the university. No one wants to wake up at six in the morning to ride around in this dusty old heap with me."

"You're the only company I'd want at six in the morning, Frankie. I told you, you're one of the few people I can talk to."

"Aw. You're such a sweet girl, Rainey. Your grandmother would be proud of you."

I dropped my gaze. "She wouldn't."

"I say she would." She twisted in her seat, giving me a firm look. "Abigail was one of my closest friends. She'd ride with me those days that old clunker gave her trouble, and always gifted me a bag of peaches like it was part of the fare. After I finished my route, the two of us would grab a beer and I'd listen to her brag about her beautiful, talented granddaughters. If she could see you two now, her heart would burst with pride."

Tears fell with every word. "I didn't know you guys were so close."

"Oh yeah," she said, a tinge wistful. "You three were pretty tucked away, working sunup to sundown keeping the farm going, but your gran got out every now and then. For a good ole bitch session."

I laughed. "Did she tell you about the goat?"

"Did she! Oh my goodness, I heard so much about the exploits of that randy goat, I started getting jealous. He had a better sex life than mine."

"We could not figure out how he was getting in the pen." I cracked up. "The girls kept getting pregnant, and when Gran found him in there, she'd chase him through the fields, shrieking about turning him into a plate of curry goat. We finally found out he was getting in because Ivy was leaving the gate open when she snuck out."

"That's the de Souza women for you. You gals do what you want, when you want. I hope your gran remembered that when she found out about Ivy's late-night adventures. Lord knows Abigail wasn't shy about hopping out a window to meet Joseph Deerfield. She was head over heels for that boy."

"Oooh, who's Joseph Deerfield?"

"Your real grandfather."

I gaped at her. Frankie saw my face and howled.

"I'm just kidding, sweetie. She gave their baby up for adoption long before your father came along."

"Frankie!"

The woman laughed so hard she nearly crashed the bus.

We spent the rest of the drive swapping old stories and laughing about the good times.

"I loved living on that farm with Gran and Ivy." I rested my cheek against the cool glass. "Mom and Dad died when I was little. I never got a chance to know them, but Gran didn't let us be sad. Life was movie nights, camping under the stars, archery lessons, and randy goats. I loved every minute of it." My smile faded. "And now they're both gone."

"You still have your sister."

"Ivy never comes home."

"Your grandmother's death was hard for both of you." Frankie rolled to a stop beside our busted-up, faded sign. "Maybe it's too difficult for her to be here. Too many memories."

"Maybe."

Frankie stopped me on the top step, grabbing my hand. "Are you sure about this, dear? Technically, you shouldn't be on the property at all, but that aside, what good is it you sitting in that empty place all alone? Why not stay with me? I know you're tired of that dreary motel. I have a spare room that's yours until you find an apartment in town."

"That's nice of you, Frankie. Truly, I appreciate everything you've done for me, and for Gran. You're a kind, loving person, and one day you'll find someone that appreciates just being with you is better than an affair with a thousand leggy yoga instructors."

"Thank you, Rainey," she said softly.

"It's sweet of you to let me stay, but I've lost Gran, Ivy's gone, and I was kicked out of the farm. There's only one of those I can do something about. Tonight, I want to be home."

She nodded. "Go, love, and fuck those jerks for making you leave in the first place. Your name is on that damn sign. That's all I need to know about who owns it."

Waving bye, I set off from the bus, down the long drive to the farm. The main gate was chained shut, I climbed over the thing and kept going.

Yes, I was kicked out of the family farm. Six generations of de Souzas on this patch of land, and the one to lose it, was me. Well, it wasn't all on me. When Gran died without a will and a farm in deep with the bank, they told me and Ivy to get our grown asses off the property. They were selling it to developers and there was nothing we could do about it.

Ivy and I tried to fight, but in every story where the poor orphan girls fight against the corporation, how many times did the orphan girls win?

We were removed—forcibly in Ivy's case. The animals were sold and the crops harvested by whoever was willing to pay the bank for the privilege. I lost my grandmother and home in a day. Shortly after, Ivy left Bedlam.

Like I told Paris, anyone who asks about my life apologizes a dozen times before the conversation is over.

I wandered up the gravel path. The farm rose out of the hill, drawing me home to fresh-baked cookies and Ivy playing her music too loud upstairs. I broke the lock on the front door and met with musty damp and silence. Sometimes, I didn't know what was worse. Being this miserable or the memories of being happy. If I had a terrible childhood, at least I couldn't count how many steps I hit on the way down.

Shutting the door behind me, I made my way in the dark. It's been years and no one's bought the farm, leaving it sitting empty for my constant visits. They had yet to put a lock on this place that I couldn't break into. I wasn't above breaking the windows either.

Down in the basement, I turned on the old generator. I only had a few things in the kitchen and living room hooked up, but it was enough for a relatively comfortable night out of the motel and in my home.

I went back up to the soft glow from Gran's favorite porcelain lamp, rescued from the estate sale, and a sweeping breeze from the tiny floor fan by the fireplace. Closing my eyes, it all came back to me.

The rocking chair and worn leather couch took their place by the front door. Rolling out from the wall, a plush brown rug covered the aged hardwood. Ivy's two-seater plopped down by the fireplace. She stretched out, legs kicking over the side, sipping iced tea through a straw. Light and warmth spread through the space, anticipating her arrival.

"Ivy, sit like a lady."

"Like this?" She flung her legs open, touching the wall and floor at the same time.

Gran laughed. "Looks right to me."

She carried the tea tray from the kitchen, setting it on the coffee table. "Rainey Day? Why are you standing there, love? Come join us. The only civilized way to end the day—"

"—is with good company and a cup of tea," I finished.

I stretched out on the rug, grabbing my throw off the armchair on the way. Snuggling the imagined threads around me, I saw Gran like she was truly there, pouring out chamomile tea and dropping two sugars for me. A spoonful of honey for Ivy.

"What's wrong, love?" she asked me. "You've got your stormy face on."

"Am I going to get these rain and weather puns for the rest of my life?"

"Fraid so." I felt the ghost of her kiss on my forehead. "Tell me, sweets. What's wrong?"

"Everything's wrong, Gran." Tears spilled down my cheeks. "You died."

"Died? Don't be ridiculous."

"Ivy left."

"Sitting right here," my sister sang.

"I'm alone."

"You're never alone, baby." Sixty years and most of them doing farm work, Gran wasn't a delicate senior gently wrinkling in an armchair. Her skin was tough and leathery from years under the beating sun. Hard labor toughened her arms, making her squeeze the jelly out of me when we hugged. Even so, I saw the traces of the young beauty she used to be. I saw the kind eyes she gave my father, then me.

"The thing about family is you can always make more."

"What will my family think of me after what I've done?" I rasped. "I had to do something terrible, Gran. Does it matter that it was for the right reason?"

"Depends."

"On what?"

"How many innocent people were hurt?"

A vision flashed of me stealing Cairo's wallet while I kissed him, and stuffing it beneath the sand.

"I should've faced the consequences, but I couldn't resist trying to hurt him one last time." My anger swelled, bringing my perfect scene under haze. "I'll never forgive the sheriff for what he did. This time, the son pays for the sins of the father."

"That's not how it works, Rainey Day."

I laughed harshly. "Isn't it? That explains why I feel so guilty I can barely breathe. Cairo's bad, Gran. He's rotten straight to his core. But what does it say about me that I let someone else face the punishment I was too scared to? I've been running from this ever since I got the first letter. Even after releasing that arrow, I'm still running."

"It's never too late to make it right. Pay penance."

"How?"

She smiled, soft and sad. "We don't get to decide, Rain. The chance will come to right your wrongs. It always does. For those who truly want to make amends, they won't miss it."

"I know what you mean," I whispered as they faded. "This is my chance, Gran. I won't miss it."

I stayed for a while—lying on the floor, imagining I heard the old sounds of this place. Fridge humming. Ivy banging around upstairs, dancing. Gran in the kitchen, mumbling to herself as she totaled the bills.

The microwave was hooked to the generator. It popped my popcorn to perfection and filled the space with warm butter—soothing as I watched a few episodes of *Special A*.

I laughed a few times. Felt like the last few days—the last two years—washed away.

When I finished, I left my things inside and headed out the back door. The entrance to the old chicken coop swung on rusty hinges. The *eee, eee, eee* followed me out in the field. It was still echoing through the night as I disappeared through the tree line.

My feet carried me over roots and around dips expertly. I knew these woods better than the critters who called it home. As I passed, I collected flowers. Little weed-like buds, but pretty in the way they were determined to survive.

Moonlight peeked past the trees, daring me to come out and enjoy its full attention.

Black Widow Hill wasn't really a hill so much as a slope. It wasn't truly dubbed after a spider, so much as it was named for the shiver that crawled up your spine as you crept near the cliff edge. This place wasn't a sweet scenic spot for couples.

It was a graveyard.

I kneeled down beneath the tree, resting my flowers where the roots stretched to touch me.

"I should probably say a few words," I spoke to the ground. "I know, I know. I've never done that before, so why start now?" I rocked back, crossing my legs to settle in. "Seems like I should say goodbye. No one knows you're here. There'll be no one to visit you after I stop coming. That must be the worst thing about dying. Having no one to miss you when you're gone.

"You're in a good spot, though," I said, leaning my head back to the cascade of glittering stars. "They'll shine on you always, communicating lovelier things than I could manage."

I got up, plucked another yellow flower at the base of the hill, and gave them that one too.

"Goodbye."

My walk back wasn't as surefooted. I stumbled over unseen roots and scratched my cheek on a low-hanging branch—cursed the damn thing too. It was hard enough making this walk without the ground tripping me up.

I'm doing this. There's no turning back now.

The woods finally released their hold, returning me to the farm. I went inside the house, got what I needed, and continued to the barn.

The busted lock lay in a tuft of grass where I left it. I pushed inside the barn, breathing deep that damp-hay smell.

Here. Definitely here.

Crossing to the old cow pen, I took the rope off the hook.

My hands were steady as I looped it around the post, carried the length to the loft, and tied the noose. They didn't waver as I threw it over the beam, and the end swung back to meet me. Perfectly, it framed my face, whispering that it would take good care of me. All I had to do was place it around my neck.

I turned away.

Finding a spot on the hay bales, I dragged my bag to me and fished out pen and paper. The average person doesn't think about what they'll write in a suicide note. I've given it more thought than most.

I wrote of losing Gran, and that without her protection, the shadows found us. I wasn't strong enough to leave like Ivy, and in the end, was too weak to fight.

I thought I'd cry while I did this. My eyes were dry.

As awful as it was to picture Ivy's face when she received the news, I knew this was right.

I killed a man. Gave him the most horrible death imaginable, as much as I wanted to plead duress, even knowing any jury in the world would agree, I couldn't forget.

A coldness seeped into my veins before I picked up that gas container. Spite and cunning burned beneath my attraction as I slipped that wallet out of Cairo's pocket. And when I loosed the bow...

Guilt, fear, and conscience plagued me to the very end. Just till the end. When the bow struck the sand, that was the beginning of a new feeling. One that had become foreign to me in the last few years, but if I was to put a name to it. The closest would be triumph.

I ripped through the page, tight grip pressing too hard. All the same, I forced myself to write:

I enjoyed it.

Scott Cavendish will never hurt another person or torture a single soul again.

If any justification of the good I've done should be said, let it be done by Jennifer Wilson. But I won't do it. I won't stand in front of anyone and say what I did was good, or right, or necessary. Even if they would say it is.

There was nothing good or right about the thoughts going through my head as he burned. And no one could question how wrong it was to place that wallet underneath him, framing Cairo Sharpe. His ass has a fair amount of karma coming, but this is my crime to pay for, not his.

Let this note serve as my final word and my confession.

Signed,

Rainey de Souza

P.S.

More people should visit Black Widow Hill. Scatter flowers. Speak to the trees. I think they'd like that.

I dotted the final period and placed the note on the bale. I set the bow I rescued from the Drumlins early that morning next to it. It was roped off with police tape, but all the busted windows and broken frames made it easy to get in. My bow hid where I left it—undisturbed.

Someone would come here and find this—me—eventually. I had a habit of breaking in, so the estate agent had a habit of sending the sheriff to roust me. Part of me hoped the sheriff was the one to find me.

And if I'm allowed one more petty thought, I hope the guilt eats him alive.

Closing the distance between the noose, I searched for a trace of regret and found none.

Maybe I could've found another way. There was hope of that until I received another black letter.

I refused to be drawn into this game again. Another human be-ing's life would not rest in my hands. Neither a life to take nor a life to save.

The new Letter Man or woman was about to lose their plaything.

The noose fell softly on my shoulders.

"I'll stay psycho to the very end, bitch," I said into the air. "But you're not going to touch my sister."

Taking a deep breath, I climbed onto the wooden banister.

See you soon, Gran.

I stepped off.

Chapter Seven

"It's not going to be that easy, sweetheart."

The rope pulled taut—wrenching my head up, and snapped.

I fell twelve feet to straw-covered concrete and landed hard. Pain zinged up my shoulder. "Ahh!"

"What did you think you were doing up there?"

Shadows moved in the dark, coming from all sides.

"What's going on?" I cried, struggling to sit up. "Who's there?"

"Who else?" They came into view.

Demons.

Darkness cloaked them. Shielding all but gleaming pools, lighting oddly in the beams filtering through the slats. At that moment, I understood why every Bedlam boogeyman story called their name. They weren't of this world.

Arsenio, Cairo, Jacques, Legend, and Roan circled me. Arsenio pocketed the knife he used to cut my rope. The others didn't.

Knives, bats, and propped on Cairo's shoulder, a crossbow.

He grinned when he saw me looking. "Like it? Is it like the one you used?"

My blood ran cold. He knew.

"What do you want?" I was proud of my voice for not trembling.

"We're going to make this real simple for you, de Souza," Arsenio said. "We know you killed Cavendish and tried to pin his murder on—"

"I—"

Jacques pounced. His arms pinned me on either side, holding the bat tight to my throat. "Don't interrupt. That's very rude."

I clenched my teeth so hard my jaw cracked. Jacques pressed hard on my hurt shoulder.

"As I was saying," Arsenio continued. "You tried to get us arrested for— What were the charges, Legend?"

"Kidnapping, negligent homicide, or second-degree murder."

I spoke through clenched teeth. "Pretty sure the first one was all you."

Cairo stepped between us. "I considered throwing you at my father, but then I thought, where's the fun in that? Whatever punishment the legal system comes up with for you, won't be nearly as satisfying as what I've got planned."

"I knew you wouldn't be arrested." My swallow bobbed against the wood. "Daddy wasn't about to put his precious son and your little boy band in jail. But even if he did, you'd walk right out after they found my note. I confessed, Cairo," I said. "I wasn't going to let you go down for my crime. You can see for yourself."

Roan broke off from the group. He came back down with my note in hand.

"See," I said as Cairo read it. "I'm telling the truth. You and I are—"

Cairo crumpled and tossed it over his shoulder.

"—good."

"We're not even close to good. Why'd you steal my wallet if you were just going to confess?"

"Alright, I admit it. The recent string of threats and assaults made the idea of you rotting in jail while your dad bawled his eyes out very attractive. I didn't want to kill him," I cried. "Why should I go to prison for that twisted piece of shit?!" The scream ripped out of my heaving chest, surprising even me.

"Ahh. There it is," Cairo said, crouching in front of me. "That look in your eyes."

I looked away, face burning.

"That's cold, Rain. You tried to run from your punishment by pinning it on me. Too pussy to follow through, you thought of another way to run." He tugged on my rope. "By way of hemp necklace."

"I'm not running. You don't understand what's going on here, Cairo." Jacques pressed harder on my throat. "I have... to do this."

"Here's what you have to do," he said. "Run."

"What?"

"You heard him," Legend said. "Run. If you get away from us, we'll let you keep running. Get out of our town, start a new life somewhere, and you won't hear from the Bedlam Boys again."

"We won't tell the cops it was you either," Arsenio added, dragging my attention to him. "You got one over on us once. Do it twice, and you'll have earned your stay of execution—to borrow a phrase."

Injured, pinned, and shaking, I trapped his gaze and hissed, "And if I don't?"

"If we catch you"—Cairo stroked my cheek—"you're ours."

"Yours?"

A smile so beautiful stretched his lips, my mind rebelled connecting it to the ferality in those eyes.

"You're going to make up for the pain and emotional damage you've caused us, and will continue to cause while we're suspects for your crime."

"For my crime?" I repeated. "You're not turning me in?"

"We have someone else in mind for Cavendish's murder trial," he said. "Till then, people will believe we're killers, and I'll need you to comfort me and my boys." That smile only got wider. "Remind us how much you *appreciate* us feeding you, getting you out of that crack motel, and keeping your secret.

"We'll own you, Rain." He continued down, sliding along the valley of my breasts, to my exposed belly button. "Mind, body, soul, and body. Did I mention body?"

"Fuck. You."

He laughed. "That's the idea."

"I'd rather turn myself in to the sheriff right now."

"No, you wouldn't," Roan said, "or we wouldn't have caught you swinging from the rafters."

"But you've got the choice now," Legend threw in. "We said you can run and that includes running to the station. You get away from us, you get your freedom."

"You don't," Jacques whispered, "and you're mine." He dropped the bat. It bounced off my knee and rolled away. "Ten seconds."

"Nine."

"Eight."

I swiveled between them. *What the hell is this? This can't be happening.*

"Seven."

Jacques picked up his bat.

"Six."

"You can't do this," I said. I got to my feet, hissing at the pain in my shoulder. "You don't have the right to keep me, or let me go."

"Four," they said. "Three."

"Cairo, stop." I backed toward the door.

"Two."

"I said stop!"

"One."

Twisting around, I ran.

I clutched my arm, biting my lip till it bled. I pushed aside the pain and ran faster than I ever had in my life.

"Whoo! This one's fast."

"Not fast enough." A hand fisted my shirt.

Screaming, I ripped away, picking up speed—bolting for the trees.

They welcomed me back with open arms, reminding me of all the places I once hid on those days I played hide-and-seek with Ivy.

Friar's Copse. If I shake them loose, I can hide there till they give up.

I looked over my shoulder and locked on to Arsenio only a few feet behind. They were not going to give up.

Crashing through the brush, I veered right to the thickest part of the woods. The trees grew close enough to share their bark. This was my chance to slow them down.

My heart thrummed in my ears, louder than their pounding and howls. The noise bounced across the leaves and it sounded like they were coming from everywhere. Behind, beside, and right at me.

"Come on, Rain." Cairo slid in my ear. "This is what you wanted, isn't it? My devotion. You wanted me to save your soul."

Devotion. Why, of all the words to use, did he choose that one? What was devotion to a wounded wolf? Why, from his lips, did it sound so much like possession?

I ached to scream they couldn't have me, but that would've given me away.

Lungs burning. Shoulder numb. Side swelling, I raced away from their thrashing—the forest muffling my footfalls in the sodden earth.

"Come back, little Rainey," Roan called. He sounded far away. "Don't you want to have some fun with us?"

Were they always this wickedly dangerous, or did they have to work at it? Either way, I was finally beginning to understand why everyone at the party dropped to their knees. These five took what they wanted. Power, respect, money, Bedlam. Now, they wanted me.

The copse emerged up ahead. There was a thick underbrush shielded by a tight collection of trees. I'd stay low and hide as they ran deeper into the forest. Then, all I had to do was make my way back home, bolt the doors, and stay there till they cleared out.

I have the generator and some food to last me a couple of days. Then I'd— Well, I'd figure out the rest later. Almost there. I—

Fingers tangled in my hair. I cried out as I was flung off my feet, pain exploding in my scalp.

"Hmm."

In a blink, Cairo was there. Straddling me, digging my hands into the dirt, pressing his full weight on my body.

I wasn't going anywhere.

"I hoped I'd be the one to catch you." Cairo bit my sore bottom lip, drawing a gasp of pain. "Were you secretly hoping too?"

"You're fucking insane, Sharpe. Get off me."

"You know, I wondered for a second while I was holding exhibit a, my burned wallet, if this was karma."

My breath caught, holding tight in my chest as Cairo laid my hand on his warring wolves.

"I've done wrong. More than the oldest man on earth could achieve in his lifetime. Was fate finally making me pay for it?"

He let go of me, only to grasp the crossbow. Light glinted off the tip pressed just below my collarbone. All thought fled my mind.

"Now I see that's not true," he continued, like we were a couple out for a lovely dinner and a chat. "You're not my curse, Rainey de Souza, you're my cure. I was bored, hungry, furious, before you came along and rattled the die on my one-track life."

His words were a steady soundtrack to the movie playing on my heart. The tip broke my skin, greedily taking my blood.

"You're going to give me what I want, Rain, and I'll give you what you need."

"You don't know what I need," I rasped, "and I won't give you what you want."

"Won't you?" He lowered himself to my chest, kissing the spot of blood. "That's our word: fate. It's what brought us together. It's the only thing that'll break us. The only thing that'll make me stop."

"I—"

He dropped the crossbow and ripped my shirt clean off.

"Cairo!"

"I dreamed about you the other night," he whispered, pressing his mouth to my ear. "We were running through town. Well, you were running. I was chasing."

My bra strap slipped off my shoulder. Helped along by Cairo.

"I caught you behind the Roadhouse. Nowhere left to run," he said. "You pleaded with me to let you go, and I put you on your knees right there in the filthy alley. I pried those pretty lips open like this"—Cairo cracked my jaw—"and shoved my cock inside like that."

His tongue found mine—tangling in a battle of wills. He demanded submission. Yanked it out of me like fevered moans, and in my fury not to give it to him, it didn't sink in that I was kissing him back.

"Till you cried," he whispered against my lips. "Like this."

Cairo tweaked my nipple without mercy.

"Ah," I cried, tears springing to my eyes as dampness spread in another part of me. My heart was racing, running, beating out of control.

Taking me in his mouth, he gently flicked my nipple—teasing it, tasting it, introducing it to one of its new owners. I sunk my fingers in his hair even before it came, knowing the reprieve wouldn't last long.

Cairo scraped the helpless nub beneath his teeth, rougher treatment than the poor thing was used to. Pain and pleasure wracked me in equal measure, so tangled I couldn't tell them apart.

Growls peeled from my wolf. He snapped, bit, sucked, and nipped my tender flesh—abandoning my breasts only to devour every part of me. Tangling in my hair, he tugged my head back and licked a stripe from neck to chin.

"Mine."

"No, Cairo. You've been waiting for someone to say it, and now it's all you're going to hear. No!" I fisted Cairo's silky, gold locks, half pulling them from the root. "You don't own me. No Sharpe ever will!"

The slap snapped my head to the side. The shock of it released my grip.

"A Sharpe will make you *beg* to be owned, bitch."

My chest heaved with ragged breaths. Shrieking, I swiped at him, and Cairo caught my hands, slamming them in the dirt. Crossing them above my head, he licked my stinging cheek.

"That's it," he said, collecting my tears. "So fucking sweet. You're my Rain now. Say it."

I met those eyes—shining even now. "No."

I didn't know where the others were. Maybe they were concealed in the trees, watching our battle of wills, and a battle it was. A down-and-out, fight-to-the-death, no-survivors for my mind, body, and soul, just as Cairo said. If I failed here, the Bedlam Boys would own me in every way that mattered—even if I one day got away.

Maybe I could've said fate and called him off, but deep down I knew that wasn't victory. It was waving the white flag. I'd be admitting their scorching burned me, and I needed their permission to leave as much as their demand to stay.

Fuck no. The Bedlam Boys can try to break me, but if there's one thing I know, it's that fire doesn't survive the rain.

"Say it," Cairo hissed.

"No."

Cairo slapped the other cheek, exploding stars behind my eyes.

"Ahh." Pressure built between my legs, contracting the muscles in my lower belly and spreading through my body. I was a gasp away from imploding in on myself like a dying star. *Holy shit. Is this normal?*

Sweat slicked my skin. My nipple was raw and achy, but inside, for the love of everything, something was happening inside me.

I bucked, yanking at my trapped wrists, and thrashed to get him off. I needed to get out of here. Away from him. Any more, and the dam would break.

"Get off!" I got my foot between us, rearing to kick him.

Cairo twisted to the side and caught my leg as it went wide. He hooked me around his waist like he thought that was what I meant to do all along.

Frustrated tears leaked down my face. "Cairo," I pleaded.

He responded instantly.

Cairo nudged my legs apart, pressing his thigh to my middle. My body took over. I rutted against him, moving in time with the cock digging into my leg. The friction rolled my eyes up in my skull.

"Say it, or I'm going to be angry with you."

Going to? Every inch of me above the waist was sore. If this was him in a good mood, heaven help the world when he gets mad.

"The last man who tried to control me died tied to a stake. What was it I told you we had in common?"

His smirk glinted in the dark.

Why? It was undoubtedly the wrong thing to say.

"Are you a virgin, Rain?"

I fell very quiet.

"Answer me." He let go of my hands and grabbed my legs, locking them around his waist. He skimmed the hem of my dress. "Did you let another man touch you? Did he take what's ours?"

I shook, swallowing hard. *This* was Cairo angry.

"What if I did? I didn't even know you then."

"That's not an answer."

"That's not a question you have the right to ask me."

"Raiinnneey."

I stiffened. No way to tell if it was Roan, Jacques, Arsenio, or Legend. All I knew was they were close.

"Come on out, sweetheart," one of them called.

I'm barely holding my own against Cairo. What do I do if they all catch me? Hold me down, hit me, ravage my breasts, rammed their cocks in my—

A moan escaped my lips. Cairo had found his way under my skirt, and slipped past the thin cotton barrier. He teased my clit under slow, soft strokes.

"Answer me, Rain." The sound of his zipper pierced the night. "Are you a virgin?"

Slowly, unable to stop myself, I nodded.

"Really?" Satisfaction laced his voice. "Because you're wet like a fucking whore."

He dipped inside my pussy, soaking himself to the knuckles. I watched, transfixed, as he licked me off his middle finger.

"Hmm. I was wrong," he said. "As delicious as your tears are, nothing is sweeter than your pussy. Taste."

"No." I smacked his hand away.

Cairo flashed. He seized my neck, squeezing till I choked—gasping for air. In went his fingers.

"Lick them clean. Don't waste a drop."

I obeyed—sucking, licking, slurping.

Cairo leaned over me. He pecked a light kiss on my nose and pushed in with one hard thrust.

"Ahh!" My cry rang through the forest.

"There," Jacques shouted. "She's over there!"

Cairo gave me no time to recover. He started pumping, angling my hips to bury to the hilt. The pain was excruciating.

"Cairo, don't," I sobbed around his fingers. "Please, no."

He groaned deep inside him. "You are so fucking tight. You did wait for me." He removed his fingers to kiss me. "Good girl."

"S-stop. It's too much."

"Oh, baby. It's not even close to enough."

He jerked me toward him. I slammed back on the dirt, my head bouncing off a root. Cairo lost control.

The green-eyed Bedlam Boy pounded me like a beast. Mouth open in a silent scream, my world converged in this single slice of space and time, Cavendish, Jennifer, the sheriff, the new letter, the dangling rope in the barn. All that existed was the wolf who claimed me, and the others coming to take me away.

The pressure was rising, taking over me. Digging my nails in his shoulder, I threw my head back, and came so hard, Cairo cursed at my squeezing down on him.

"Holy fucking shit, woman."

Jerking and flopping on the ground, I rode the crest of pleasure and pain till they threatened to choke me themselves. I sucked in deep lungfuls of air, gazing up at the trees, wondering what the hell happened. What the hell was still happening. Cairo was far from done.

"Cairo," Arsenio called. "Do you have her?"

"I've got her."

I dropped my head, eyes alighting on something.

"She's ours now."

"I'm not," I whispered. "You don't get to keep me. It won't be that easy."

"She says while her cum lubes my—"

I smashed the crossbow over his head.

Cairo pitched forward—dropping on top of me. He was out cold.

"Where the hell are you?" Roan demanded.

Pushing him off, I fixed myself as best I could and disappeared into the trees. This was my forest. I've run around inside her since I was old enough to get my wobbling new legs underneath me. My interlude with Cairo aside, there was never a question of if I could lose them in the woods. I was destined to the minute I crossed the tree line. It just took some creativity toward the end.

But now what?

I headed away from Black Widow Hill. If I continued in the direction I was going, it'd skirt the rim of the canyon, then drop me off at Chaney Bridge. From there, it was a six-hour walk to the next town, and I'd be limping the whole way.

Cairo fucked me. There was no sweet or cute way to put it. He got me in the dirt and fucked me like an animal. My cheeks stung, my nipples throbbed, and I'd fall asleep in an Epsom salt bath with dreams it'd help the soreness in my middle.

Did I keep going? The Bedlam Boys made it clear there was nowhere in this town I'd be safe from them.

I touched my neck. Did I finish what I started?

No.

The denial rang clear and true in my mind. What had changed since I stepped into that noose was hard to put into words. I just knew there was another way now.

My fingers moved down, brushing the tiny pinprick wound of the crossbow.

"You're not my curse, Rainey de Souza, you're my cure."

Once more, I asked my grandmother what to do. The wind carried her whispers in my ear, showing me the way.

CAIRO

"Let me get this straight." Legend's dry voice grated on my ears. "You had her, and somehow she got your crossbow, hit you over the head, and left you in the dirt with your pants down?"

I probed the welt on my forehead, grimacing. "That about sums it up."

"How exactly did she get your bow?" Roan asked. He wasn't trying to hide his amusement.

The five of us tramped through the forest—lost as hell, but figuring if we didn't go over a cliff, we were heading in the right direction.

"Ever been knocked unconscious mid-ejaculation, Banks?"

"Can't say that I have."

"I'll arrange it for you."

Roan cracked up.

"What are our chances of catching up to her?" Arsenio asked. The question wasn't for me.

"Approximately six minutes since Cairo confirmed his location and we tripped over his body. Average healthy female— Above average due to years of farm work puts her a mile ahead in those six minutes. Prior knowledge of this area and a... high... motivation to escape," Jacques said. "We have a slim-to-nil chance of catching up to de Souza."

"Think she'll do it?" Legend asked. "Leave town."

"I read the suicide note," Roan said. "Parents and grandparents dead. Sister fucked off. She's got nothing keeping her here."

"She's got the university." I grimaced again. What the hell? Didn't I sound like a hopeful cuck wishing and praying my girl doesn't leave me? *That hit did more damage than I thought.*

Even so, visions of her floated before my eyes. Her fleeing through the forest when I spotted her. Pouncing on my sweet little prey. Drinking the fear in those big eyes. Feasting on her screams. Absorbing her hits, smacks, and hair-pulling. The rage that burned beneath the surface even as she surrendered her submission.

I hitched my step, suddenly so hard I was limping as bad as my Rain would've when she ran from me. Yes, mine.

I didn't care what deal we made. I couldn't give a shit if she made it to Hunter's Crest and was currently buying her bus ticket to her sister. I would find her wherever she was. We were bound together in blood, pain, and fire. As I promised her, only fate would break us.

"Up ahead," Arsenio spoke up. "It's the barn."

"We follow her," I stated. "She won't want to run through the woods all night. Eventually, she'll come out on the road and follow it out of town. We'll pick her up there."

"Three roads out of town," Legend said. "Which, Jacques?"

"We're closest to Abbey Road. If she heads in that direction, she'll get as far as the river before she has to come out and cross the bridge."

We broke free of the woods, riding the surge of renewed lust.

Now that I tasted that pussy, I wasn't letting it get away. I nearly blacked out from her squeezing my cock alone.

"She's on foot," I said as we rounded the barn. "Legend, we'll drop you and Roan off. Arsenio, Jacques, and I will wait out on the..." I trailed off.

The five of us ground to a stop, staring at the truck's new hood ornament.

"Took you long enough," Rainey said.

She munched on a bag of popcorn, of all things. Leaves and sticks tangled in her hair. There were smudges of dirt on her cheeks, cut through by tear tracks and decorated with my red handprints. Somewhere she found a baggy shirt that didn't match the skirt, and a makeshift sling for her shoulder.

She couldn't have looked more banged up and ridiculous if she tried, but reclined on my windshield, looking at me with that half smirk on her lips, it was everything in me not to tear those clothes off and have my fill for the second time that night.

And this time, I'll get it right. I circled her. *Keep those pretty hands tied.*

"Surprised to see me?" She shrugged. "I told you I'd come back to you, Cairo. You didn't have to be so impatient."

"What can I say, baby?" I replied slowly. "The noose gave me pause."

"A momentary lapse in judgment. It won't happen again."

She sat up and the guys twitched for their weapons. For the first time in our lives, we stood dumbfounded as she plucked the keys from Legend's hands and climbed in the car.

"Well," she prompted when we didn't make a move to get in with her. "I considered my options, and I'm staying. Nothing and no one is driving me out of my town. If that means you and I are roomies for a while, so be it. I've been itching to get out of that motel anyway."

"You understand what this means," I said.

"I do."

"The offer is off the table from here. Stay or run." I leaned on the door, skimming my hand down her cheek. "You're ours now."

"We're going to discuss this 'yours' thing."

"No, we're not."

Chapter Eight

R*ainey*

Large, painted eyes tracked me—watching. Judging.

Fed up, my hand shot out of the covers and twisted the lucky cat around. Why did Cairo keep that creepy thing on his nightstand? Who'd want that to be the first thing they saw when they woke up?

All right, maybe my problem wasn't really with the cat, as it was those eyes kept asking me what I was doing here.

I was free of them. I could've made it to Chaney Bridge and been halfway to the next town while those guys were still stumbling through the woods. Free of Scott Cavendish, Sheriff Sharpe, and the new Letter Man. The Bedlam Boys were giving me a gift.

But a gift isn't what I deserved.

The crushing, stomach-twisting guilt ate me at the very thought of packing up and starting over like nothing happened. Leaving Cairo and the boys to face suspicion over my crime. Keeping the Letter Man a secret in fear of my motives being discovered, while they're free to torture someone else. If I picked a life of running, I'd never stop.

It wasn't until Cairo caught me. Dominated me. Punished me, that I felt something else. Actually, I felt many things as my virginity was brutally taken from me. What I didn't feel was guilty. For the first time since the arrow flew from my bow, I could breathe.

I betrayed Cairo, and he took what he wanted while giving me what I needed.

"We don't get to decide, Rain. The chance will come to right your wrongs. It always does. For those who truly want to make amends, they won't miss it."

No, my ghostly apparitions didn't count as Gran giving me advice. Even so, she said things like this my whole life.

"We don't get to decide when we're forgiven, Rainey."

"It's not a punishment if we choose how and when it's over."

Wisdom she dropped on me after petty fights with my sister, or the many times I complained about being grounded. Did they compare to murder and framing not-so-innocent men? Would she have given me the same advice about giving myself up to the man who repeatedly assaulted me and played out his rape fantasy in the woods? Not just him, all of his friends.

I knew what any sane person would say, and all I could reply in response is I don't get to say when I'm forgiven.

I don't choose my punishment.

I burrowed deeper in Cairo's covers, inhaling the piney, spicy-sweet scent. I was brought here after a long, silent drive, during which the guys looked at me like I'd try to set someone else on fire at any moment.

They brought me straight up here. Legend checked me out, gave me a real sling and painkillers, then the lock clicked shut on my new prison. Yes, I've asked myself many times why Cairo's room locked from the outside. Was he so dangerous even his housemates slept better when he was contained?

It was a question I planned to ask when he came to me. When any of them did. I sat in the room for hours, watching the sun come up from his bed, and no one came. Not so much as a whisper on the other side of the door.

I swept the space, taking in all that was Cairo. I didn't get a proper look the first time I was here.

I missed the band posters on the wall. The pitch-black bedspread even softer than it looked. The waving lucky cat, and a collection of dream catchers covering an entire wall. They all said something about him, but did they say it as loud as the throbbing ache between my legs, or the blood that drained down his tub.

Shutting my eyes, I drew my legs to my chest, feeling him in every part of me. Here I am wondering who Cairo was, when I should be asking who the hell am I? He hurt me. Hit me. Shoved inside me without preparation or mercy.

I should hate Cairo Sharpe, and I did. I hated him for making me come.

My first orgasm that I didn't give myself, and he exploded every one of my nerve endings, blowing a bomb in my mind.

The night before played on a loop, asking me if their ownership meant Cairo would hold me down and fuck me till I screamed every night. Would they all?

Wetness dampened my panties—bringing equal embarrassment and anticipation.

"Yes, cat," I said. "I am fucked up."

The doorknob rattled. I poked my head out of the sheets as Jacques came into the room. He shut the door behind him.

"What?" I sat up, scooting back against the headboard. Those mirrored eyes just watched me. "What do you want, Stone? Where's Cairo?"

"Why?" he asked, tone measured. "Are you looking for a protector?"

"Do I need one?"

"Yes."

The snappy comeback died on my lips. A yes to tease me, sure. A yes in such a matter-of-fact way, I didn't have a reply for that.

"Get up. Come to me."

I kept scooting, though there was nowhere for me to go. "No, I'm good here."

"It wasn't a request."

"Frame it like one, so I can again say no."

"De Souza." He said my name like I was a naughty child. Jacques pointed to the floor in front of him. "Here. Now."

"Oooh, I kinda want to see you make me," I snapped.

Inexplicably, he grinned.

"What have they told you about me?" he asked.

"Who?"

"Paris Keller and her hair-flipping, perfumed horde. They are always clucking about something. I know I've come up."

"Arrogant much? And clucking? Why, because women are chickens?"

"Women are cattle."

I reeled back and he made a *tss* sound between his teeth.

"Don't be offended. Men are cattle too," he said. "Slow. Stupid. Driven by eating, shitting, and mating, and never considering their value to the world beyond that."

"Douchebag," I said clearly. "The hair-flipping horde warned me you were a douche."

He closed the distance, advancing on the bed, then stepping around and moving to the window. I gathered the blankets tighter, heart thrumming as he closed the blinds.

"People don't agree with their true designation, of course," he continued. "You all believe your precious thoughts, opinions, and problems are unique. You, for example, put on a tough act to cover grief, loneliness, insecurity, and a touch of sadism."

"I'm not sadistic."

"You planned and carried out burning a man alive, and you enjoyed it. What would you call that?"

I pressed my lips together.

"Exactly. You're all textbook," he said. "Literally lines on a page explaining human behavior down to the last mommy issue. You never veer from the case studies. So, what will a blustering clucker do when I jump over this bed and *make* her face me?" He paused. "That wasn't a rhetorical question, de Souza. What will you do?"

"Break your nose."

"I say you'll do absolutely nothing. If you could truly face up to someone stronger than you, Cavendish's eyes would've crossed staring down your arrow. Instead, you struck from the shadows and shifted the blame on us."

"Stone, I appreciate that a high IQ left you with a low EQ. Everything you know about people and social interaction, you read in a book," I said. "Sad, but there's one thing I can promise you. You don't understand what happened that night between me and Caven—"

"He challenged you to find and stop him before he killed Jennifer Wilson," Jacques sliced in. "Don't look so surprised. We read your suicide note."

Of course. I guess I did put enough pieces in that they added up to that conclusion.

"If you discovered some random person was plotting to kill an innocent woman, you would've reported it to the police, and warned her Scott Cavendish was after her. Neither of those things happened. Instead, Jennifer Wilson was surprised to wake up in a freezer one night, and even more surprised to be rescued.

"You knew she was in danger, but by threat or coercion, could not report it. Aligning with society's moral code, you could not let her die if there was something you could do to stop it. You killed Cavendish, rescued Jennifer, and laid the trail to someone else.

"My only question is, how did you get involved? Choosing a worthy opponent and taunting them to catch before they kill again is a classic serial killer profile. They get off on staying ahead of the chase just as much as they do the killing. But they usually choose cops, detectives, or journalists. Maximize the chance of their cleverness broadcasted on the media. They don't go for farm girls. What makes you so special?"

I looked away. *Great question. Let me know when you have the answer.*

"Did you come in here to tell me this?" I asked.

"I'm here to make something clear to you." Jacques bore down on me. "The single thing cattle have in their favor is they can be trained. They do something they shouldn't, you take out the cattle prod, and the message sinks in. Maybe not the first or fifth time, but inevitably—"

Jacques snaked an arm around my waist. He didn't grab or force. He simply slid me out of bed and dropped me on my feet before him—as ordered.

"Inevitably, they learn."

I hardly heard him, or the contempt lacing his words.

Up close, Jacques Stone was more coldly beautiful than ten feet away, or one foot from my seat in class. Chin pressed to his chest, I skimmed his cheeks for a trace of a blemish, large pores, or one slight imperfection to tear him down and bring Jacques to earth with the rest of the mortals.

But no. His skin was flawless, and the shadow's beard darkening his jaw appeared too soft to resist stroking. So, I didn't.

I traced his jawline—dipping with his cleft chin and continuing my path to his lips. Sense stopped me just short.

I peeked at Jacques. He displayed no reaction to me touching him.

"You live here now," he said. "You will obey our rules."

"Rules?"

"You do not go where you're not wanted. You don't touch what's not yours. No talking back. No disrespect. No false bravado unless you want your bluff called—mercilessly."

Jacques took my hand and placed it on his lips. I felt every horrible word fall from them.

"When you're told to do something, you will obey without argument. You do not share what goes on in this house with anyone. What's between us is between us."

"Us?" I whispered.

"You're our girl now," he dropped like it was a fact of life. "Quinn is out. Now there's you."

"Your girl. Mind, soul, and... body."

"Yes."

I brushed the sharp ridge of his nose, continuing to his brows. Impossibly long lashes tickled me as he blinked.

"I wouldn't have thought you wanted either," I said. "You seemed a bit ticked off about the surprise shower in the middle of class."

"Yes."

The slight smile froze on my face. "But you're over it, right? Chasing me through the forest and scaring the shit out of me makes up for it. We can move on to bigger things."

"No."

A flush crept up my neck. "Put it down to not being a genius, but I'm going to need more than one-word replies to understand what you're getting at."

"I see. Then, let me be clear. You haven't made up for your unfortunate choices that morning. I planned to handle it Ruckus night, but instead you handled us."

I lowered my hand, taking a step back.

"Another unfortunate choice, and this one with bigger consequences. After your shoulder heals, I'll deliver those consequences."

"Why after my shoulder heals?"

He cocked a brow. "Would you prefer I do it now?"

Heat stained my cheeks. "What are the consequences? What exactly are you going to do to me?"

"Cairo's in the process of setting up your space," he said, ignoring the questions. "You'll stay in this room till he's done."

"My space? Did you guys get my things from the farm?"

"We have everything you need."

"Why am I locked in here? I chose to come with you guys. I'm not going to run."

"Why is that?" His tone sharpened. "We had little chance of catching up to you, despite Cairo's plans to catch you on the bridge. You were free of us, and yet you handed yourself over on a platter. Explain."

I grinned. "Huh. Well, isn't this interesting."

"What?"

"You really don't know, do you?" I laughed. "None of you do. You spent all last night in the living room, arguing about what the farm girl is up to.

"Even better, Jacques Stone, the cattle wrangler, has no idea why I hopped in that truck." I leaned in, whispering against his lips. "I guess I'm not so textbook after all."

His cool, if narrowed, gaze surveyed me. "Eight."

I brushed past him and slid into bed. "I'm cool to stay in here till you set up my digs. It's much nicer than my last place. Oh, and I'll take breakfast while you're at it."

"Nine."

Jacques left me with that and returned me to my locked solitude. I suspected I'd soon find out why he was counting up. Nothing would be able to help me then.

ARSENIO

Jacques climbed off the stairs.

"Well?" I asked.

He shook his head. "No explanation for why she chose us. Accurately, she found the question amusing."

"What business have we had with the de Souzas?" Roan asked. "If she's up there plotting to slit our throats while we're sleeping, I'd at least like to know why."

"She looks familiar," Legend said. "I think Dad did business with her grandmother. He did with most of the local farms."

"Did he screw her over?"

"If he did, it would've been my wallet under that container."

Our attention shifted to Cairo, who reclined feet up on the coffee table and stretched out on the couch, digging through the bags we went back and took from the old farmhouse.

"It's me she has the problem with," Cairo said. "Or I should say, with the sheriff. She hasn't come clean, but I've seen that look. She hates him."

"There it is," Roan said. "So, that's why she came back. She wasn't leaving till she got another chance at fucking over the sheriff."

"Possibly."

"You're not worried?"

He mouth-shrugged without stopping in his task. "Enemy of my enemy, as they say."

"The sheriff's not the enemy," I said. Funny how we'd all taken to speaking of Cairo's father by title. We've known the man our whole lives—which had something to do with it.

"Wasn't talking about him."

I inclined my head, letting the matter drop. "What's she got?"

"Nothing." Cairo fished out an album. "Clothes, books, toothbrush. The regular stuff. She's got a laptop. It's not password protected, but she deleted the search history. Everything else on there are old school assignments. No weapons. No notebooks with our names scribbled a thousand times."

"But she killed Cavendish."

"Yes, there is that."

Our gaze shifted again—peering through the ceiling at the surprisingly attractive little assassin, kicking back in Cairo's room.

"Old history makes no difference," I said. "She's our girl now. Her days of plotting against us are over."

"She won't be easy to break," Cairo said. "Rain took my cock like a good girl, then she took a crossbow to my head. She's going to make this interesting for us."

"Looking forward to it," I said. "Now on to shit that matters. Roan, did you find out who those guys were that hijacked that party?"

"Nah." He flopped down next to Cairo. "I asked around. They're not from Bedlam. No one knows who they are, or they're not saying."

"Think they're connected to Foundry?" Legend asked.

"I'll assume everyone is until we root those bastards out."

"These guys are smart," he said under his breath. "Who knows how many people they got to before we heard their name. We're running out of money, but if we up payments in retaliation, it'll just drive more people to them. We can't do this on our own."

"We have to, sweet cheeks," Roan said. "She's not going to help us."

"Arsenio," Legend began.

"No," I said. "Don't bother asking. She's opting for plausible deniability. As long as she doesn't know shit, she can't get taken down for it. Besides, she's blaming us for letting the problem get out of hand in the first place. These guys moved in on our turf and we didn't know a fucking thing. Ruckus Royale is further proof we're losing our grip.

"Those guys knew to find us at Westchester Drumlins. They knew who we were and what we do, and we can't dig up their damn names." I leaned back against the counter, folding my hands across my stomach lest they found something to punch. It was times like this I needed stress relief. Unfortunately, or fortunately, depending on who you asked, Quinn was out and the new girl wasn't ready for me. I didn't do the breaking.

My methods were outlawed.

"We're on our own," I said, finally stating what we all knew. "Ideas?"

"We can't up payments?" Legend asked.

"No."

"We're locked out of the databases."

"Yes," Roan confirmed. "Oooh, nice bikini."

He plucked a photo from the album, unzipped his pants, and fisted his cock. I slid to Cairo as he jacked off.

"Then, it's simple," Legend said. "If diplomacy doesn't work, we switch to violence."

"We would've chosen that option a... long time ago, sweets—ahh." Roan tossed his head back, moaning. "But, we don't know who to take the fight to."

"The fight's coming to us now." Jacques finally added his opinion. "Don't have enough information to say if those guys from the party were with Foundry, but they have it in their head they're taking over our town. While they're happy to come to us, we start with them."

I nodded. "The sheriff," I said to Cairo. "He's questioning the crashers about Cavendish. We need to know what he finds out."

"We will." He dropped his feet on the floor. "In the meantime, we have a guest. Our focus is on making her stay as comfortable as possible."

Again, I said nothing as he headed up the stairs. There was no point getting in Cairo's way when he had that look on his face.

RAINEY

One week.

One week since the Bedlam Boys brought me back to their frat-boy home. One week I'd been kept in Cairo's room with minimal contact with any one of them. My food was placed on a tray they set just inside the door. Jacques stopped by every day to check my shoulder, ignoring questions of when I'd be let out and my demands to go to class.

All I got was a, "your classes have been taken care of," and nothing else.

Cairo didn't come to me. Arsenio didn't so much as cough outside my door. Roan stuck his head in once when delivering my tray. Licking his lips, he blew me a kiss and ducked out.

I snuggled into Cairo's pillow, watching a *Golden Girls* rerun on TV. It was losing the smell of him and starting to smell like me. Even though I was bathing with Cairo's body wash. It wasn't the same.

Roan came in with another tray. "Uh-oh."

"What?"

He pointed. I followed his line of sight to my sling, lying innocently at the foot of the bed.

"Just as well," he said. "We were starting to get impatient."

I snatched it up, though it was far too late.

"Impatient for what?"

"For you, Rainey de Souza." He grabbed my neck, yanking me to him. Roan's hot, wet tongue licked my cheek. "I've been waiting for my taste."

"Yeah." I flung away from him. "I've been told I'm your girl now. So far, that looks like lying around and being waited on hand and foot. That'll teach me to listen to small-town gossip. Your reputation is blown way out of proportion."

Cardinal curls danced with his laugh. What I mistook for a slender body from a distance, transformed into the hard, discrete muscles of a swimmer.

"You don't ride a wounded horse, sweets. Now that you're all fixed up, you'll take your rightful place with the guys. Me, on the other hand, I'm a bit choosier about my playmates. Hold out your hand."

"Why?"

"Why not?"

Cautiously, I raised my hand, palm up. Roan moved quicker than I could react.

A flash of silver and sharp pain blossomed in my finger.

"Ow!"

"Shh," he crooned.

Blood pebbled from the pinprick wound. Wide eyes trailed the knife to his lips where flinty green orbs trapped them. Roan licked the knife's edge, and I gasped, stunned at the cut he sliced into his own tongue. He lifted my hand.

"Roan, no…"

He sucked me into his mouth, bobbing up and down to the knuckle. It was the most erotic thing a man had ever done to me. My nipples were so hard, they could've popped off my breasts and made little *tick, tick, ticks* as they bounced across the floor.

"Hmm." His moan turned the heat on deep inside me. "We taste sweet together, baby. You try."

It wasn't a conscious decision. One moment, we were separated by a foot of distance, the next I was crawling on my knees toward him—pulled in by that devil's grin.

I slid my hands over his pecs, hesitantly like he may stop me. Instead, Roan cupped the back of my neck, drawing our lips to meet.

Kissing Roan Banks was nothing like kissing Cairo. Cairo was roving beasts, wildfires, lightning storms, and forces you couldn't hope to control.

But Roan, he was that piece of chocolate cake that wrecked your diet. He was sneaking and opening your Christmas presents early. Secret flings with that guy you know you're not supposed to be with.

Slipping the odd thing or two in your pocket under watch of the security cameras.

Everything wrong and sinful in this world, distilled into one deep, plundering kiss, and topped with the sharp metallic taste of our blood. Did it taste particularly sweet? Couldn't say. All I knew was Roan for fuck sure did.

I melted into the kiss, moaning as Roan deepened it.

Something pressed against my side.

He broke away, grinning that grin. "I said I do my own vetting. You've definitely got the wanton slut vibe I go for. You don't even know me and you're licking me up like the last squirt of cream."

I might've pushed, slapped, or shoved away from him. If it wasn't for the blade digging above my hip—held back by a single layer of cloth.

"Turn around."

I did, putting my back to him. The knife moved with me.

Roan leaned me against him and propped his chin on my shoulder. "Cairo said he claimed your virginity. Is that true?"

I nodded.

"Just how fresh and unspoiled are you, Rainey D? Anyone spread those ass cheeks and plunder for gold?"

My face burned. "No."

"What about these juicy little treats?" He kissed the corner of my mouth. "How many cocks had the pleasure? How many pussies?"

"Stop it," I hissed.

"Oh, am I embarrassing you? That's too cute."

"It's none of your business."

Roan gathered my shirt from neck to hem and sliced it in one stroke. The tatters slipped off my shoulders, revealing my complete lack of underwear. Cairo hadn't seen fit to return my clothes. I'd been making do with his, and his briefs didn't fit.

"There's nothing about you that's not our business." He cupped my breast, flattening the blade against my nipple. I wanted to believe he wouldn't cut me, but he already did. "You're going to tell me everything, de Souza, starting with... what was it like?"

"What was what like?" I gripped his hips, digging in to be painful, though he didn't react. Roan shifted to cradle me against his collarbone. The smell of honeysuckle shampoo floated in my nose.

"Killing Cavendish."

I stiffened.

"Be honest."

"It was awful," I snapped. "The worst thing I've ever had to do in my life."

"I told you to be honest."

The knife dropped on the sheets. Roan found a new thing to fondle.

I bit hard on my lip as two fingers slipped past my folds.

"The awful part wasn't killing him. It was enjoying it. Tell me what it was like." Fervor leeched into the whisper. "The moment the arrow left the bow, soaring for its target."

He moved inside me, palm rubbing firm on my clit. Electricity zipped up my veins.

"What did you do when the container exploded and engulfed the murdering shit in flames? The truth, baby." Roan picked up speed.

"Ahh," I cried, arching my back.

"Did you tease this sweet pussy like I am?"

"No."

"Yes," he hissed. "You had the best orgasm of your life that night. Admit it."

"No! It wasn't like that. That wasn't what I meant—"

"I know exactly what you meant. That was the first time in your pathetic life you had a taste of power." Roan's tone changed in a snap.

"You weren't just the farm girl mucking around in chicken shit, or another orphan everyone forgot about."

"Roan," I cried.

"What? Am I wrong?" He grasped my chin, twisting my neck to face him. The other hand didn't stop its activities for a second. "You lived in this town your whole life and no one knows who the fuck you are. No one cares. No wonder you made yourself a hemp necklace and went for a dive."

"Shut up!"

"You felt your first taste of importance while you watched the flesh *melt* off his skull—"

"I said shut up, Roan." I snatched his wrist, trying to pull him out of me.

"But after he was dead, what did you have? Nothing." Each horrible word pelted me like machine-gun fire. Every one a fatal blow. "Your sister still fucked off and abandoned you. Granny died to free herself from the burden of you. Did she hang herself too? Is that where you got the—"

Whipping around, I smacked him across the face. The blow snapped his neck—knocking him back and freeing me from his hold.

"Don't you ever! Ever! Talk about my grandmother."

Roan spun around, eyes flashing. He launched at me.

"Crazy, sadistic asshole," I screamed.

We scrapped like WWE fighters. Roan pinned my arms over my head, sinking a knee on my thigh. I broke free and backhanded him across the face.

"I got it right, didn't I?" His laugh bordered on insane. "Gammy left via razor blade and now you're all alone. Oooh, poor baby. Did Mommy and Daddy kill themselves to get away from you too? Their birth-control-fail mistake."

"Ahh!" Surging up, I drove my skull into his nose.

"Fuck!"

Dazed and in pain, he couldn't stop my next hit.

I tackled him around the middle and threw him back on the bed. Scrambling up his body, I straddled him as my hands closed on his neck.

"Take it back!" Scorching, incendiary fury burned every trace of me down to the last molecule. "Take it back, you fucking monster!"

I squeezed tighter, popping his eyes from their sockets. Roan gagged, hand flying to grip my wrist. He knocked something aside, and there was the knife.

I grabbed and pressed it to his cheek. Leaning over him, I hissed in his face, "Say you're sorry."

Roan's mouth worked. He strained to get it out. "Do... it," he gasped. "Do it, you gorgeous, crazy fucking thing. You know you want to."

Surprise broke through my rage, then he did.

Roan dipped inside my pussy again, setting a furious pace. *Slap, slap, slap, slap, slap.*

"Come on. Hurt me, baby."

Yes, in that moment, it did cross my mind that I had lost complete control of my life. I didn't know who I was, or what the hell I was doing, but I did know this: I really, really wanted to.

The tip split his skin, coming apart as a seam, and my hand drawing red ribbons down his cheek. Roan groaned—a glare of such ecstasy on his face, it undid me.

"Say you're sorry," I repeated. I moved the knife beneath his collarbone. "And mean it."

"I'm sorry." Roan let go of my wrist, leaving me to choke him as I saw fit. I heard the zipper yanked down to free his cock. "Course I'm sorry."

I cut a slow, steady line down his chest. "More."

"Your parents are freaking saints. Songs should be written about them. Let us bow down and worship at their statues for bringing you into this world."

I rocked back on his fingers. I couldn't help it. Roan had found a particularly interesting spot and was hitting it relentlessly.

Blood poured from his wound. A shallow cut that dripped uneven red lines down his chest like running paint.

"May your grandmother rest in peace," he continued. "I know she was a strong, fierce woman who raised you to be nothing less. She'd be proud of who you are, Rainey de Souza. A woman who doesn't let anything or anyone get in her way."

The room was thick with our moans and the heady sounds of us getting off. My lower belly was tightening. Orgasm was swelling fast. I bounced faster on the balls of my feet, eager to bring her on.

"She'd be proud of what you did," Roan gruffed, "so don't feel an ounce of guilt. What you did was divine, baby. You're a damn goddess."

I seized—body jerking as an orgasm the likes of which could put me in the hospital, hooked and dragged me under.

"Not," I rasped, "good enough."

Holding the knife above his hip, I reared up and stabbed.

"Argh!" Roan bellowed, arching off the bed. Cum exploded on my back.

"Holy fuck," he cried. Blood poured from the cut, soaking us in ichor and cum.

I collapsed on him, falling boobs-first on his face. My strength leaked out, leaving me a boneless, sated mess of limbs and sweat.

"Oh, yeah," Roan said. He slid me down, pressing his already hardening cock to my entrance. "You'll do just fine."

"Wow."

The dry voice snapped my head up.

"Can't get a show like that on Pornhub." Cairo leaned against the door. Who knew how long he'd been standing there. "Rain, come."

I didn't think twice. I clambered off the bed and ran to him, burrowing my face in his back. That spicy pine scent enveloped me as I did Cairo, hugging him from behind.

"Didn't miss me too much," he breezed. "Made yourself right at home.

"You," he said to Roan. "I told you to quit coming on my sheets."

"Don't blame me." Roan stretched like a lazy cat. "She did it."

"Then, she'll be punished for it," Cairo replied, peeling my hands off. "Let's go. I worked all week to get everything ready for you. You can finally move out of this room."

Cairo stepped out, holding the door for me to follow.

I quickly grabbed a shirt and baggy sweatpants from his closet. Cairo led me down the hall. If he felt my eyes drilling a hole in his head, he didn't give a sign.

"I'm going to class tomorrow," I said. "I can't miss any more."

"Your lockdown is lifted. You can come and go as we please."

"What does that mean? That I need your permission?"

"You catch on quick."

I grabbed his shirt, stopping him before the stairs. Cairo twisted, gazing down at the appendage holding him back and wondering what the hell it was doing there.

"Why haven't I seen you all week?" My grip tightened. "Are you mad at me?"

"Shouldn't I be?" He gestured to the bruise on his forehead that shifted away from purple and blue, and was now a sickly yellow.

"I did what I had to do to get away. You would've done the same."

"The lists of things I'm allowed to do without retribution is much longer than yours."

"That's a ridiculous double standard."

He laughed. "Isn't it?"

I pushed down on my temper. "You can't just take someone's virginity and then ignore them for days. Who taught you manners?"

"No one, sadly. Daddy worked all day. Mommy ran off." Winking, he grinned. "You know how it is."

"Then, you need someone to teach you."

"Oh?" Cairo advanced on me, flattening me against the wall. "Are you going to teach me manners, Rain?"

"I'll give it my best shot."

He nipped my lips. The quickest kiss—over as soon as it started. "You first," he said. "On your knees."

"Kiss me first. Properly."

"You don't give me orders."

"Please." I kissed the corner of his mouth, chin, nose, and everywhere. It wasn't too much to ask that the man who claimed more of my firsts than he was entitled to, should give me a single kiss that wasn't forced or stolen. "Please, Cairo. Kiss me."

Cairo complied. He swiped the roof of my mouth. The tickle made me start, and he caught my tongue on its skittish retreat, drawing it back to play.

I untethered from him, breathless and dizzy.

"Ugh," he said, dragging me down to earth. "You taste like Roan."

"And you know what he tastes like?" I flung.

"I know I told you to get on your knees."

Sliding down the wall, I landed softly, crossing my legs at the ankles.

"Truth is, I have missed you." Cairo brushed my mussed hair from my eyes. "Been thinking about nothing but that tight pussy. You know, it took me a whole day to finally wash your blood off my cock. What can I say? I'm a sentimental guy."

Cairo caressed my mouth. "We didn't get to finish what we started. And these tasty lips have been begging for me. Haven't they?"

I bobbed my head.

"Aching for me to force through your lips, and fuck your mouth till you choke on my cock."

I nodded harder.

"Say it," he ordered.

"I want you to fuck my mouth, Cairo," I said it, though it heated my skin. "Make me... choke on your cum."

"Hmm. Well, if you want it that badly, I can't do it. Why should you be rewarded after this?"

He motioned to his bruise, and I understood at once what he was driving at.

He wants me to apologize. Beg and plead for forgiveness after he had me like an animal in the woods.

I lifted my chin and took Cairo's thumb in my mouth. I looked him in the eyes as I swallowed him, pulling back with a *pop*.

"You probably shouldn't," I said, "since I'm not in the least bit sorry. But we both know you will because you can't resist this mouth. It's in your dreams, Sharpe."

He released a low, labored hiss. "Fuck, the things I'm going to do to you." Cairo leaned down and poured the words directly into my soul. "I'm going to tear you apart."

I rose up, seeking his kiss. Cairo was gone.

"But not today," he said, descending the stairs. "Some other time when you're not covered in the blood, sweat, and cum of another man."

I bit my lip to pen in a harsh response. Cairo gleefully announced I'd be their shared treat, but somehow, I was also being punished for it.

Get used to it, Rainey. They rigged this game for you to lose. Every move would always be the wrong one. Every word a mark for sentencing.

"Till then, I've got this little lovely as the perfect ringtone." Cairo held his phone over his head, playing it as he descended. "I want you to fuck my mouth, Cairo. Make me choke on your cum."

"Asshole," I said under my breath.

"Let's go."

"What's my room like?" I asked, clambering down the stairs. "Does my door lock from the outside too?"

"Course not."

"Good."

Cairo slipped his hand in mine, surprising me—in a good way.

"I'm not going anywhere," I continued. "I made my choice."

"So did I."

The two of us entered the living room, walking in on Arsenio, Jacques, Legend, and the living room's newest addition.

"What's this?" I asked.

"Your *room*, obviously."

I opened my mouth, but nothing came out.

Pushed into the corner between the couch and fireplace was a large red doghouse. And if there was any confusion, hanging above the circular entrance was a sign saying "Rain."

"You can't be serious," I breathed.

"Where else would you sleep?" Legend asked. "Beds aren't for pets, love."

I got closer, eyeing the thing in disbelief. Maybe I should've been thankful they put in some effort to make it comfortable. A blue dog bed was stuffed inside and covered with a blanket.

Wait? I squinted. *Is that...?*

I reached in and pulled out a shiny pink collar.

"No. Fuck no!"

"You're hurting my feelings, Rain." Cairo's wicked smirk said nothing of the sort. "I put a lot of effort into making this perfect for you."

"Fuck you." I flung the collar across the room.

"Ten," said Jacques.

"Fuck you too!"

"Eleven."

"You will sleep in your house like a good pet," Cairo said. "Good girls get treats. Bad girls—" He tsked, shaking his head. "But you're not going to be a bad girl, are you, Rain?"

"Why are you doing this?"

"The cell you picked out for us." Arsenio's deep voice dispersed through the room. "Wasn't much bigger."

I pressed my lips together, shaking.

"Better," Jacques said.

I flipped him off.

"Twelve."

"Take off my clothes," Cairo said. "You have your own."

"Where is my stuff? I want my laptop and phone too."

Arsenio nodded at Legend. The raven-haired Adonis rounded the kitchen counter and returned loaded with shopping bags. "Hope you like them." He winked. "We picked it out ourselves."

"What is this?" I didn't touch the bags. "I have clothes."

"No, you don't," Cairo said. "I tossed out the farm-girl chic. I warned you about shit that reminds me of what kept us apart."

"That was both disturbingly possessive and insane. They're just clothes, Cairo. *My* clothes." I squared him down, folding my arms. "I want them back."

"I don't think you do. I shredded them before they were deposited in the nearest dumpster." He pointed. "You wear these, or you go naked. Never say we don't empower you to make your own choices."

My nails pierced my arms. It was incredible to me that I believed for a second there was a special connection between me and Cairo. With the other guys, I had no illusions that they just wanted to punish me. The only thing they knew about me was I nearly got them locked up as accessories to murder—although Roan seemed fond of me now.

With Cairo, I thought it was different. I said no to him. I challenged him. Fought him. I was tied to him by fate. He was supposed to want more from me than revenge.

"Don't fall for it. Cairo Sharpe is many things, but a wounded bird is not one of them."

"You tried to warn me."

"What was that?" Legend asked.

"I said, what did you buy me?"

"Everything you need for all occasions."

I took the clothes out of the bags one by one. They were looking for a reaction, so I refused to give them one. Despite wanting to throw up.

"These are all lingerie and club dresses," I said evenly.

"School clothes." Cairo held up a tight, slinky black, sleeveless dress. "Home clothes." A purple lace bra hung off his finger. He tossed it at me. "Put it on."

I tossed it back. "No. I'll wear the dress."

"Didn't you hear me? The dress is for when we go out." Cairo stroked my cheek. "Can't have you looking less than perfect, pet. But now, we're home, and these are your clothes."

Glaring at the dental floss called sleepwear, I said, "I might as well be naked."

"You can be."

And they win either way.

I shifted to each of them. Roan too when he came in, bandaged from cheek to hip, and looking plenty proud of himself.

"Let me stay in this," I said. No, I asked. Like the whimpering bitch they wanted me to be, I was asking for permission. "Don't you like me in your clothes?"

I reached for Cairo and kneaded his temples. Firm, slow circles to bring him to me.

A strange sort of frozen expression crossed his face. He gave me a look like he didn't know me and shot away.

"No." He was angry. "I like you not wearing clothes at all, and that's about to be your only fucking option. What's it going to be, Rain? 'Cause my clothes are coming off if I've got to tear them off myself."

There was no point in arguing with him. In full view of my pleased captors, I stripped off the shirt and sweats. Digging through the pile, I fished out the least revealing pair. A two-tone silk top with matching bikini bottom that covered a quarter of my ass cheeks.

"Final touch."

Roan tossed Cairo the collar. My lips peeled back as he approached.

"No biting," he said, winking at me.

This isn't a battle worth fighting. I can always take the damn thing off when they leave. And, I don't get to choose my punishment.

I ran a finger down Cairo's arm as he fastened my mark of ownership around my neck.

I didn't decide. These wild, dangerous men did. In exchange, I atoned for my crimes, and the ones to come.

Impossible to believe now that I sought to find a way out by killing myself. Gran would never have whispered that option in my ear—the real or imagined. She always told me to fight. Reminded me the blood of revolutionaries burned in my veins. And finally, I understood what I had to do, and naturally it came from the mouth of a genius.

"Choosing a worthy opponent and taunting them to catch before they kill again is a classic serial killer profile. They get off on staying ahead of the chase just as much as they do the killing. But they usually choose cops, detectives, or journalists. Maximize the chance of their clev-

erness broadcasted on the media. They don't go for farm girls. What makes you so special?"

Obviously, I'd been asking myself why the Letter Man chose me from the very beginning, but I didn't stop to think what him choosing me really meant.

If Scott wanted the glory of the hunt, why didn't he post his letter to the local PI? If he wanted to die, why not choose someone with a badge and gun who'd take him out as a public service?

But then, I didn't need to ask why he didn't choose those people. Cavendish said himself that this was all about me.

Not infamy. Not glory. Not the joy of holding a town's fear in his grip. The last letter said this wasn't the first time they killed, but it was the first time it was personal. I had to find out why.

There had been three tragedies in my otherwise happy, normal life. Losing my parents when I was three. The knockdown, drag-out fight between me and Ivy that sent my sister packing and ruined our relationship. And last, the circumstances that led to that fight, our grandmother's death.

I know what happened to her, and I knew the enemies I made in the wake of losing her. But Scott Cavendish wasn't one of them. I never met the guy before I spied him across the street. Ivy's tales of his exploits with Douglas Herbert were as far as he penetrated my radar. He had nothing to do with my life, and he wasn't involved with my gran's death.

So why did he look at me, sneer dripping with hatred, when he said it was his honor to die in the name of destroying me?

A stabbing pain pierced my temples. I massaged them the way I did for Cairo.

Thinking about this spun my mind in circles. Everything was telling me there's no reason Scott Cavendish and his friend should've targeted me.

But they did. So, everything I knew was wrong.

I'm here. The Bedlam Boys stopped me. They brought me here, where if it's not completely safe, I'm still no longer living in an abandoned farmhouse or dank motel room while a new, unpredictable threat is after me.

Jacques said there's a classic serial killer profile, which meant something nudged Cavendish outside of it. I was asking the right questions now. Searching the right path. It would lead me to the answers to end this once and for all—without killing or anyone getting hurt.

I let Cairo guide me to my knees.

This is where I need to be.

"To your bed."

I crawled inside. It was a tight squeeze. I lay at a ninety-degree angle, shoving my head in the corner to let my legs stretch as far as they could.

Cairo stuck his hand inside. The shout wasn't out of my mouth before the metal hooked my collar, chaining me to the doghouse.

"Cairo!"

"Night, Rain."

The lights went off one after the other, surrendering me to the dark.

Chapter Nine

A loud noise woke me the next morning.

Jacques stood over the countertop, chopping various things and throwing them in the blender.

I pushed myself up, stretching out my kinks and coils.

"Thirteen."

Mumbling under my breath, I shoved the dog bed back in the house and tossed the blanket in after it. I didn't bother asking why I got another number.

After the house went quiet, I grabbed one of the dresses they left on the coffee table, tore off the collar, and carried the bed and blanket to the couch. The bed ended up being my pillow for a surprisingly restful sleep. Not as comfortable as Cairo's bed, but far better than the night they planned for me.

"Thirteen," I repeated. "What's that supposed to be?"

Jacques finished his smoothie and took a sip. It looked awful. A thick, green sludge with floating black bits I couldn't identify. Jacques, though, was another story. This guy did not spend the night on a frat-house couch, cuddled with a dog bed.

His hair was brushed back that morning. The tufts above his ears curled, at odds with the rest of his thick, straight rows of ebony. He opted for another outfit from the neutral side of the closet. Light gray sweater and black pants. Behind those thick frames, steely eyes watched me watch him. He was likely used to scrutiny. Gorgeous and a prodigy. People never took their eyes off him.

"That's how many times you've broken the rules."

"How? You started me at seven."

"You framed us for murder," he shot back.

"Fair enough. But still, after you guys went to bed, you couldn't have expected me to sleep in a bikini in a doghouse. Now that we're up, I'll continue playing your humiliation game until you get bored of it."

"You will tell me why that is," he said. "Your willingness to play our humiliation game."

I tugged the pink sheath dress over my head. The lingerie underneath shone stark in its revealing glory.

"Did Legend buy me shoes too? Show mercy and do not make me wear heels. I grew up on a farm. The only use for them is hammering a tilted post for the goat pen when I'm too far from the toolbox."

"Collar," he said.

Dutifully, I slipped it around my neck, flicking my name tag against its neighbors. Cairo saw fit to stamp the name of my *owners* on metal pieces to hang next to mine.

"What's for breakfast?" I asked.

"Hands and knees. Face the doghouse."

"Why? What's this punishment, Jacques?"

"Hands. Knees. Doghouse."

I was slow to move, so he stepped out from the kitchen.

I didn't know Jacques. I couldn't say if the Artic chill that frosted his glasses and put a shiver up my spine whenever he looked at me was an effect he had on everyone, or if it was just me who set him on edge.

"What are you going to do, Jacques?" I whispered.

The first real smile curled his lips. "Reason dictates you'll soon find out."

Swallowing hard, I dropped to my hands and knees and crawled to the doghouse.

A metal ring was screwed in the wall by the entrance. Jacques looped the leash through my collar and secured it to the ring. I wasn't going anywhere.

I quivered as his shadow fell over me. I had a sense of Cairo and what made him tick. Jacques, on the other hand, was a silent unknown, counting down to a punishment I didn't know if I could handle.

I tried to hold on to my resolution as metal clinked behind me. The Bedlam Boys choose my punishment. They hold me to the fire so I can breathe again. I can handle what they throw at me, but maybe it's okay if some things I can't.

"Stone, if you're trying to torture me with anticipation—"

Thwap!

Stinging pain erupted from my left cheek.

I jerked, crying out, then choked on it as the right lit on fire to match.

"Two," said Jacques.

I twisted to see the leather belt fall. I shrieked over the sound of flesh on flesh.

"Three."

Oh no, please don't let him be counting to thirteen.

He belted me again.

"Ah," I cried. "Jacques, no, p-please, don't—"

Thwap!

"Five."

I clenched my teeth, viciously penning in a whimper. It burst out with the next hit.

"Six," he purred. "What are the rules, de Souza?"

"I— I don't remember."

Thwap!

I spasmed—rocked by a burst of heat in my core. I felt my folds slickening, and in this getup, Jacques would see everything.

"Seven. What are the rules?"

"I don't fucking remember!"

Thwap!

"Oh, Jacques. Holy shit," I breathed.

Thwap!

My back arched. Trapped by my collar, it held me fast, branding its possession in the marks left on my neck.

"Tell me the rules," Jacques said. He ripped my thong off, tossing the fabric on my back. I whined at his belt pressed to my pussy—the leather sliding over the wet, engorged flesh. "Now. You won't like it if I ask again."

I searched my mind for the speech he gave that day in Cairo's room. I lost most of it around his statement that everyone on this planet was cattle.

What did he say?

"No... disrespect."

Thwap!

"Jacques, please—"

"I still haven't given you permission to use my name. That's fourteen."

I bit my lip, both so frustrated and sore I could cry, and so turned on I might explode with the next hit.

"No talking back," I rasped. "No—"

The conversation came back to me. I glared in his eyes, and slowly, pointedly, trailed down to the bulge straining his zipper. "No false bravado unless I want my bluff called," I said. "But what's the rule on calling yours? I remember a certain cattle wrangler saying he had no interest in my body."

"This isn't sex, Rainey." My name was sinful on his lips. "It's punishment."

A light slap hit my clit, pulling out a moan.

"Fifteen."

"Fifteen?" I spread my legs, resting my cheek on the floor, rocking side to side as his belt was made intimately familiar with me. "What did I do?"

"Your filthy pussy is dirtying my belt."

"My filthy pussy is dirtying your pants," I shot back.

Thwap!

"What's this?" Legend traipsed into the living room. "A snack before breakfast."

He dropped down next to me. "Don't mind me. Continue with what you're doing."

Before I comprehended what was happening, Legend slipped my boob free and sucked my nipple between his teeth.

My mouth froze in an "o," shock trapping the moan just short of freedom.

For years, I hitched a ride on Gran's trips to the factory to sneak glances at Legend St. James. A face from a magazine. The kind of affable charm that came from something more than confidence. Not for a second did I delude myself that I had a chance with a guy who couldn't be bothered to remember my face or name.

I was quite content with those stolen glances, and then just my fantasies when it became clear Legend was someone I needed to stay far away from.

And now here we are, and the guy who didn't give a shit about my existence a week ago is tormenting me with an expert tongue.

"Legend, wait. I can't."

Thwap!

"Oh," Legend said. "How rude of me. How's that?"

Legend found my clit. He rolled it between fingers more calloused than a rich boy's should be. The deceptive bastard ripped a moan from me that ended in a scream with my eleventh slap.

Another strike of the belt knocked me to the edge. Any more of this and my humiliation would be crowned for the enjoyment of all witnesses.

I burned with shame. I was on my freaking hands and knees, collared and chained, while one enemy milked me like a cow and the other whipped me like a horse. I was, in every single sense of the word, their pet. Used, abused, and—

My heart shot in my throat.

—destined to be discarded.

"Was that what you were looking for?" Legend asked, the smirk plain in his voice. He sharply flicked my helpless bundle of nerves, sending a jolt that lifted me off my knees.

"No, you twisted, sadist fucks, that wasn't what I was looking for. This is what you want and when are you going to have enough." I spun on Jacques. "How many lessons will it take to train me? How long till you get bored of your little game?"

"Reason dictates you'll soon find out."

"Fuck you," I hissed. "I hate you. *All* of you. I was willing to confess. I still am! That should be enough for you."

"It's not."

Thwap!

My arms buckled. A wave of pain and pleasure bowling me over.

"You wait, Stone. Reason dictates consequences are coming for you too."

He raised a single, dark brow. "Is that a threat?"

I burned a hole in his skull. "I don't make threats anymore. False bravado is against the rules."

The genius he was, he caught on to my meaning almost immediately.

The belt rose high to deliver its judgment. Defiant down to the last, I arched my back to meet it.

"Jacques." Cairo strolled in dressed in the same clothes he made me take off the night before. "What did you do that's got our pet so upset? I can hear her bitching you out from upstairs."

"Whatever he did." Jacques hadn't stopped indulging his treat for a minute. "He should keep it up. I'm digging this delicious irony of her swearing she hates us, while her pussy's so wet she's got me drowning down here."

Cairo paused, pouring his coffee. "Hates us, does she?"

A dangerous edge poisoned his tone. Shuddering, I almost broke and said I didn't mean it.

Almost.

Why should he get assurances of my feelings for him when I'd get none in return? If Cairo, Jacques, Arsenio, Roan, and Legend did throw me out after getting their fill, I for fuck sure hated them.

"That's right," Legend crowed. He slipped two fingers inside me, finding that spot with expert precision. "Go on, de Souza. Tell me how we're all going to pay for bringing the cowgirl out of the farm girl."

"No."

Legend's fingers disappeared and his mouth followed. Jacques slid him out from under me.

"No, you don't get to come, and don't you dare touch yourself. Good pets get treats. Bad ones mouth off to the hand that beats them."

"Shove a pineapple up your ass, Stone. If there's room in there with the stick."

His laugh was deep and throaty music. It made me want to curl up and purr, then kill him for having that effect on me.

Jacques slipped his belt on, denying me in every way.

"One," he replied, and left me on the floor.

Shutting my eyes, I rested my forehead on the wood-mimicked plastic, sucking slow lungfuls to steady my heart. I don't know why

I kept goading Jacques. I'd been butting heads with the guy since he sat down next to me in class.

Something about him ignited a rarely used side of me. Watching him push around Professor Valdez and calling the first sorta friends I made clucking cattle, made me want to show the genius he wasn't as smart as he thought. He certainly didn't, and never would, know enough to break me.

And in that battle, it's Jacques: 3

My sore backside: 0

"With me," Cairo announced. He unhooked my chains and led me off by the leash. "I've got a nine-thirty class."

"You go to class?" I tugged the rein in irritation. "Why bother? You've got everyone bowing and scraping. I figured you sat around all day dipping your honey stick in everything that moves, and intimidating professors into giving you As."

"Honey stick," he repeated, setting foot up the stairs. "I like that. I'm gonna use it."

"What do you even study?"

"Bioengineering."

I stopped dead. "Wait, for real?"

"Do I detect a tone of surprise?"

"I— I thought—"

"That my aggression is a sign of low IQ, or the result." He faced me, that handsome face chiseled to express a rare emotion—amusement. "A lack of emotional self-control would indicate the lack of discipline required for an intensive academic workload." He winked. "Psych double major."

I opened my mouth a few times, finding my voice. "Why?" was all I came up with.

"Bedlam doesn't have a hospital. We have a local practice and Doc Nash, who turns off his phone when he goes fishing. A fact which almost killed me." Cairo came down, casually looping his arms around me. "For the last two years, I've been developing a stent that reduces the risk of blood clotting to virtually zero percent. Patent in the works.

"After I sell the design to the major medical companies, I will have enough to open Bedlam's first general hospital," he said.

There was something to say in response to this shocking and truly selfless revelation, but my mind refused to supply it.

Cairo swept my legs up, carrying me the rest of the way. "As for psychology, I've been called many things in my life. I was curious if they were true."

"Psycho. Sociopath. Sadist."

"Basically."

We entered his room. Cairo kicked the door shut behind us.

"Well?" I asked. "What's your diagnosis?"

I was dropped on my feet and slammed against the door so fast, my cry wasn't half off my lips as he towered over me.

"Completely normal, functioning member of society, gorgeous. No psychopathy, or compulsions. I just really"—he licked the tip of my nose—"really enjoy hearing you scream, tasting your tears, blacking out from you throttling my dick while begging me to stop.

"We all need a hobby."

Cairo tugged off my top. The collar also made a blessed new home on his bed. Hooking me around the waist again, he towed me to the bathroom.

I let him turn on the shower and put me in without a fight. Cairo's bathroom was a small, but clean space. There wasn't much to say for it. Decorations consisted of black towels, black bath mat, and damask wallpaper that likely came with the house. It was just a bathroom, so it made sense he didn't put as much effort as he did with his bedroom. Still, I noted he could be bothered to label place markers for the items under the sink, and line up his body washes and shampoos by height.

"No psychopathy, huh?" I muttered.

"What?"

"Nothing."

Cairo squirted shampoo on top of my head.

"I can bathe myself, you know. Been doing it since I was four."

He didn't bother to respond.

My eyes fluttered shut as the pads of his fingers kneaded my scalp. I moaned softly.

"Why?" I asked. "Why did Doc Nash's fishing trip almost kill you?"

"Why do you think you can ask me that?"

"Because you wouldn't have brought it up if you didn't want me to ask. I took a few psych classes too."

"Really want to know?" Cairo moved down my neck, digging magic fingers into my shoulders.

"I do," I said. "I want to know who you are, Cairo Sharpe."

He kissed the tip of my ear. "I'll tell you."

I twisted to face him, placing my hands on his hard, sudsy chest. "You will?"

"You'll know everything, my Rain," he said, "after I do."

My smile dimmed. "What does that mean?"

"What evidence do you have against my father?"

"Don't bring him up to me."

"Rain," he said, heavy with warning.

"We don't talk about him, Cairo. Ever. As far as we're concerned, when we're together, Jack Sharpe does not exist."

Cairo grasped my chin between two fingers, tipping me up. A gentle touch, but unbreakable.

"You don't set the rules, Rain."

"I set that o-one." My voice cracked. "We don't go there, Cairo. Don't ask me again."

"Don't ask me again. Who, what, when, where, or how in regards to my life. It's my terms or nothing. You're a bit slow to understand that, but you'll get there soon enough."

I tore away from him, snatching the curtains to climb out. Cairo snatched me back.

He hooked the back of my leg, and we both went down. Landing back to the rim, I struggled and fought, more furious with him than I'd ever been. I'd take a lot in my path for redemption and understanding where my life went wrong. But not this.

Using Sheriff Sharpe against me after all that man had already done. After all he'd taken.

That was unforgiveable.

"Unforgiveable, Cairo," I barked. "You play your little game of kings with everyone else, but not with me. I'm different. You know I am, or you wouldn't have brought me here. Don't ever use your father against me. Promise."

He said nothing, and a burst of anger rocked me.

I slapped him across the face.

"Promise!"

"I promise you this." His expression didn't shift. "If you don't calm down, I'll make that spanking you got seem like a tickle. You won't sit for a week."

Chest heaving, I quieted—though my glare had plenty more to say.

"I won't bring up the sheriff."

My arms dropped, opening to accept him as he slid me closer, easing me on his lap.

"You won't?"

He shook his head, resuming my bath. "I won't have to. You'll tell me everything. All on your own."

I tucked in the crook of his neck, threading my arms around him. "Why would I do that?"

"Because you're different."

ROAN

"No, Cairo!"

A low murmur sounded from the other side of the door.

"You can ask how many times you fucking want! I'm not walking around campus on a leash!"

Another murmur. Then a crash.

"Fuck you. Fuck your leash. Fuck this pet shit. Fuck—"

I eased down the stairs, bypassing the impending homicide—against who, I couldn't tell.

The lady did stab me.

I touched my bandaged side. My cock twitched in my pants.

I was known for eclectic tastes in the bedroom/car/closet/woods. Which is why I picked people who could keep up with me. That said, in the revolving door of freaks, s_uts, and delectably delicious skanks, none of them could push past a pinprick of the finger before skeeving out at the blood and shouting the safe word.

Not Rainey "Yummy" de Souza.

She wielded that knife like a warrior—a sex goddess. Riding and bucking on my fingers as she delivered justice. And when she decreed that my punishment wasn't over, she sheathed her blade in my skin without a moment's hesitation.

"Not good enough."

I've jacked off to the fiery-eyed, dark-haired beauty bringing the knife down half a dozen times since.

I now understood Cairo's irritation with anything that reminded him of why it took so long for Rainey to come into our lives.

If that woman's not my soul mate, who is?

Legend waited in the living room, riffling through his shoulder bag.

Well, one of them.

"Hey." I slid in next to him, slipping my hand up his shirt. "How long has it been since I sucked your dick?"

His grin was wolfish. "The answer will always be too long."

He slipped his hand up mine—for a different reason. Legend's touch tickled around my bandage.

"Sure you're up for it?" he asked.

"When am I not?"

"I warned you one of these days, you'll piss someone off who is more than willing to carve you up," he said.

"—humiliating. How am I supposed to face people? How will you?!"

Cairo came down with a raging vision in a clinging silver dress cut way low and ending way high. All her assets and curves shown on full display, along with her single accessory—a pink collar.

"And how lucky am I that I finally found her," I said to Legend.

Arsenio and Jacques tromped down a step behind. Those two were frosty bastards who didn't give off any emotion when standing there waiting for you to be worth their time, worked as well. Still, I'd bet another go with Rainey and my knife, they were checking her out too.

Full, sweet lips pinched in annoyance. A rack I was looking forward to falling asleep in strained against the tight fabric. Long sable hair was swept into a bun—Cairo's idea, I wagered. It left everyone free to see the collar for miles around.

"I have a ten a.m. class," she said. "I'm not walking in there like this."

"Aww," I cooed. "It's adorable that you think you have a choice."

"I'm serious. I need law school recommendations from these professors. They have to take me seriously."

"Aww. It's adorable you think this is a debate."

Rainey flipped me off.

"Two," Jacques said, brushing past her. "Let's go. We have matters to handle."

Rainey tried digging her heels in. Arsenio scooped her over his shoulder and carted her out the door.

The house my mother gifted us on Greek Row was a five-minute walk from the student union. One or all of us went there in the mornings. Bagel Glory and all the breakfast shops in that place were overrun by students who didn't think about what would happen after they moved out and Mommy stopped cooking for them.

Those students, at some point, ended up on the terrace where we sat every day, holding court. We never called it that, but I liked it all the same.

Arsenio set her down as we neared Homer Green. All eyes of those studying, lounging, frisbeeing on the grass found us, then they found her.

Rainey flushed redder than a maraschino cherry.

"Just smile, gorgeous." I came up next to her, planting my hand on her ass. "Anything's a fashion statement when you wear it with confidence."

"A leash tied around a guy's wrist is not a fashion statement."

"You're right, it's a kink." I licked the shell of her ear. "You keep walking around looking this damn good, I'm going to introduce you to another one of mine."

"Not here," she hissed when my hand traveled lower. "Later. At home."

It was cute she thought she got to decide the when and where. It was even cuter she didn't question I'd be coming on that ass again, or that it was our home.

In spite of her flaming cheeks, Rainey lifted her chin. Head held high and gaze straight ahead, she marched on Cairo's firm lead.

The Bagel Glory lady dropped her tongs at the sight of us.

She stared openly at Rainey, who suddenly found a spot on the wall extremely interesting.

"Cinnamon sugar bagel," said Cairo. "And a water. You can put it in a bowl."

Her eyes bugged. "Listen here, whatever you want to get up to in the privacy of your home is your business. But do not bring that nonsense outside and involve decent people," she snapped. "Shameful."

The lady flounced off to have a fit in the back—super angry she wasn't getting any.

"I'd be mad too," I called after her.

Someone else came up and served us. "I'm sorry, sir. The way she spoke to you was unacceptable. Your food is on us."

"Everything bagel with walnut cream cheese," I said. "Oh, and fire her."

Debra, as the name tag read, didn't argue. "Of course, sir."

"Roan, no," Rainey cried. "You can't get her fired. This is her livelihood."

"This is the service industry, and she just shamed customers—literally—and refused to serve them. If you don't think that's a fireable offense, you've been on the farm too long."

"You five are shameful," she muttered, "and when are you going to quit with the farm-girl stuff? My clothes had to go because they reminded you of it. If you're going to keep reminding yourself, I get my stuff back."

I molded myself to her backside. "It's a crime to let you walk around in that many layers."

Rainey turned to me, smirk playing on her lips. "Shouldn't be a problem, then. Since when are you guys law-abiding citizens?"

My brows shot up my forehead. *Holy hell. Flirty, witty, and unwilling to take an ounce of shit. You can dominate me anytime, baby.*

Damned if she isn't already, another voice said. *Part of me was happy to buy out the farm-girl aisle, and hold the clothes hostage till she whipped my surrender on the edge of a riding crop.*

Alright, all of me was.

"You want out of these clothes so badly, we can arrange something."

Rainey pinked, assuming I meant something else. Fine with me.

We got our food and went out onto the terrace. Paris looked up from her breakfast and spat her drink in Amy's face.

"Rainey?"

"Oh ho," someone called. "That's the way to do it. You guys are fucking legends!"

He kicked off a roar of hooting, hollering, and wolf whistles. Rainey tried to duck behind Cairo.

She was still learning.

Cairo dragged her out by the collar, positioning her front and center. "What do you think you're doing? You hate us *and* you're ashamed to be seen with us?" He tsked. "I'm starting to feel undervalued in this relationship."

"Don't invent reasons to be mad at me, Cairo. Take the collar off. Please, you made your point. I want to curl up on the ground and die."

"The ground? Well, it wasn't like you were going to get a chair. You're a pet," he said, bringing her to the table. "Hands and knees. Now."

"And if I say no, Jacques says three and the world keeps spinning. I can live with that."

"If you say no." Cairo spoke in her ear, but not too low for us. "*I* say five and deliver your punishment right here. Right now." He kissed the tender spot on her neck. "One peek at those red cheeks is Viagra on steroids. These repressed shits would love a look."

Rainey's throat bobbed visibly. I read her internal struggle clear on her face, and naturally did nothing to help her. She was lucky to have a strong, handsome beast like Cairo put her on her knees. As lucky as I was to have Legend, and now her.

Fixed on us, she dropped to the floor, sitting on her legs like kneeling before an altar. She didn't drop her head or break contact.

We did that. Though, we had taking our seats as an excuse.

"Rainey?" Paris ran up to her. "What the hell is going on? We were supposed to hang out at my place last week and I didn't hear from you. What happened?" She spun on Cairo. "What did you do?"

Cairo didn't see his sister as reason to look up from his breakfast. "It's what she did, not me."

Panic flashed on Rainey's face.

"She disrespected Jacques in front of their entire class," Cairo finished. "The TikTok video is still trending. You know better than anyone, Evie, that shit like that doesn't stand. You should've warned your friend."

"For that, you're putting her through this? You've finally lost it. You fell off this ego trip and cracked your head!"

"You should be happy. This is us showing mercy," he said. "Ask her if she's grateful."

"Shut up." She put her arms around Rainey. "I'm so sorry, you're not putting up with this for another second."

"It's not your fault." Rainey grasped her arms, stopping her. "You warned me. Wounded wolf, remember? I agreed to endure this so they wouldn't make my life difficult in other ways," she said simply. "Eventually, they'll get tired of this humiliation game and everything can go back to normal."

Don't bet on it, sweetheart.

"This is demeaning. Whatever Cairo threatened to do—"

"Hilarious." A raucous guffaw cut her off. "I see you finally put the bitch in her place."

Alfie strode up with a drink and egg bagel. He munched on it, the masticated egg and bread in full view with his horse chewing.

"New girl thought she was better than us. Didn't have to follow the rules."

"I'm not new, jackass," Rainey said. Still on her knees, but damned if she didn't tower over Alfie. "And I don't have to follow *the rules*. There are no rules or anyone with the power to enforce them. There's just a bunch of guys ballsy enough to take charge, and the chickenshits who 'yes, sir' and 'no, sir' 'cause standing up for themselves never occurred to them."

"What did standing up for yourself do for you?" Alfie snapped.

"Fonsie," Cairo said. A wrinkle marred his perfect brow.

"That's a nice collar, Stormy. Windy. Whatever the fuck your name is."

"Alphonso," Jacques spoke up.

"They brought you to heel, you little bitch, so let me teach you your first trick. Catch."

Alfie threw the iced tea at her, exploding the drink in her face and down her chest.

The table rocked, nearly tipped by all of us jumping from our seats at once.

Cairo got to Alfie first, sinking a punch in his gut that doubled him over. The next hit was mine.

I tackled him, dropping him flat and jarring agony through my sore thigh and chest. It heated up my excitement, stoking just beneath my rage and granting me a semi as I punched him once, twice, four times in the face.

Legend lifted me up, only to deliver a savage kick. And then we were all on him, forming a ring and stomping the shit out of the moaning, crying heap.

"Stop! Guys, please, he's had enough."

Rainey and Paris pulled us off one after the other. Paris went for Cairo and got hoisted up and dropped behind him. He grabbed Alfie's collar and reared for another blow.

"Cairo." Rainey shot between them. "It's okay. I'm okay. You don't have to do this."

Rainey murmured to him, easing him back as her fingers found his temples, gently kneading. "Don't be this man for him. He's not worth it."

Ragged breaths tore his lungs. He clutched her waist. To move her aside, I wasn't sure, because he stopped short.

Interesting.

My brows crowded together, watching Rainey de Souza do something I'd never seen anyone do.

Defuse Cairo.

"Get him out of my sight," Cairo barked.

Three guys picked up the broken, bleeding mess and carried him away.

"Listen up." Cairo faced her to the silent crowd. "Rainey de Souza is our girl. Standard rules apply. You don't touch her. You don't speak to her unless spoken to. You do not disrespect her. Am I understood?"

"Yes."

"Am I?" he shouted.

"Yes," they chorused.

"Spread the word. If I have to repeat myself, everyone pays for it. Paris," he said.

"What?"

He tossed her his keys. "Take her to get cleaned up."

"You don't give me orders," she said, even as she hugged Rainey and led her away.

It was such a Cairo thing to say and do, I asked myself why those two swore they had nothing in common.

We went to retake our seats, and slow clapping shattered the quiet.

"Wow. I definitely take back what I said."

The familiar voice was quickly attached to the face, coming up the back entrance leading from Homer Green. His friends trailed him.

Arsenio stepped out in front, sizing him up, but saying nothing and giving even less away.

These crashers were going for a surprise entrance. Why give them the satisfaction of seeing they caught us unawares?

"What?" The green-haired guy grinned. "No hello?"

"No," said Arsenio. With that, we reclaimed our seats and our breakfast.

"Are we sure Fonsie got the message?" Cairo asked. "He got half the beating he was owed."

"Alphonso did two years at community college and then transferred," I said. "Obviously, he spent enough time away from us since high school, he forgot..."

Screeeee.

Five chairs scraped across the concrete. The crashers dropped their seats between us and plopped down.

Legend's left brow twitched—sign of something the mortals rarely got to see. Legend St. James shedding that manicured, high-browed personality for the true man beneath.

And it's an arousing sight. Worth bringing out for sure.

"You clearly want our attention," I said. "Why don't you get to the point and tell us why you're in my school?"

"Thought you'd know by now." Green Guy kicked back in his seat. "Looked us up down to our blood type and birth weight."

"You overestimate your importance. Going forward, you should rate it on the level of the piece of lint I found tangled in my pubes yesterday."

They howled, smacking the table.

"Roan Banks," Green Guy said. "So, you're the funny guy, and son of the dean. Let me continue the introductions. I'm Jeremy Ellis." He pointed across to the guy sandwiched between Legend and Jacques. "That's my brother, Micah."

My brow lifted just a fraction. *Damn. Maybe I shouldn't have dismissed these guys so quickly.*

Jeremy was handsome—now that I was bothering to look at him. The green hair worked with his blue, swimmable eyes, angular cheekbones, and the crow lying on his neck. He had a rich biker look going on. Leather jacket partially concealed a screamingly expensive watch. But his brother, Micah...

Micah's long, dark hair was as inky as nature intended. It fell in soft curls to his shoulders and wrapped around his fingers when he brushed it back. His full, pouty lips weren't made for sneering, and contempt didn't sit well in his big, maroon eyes. Micah Ellis was too pretty to look mean.

I raked him up and down. *Very, very pretty.*

Micah caught me looking on the way up. Flashing him a small grin, I winked.

He pulled a face, looking around like I must've meant that for someone else.

"That's Gael Stoll," he continued, pointing out a burly guy with little hair on top but plenty on his arms. "Jonah Hayes."

A blond guy in a leather bomber jacket and shades saluted us.

"And Bentley Levine," Jeremy finished out.

The last guy rivaled Jacques in height, and almost in looks with the glasses he was rocking. Their similarities ended at the lack of beard and the nasty glare he was giving us.

"We're from Hunter's Crest," Jeremy said, "where they call us the Crows. We transferred in at the start of the semester, but took our time getting to know everything, and everyone." He leaned back in his seat, spreading out his hands. "You five run this whole town like you're bangers and this is your turf. Everyone is too afraid to do anything about it because of your mommies and daddies."

The guys didn't say anything. They didn't pause eating their food either. Jeremy was the equivalent of elevator music, and even I was about to change the tune.

"I know, I know," he sang. "These jokers are interrupting your breakfast to tell you what you already know. So, here's the point: thank you."

Cairo dipped a napkin in his water, using it to clean blood off his knuckles.

"Seriously, thank you for all the work you've put in with these people. Fuck knows it's easier to take over the masses when they're already lying on their backs with their bellies exposed." Jeremy's tone changed. "This is our town now, *Bedlam Boys*, so take my advice and accept defeat before you start the war. This is one fight you can't win."

Hands returned to pristine, Cairo snapped his fingers. "You guys," he said, pointing to a table with half the football team. "Escort these gentlemen out of here."

"Wha— Hey!" Jeremy shot up, drawing his knife on the advancing linebackers. "Back the fuck off!"

"You see, Jeremy?" Bentley said. "These guys are stupid. A waste of our time. Here we are dangling it in their faces, and they're too dumb to ask. Don't you want to know why we're certain this dump will be ours?"

"Because you're with Foundry," Arsenio stated.

Their smiles wiped away.

Sighing, Jacques pushed his glasses up his nose. "Jeremy and Micah Ellis, son of Steven Ellis. Your father made his millions playing the stock market. He was on the short list of people we suspected of silently, and financially, backing Foundry. We've been unable to hack the company records to confirm it, but you've just done that for us."

"Foundry's been buying property all over Bedlam," Jacques took over. "It started with the fifty acres out by Westchester Drumlins. Foundry tried to petition to build a factory out there, banging on that it would bring in jobs and enrich the community."

"Town hall rejected you," Legend said, "and Foundry retaliated by coming hard at farmers, pensioners, and anyone hard up with above-market offers on their homes and property."

"You're carving up Bedlam piece by piece," Cairo threw in. Their eyes ping-ponged between us. "Word is you're taking the next vote straight to the people. You need fifty-one percent of eligible voters to back the creation of a brand-new town—independent from Bedlam. And how fortunate you'll have the land, homes, and conveniences for your new citizens to move right in."

"You're convinced they will," Arsenio finished. "Free themselves of this lawless place run by a couple of young, if handsome, men who keep the boot on their throats. Actually, you're certain the vote will go your way because Daddy's money is greasing the road. I'd ask why he and Foundry care so much about an out-of-the-way town deep in the bush, but I know that too.

"And so do you." A smile stretched across his lips. "You know why your old man wants this town, Ellis. Wants it so bad he sent you and your Girl Scout club to intimidate the only ones who could stand in his way."

Jeremy paled. He lowered his knife hand, stepping back.

"You can't have it," Arsenio sang. "Even if you succeed, you'll never get what you came here for. But go ahead and give it your best shot. While you're doing that, pick up a history book and research what we do to tyrants in Bedlam."

I playfully cuffed Jeremy's shoulder. "So? How'd us dummies do?"

Jeremy laughed. Couldn't have been more forced if he *wasn't* trying. "Terrible," he said. "Totally wrong. Don't know where you got all that bullshit from, but my dad doesn't want this shit heap. Just a part of it, and the whiskey distillery on top."

He sneered at Legend. "Did you tell your boys the business is going under and you won't be able to pay them to be your friends anymore?"

The mask broke. Legend rose from his seat, and the charming son did not rise with him.

"This is what I'll tell you," he hissed. "Tomorrow, you're going to wake up and find something missing. Something you can't live without. And when you do, you'll crawl back here sobbing and licking my fucking boots, dripping apologies. I suggest you make them good."

"You don't—"

"Tomorrow," Legend said. "Set your alarm."

Reddening, Jeremy retracted his blade, shoving it in his pocket. "We're outta here," he said. "Oh, one thing. I wouldn't get too comfortable. Crystal Canyon is making a comeback."

Arsenio raised his voice. "Bedlam now."

"Bedlam forever!" rebounded our audience.

Cairo grinned at him. "We're pretty comfortable."

Jeremy stormed off, muttering something about cults and pistol-whipped dogs. I stood as Micah streamed past, brushing my finger across the back of his hand.

He knew without a doubt that was for him, and he didn't say anything. Not to tell me off or holler for his brother. Micah cast one last look at me, then picked up the pace to catch Jeremy.

Promising, I thought as I claimed the empty seat by Legend. *Never slept with the enemy before. That's another one off the bucket list.*

Chapter Ten

R*ainey*
  "I'm so sorry. I swear, Rainey, he's not going to mess with you anymore. Jacques either."

Paris kept up a string of apologies, promises, and vows of retribution all through the car ride. Understandable, since the story we were going with was the Bedlam Boys blackmailed me into a leash for a little viral video.

How do I explain it's bigger than that? And so are my reasons for staying.

"You don't have to apologize," I said. "Cairo is responsible for his actions. It looks bad, but they've agreed to leave me alone after everyone's seen me made a fool of, like I did to Jacques. I'd rather that than they keep coming after me, and it damages your relationship with Cairo if you stand in the way."

"You're too nice, Rainey. My relationship with Assface is hardly the issue here."

Paris veered off Lincoln, turning onto Bay Avenue. The street sign forced me to take note of where we were going.

Bedlam wasn't a wealthy town, and like a lot of places, when someone hits it big, they tend to move to a larger city with larger houses and a larger community of moneybags to schmooze and impress. Unless your money is tied to Bedlam, then you tend to stick around.

Where they stuck around was Bay Avenue.

The big houses— Mansions I believe the rich call them. Infinity pools next to the hot tub. Four cars in the drive for the two people who live inside. That was Bay Avenue where the owner of the distillery, dean of the university, and apparently Paris got to live.

"Uh, Paris? We're going to your place, right?"

"Of course we are. We're about the same size. You can shower and change while I convince you to let me take care of this thing with Cairo." She blew out a breath. "At least he likes you. He won't go too far."

I blinked. "Excuse me? Did you just say he likes me?"

"Yeah." Paris slowed down, rolling to a stop by the curb. "They beat the shit out of Alphonso. Do you think they do that for everybody? Plus, he told everyone you're their girl."

"That means something other than I have to wear a collar?"

"It means what they said. No one messes with you. No one disrespects you." She shook her head. "Except for them, I mean. Small comfort.

"Come on," she said. "We'll be quick and back in time for class."

I hopped out a step behind her, walking up a hill to the main gate. A collection of pinkish stones topped by a gray roof unveiled before us. They weren't quite turrets, but they came together to form a collection of As. It looked like a Barbie dream house that grew up to be a big-girl mansion.

"Wow. Nice place," I said.

"Thanks." She let me in the door ahead of her, came in and kicked her shoes in the direction of the rack. "Mom and Dad aren't home, so we're cool."

"Would we not be cool if they were home?"

She laughed. "No, we wouldn't. Mom would follow us around, asking a million questions about you, your life, and your family. Dad hasn't forgiven me for when I was fourteen and said I can't bring friends around 'cause he's a massive dork. He's now made it his mission to prove to all my friends he isn't one... by being a massive dork."

"At least your dad doesn't come inside on a hot day, flapping his arms, and going 'don't mind me, just airing out my pits.'"

We howled, nearly tripping on the grand staircase. Yeah, I said grand staircase.

Paris's home was as magnificent inside as it was on the outside. Peeking through the entryways on the right and left, I spotted a kitchen that could fit the entire farmhouse bottom floor, and cost more than both floors put together. The other side granted me a look at their dining room with crystal chandeliers and a hanging painted portrait of the family, smiling down on their china place settings.

We topped the landing and Paris went through the door in front of us, padding inside a large, airy suite boasting a king-size bed, lounging area, and a big-screen television outfitted with pink diamonds around the edge.

"Sweet digs."

"You can stay over anytime." Paris flopped back on her bed. "Like now, while I sort this shit out with Cairo."

"Can I ask you something?" I wandered into the bathroom, hunting down a towel and washcloth. "Why does Cairo call you Evie?"

"My middle name is Evelyn," she called back. "He always thought the 'named after our favorite cities' thing was stupid, and he wasn't shy about saying so. Announced when he was five that he was calling me Evie, and no one could make him stop. I really don't mind."

"But you still call him Cairo?"

"I call him Assface."

I barked a laugh. "True."

The washcloth and towel were found in a little closet between the shower and bidet. I peeled off my sticky clothes and stepped into the steamy spray. Paris came into the bathroom to continue the chat.

"When he's just being garden-variety irritating, I call him Cairo. When he's sweet, I call him Danny. His middle name is Daniel."

"Daniel," I said, trying it out on my tongue. A simple, common name, and somehow perfect for him. "What about Jacques, Legend, Roan, and Arsenio? You've known them your whole life? Do they have the little-sister thing going with you too?"

Maybe it was cheating to get what the guys wouldn't give me from Paris.

But I didn't care.

"Hmm. I'm not sure if they see me like that. They don't mess with me like they do everyone else, but that's likely because of Cairo. Still, they're pretty chill guys when you get to know them."

"Yeah?" I edged closer to the glass, hanging on her words. "In what way?"

"My folks hated my high school boyfriend, so they got Arsenio to take me to prom instead. He showed up in a tux with a corsage and everything. Smiled nice for the cameras, then drove me to my boyfriend's place and covered for me.

"Jacques helps me with homework, but that might be because he never misses a chance to prove he's the smartest guy in the room. Legend sneaks me whiskey. Roan and I like the same music. I'll catch rides with him out of town to see our bands play in Hunter's Crest."

I caught myself smiling. It did sound a treat to see the side of the Bedlam Boys that Paris got to see.

Paris ran out to get me clothes. I changed into a pair of jeans and a loose sweatshirt, and imagined Cairo's face when he tore it off.

"We've got an hour before we have to head back. Want to—?"

"Cairo? Cairo, what are you doing here?" Rapid footsteps approached the door, and a blonde woman burst inside. My eyes widened, trying to take her all in.

She was beautiful. From the short, platinum locks, to the lily-green eyes, to the trim pantsuit that cut perfectly on her figure. I saw

Paris in her at a glance, and looking in those eyes and the curve of her frown, I saw Cairo.

"Paris, where's your brother? Why is his car parked out front?"

"He's not here. He let me borrow it. There was an emergency and mine is in the shop."

"Emergency? What happened?"

"Rainey happened," she said, throwing her arms around me.

"I swear I'm not an emergency. Just a wardrobe malfunction." I stuck out my hand. "Nice to meet you. I'm Rainey de Souza."

"Rainey, this is my mom, Nora."

"Charmed, dear." She shook my fingers, still fixed on Paris. "Why would you borrow your brother's car, Paris? You know you can take one of ours. Is he coming over to get it? Every time Cairo comes into this house, it is such chaos. He always picks a fight with Isaac."

"You mean the home-wrecker that whisked his mother and sister away in the middle of the night and refused to consider split custody of him?"

"Paris," she cried. "That's your father you're speaking about."

"That changes what I said how? Cairo hates Isaac. Isaac hates Cairo. The feeling is entirely mutual," she said. "The picking fights goes to both sides."

Paris had a pretty firm hold on me, or I'd have drifted out of the room a long time ago.

"It's darling how you stick up for him, but Cairo is responsible for his own actions, and his behavior when he steps in this house. When he comes by to get the car, I will not have any nonsense." She stuck out her hand. "Give me your phone."

"Mom, please, no. Cairo's going to stop giving me his number if you keep using my phone to call him."

Nora flushed deep red. "I'm his mother, I have every right to call him. Phone. Now, young lady."

Goodness, that authoritative bark is genetic.

Mumbling under her breath, Paris handed her phone to her mother.

Nora marched out, answering "Hello?" on the click of the lock.

"Ugh. Is family like this for everyone? Dad thinks Cairo is a behavioral problem and bad influence on me. Cairo winds him up because he won't forget for a second that my dad stood up and flatly said in court that Jack was to have full custody of him and he wouldn't even do weekends. And Mom forgot how to talk to Cairo a long time ago. All they do is argue, then they weren't even doing that 'cause Cairo blocked her number and stopped coming over for dinner.

"Now she takes my phone and uses bullshit like borrowing his car as an excuse to speak to him. But, of course, she doesn't use the time before he hangs up to say what she really wants to say."

"What does she really want to say?" I asked softly.

Paris's eyes filled. "That she's sorry. She can't say it because..."

"Because saying sorry means admitting to yourself you did something wrong," I finished. "The words are easy. It's what comes with it that lets years go by unsaid."

"Yeah." She laid her cheek on my shoulder. "I'm sorry I said all of that. You're dealing with enough. No need to throw my family drama on top."

"Don't say that. We're friends." As much as I didn't want it at first, I couldn't deny it. Someone who wasn't your friend didn't rant for a thirty-minute car ride on their brother's treatment of you, and that they'd defend you.

"Family is like this for everyone. With Ivy—" Pain crept into my temples. I rubbed it away, wishing the memories went as easily. "My sister and I got into a fight, and now she refuses to speak to me. I can't blame her, though. I was wrong." My voice grew thick. "In every way, I was wrong for how I treated her. I don't deserve her forgiveness till I give an apology she can trust."

Paris rubbed my arms. "It can't have been that bad," she said, pulling me in for a hug. "This is what siblings do. They fight. They literally try to kill each other. But you make up because no one is going to understand you like they do."

I swiped a stray tear away. "Damn, we like to get heavy. Should I write you that check for therapy now?"

"Nah, you can give it to me at the end of the week." She popped a kiss on my cheek. "Did you get any breakfast between all that drama? Our housekeeper makes a fresh batch of muffins every morning. Interested?"

"Interested? There's a very good chance I'm not going to save any for you."

"Oooh," she crowed, backing toward the door. "How you gonna do that when"—Paris took off running—"I'm getting to them first!"

I chased her out the door, laughing my head off.

After a breakfast of delicious fresh-baked muffins, Nora told us to drive her second car to campus, leaving Cairo's on the curb. I saw it for the obvious attempt to lure her son there that it was, and damned if I didn't feel bad for both of them. It was a hard, difficult road for them to end up where they were.

Back on campus, I met my professors after class for the work I missed. The guys told them I was traumatized after the events of Ruckus Royale and needed time off. Actually, they weren't the first to call out with that excuse. Professor Valdez was taking a short leave of absence. There was speculation on if he'd come back at the end of it.

End of Civil Rights, I waved bye to the teaching assistant, turned off my phone, and ducked out of the building through one of the side entrances. I didn't put it past Cairo to be waiting outside the door with leash in hand. I couldn't go back to the Bedlam Boy house just yet, and I wasn't about to get in the argument about me needing to head out and they not knowing why.

I made it off campus and passed through the square. My bus stop waited for me with its pack of hopeful pigeons and a bus schedule that faded to blurred text years ago. Frankie honked her way up.

"Rainey, love. Good to see you."

"Good to see you."

"Out to the farm again," she said. "What do you do there all day?"

"Between you and me, I've got the old generator and some swap shop appliances tucked away. I'd move back in if it wasn't for the whole no-running-water thing."

"Right," she said with a laugh. "That thing."

I settled in for the forty-minute ride. Frankie carried me all over town, dropping off elder riders pulling shopping wagons, and university students making it back to their student apartments.

This was the part of the trip I loved—other than talking to Frankie. Seeing my town pass by the window was the most relaxing part of my day.

There was still something of the old Crystal Canyon about Bedlam. Historical buildings survived like Westchester Drumlins, a general store, an old-timey barbershop, and a hotel that they renovated inside, but outside maintained the original stonework. It was trippy passing a structure that stood before your grandparents were born, sandwiched between a vegan restaurant and yoga studio.

But that was Bedlam. A town moving forward, and dragging its past along for the ride.

"Looks like you're feeling better."

I raised my head, catching Frankie's knowing smile in the mirror.

"I am better than I was," I admitted. *Last time I stepped off this bus, I resolved to kill myself. I'd say I'm doing much better.*

"I moved in with some—" My tongue stuck trying to say *friends*. It wouldn't move at all for *boyfriends*. "—guys," I finished. "I was in a bad place. They're helping me see that I can be forgiven."

"Course you can. Everyone deserves forgiveness, love."

"Even—"

"No," she sliced in. "Not my son-of-a-bitch ex."

Giggling, I hopped off the bus, waving bye to Frankie rattling down the dusty road. My smile faded, turning back to my gate. It wasn't being home. It was the reason I was here.

Climbing up the rickety porch, I lifted our mailbox lid and found three black letters waiting for me.

The letters have always come to the farmhouse. Despite me having moved out a long time before they began coming. It was proof of how long Scott Cavendish had been following me. He knew how often I came out to my abandoned farm far out of town. It was the perfect place to leave messages for me without being seen.

I broke the new lock on the door and went inside.

"Fuck!"

The estate agent hadn't stopped with the door. My microwave, lamp, and the little things I snuck back inside were gone. I ran downstairs to check the generator and found that gone too.

"Point Cruella," I hissed.

The woman's actual name was Ella Franklin, but that's because someone would've called child services on her parents if they wrote her full name on the birth certificate.

Heart pounding, the unopened letters crumpled in my hand. It had become my routine to sit in the place where I'd always felt safe and read the next horrible letter. The smell of warm, buttery popcorn and the soft glow dispelling the dark around me gave me the strength to break the seal.

Dropping the letters on the floor, I headed out and went straight to Black Widow Hill. The flowers I collected on the way were laid on the unmarked grave.

"Sorry I've been gone for a while." I sat cross-legged on the ground, plucking blades of grass. "My suicide attempt ended in a chase through the forest and then semi-voluntary imprisonment. That sounds like an oxymoron."

I fell back on the sea of green, gazing up at the evening sky. "Is it weird that I named you in my suicide note? The thought of you lying here until the next town rises in place of Bedlam and no one knowing you're here was too sad to bear.

"I can't help wondering about your family. Where are they? Are they looking for you? Did you have a job that you one day didn't come back from? A home? Are you from Bedlam, or just a traveler blowing through town? And of course, who are you? What's your name?"

There were even bigger questions than all of those. Like how I ended up lying next to the grave of a stranger. I wish I knew.

"The day I found you is still fuzzy," I said. "After Gran's death, something in me snapped. When they talk about going off the rails, they've got a photo of me in the case study. I was not doing okay, and wound up with a doctor and a bottle full of pills."

I latched on a cookie-shaped cloud and followed it through the sky.

"That's the real reason I didn't go away to college. The pills Doc Nash put me on were supposed to balance my emotions. Some days they mellowed me out so much they took my brain offline. I'd have these blackouts. Hours would go by, and I'd come to somewhere else, not knowing what I'd done in that time.

"But the day I found you..."

I stopped, digging the heel of my palms in my eyes. It didn't work. Visions of the blood, the body, and the terrible scene I stumbled into shone in stark clarity. The only thing about that day that was clear.

I recalled bits and pieces of dragging the body from the barn and taking them out into the woods. A blank eroded my memory, skipping over the time I must've gone back for a shovel. The last thing I vaguely remembered was scooping dirt into the hole I dug for them.

Maybe if I'd been in real control, I'd have checked them for ID, called the cops, gone about it in the right, sane way. But as it was, I couldn't even say if they were male or female.

"That was my last day on those pills," I said. "I wish I could say things started making sense afterward, but nothing did. Gran is still gone. Ivy's gone. And I'm no closer to remembering if I— if I was the one—"

I cut myself off, got up, and left. Why did I think coming out here would make me feel better? Why did I think for a second I was regaining control of my life? Being with Cairo and the guys may have helped me not feel guilty. They didn't help me forget.

I returned to the bare farmhouse and found the letters where I left them. Sitting down on the past living room floor, I opened the first one.

I stood outside the police station today, thinking all I had to do was go inside and point Sheriff Jack in the right direction. Tell him I saw a girl go inside Westchester Drumlins carrying a bow.

How much would you love that? Sitting in an interrogation room across your old friend Jackie Boy.

Don't test me, bitch. You can't ignore me.

I let the note flutter to the floor. That must've been letter number three, left when they found number one and two still sitting there unopened.

I can't wait to see who you've chosen. Use another arrow.

The medieval Braveheart thing you've got going on is such a turn-on. I've masturbated twice to Scott's death video. If you slow it down just enough, you can almost make out the slim piece of wood flying toward him.

I wonder why no one else has thought to do that? Maybe I should plant the idea in the sheriff's head.

I will if you warn them, or tell anyone about me. The sheriff will know about EVERY death stacked against your name. He may let you slide on Cavendish, but what about the sweet little innocent you threw in a hole and covered with dirt?

You'll be thrown in a cage, and I won't stop killing the people you love. I'll never stop. I've been here since Bedlam began, I'll be here long after it's ash.

I want that name.

Stay psycho.

XOXO

The final letter lay flat on my palm. The one I assumed would tell me what my new tormentor was referring to. The letter that was bound to demand more than I'd give.

I set it down in front of me.

I had to decide right then what I'd do. They said they didn't have Scott Cavendish's death wish, so I suspected they weren't going to order me to kill them. They also said they'd put someone I care about in danger.

I won't let it happen this time. No one is going to wake up in a freezer, and I won't be forced to hurt anyone.

I'll take these letters to Hunter's Crest. I won't go anywhere near Jack Sharpe, but someone there is bound to be a decent cop who'll take the steps to catch this lunatic. Possibly set up a real sting to catch them leaving these notes by my door.

Mind set, I picked up the letter.

I promised you no more silly rhymes or games. I figure old friends like us can skip the tricks and get straight to the point. We deserved that.

My forehead crumpled. *Old friends?*

What the hell were they talking about? I knew my friends, and none of them were deranged psychopaths.

What is this guy playing at?

You disappointed me, de Souza. I thought of all people, you understood the meaning of sacrifice. It isn't about malice or superiority. A fact is some must die for a greater purpose, and in that purpose they are honored.

Once, you knew that, but you forgot who you were. As your friend, I will remind you.

I'll bring you back to who you were.

I flipped the note to the back, foreboding settling deep in my bones before the rest was read.

You will choose someone in this godforsaken town and put them out of their misery. I don't care who you pick or why. You have two weeks and I want the name of the person you've chosen sitting in that mailbox in two days.

By Saturday the 13th, if their gruesome death isn't trending in national news, the death of someone you love will be.

Paris Keller. Bella Hope. Francesca Lopez. One of Francesca's brats.

Bet you thought you didn't have anyone left to care about. We'll find out how true that is in two weeks.

Stay psycho, bitch.

Love ya. XOXO

The note slipped through trembling hands. Gasping, I fought for air, but none was in the room.

The bastard was right. I did think I didn't have anyone left to care about. Leave it to a killer to rip open a healed wound.

Francesca was Frankie. Gran's friend, and some days, the only person to make me smile. My mind rebelled at the thought of them hurting one of her kids. Those sweet little ankle-biters who showed off all their missing teeth when they smiled, and kissed me hello the days Francesca went off-route to pick them up from the babysitter.

Bella Hope was the receptionist from the motel. Her father opened it forty years ago, and though she only worked there to save money while completing night school, she treated everyone who came through the door like family. I couldn't count the times she got me out of my room to watch Netflix and eat Chinese food at the desk.

And Paris.

Tears dripped down my cheeks.

I did care.

I couldn't let a single one of these women die, nor would I let a single hair on those kids' heads be harmed.

You'll be thrown in a cage, and I won't stop killing the people you love. I'll never stop. I've been here since Bedlam began. I'll be here long after it's ash.

What do I do?

"Fuck!" I flung the letter away from me.

This was supposed to be over with Cavendish. I did what he demanded I do. I killed the bastard, and it was supposed to get me my life back. How could there be another one? What did these people want from me?

"Rip out a piece of my soul," I whispered.

That's what this is about. That's what it's always been about. They want to make me a monster.

I thought of the grave at Black Widow Hill. *For all I know, I am one. What if this is punishment for a crime I don't remember committing?*

Then why not just punish me? Why bring Jennifer, Paris, or Frankie into this? Why would this be revenge Scott Cavendish was willing to die for? And what did they mean they've been here since Bedlam began?

A dull, throbbing pain formed behind my eyes.

The headaches were constant these days. Advil barely made a dent in them, but I refused to go back to Doc Nash and be prescribed anything stronger. For better or worse, I was facing my horrible, screwed-up life unmedicated.

What to do about this fucking headache isn't the question, Rainey. It's what to do about the mad Letter Man threatening to turn you in if you don't give him the name of the innocent person you're going to kill in less than a week.

I froze.

I heard something. A creak from outside.

This is an old house. It creaks. I stood even as the thought went through my head, creeping toward the front door.

Thud.

My breath trapped in my chest. Peering through the cracked blinds, I laid eyes on the black-hooded figure standing on my porch.

I shot away and tripped over my feet. Panic blotted out my senses as I went down, hitting the floor with an ear-splitting crash.

Oh my god! He's outside!

It wasn't possible he didn't hear that noise. The Letter Man was on my porch and he knows I'm here.

I scrambled across the floor, shoving my back in the corner.

He'll leave. He won't want me to know who he is. His plan to stalk and kill my friends won't work if his face sketch is posted on every corner.

That was before he believed you were ignoring him, a chilling voice said. *He thinks I'm refusing to play his game. What will he do now? What's the letter he's leaving supposed to say?*

"Please go," I whispered. "Please, just go."

I forced myself out of the corner, crawling to the door. If he's been watching me, let him have seen my debut with the Bedlam Boys. I wasn't ignoring the letters. I desperately wanted to keep my friends and their children safe. *The situation doesn't have to escalate—*

I glanced through the blinds and saw no one.

—before I found them myself and put an arrow in their heart.

Shaking, it took three tries to open the door and step out. I swept the farm for a sight of a person running away and saw no one.

I still didn't know why Cavendish and his buddy chose me. I didn't know who the Letter Man was, or how I'd find them in my shortened time period. I just knew two things. They wouldn't get anywhere near my friends, and if I had to pick up my bow again to ensure they were safe, this time there'd be no hesitation.

I'm going to find your ass, bitch.

I stomped back inside, shoved the letters in my pack, and hitched it on my shoulder.

The laughing jackass, Douglas Herbert, had a whole crew of guys who got off on their sick pranks. Wasn't a stretch to think there may have been more than one sociopath in the bunch other than Scott Cavendish.

The Letter Man could be one of them. Someone who has history with Cavendish. Someone he trusts. Nathan Wade and Sam Dillion.

I closed on the door handle.

Last I checked, Sam Dillion left town. All the same, he was the one I put my money on. Dillion called in a bomb threat, then fired blanks at a panicking crowd of teenagers. His goal was to incite true, honest terror, and two girls ended up in the hospital, so he'd get his kicks.

Tonight, I mused as I stepped on the porch. *I'll head to the library and see if I can find out where that guy really is. If I can't find a trace, that's suspicious enough to—*

A hand clamped over my mouth.

"Hmph!"

I was yanked off my feet, flying back into the house. The door slammed on my muffled scream.

No!

I kicked and thrashed, bucking in his viselike grip. My head smashed against a hard chest. The Letter Man was correctly named, and now he had me.

"Hmm!"

"Where do you think you're going?"

My eyes popped. *That voice...*

"I told you to wait outside for me after your last class, and I'd walk you home," Cairo hissed. "You disobey me, refuse to answer my calls, and then I find you here."

"Cairo, no," I cried. "You don't understand."

He slammed me front-first against the door.

"Who you belong to now doesn't seem to be sinking in." Cairo bit my ear. "Seems you need another lesson."

"No, I do. It wasn't like that. I wasn't ignoring—"

Cairo ripped my borrowed pants down.

"Please, Cairo."

His hand snaked around my waist, dipping between my middle. Cairo shoved two fingers inside without ceremony. I gasped on a cry.

The sound of his zipper dropping filled the room.

I shot away, knocking him out of me. I raced into the hall with no real idea of where I was going. All I knew was this was a hunt.

I had to run.

Cairo was on me in three bounds.

We collapsed before the door to the guest bedroom.

"Get off!"

"Keep struggling. I'm going to fuck you right here while the Ghost of Nanas Past watches. If you wanted to get away from me, de Souza, you should've run faster."

There's nowhere I could run to be free of you.

Seizing my ankles, Cairo dragged me across the floor.

"No!"

I latched on the doorframe, kicking to get free. All it did was help him get my pants all the way off.

He pulled me free of the door and hauled me bare-assed over the splintered wood. Cairo dove between my legs, descending on my pussy like a ravenous beast.

Have you ever been eaten out by a wild animal masquerading as a man? I would assume not unless that man was Cairo Sharpe.

Mercy was not in his vocabulary.

He tortured my clit between his teeth—reducing me to a moaning, quivering mess in seconds. His tongue forced its way past my folds, licking and collecting every drop of juice from my traitorous sex.

"Uh, it hurts." I slapped him. "Stop!"

"I don't have to stop taking what's mine."

He rose up, snapped me to him, and pushed in with a single thrust.

"Ah!"

Cairo gripped my neck, pinning me to the floor as he started pumping. I grabbed his wrist—to pull him off or to hold him, I couldn't tell. I couldn't think.

The pain was mind numbing. Ripping, tearing, rending the last pieces of the Rainey I used to be to shreds.

"C-Cairo... no, please."

Sweat covered my body, easing my slide on the unforgiving floor. Cairo lifted me, burying his face in my neck. I whimpered as he licked a stripe along my collarbone, then sucked to mark his claim.

"Take it, you tasty little slut. And say thank you." He bent my head back. "Say it."

"Fuck you."

I reared. Cairo caught my wrist and bent it behind my back, making me cry out. Pulling out, he twisted till he forced me on my knees. One hand securing my wrist. The other forced the back of my head down, pressing my face to the floor.

He sank inside with a deep, satisfying hiss—fed by my whimpers.

"Cairo, please. I can't take any more."

"You take what I fucking give you, and what." *Thrust.* "Do." *Thrust.* "You." *Thrust.* "Say?"

Each snap of his hips molded our bodies together, driving him deeper inside than I thought possible. My knees scraped the wood, splitting open to weep their own red tears. The pain anchored me. Gave me a safe place to harbor as my orgasm swelled and fought to drag me under.

"Thank y-you," I rasped. "Thank you, Cairo."

"For what?" he asked—his smirk so damn obvious, I didn't need to raise my head and see it.

"For... owning me— Ah!" Cairo struck that spot, lifting me off my knees. "For giving me what I deserve."

"What do you deserve?"

"You," I said so softly, his grunts washed it away, then I was gone.

I came so hard black spots danced in my vision. Cairo drew away, leaving me to jerk and bounce on the floor.

Every part of me from the knees up ached. Blood stained my legs. All that being tossed around gave me a few dings and dents. As for the fire burning between my legs.

I wasn't getting up and walking anywhere, anytime soon.

My eyes blinked as open arms slid under me. Cairo cradled me in his arms, picking my bag up on the way, and carried me out the door to the waiting car. Not his, so I suspected the showdown on Bay Avenue hadn't happened yet.

Cairo took me home and left me in the tender care of Roan, who got hard bathing me and tending to my scrapes. He jacked off in the shower a few times, but otherwise didn't shove another dick inside me, or try to goad me into spilling more blood.

After my bath, I shimmied into one of his T-shirts and crawled into his bed. My eyes nailed him over the covers, silently daring him to make me move.

He chuckled. "It won't be me who hauls you out of that bed and deposits you in the doghouse. Jacques, Arsenio, or Cairo will have that honor. Though, I'm leaning toward Cairo since he's always in a particularly foul mood after visiting his mother."

"I'll be the one watching and silently rooting while Jacques spanks you again, but this time for me to enjoy."

"You get off on pain, don't you?"

I swept an eye around his room. The whole place was a shrine to sadomasochism. Whips and chains hanging on the wall. Posters of various people wearing leather and metal, flashing their red bare asses, clamped nipples, ball gags, and saucy winks as they wielded their riding crops.

Such a sweet, charming grin stretched his lips, you almost believe he was as harmless as he looked. "There is no pleasure without pain, darling. Anyone who says otherwise is repressed."

I stifled a laugh. "Not sure it's that simple."

"No, but then you're still learning." Tossing me a wink, he backed out the door. "We'll complete your education soon enough."

CAIRO

"Give me the keys."

"Cairo, watch your tone."

Nora stood on the other side of her gilded fence. My car keys dangled from her fingertips.

"How are you, sweetie?" She tilted her head, gaze softening. It was the perfect mimic of someone who actually cared. "Are you eating enough? You look thin. Come inside for dinner. I'll have Chef make your—"

"This is low, Nora. Even for you."

"Do not call me Nora," she snapped, a flash of my true mother returning. "I am your mother. You will treat me with respect."

"You're my mother," I repeated. I made a show of looking around. "Is that why you'll only speak to me through metal? Are you afraid of me, Mommy dearest?"

"Don't be ridiculous. I am going to go into this house, Esteban will open the gate, and if you want your keys back, you'll come inside and have a civilized dinner with your family." She stroked my cheek through the bars. I could've been chipped from granite for all the reaction I gave her. "I have missed you, Cairo. My sweet baby. Come inside."

Nora turned away and did as she promised. She strode into her grand house, taking my keys with her. The security guard hit the button to open the gate.

I headed off in the opposite direction. Walking past my car, I saluted the rusted can goodbye and continued down the street, leaving Bay Avenue.

I didn't stop till I was three miles and an hour away.

The modest two-story bungalow loomed at the end of the curb. I found the spare under the flowerpot and let myself in. A fetid, demanding stench hit my nose before I stepped over the threshold.

Kicking aside stray beer cans, I passed through the short hallway, nose wrinkling as the smell got worse. I rounded the corner and there he was. The great and honorable Sheriff Jack—defender of the city and upholder of all true and lawful—slumped on the dining table.

A puddle of vomit decorated the floor, spreading to mix with the whiskey dripping off the table, flowing freely from the upturned bottle.

"Dad." I shook his shoulder. "Dad, wake up."

"Wha—?" He swiped at me and flipped over, mumbling something I couldn't make out.

"Dad." I grabbed him under the shoulders, grimacing as days' old sweat and tequila enveloped me. My father didn't discriminate. If it was alcohol, it was going straight to his liver. "Wake up."

His head lolled. Dad peeled open bloodshot eyes, gazing at me for a second like he didn't know me. "Cairo?"

"Who else would it be?"

I moved into the kitchen, taking the whiskey bottle with me. I returned with a glass of water and a bowl of pretzels. He didn't even argue. We had our routine down by now.

Dad sipped his water—swaying slightly, and splashing some on the floor while I cleaned.

"I'm sorry, son," he rasped.

"Just give me the name."

"I... don't want it to be this way."

"Name, Dad." My voice was hard. I was entitled.

"It's just— It's just—" He burst into tears. "I can't say no. I w-want to. I do."

"We've done this for ten years and you're still singing the same song," I said.

I wiped up the last of the sick and tossed the paper towels in the trash. Going back to my father, I made him eat a handful of pretzels. I made sure there was always food in the house. Didn't stop him drinking himself to death on an empty stomach every time.

"But this is what a son does, steps into his father's place. What you can't do, I can."

He sobbed harder. Tears and snot ran down unshaven salt-and-pepper scruff.

"I'm sorry. For everything. I wanted to be a good father. A good man. I wasn't strong enough."

I wasn't about to dispute that.

"Let's go. Time for—"

Dad grabbed me, burying his face in my shirt. "You're a good son. The best I could've asked for," he wailed. "I love you."

"Jesus Christ," I muttered, trying to peel him off me.

"I do. I love"—he hiccuped—"you. I don't say it enough. I don't tell you how proud I am of you, but it's true all the same."

I got out of his hold and slung his arm around my shoulder.

"You're all I have."

He tried to hug me. I put a firm hand on his chest, keeping him back.

"Give me the name, Dad."

Jack sniffled. "I'll do it this time. I can—"

"No, you can't. You couldn't then, you can't now." I made him look at me. "Tell me the name."

When the words came, they came slow.

"Axel. Axel Verlice."

"What did he do?" I asked tonelessly.

"Started a side business. Cut us—*her* out of the profits."

"Unwise." I half carried him out of the dining room. "The situation will be taken care of."

"Just don't hurt him."

"Don't tell me how to do your job," I bit off.

Jack fell silent.

He didn't speak during the time I helped him out of the uniform and holster, cleaned him up, and pulled the covers to his chin. I left once to get another cup of water and put it by his bedside. I checked to make sure his pillows propped him on his side, then eased onto the rocking chair in the corner, picking up a book on the dresser.

I'd most likely be here till the morning, ensuring he didn't choke on his vomit or die of alcohol poisoning.

Settling in, I picked up *The Picture of Dorian Gray,* where I left off.

People asked why my bedroom in the Bedlam House locked from the outside. The answer was simple and not shared.

It was so no one realized how rarely I slept in my room.

Chapter Eleven

R*ainey*
I woke early the next morning and watched the sun rise on Bedlam University.

Roan was correct about my short reprieve. Jacques came home and brought me down to the doghouse. He wasn't shy about making me change into my home clothes, either.

It didn't bother me as much as it should.

Which bothered me.

I dozed on and off throughout the night. Sleeping, I lay half in the doghouse. Awake, I snuck snacks from the kitchen, munching and thinking.

What did it say about me that I didn't put up much of a fight at wearing a collar and sleeping on the floor in the living room? What did it mean that I looked at Roan and saw both the devilish imp and the vicious manipulator? I saw cold, arrogant Jacques and the man who cracked his knuckles, beating a guy who threw a drink on me. What did it mean that violent, rough rape-fantasy sex had become the staple of my relationship with Cairo, and as much as years of social programming said I should, this didn't make me fear or hate him?

There was a darkness in these men I both responded to and was able to see past to something more underneath. I kept asking myself why both Letter Men chose me, and now I had to ask if it's because they saw darkness in me too.

Jacques came down into the kitchen while the sun was still rising. He didn't say another number at the sight of me, so I guessed sitting out, leaning on the doghouse, was allowed.

"You couldn't sleep either?"

He slowed, cast me an unreadable look, and continued on. I watched him move around the kitchen, setting up the blender.

"What's in that shake you make?"

I didn't expect him to answer. I was mostly just talking at him after too long a night in my head.

"Kale, spinach, banana, cucumber, apple juice, and cocoa nibs," he replied.

"Wow. That sounds... gross."

He made a noise in his throat. Was that a laugh?

"Can I try it?" I asked.

"Yes."

"Really?"

"Yes," he repeated. "Starvation isn't a part of your punishment. Besides, it is only logical to consume a diet that provides the maximum nutritional value in every meal."

"Sure, but everything doesn't have to be logical, does it?"

"Explain."

"Well, uh." *My goodness, is this the longest conversation I've had with Jacques that doesn't include fighting?*

"Comfort food, for example," I said. "Hot, greasy, salty, fried loveliness. We all know it's not good for us, but when you had a terrible day, it makes you feel better to veg on the couch with buttery popcorn. Couldn't you say the positive impact on your mental health is worth it? What good is it being the healthiest man on earth, if you can't enjoy the little things in life?"

"Interesting theory." Jacques threw a handful of spinach in the blender. "The production of dopamine and serotonin from junk food derives its own benefits in regards to stress relief. Stress itself is a negative factor toward health, so the pros and cons should be weighed," he said. "Your supposition has merit."

My brows shot up my forehead. Did he just say I was right in genius-speak?

"Although," Jacques continued. "The continued overproduction of dopamine lessens its impact on the human body. Therefore, to reach the same high, we must consume more and more junk food. Leading to addiction."

"Absolutely the 'eating junk food to feel better' idea can only go so far. But that's why we say everything in moderation. You can drink your green smoothies every day, but once a week, eating your favorite maple donut can do you some good too."

"I agree with your reasoning."

Holy hell. That was definitely genius-speak for you're right.

I studied him. "What's it like in your head, Jacques?"

"I've been asked that question many times."

"I'm sorry. Does it make you uncomfortable?"

Now he studied me—a long, probing look that made me shift on my dog bed. "Now that question, no one has ever asked me."

"Curiosity can make people insensitive. We forget just because we want to know something, it doesn't mean we treat people like animals in a zoo."

"Yes, courtesy is often discarded in favor of intrusiveness," he agreed. "But to answer your question, no. It doesn't bother me. I understand humans are naturally curious beings. They seek to understand so they can categorize. Labels make people comfortable. Once I was given the title genius, people felt less uneasy around the small child spouting facts he shouldn't know or understand."

Jacques spoke about people like we were a different species. To be called humans was better than cattle, though it made me wonder if it stemmed from people treating him differently.

You're doing it again, de Souza. Trying to make a wounded bird out of an emotionally closed-off man.

"I can't speak to what it's like in other people's minds, but the closest comparison I can think of is a warehouse of file cabinets," Jacques said. "Some are small, labeled, and near the entrance. Others are miles back and ten stories high. Every event, detail, fact, and the resulting conclusions I've made or experienced in my life are in the cabinets, but I do not have an eidetic memory. I cannot recall them at will.

"I have to build systems, networks, and shortcuts to get through the maze. I create ladders to get the information high above me. It is not a simple process, nor is it painless," he said. "But to disregard sections of it like others can is impossible." Jacques touched his temples. "I can feel it. Always. Every day. Every minute. My life will not be deleted."

"I can't imagine what that's like," I said softly.

Jacques hit puree on the blender. It seemed our conversation was over.

I watched him while he made his breakfast, and a few times he glanced up and looked back at me. Smoothies done, he brought over two mason jars and handed me mine.

It was disgusting, just as predicted. He must've used unsweetened dark chocolate nibs, because they made the situation worse. Even so, we slurped in an almost companionable silence. I wouldn't say I understood Jacques Stone completely, but in one thing I could relate.

No one knew what to do with him till they found a comfortable, recognizable label to slap on his head, and what had I been doing the entire night if not looking for a similar solution for the Bedlam Boys? And for me.

Maybe I didn't need to understand why I craved every woman's worst nightmare as a fantasy. Obviously, I didn't want sex forced on me in a situation I couldn't control with a person I didn't want. But with Cairo, Jacques, Roan, Legend, and Arsenio, it was different. With them, I was in charge of my fate. I decided when it broke us.

I thought of losing Gran, Ivy leaving, the Letter Man's grip on my life, and the body at Black Widow Hill.

When in my life have I ever had control? When have I been able to make the bad things stop?

Jacques set his empty glass on the table. "Hands and knees. Face the doghouse."

I did as ordered. I was up to ten for running off and not telling the guys where I went yesterday.

He secured my leash to the hook, then tugged my thong down. It was hardly getting in the way, but by Jacques's erection the day before, he liked the view.

Thwap!

Stinging pain ricocheted through my cheeks. My body responded even as I hissed.

"One."

Over and over, the leather tasted my skin, drawing my arousal to dampen the belt and get me in trouble once again. It was a never-ending cycle my wanton pussy was more than happy with.

"Six."

A moan escaped. I bit my lip harder to hold them back.

"Don't do that." Jacques slipped his fingers inside me. "You don't get to hold back what's mine."

He worked me effortlessly—crooking his fingers and teasing my clit with his thumb. Did you have to be a genius to achieve that level of dexterity while whipping someone's ass? Because I was very impressed.

"Holy shit," I breathed.

"You shouldn't be enjoying this so much."

"You shouldn't add a third finger. Ugh, I *hate* that."

He chuckled, and the sound was a straight shot to my core. No matter what he did. Even if you witnessed him burn the world down. You could not think of Jacques Stone as anything but an angel when he laughed.

Jacques gave me my third finger, stretching me to the limit. Soft sounds fell from my lips, mixed with hisses from each snap of the belt. It hurt so terribly and felt so amazing at the same time, and yet I knew I couldn't have one without the other.

Roan was right. Pain and pleasure were two sides of the same coin.

Thwap!

I came screaming, waking the whole house up. I reached behind and grasped his zipper to return the favor.

Jacques caught my wrist and gently returned it to its place.

"One," he said.

He walked off, eroding my bliss with confused frustration.

What did I tell you? The other guys tromped down the stairs, filing past him. *Jacques is not a wounded bird. He is never going to make it that easy for me.*

I eased onto my sore backside, waiting for one of *my* boys to bring me breakfast, then carry me up for a thorough, intimate bath.

Yes, they were mine. The fact was setting in stone with every day I spent with them.

It was a mistake to think of them as soft men underneath who needed love to bring them out, but it was becoming clear how they saw me. I was their wounded bird—albeit wounds of their own making. I was theirs to tend, to cage, to punish, and to defend.

And although they did not understand it now, that kind of devotion led down a single path. One day, they would be as much mine as I was theirs.

I decided our fate.

We don't end until I say we do.

"DO YOU GET BAGELS EVERY morning?" I asked as we entered the student union.

"It's not about the bagels," Legend said. "You can't keep a close enough eye on your kingdom from the tower."

"Ah, I get it. You're surveying the serfs." I mumbled something uncomplimentary under my breath.

"Heard that."

Legend snaked an arm around me, drawing me close and pulling taut the leash around Cairo's wrist.

"Has anyone told you that those lovelies are the perfect little handful? Not too small, but still big enough a man can suffocate between them." He brushed his finger over my nipple, discreetly, so you could almost believe he wasn't feeling me up in public. "Can't wait for another go."

"So, just to be clear," I said, "your whole gentleman routine is a complete act."

"Yes, ma'am." He popped a kiss on my lips. "Actually, after this let's..."

Legend trailed off as he stepped out onto the deck.

The New Boys gathered up the remains of their breakfast, getting up to toss it.

The New Boys was the name I gave Jeremy, Bentley, Micah, Gael, and Jonah that morning while I overheard the guys discussing them. It seemed like the appropriate name for a band of violent, hot troublemakers threatening to take over, and currently sitting at their table.

There were only four of them that morning, and they weren't alone.

A group of people were chatting with them, leaning on their chairs and laughing like they just hit the punch line of the joke.

"Oh." Green Hair— Jeremy made big eyes, clapping his hand over his mouth. "I'm so sorry. We meant to be out of here before you arrived."

The crowd dispersed quickly. Some of them moving too fast for people just hanging for a friendly chat.

What do you look so guilty about?

"What's this?" Jeremy fixed on me. "If it isn't Miss Get The Fuck Off My Property. I wouldn't have pegged you as a woman who lets someone put her on a leash."

"Two," said Jacques.

"What's that supposed to be?" Jeremy asked.

"That's how many teeth you'll lose if you keep talking to our girl," Cairo replied. "And what was it you said? Oh yeah, get the fuck off my property."

"Oooh," one of them crowed.

"Yes, master."

"Sorry, master."

Bowing and scraping, they got up from the table, eliciting a few chuckles from the crowd.

"Kind of you," said Arsenio. "Hey, what's the update on the murder investigation? Just spoke to the sheriff and he mentioned you five were his main suspects."

The smile froze on Jeremy's face. "Don't know what the fuck you're talking about."

"Of course you do." Arsenio's grin oozed charm. "Ruckus Royale. The guy you stabbed was set on fire after swearing he'd kill you. Sheriff said something about how strange it was you sank a knife in that guy, but the other sacrifices were just hassled. You two must have a history."

The deck fell silent. Even the bugs in the trees stopped making noise.

"There is no history," Jeremy gritted. "I never met the guy, and my lawyer told your hick sheriff the same thing. The Crows had nothing to do with his death."

"Soooo," Arsenio drew out. "You just go around stabbing innocent people for fun? Totally random guy already having a bad day, and your first thought was to carve him up?" He shook his head. "I'm not buying it. No wonder the sheriff didn't either."

"I didn't do that because I had beef with the fucker," he snapped. "That was to teach you—"

"Teach me? Let me get this straight, you stabbed an innocent man just to intimidate us? You needed to prove how tough you are that badly?" Arsenio whistled. "Wow. Maybe you are worse than we'll ever be. I mean, not even the Bedlam Boys attack unprovoked."

I bit my lip, afraid a "Damn" would come out.

Arsenio maneuvered him so expertly in his place, if I wasn't watching, I would've missed it.

Jeremy's eyes flicked around, seeing in those faces what I was seeing.

Doubt.

New Kings were all well and good, unless you're next on the stake.

"The Crows didn't kill that man," Jeremy said. "I believe he died from the fire your boy lit under him. That's for sure the cause of death Sheriff Daddy has written down. Not stab wound. I don't know what you're trying to pull, pushing the blame for your crime on us, but thank you for confirming this for me—you don't attack unprovoked. When I figure out your motive, we'll see how far nepotism gets you."

Arsenio clicked his tongue, grinning. "It's gotten us pretty far," he said, not letting his words float to our audience. Louder, he replied, "Doesn't matter because we've been cleared. The cops know we were framed by someone who wants the Bedlam Boys taken out."

Not quite the reason.

"We'll be watching you." Arsenio closed the distance, towering over Jeremy with all six feet, one inch of him. "We won't let you hurt anyone else in this town."

"Yeah," someone said.

Nods went around the deck.

Jaw ticcing, Jeremy came closer still, leaving a hair between their chests.

"You're smooth, politician's boy. Got a nice way with words that have even me almost doubting myself, but that only works for so long. Eventually, this town is going to wake up and remember they hate you. They hate running when you snap your fingers and bending their necks for you to wipe your feet.

"Between you and me, the wake-up call is coming soon, and when it does, I don't actually have to be a nice guy as long as everyone thinks I am." He flicked to Legend. "By the way, that was a sinister show you put on yesterday, but I set my alarm, and I'm not missing anything."

"Aren't you?" Legend brushed past me and leaned over Jeremy's ear. "Where's your brother?"

"Micah? He went home to get something."

"Did he?"

I'd never seen that expression on Legend's face. It kicked my fight-or-flight impulse into gear.

"Yes," Jeremy snapped. "He texted me that—"

"—he couldn't find his watch and took a quick trip back to HC to see if it's home," Legend finished.

Jeremy blanched.

"Oops," Legend breezed. "Hope he finds it."

"You piece of shit! What did you do with Micah?!"

Legend threw up his hands, the picture of innocence. "Do? What could I have done?" His voice was too low for anyone but us to hear. "I was home all night and morning. Wasn't I, guys?"

The boys nodded.

"Tell me where he is or—"

"I've already told you." The sickly sweet tone clashed violently against the glint in his eyes. "You can skip the blustering and shouting, and drop to your knees now. I'll take a kissed boot and a 'Sorry, Mr. St. James' while you're down there." He lifted his foot, wiggling it at him. "Chop, chop."

Jeremy flew at him. A wild punch cut the air, heading for Legend's jaw.

Legend snapped back, caught his arm, and used the momentum to spin him around and secure him in a headlock. The whole thing happened so fast, Jeremy couldn't stop it.

"Son of a bitch! If you hurt my brother, I'll kill you!"

"Whoa," Legend said, lifting his voice. "Calm down, buddy. We're just talking."

"Where's Micah?!" He thrashed in his grip. "What did you do to him?!"

The Crows tried to help him and Arsenio, Jacques, Roan, and Cairo blocked their way four to three. Actually, eight to three as other guys jumped to break off the impending fight. Suddenly, they remembered who they served.

Legend tossed Jeremy at a pair of guys. "Escort them out. They're done ruining everyone's morning."

"You're next, St. James!" Jeremy's spittle showered the deck, his shoes leaving scuffs on the deck. "You'll burn! You'll all fucking burn!"

I watched him go, mouth hanging open. Arsenio maneuvered him into losing the chess match, then Legend got him to blow up the board. There was no coming back from a scene like that. He may turn sympathy by saying he lost it over his brother, but that was real, frightening hatred in those eyes. You don't forget a look like that for as long as you live.

I can promise you.

"Legend," I began, "what did you do to his brother?"

The *more than just a rich boy* slung his arm around me, giving my nipple another quick tweak. "Had a couple guys pick him up this morning, drive him out of town, and drop him on the side of the road. No phone, of course. It'll take him a good ten hours to walk back. Long enough for Jer-Bear to learn some humility." He nuzzled my cheek. "Like I was saying before we were interrupted, I'll have another go on those lovelies before class. Eat fast."

The Bedlam Boys reclaimed their table with a smugness that bordered on obscene. I had mixed feelings, to say the least. Legend didn't hurt Micah, but then the lesson was for his brother, not him. If it was my sister, I wouldn't make it ten hours before dropping on my knees and begging Legend to tell me she was safe.

A brutal lesson. Even so, I can't forget the Bedlam Boys didn't start this war with the Crows, and they're not interested in being in it. These guys keep getting in their faces. If they want so badly to play on their level, they'll face the consequences like the rest of us.

Joining them, I lifted Cairo's hand and sat on his lap. My butt still hurt like a motherfucker, so it took some wiggling to get comfortable. His cock twitched a hello.

Once I was settled, I faced him full on, silently challenging him to move me onto the floor.

"You're getting bold, baby." He gave me a quick nip kiss that was over too fast. "I don't dislike it."

Cupping his jaw, I turned him back to me and molded his lips to mine—stealing the deep, dizzying kisses he denied me. Cairo responded, moving in rhythm with me, teasing my lips apart.

He clamped on my bottom lip, breaking the skin.

"Ow."

Cairo licked my blood from his mouth, looking every inch the wolf I named him. "Don't get carried away."

"Asshole," I muttered.

"—leave it."

"No!"

A cloud of Shalimar perfume invaded my nose.

"So, it's true." Quinn Cunningham planted herself in front of us. "You dumped me for this bitch."

"No," Roan said. He didn't look up from his texting. "We dumped you. Then we hooked up with this bitch. We were through with you before we met her. Two separate events."

That didn't stem the rising color in Quinn's cheeks. I don't think it was meant to.

"I thought this was a joke. Another one of your stupid punishments for whatever shit you imagined I did wrong."

Quinn really was beautiful. I didn't know many people who still looked pretty with a curled lip and tomato-red cheeks.

"I'm not putting up with this. You don't get to throw me over for farm-girl trash over here—"

"Hey," I said.

"—and think I'm going to let you get away with it."

"What are you going to do about it?" Legend asked.

Cairo's phone went off. "I want you to fuck my mouth, Cairo." His ringtone sounded clear as day. "Make me choke on your cum."

Now I wished I was on the floor. It would be easier to hide my face.

Poison burned her glare. "You'll see."

She stormed off and was dismissed as quickly as she left.

Legend eyed Roan. "Who are you texting?"

"Oh, you know." He winked. "A boy."

Legend moved under the table, and Roan hissed—face screwing up in pain even as his eyes glazed in pleasure.

"Just kidding, baby." Roan tugged him by the collar. The X-rated kiss he gave him made me cross my legs. In the tiny little black dress the guys squeezed me into, they could see I was wet from space.

Cairo's phone went off. He glanced at the screen and something flashed across his face.

"Hello?" He listened. "Yeah. Yeah. I got the message."

My ears perked up, listening for a hint of who was on the other end.

"No," Cairo said. "He forgot to mention that. Yes, we'll take care of it. I said we'll take care of it."

He ended the call.

"Off," he ordered. "Go to class, Rain."

Cairo helped me along by standing and tossing me off his lap.

I headed out. I needed to find something less nightclub to wear to my bankruptcy class anyway.

"We have a problem," I overheard him say. "Must be dealt with tonight..."

You have problems?

Out of their orbit, my attention focused on my impending deadline, and the increasingly angry psychopath waiting for a name.

I have to warn them. His threats be damned. They have to know their lives are in danger. Especially Frankie. Her husband is a walking shitbag, but he wouldn't refuse watching the kids and getting them out of town until I find this guy and stop him.

In four days.

The majority of my two weeks were eaten up and there was nothing I could do about it. All I had was a theory about Sam Dillion, and if I was wrong, there was the final guy in their old crew and Cavendish's girlfriend.

What do I do if looking for these people turns up nothing?

I didn't know Cavendish. Who knew how he spent his time, or who he got close to after he killed his best friend and the others drifted away? The Letter Man could be his long-lost frickin' brother who recently bonded with him over their shared love of blood and torture, and after big bro died, he decided to take up the mantle.

I stopped outside the building, taking a deep breath and holding it. Playing the what-if game wouldn't do me any good. I needed a real, solid plan that didn't rely on sudden mania and a perfect window of opportunity. The Bedlam Boys were hardly going to set that up for me again.

I'd change, spend the last hour till class in the library, and put together the pieces of Scott's life. That night, I'd break away from the guys—punishment be damned—and tell Paris, Bella, and Frankie they were in danger and why. A twisted sadist stalking and threatening to kill you wasn't something you shot off in a text.

They'd most likely demand we go straight to Sheriff Jack. Hell would open up at my feet before I sat in the same room with the man. I was prepared to tell my story to one of the Hunter's Crest officers and show them the letter detailing in no uncertain terms what they'd do if I didn't kill someone in two weeks.

The cops would assign them protection. My friends would be safe.

For how long? a chilling voice sounded. *How long can any of us be safe from a shadow?*

I looked down, throat tight, as doubt fought its way in.

It's always behind you.

MY FIRST TIME IN THE university library, and it was becoming my favorite place.

A light scent of vanilla wafted in and out of the stacks. This library wasn't like most I'd been in. Huge overhead windows and skylights dispelled the dark corners. There were study tables and couches placed everywhere, and in the front of the building, a little café that served me a chicken pesto panini that hit the spot better than Jacques's logical breakfast smoothie.

I was dressed in a hoodie and sneakers from a girl who literally gave them to me off her body. I went up to her in Homer Green, asked if she was a size seven and how she felt about a trade for my pair of Manolo Blahniks. She whipped them off so fast, she took off barefoot so I wouldn't have a chance to change my mind.

A thousand times more comfortable, I found a spot near the back and did a deep dive into the life of Sam Dillion.

Local Teens Injured During Fake Bomb Threat.

Sam Dillion's name was added to that piece of news after Douglas ratted out his friends. That was years later, and another year after that, he left town.

My search into Dillion ended there the first time around. He wasn't around, so I focused on the friend that was: Scott Cavendish.

Where did Dillion go? What finally drove him to leave?

And did he come back after a certain man's death?

I typed in "Sam Dillion Hunter's Crest."

Most of us Bedlamites had a hard time getting too far. It was worth a shot.

Munching on my sandwich, I poked around the top articles. Two mentions of Sam Dillions, none were him.

My next try was the nearest town to the south, Beckerburg. I scrolled down and clicked the LinkedIn page for Samuel Noah Dillion.

I sat up straighter.

Clear under education was Bedlam University.

This is him.

I clicked out and typed in his full name and town. The top result was the Beckerburg Journal. I realized what it was before I clicked on the article. I opened it anyway.

***Samuel Noah Dillion, age 25, passed away last Sunday. He is
survived by his parents, Donna and Jerald, and his siblings.***

I stopped reading there. Why go on? Samuel was not the Letter
Man. My last hope hung on the chance the Letter Man was now the
Letter Woman.

What was his girlfriend's name again? Hannah? Hailey?

Stomach churning, I put in Scott Cavendish. The first thing a
vulture reporter would've done was run to their house to interview
the grieving girlfriend and ask why would anyone want to burn her
man alive?

There was always the chance she was involved in this. I considered it when I was standing outside their house, watching the two
pull into their driveway and move about through the windows. The
more I learned about Cavendish, the more I let suspicions of her go.

He had a shady past and death connected to his name. She spent
most of her time chatting animatedly on the phone in her living
room and blasted music on her way home. It was too hard to see that
happy, social person as the sad, sick man who sent me those letters.

*Maybe I dismissed her too quickly. For all I know, they were a
match made in heaven.*

Heather.

The name came to me just like that. Heather Mitchell.

I typed in her name. My eyes widened at the top result.

Heather Mitchell Commits Suicide.

I stabbed the button, opening the article. Nestled in between her
history, family and friends, was the story of losing her boyfriend and
how she couldn't recover from the shock. Last week, Friday morning, her body was found in the bathroom by her mother.

A chill set in my bones. I had no proof. There was less than
nothing to go on. Still, I couldn't shake the feeling it wasn't bad
luck, depression, or coincidence that explained why people kept dying around Scott Cavendish.

Did the new Letter Man kill Scott's girlfriend? Why would he do that?

Why would he ask me to kill an innocent? I am not dealing with a person who—

A shadow moved on the other side of the stacks.

I shot up, quickly clicking out of the window. "Who's there? I'm warning you. Don't fuck with me today."

"Whoa. Easy, mama." Jeremy's smooth baritone floated through the books. "I just want to talk."

Clutching my chest, I dropped back in my seat. The chances weren't high the Letter Man would leap through the books and attack me in a brightly lit library with dozens of witnesses around, but you couldn't blame me for being jumpy.

Everyone with the misfortune to know Scott Cavendish ended up dead or gone. Now his replacement had me in his sights.

My days of fooling around at the farm without a weapon or people knowing I'm there are over, I thought as Jeremy came around to face me. *My days of going anywhere at all without a weapon or backup had to be over. The next obituary in the Bedlam Post would not be mine.*

"I don't know where your brother is," I said.

"I didn't think you did."

"Then what can I do for you?"

"I'm here to ask you that."

Jeremy slid in his seat, draping one arm behind the chair and adopting a casual air beautiful people make look effortless.

"What's that supposed to mean?"

Jeremy looked me up and down. "The girl who ran into me in the woods is not the same one shivering on a leash in the corner like a whipped dog."

"You don't know me, New Boy."

"I know the Bedlam Boys chained you. I can set you free."

I pushed aside my borrowed laptop. Jeremy had my full attention. "How exactly can you do that?"

"Tell me what you want," he said. "Name it. It's yours."

"You can't give me what I want." I turned away, gathering my things. "And if you haven't learned by now, here's a tip: the Bedlam Boys have minions everywhere and they're not above reporting your movements. Jacques told you what will happen if you talk to me," I said. "I'd warn that those guys don't bluff, but you figured that out by now."

He grabbed my arm. Gentle, but firm. He towed me back in my seat.

"Money," he said. "My dad's loaded. I can transfer fifteen grand into your bank account by the time you finish your panini. And that's just my daily limit. Another fifteen grand could be yours tomorrow."

I flashed him a hard look. "And you want to give me thirty grand why? Because you feel sorry for me? Why don't we start with what you want, and then I'll decide what it's worth."

He smiled. "If it's not worth thirty thousand, then it doesn't look like you come at a price. I'll skip ahead to what you truly want.

"De Souza Farm."

I stilled. "Excuse me?"

"You heard me. The farm's been tied up in legal issues and murky questions of ownership since your grandmother passed and the company that was supposed to buy the farm went under. The bank isn't about to hand it back to you, so it's just sitting there waiting for someone else to move in. Your family home. The de Souza name on its sign for six generations."

Each word stuck a pin through my heart.

"Don't tell me you wouldn't give anything to get it back. At the very least, if you had somewhere to live, you wouldn't be bunking in a doghouse."

I yanked free of him. "How do you—? Of course. You broke into their place."

"One of the school's custodians cleans their house. You may not have a price, but they do," he said. "I know how awfully they treat you and that you want to get away."

You know nothing, New Boy.

"My father is on the board of a few development companies. One word and they cut through the red tape, buy the farm, and put the deed in your name. No one will take it from you again."

"Let me see if I'm understanding this. You're going to convince your dad to buy my farm... and then hand it over to me. De Souza Farm is twelve acres for eight thousand and seven hundred dollars an acre. That's just for the land.

"To get the farmhouse, barn, chicken coop, and animal pens on top, it's five hundred grand," I said. "That's not a guess. It's a quote from Cruella herself. Over half a million dollars, and it'll be a gift? Daddy Warbucks is going to make that happen?"

Jeremy didn't blink. "That's what I just said, isn't it?"

"Then again, I have to ask, what's in it for you?"

"Nothing sinister. I just want you to keep an eye on things for me. You're living with— under them," he corrected. "You overhear their conversations. You snoop in their rooms. You're as close to the Bedlam Boys as anyone can be. Tell me what they're planning, and you get your farm back. Simple."

The first crack in his mask appeared. "You can start by getting St. James to tell you where my brother is. I broke into their house and he's not there. I've sent my guys to their houses too. If I'm missing a place, find out where it is."

"Everything you said sounded simple, but it's not," I replied. "You know what is? Giving Legend what he wants. I'm surprised you haven't swallowed your pride by now. This is your brother we're talking about."

"So help—!" He cut the shout off, clearing his throat. "Help me. We both hate these guys. Help me take them down."

"Why do you want them out of the way? What are *you* planning?"

The frown twitched. "Honestly, I didn't think you'd make it this difficult. I'm handing you everything you want on a silver platter. Don't tell me— Shit. Are you in love with those guys? They treat you like garbage. Scratch that. They treat you like an animal."

"Thanks for the reminder," I said, tone even. "No, I'm not in love with them. It's not about them. You haven't asked me why I call you New Boy. It's not because you just transferred here. New Boy is short for New Bedlam Boy. Far as I can see, your Crows are no different from them. Getting deep with you would be taking the leash from their hands and putting it in yours."

"That's not true." Jeremy ran a finger up my thigh. "I'd never treat you the way they do. You're a goddess, Rainey. The Crows would worship you."

I folded my legs, knocking him off. "If you're so different, prove it to me. The Bedlam Boys aren't honest with me. They haven't told me a thing about what they do in this town or why. If I'm supposed to trust you, then you can trust me. Tell me what you guys are doing here."

Jeremy held my gaze for five, ten, fifteen seconds. He looked away.

"That's what I thought." I stood to go.

"Wait," he hissed. "Obviously, I'm not going to spill my guts in a crowded library when you just told me their spies are always watching. You can trust me, de Souza, I swear. Agree to help me out and everyone gets what they want."

I hummed. "If you did that much research on me, it should've come up that I'm prelaw. I'm not entering into any land agreement without a written contract signed by your father and his company stating upon purchase of the farm, ownership will transfer to me. Once that contract is in my hand, I'm willing to hear *exactly* what you want from me and why. If that's not possible, you weren't really serious in the first place.

"As for your brother, stop racking up breaking and entering charges and go to Legend. He's your freaking blood. He should not have to wait as long as you've made him."

Picking up the laptop, I marched off.

"Bitch."

"Not off to a good start," I tossed over my shoulder.

Jeremy's unwelcome distraction aside, it was still an unproductive morning. Sam Dillion was dead. Heather Mitchell was dead. There was the final friend of Scott and Douglas, Nathan Wade. I didn't expend too much energy looking him up again.

I found out the first time around he got married after his expulsion, and his wife was currently expecting a baby. His Facebook photos put the two of them in Hawaii for a babymoon on Ruckus Day. According to the pics, they were still there.

These letters are hand delivered. It's not Nathan Wade. What now?

Questions went round in my head all through my classes. Bankruptcy and land transfer were small classes with less than twenty students. Unfortunately, it was easy for my professors to tell my mind was elsewhere. They called on me more than usual. It was a relief to get out of my last class and walk across Homer Green.

There was no air in those damn rooms. How could I do what I had to do next if I couldn't breathe?

I lay flat on the grass, watching the shapeless white blobs dancing in a blue, red, and orange sky. Once, when I was little, I told Ivy I wished I was a cloud. She said that was silly. Why would I want to be something that wasn't alive? I told her they were alive. I could see them move. See them change. See them bloat with rain and stamp out the sun. Maybe the clouds looked down on us dots, flapping about all day doing nothing, and wondered if we were real.

She said I was a cute little weirdo and kissed me on the forehead. Two weeks later, on my birthday, I woke up and discovered she made clouds out of fairy lights on my ceiling.

That's Ivy. She teased me like all big sisters did, but when I needed her, she always knew what to do.

I dialed her on the off chance. Who knew? Maybe today was a day for forgiveness.

The dial tone rang and rang till the voice mail picked up. I didn't leave one. I had other calls to make.

No more stalling.

Ring. Ring.

"Hello?"

"Hey, Paris. Is now a good time?"

"For sure. What's up?"

"I was wondering if we could meet up tonight? Dinner at Sassafras on me."

"Oooh. Is this the big date to tell me you're into me? You're hot, Rainey D, but it takes a gear shift to rev this engine, if you know what I'm saying."

I snorted, braying an unattractive noise. "Not at all. You don't know much about cars, do you? That's not how that works. Don't guess what tonight is about. I promise you, you'll get it wrong."

"Mysterious, but I think I can guess. It's something to do with my brother, isn't it?"

"It's complicated. I'll tell you everything tonight. Are we good for eight o'clock?"

"Yeah, eight's fine. Do you want me to—"

The phone slipped out of my grip.

"Cancel that. Rainey's got plans tonight."

I flipped over, gaping up at Arsenio.

"Trust me," he said. "It can wait."

Arsenio hung up the phone and slipped it in his pocket.

Looking at him from that angle, I traveled up and up and up—skimming over his dips, curves, and bulges. Climbing his full lips. Sliding past his deep, unreadable eyes, and then getting lost in the halo of curls shining in the setting sun.

"—with me."

I started, coming back to reality. "What? Arsenio, give me my phone. You don't understand. I need to speak to Paris, it's important."

"Nothing is more important than what we have to do now. Don't argue. Get up and follow me."

He strode off, expecting me to follow. With my damn phone in his pocket, what else was I supposed to do?

I had to call Bella, Frankie, and Paris to tell them to meet me at the diner. Telling them all at once made more sense than wasting even more precious time running all over town.

"Arsenio." I raced to catch up to him. "This is serious. Give me my phone and then give me a ride while you're at it. I need to be at the diner at eight."

He stopped dead, pulling me up short. "Let me make something clear to you. The amusing back-and-forth you have with Cairo, you do not have with me. I told you two things. Do not argue and follow me."

I folded my arms. "Or?"

Arsenio looked around us, catching sight of all the people watching the perfect mayor's son. "I don't make threats," he said. "I don't give ultimatums or second chances. There is no or. You will come with me."

He leaned back, an amused glint lighting his eyes. "But not because you're afraid of me. You'll come"—he put his lips to my ear—"because you're curious."

Arsenio set off.

I stood there—determined to make a point, and damned if I knew what. Cursing, I chased after him.

"Will we be finished before eight?"

He narrowed on me.

"That wasn't arguing. I was asking a question."

To which I didn't receive a reply.

I blew out a breath. "Would it make a difference if I said this affects Paris's safety? She's your best friend's sister. I know you care about her."

"No. It makes no difference." He pointed to a vintage Chevrolet Corvette shaming every other car in the lot. "Get in."

Penning in my retort, I slid in the car. Why was I arguing with this guy? If I had to, I'd slip away when we got to wherever we were going.

I would be at that diner tonight. I had the short version of my torment under the Letter Man, proof to show the police, and four days to get them off their asses and arranging protection for three women and two children. If the Letter Man wasn't going to stop me protecting them, neither was Arsenio Creed.

"Where are we going?"

"Ever been to the Highland Arms?" he replied, surprising me.

"Old-fashioned Scottish pub on the other side of town. Never had a reason." I ran my fingers over the dash, swallowing what would've been an embarrassing sound. "1957, right?"

"That's right."

Was I imagining it, or did he sound the tiniest bit impressed?

"My gosh, I can't believe I'm sitting in this. This car is a work of art, Creed. It is an act of blasphemy to put a single scratch on it."

"On that, we agree," he said. "When I fuck you over the back of the seat, I expect you to be careful."

"Is that what you're whisking me away to do?"

"No. Highland Arms, like I said."

I eyed him. "Why haven't we...?" I trailed off, leaving him to pick up my meaning.

"You're not ready for me yet."

"What's that supposed to mean?"

"It means what I said." Arsenio looked me in the eye, traffic and all. "You're not ready."

A sensation went up my spine. Good or bad, I wasn't sure, but I believed him.

"When will I be ready?"

"When you obey without argument."

I shook my head, leaning into the leather. "Did Quinn hop, skip, and jump before you gave the order? Because looking at the girl who bitched you out today, I didn't get that impression. You guys don't actually want submissive women," I stated. "You want women who'll argue, and fight, and push back to make it more satisfying to break them. It's no fun punishing someone who just sits there and takes it."

"How would you know?"

He weaved in and out of traffic. Arsenio stayed under the posted speed limit, and still the engine revved and hummed, blissed for its day out.

"So that's what you want," I whispered. "Obedient. No fight. No struggle. I drop to my knees for master. I put my ass up when he demands. I spread my legs on his order. You want me when I'm broken in."

"Hmm. Interesting."

"What is?"

"Going by the dripping pussy I'm smelling from here, you want that too."

"I didn't say that."

"The first time I have you, I'll make you come all over these seats, then make you lick every inch clean." He could've been talking about the weather for all the inflection. "I'll walk you around town on your leash and fit you in vibrating panties. You'll sit at my feet like a good girl, not making a sound while I claim every drop for all of Bedlam to see."

"Arsenio." I squeezed my knees, pulling my borrowed hoodie lower. "Stop."

He tsked. "I thought you knew that wasn't how this worked. Open your legs."

I opened my mouth to argue. Arsenio flashed.

He pinched his fingers in my cheeks, hooking my open jaw. "Don't even think a refusal. Panties off. Now."

I didn't think a refusal. Wiggling my thong down my hips, I let it pool around my ankles.

"Feet up," he said. "Give me a reason to be... impatient."

The word poured like honey from his lips. My feet dug in the red leather. Letting my legs fall open, I was as exposed as the open-topped car.

"Ask me what else you want me to do to you."

What is happening?

We drove by the square, zipping around the lovely couples and families enjoying an evening stroll. The most wholesome picture, and Arsenio was getting me wet to slide me off this seat.

Why is this working? I am not the "yes, sir, no, sir" girl.

"What do I want you to do to me, Arsenio?" I asked, cheeks flaming. The Bedlam Boys were teaching me a lot about myself.

"You want me to put a glass of water on your back, and fuck you from behind. Every time you spill, that's longer I'll hold back your orgasm. You don't come until I say."

"Ah." I flicked my clit, nipples pebbling in their safe cocoon.

Arsenio stopped at a traffic light, which reminded me of the half dozen we had to go to get to the Arms.

"You think Cairo, Roan, and Jacques haven't shown you mercy? I'd have you drink from a real bowl. Ass up and butt plug tail wagging."

I jerked—an involuntary muscle contraction that drove my fingers deeper. Were butt plug tails a real thing? I was more curious to find out than I'd admit.

I don't have to. Arsenio isn't asking. He's telling.

"Faster," he ordered. "Four fingers."

Head falling back on the seat, I stretched my cunt to the limit. My face relaxed and I caught it, scrunching into a grimace. If the person in the car idling beside us looked over, she'd see a woman about to hurl, not a woman about to orgasm.

I picked up speed, soaking myself in my own arousal and skin tightening at the sound. I was getting turned on, from Arsenio turning me on.

"I told you to persuade me."

Shifting on the seat, I leaned on the door and faced him.

Arsenio was rock hard and desperate to replace these fingers with himself. Even so, I sensed the kind of patience in him that I wasn't familiar with.

He wouldn't touch me until I gave him exactly what he wanted. No compromises. No settling for a quickie on the couch. A man like this had to own me body, mind, soul, and body.

"I'm ready for you, Arsenio. You can have me anywhere and any way you want." I spread my folds, drawing his eye off the road and nearly killing us. "I'll be your faithful, obedient pet." My foot slid across the seat, seeking his crotch.

He shoved me back. "Not interested in a pet. These lapping dogs are on every street corner, begging to please the mayor's son."

"I'll be your whore." The words felt wrong coming out—because they came so easily. "I won't beg for it. I'll wait for you to give me whatever I deserve. Hurt me. Punish me. Spank me. Slap me," I moaned. "I'm yours, Arsenio. The girl you've been waiting for."

He made a noise low in his chest. "I'll find out."

I sensed I pleased him whether he'd admit it or not.

"Come."

The command was a second ahead of me. I came screaming, uncaring of the cars driving past, my head hanging dangerously out.

Arsenio curled around my wrist, and licked me clean one digit at a time. My skin heated all over again.

"Give me your thong."

I did. Arsenio stuffed it in his pocket without a word.

Sore-assed and bare-assed. My life was not this intriguing when I was just a farm girl chasing my feathered bobbleheads.

"What's at the Highland Arms?" I asked after a spell.

"A guy named Axel Verlice," he replied. "What have the guys told you about what we do?"

"They've told me exactly nothing. I've been going off the rumors I've heard over the years, and they aren't flattering."

"Then, this should be a treat."

"Are we collecting money from him? Cairo said during Ruckus that everyone in town pays you a cut."

"They do."

"And..." I chose my words carefully. "No one has complained to Mayor Creed?"

"I don't go on collection runs. They want to claim I'm involved, they better have proof. Why would my mother entertain anything less?"

I bobbed my head. "Why are we going to the Arms if you don't do collection runs?"

"Who said this was one?"

I stopped asking questions, because he might just answer me.

Why meeting Axel Verlice was the most important thing we had to do today—more important to Arsenio than Paris's safety—wasn't something I wanted to know. Heavens knew why he sought me, of all people, out and dragged me along. It didn't matter because the plan remained the same. Wait for a good time to duck out the door and not return until my friends were safe. When the truth came out about the shadow stalking Paris, the guys would understand. Some things were bigger than penance.

Like Redemption.

Arsenio was a handsome blur out of the corner of my eye. I avoided looking at him directly, half afraid he'd glance at me and see my escape plans written all over my face.

Another secret to hide: my conversation with Jeremy.

What if his father truly could give me the farm back all in exchange for the snippets of nonvital conversation they have in front of me? Could I really pass that up?

Another selfish choice made at their expense. Yes, I could pass that up, but not when it came to Gran. She wanted a de Souza on that farm till a meteor struck and ended the human race. If there was even the slightest chance Jeremy was writing up that contract, I wouldn't fail her again.

"Arsenio, did your spies tell you what happened in the library?"

His tone sharpened. "What happened?"

"One of the New Boys came to see me," I said. "Jeremy. He offered me a bribe to report on the Bedlam Boys for him."

"Makes sense. You are the only person he can hope to turn. I'd respect him even less than I already do if he hadn't approached you."

"That's not the reaction I was expecting." I fixed myself better, smarting up in the mirror as we neared the Highland. "I thought you'd be calling the guys to break his teeth."

"Did you agree to do it?"

"I told him to come back with a better offer. If he does, I'll agree and pass on whatever bullshit you guys tell me to."

"Hmm."

I was beginning to understand his grunts and hums. That was definitely pleased.

"You might be worth keeping around, de Souza."

"That was never in question." A sassy reply for a man who stood no back talk, but we covered that a meek little flower wasn't what the Bedlam Boys wanted.

His chuckle proved it.

"One more thing," I said. "You may want to hire someone else to clean the house. Or skip the cleaning services completely. Thirty-thousand-dollar bribes are pretty effective."

"Noted."

Arsenio turned on the street leading to the Highland, and drove past it. He parked in the lot for a restaurant movie theater and came around to open my door.

"The Highland is closed right now. Verlice shuts down every Tuesday for a private event. He'll be inside prepping."

"Is he expecting you?"

"I'm sure he is."

Arsenio took us in through the back. A cinder block wedged in the door, leaving it open for all looking to skip the breaking and entering charge. We came in by the kitchen entrance, stepping out into the main pub. The Highland Arms was a stately place with a long bar, red-topped stools, a wall of every kind of alcohol you could imagine on one side, and a parade of flags on the other.

"Nice place," I said.

"Yes, it is." Arsenio was a massive presence filling the room. That didn't make sense till you met a man who owned every space he walked in. It wouldn't make sense till you met Arsenio Creed. "That bottle of Macallan is worth two million dollars."

I choked. "Excuse me? Did you just say two *million*?"

He nodded.

The slim bottle with its simple white label hung around the rest on the whiskey shelf like it was no big deal.

"He has two million dollars behind the bar, and he just leaves the back door open? What kind of insurance nightmare is this guy?"

"He's counting on his patrons being too ignorant to know what they're looking at." His Oxfords were soundless on the hardwood, brushing past me. Arsenio slipped a finger under my shirt—the briefest touch burning through my skin and tingling after he went away. "The whole place is a fuck-you to the IRS. Even the walnut bar top set him back a good amount."

Glancing over my shoulder, I eyed the door we came in. Once Arsenio was absorbed in talking to this Axel guy, I'd duck out. I wasn't too far from Frankie's place. Once there, I'd called the other women to come meet me.

"Where is he?" I asked.

"Downstairs. Prepping for his guests like I said." Arsenio picked a pool cue off the rack. "Let's bring him up."

"Why do you need the—?"

Arsenio swung at the top shelf—Macallan sitting pretty—and busted the bottles in a shower of glass and alcohol. My scream was a squeak beneath the unholy noise.

"What's going on?!"

A middle-aged man with flecks of gray in his full beard burst from a door on the other side of the room. He ground to a halt—face frozen in horror at the millions lying in pieces on his bar top.

Arsenio tossed the pool cue on the floor, rolling up his sleeves as he rounded the stools.

"Good afternoon, Axel."

"What did you do?!"

"The more appropriate question is what did you do?"

I clamped a hand on my mouth, smothering my ragged breaths. This was not a friendly conversation. It was the start of something that was going to get very bad. I would not be a part of it. I was backing out of this room and leaving before either one remembered I was there.

Inching toward the door, I paused as Arsenio kept coming, planting himself in my way.

"I didn't do anything!" Verlice could be forgiven for his shouting. This was a stressful situation. "I paid on time. Ask Cairo, I paid."

"You paid our cut of the bar profits," he said. Arsenio hooked through my jeans, bringing me over to him. My heart raced being molded to his side, drowned in black currants and apple cologne.

Maybe he did read my mind.

"We got word you were running a side business and made plans to return for another visit to collect our back pay. That's until we found out what your side business is." The temperature dropped ten degrees. As fast as Verlice's expression.

He drew blank. "I don't know what you're talking about. I don't have a side business."

"You're stocking two-million-dollar whiskey from the unpaid tabs and five-dollar tips from guys stumbling in after a shift in the factory?" He tsked. "Why would you insult my intelligence, Verlice? How is that the wise move?"

Arsenio slipped under my shirt again, drawing circles on the small of my back. It was a highly distracting, intimate gesture that popped goose bumps on my flesh.

"I'm not insulting you, Mr. Creed. I'm simply suggesting there's been a mistake. I assure you my business is completely aboveboard." He gestured to the mess. "I had a wealthy uncle who passed. He willed those bottles to me. I sold a few. Put the rest on the shelf."

Arsenio bobbed his head. "A reasonable explanation."

"See." His relief was palpable. "Just a misunderstanding. Please, don't worry about the bottles. I'm insured. I—"

"Verlice, let me stop you while the hole is half dug. I know," Arsenio stated. "Everything. I know why you close this bar down every Tuesday. I know who's coming through that door after midnight, and why. If you stop playing games, we can skip the stuff we already know and move on to how you'll fix the problem. If so, I won't have to do what I came here to do.

"But you open your mouth and lie to me one more time, I'll be forced to spell out the entire horrible truth, and sully my girl's ears. This will upset her—which will upset me. I cannot be held responsible for my actions then."

"But I—"

"Think very carefully about what you say next."

Verlice's Adam's apple visibly bobbed. "Mr. Creed," he began, "I assure you I don't know what you're talking about. I don't have a side business. The party coming tonight are just a few friends of mine. We— We play poker, drink, and mess around in the basement." A strained, shaky laugh burst out of him. "Oh, I see. You're here because I haven't included my poker winnings in the payments. That was my mistake. I'll write you a check right now."

He crossed to the bar, pulling out a checkbook and pen. "Would two thousand cover it?"

I flicked to the pen. It shook on the paper.

Arsenio gave him a long look, stretching the silence till it pressed on us, and Verlice's hand shook harder under its weight.

"Three thousand?" he croaked, skin paling. "Or four— five thousand. Five thousand dollars is what I owe you." Verlice wrote the check and held it out. Arsenio didn't look at it.

"Shall I tell you the truth of the Tuesday Nighters, de Souza?"

I looked from him to Verlice. *If this was about poker games and goofing off with his buddies, he wouldn't be shitting his pants. This is not the look of an innocent man.*

"Yes," I said. "What really goes on tonight?"

"Axel Verlice and his precious bar are what some in the business call a way station."

"No. No, it's not true!"

"What's a way station?" I asked, ignoring him.

"Not all human traffickers have the benefit of owning docks and shipping yards to receive under cover. Those out here who are land-locked with the rest of us, rely on trucks, back roads, cabins, and safe places to stop—or way stations.

"Verlice here works for a particularly paranoid trafficker who de-mands his drivers make no stops other than gas and the one trip here on Tuesday nights to stock up on food and crash. The trafficker in question allows this, because Verlice is his brother."

"Lies," Verlice barked. "All lies! I have nothing to do with this!"

"It's a three-day drive from the pickup location to the drop-off, and his brother times it. If they're late, the driver is killed," Arsenio finished. "That's why they arrive at this bar and leave at the same time—"

"Every Tuesday," I finished.

"You must be wondering what Axel's stake is in this racket—be-sides the money." Arsenio dropped his hand, moving away from me. "While the driver is passed out, Axel takes a girl or two out of the truck, brings them down to his basement, and invites a few of his buddies to have a little fun."

"Oh my goodness." My stomach heaved. "Are there— Are there women trapped down there right now?!"

I took off running. Arsenio stopped me.

"No. There's no one down there, or a truck parked in the back," he said. "It's still a few hours out."

Sense returned to me, calming my heart rate. Of course, we came in the back. No one was there and the sun was still up.

"But what Verlice doesn't know is the truck isn't going to make it."

The disgusting old man's jowls quivered. "What? What are you talking about?"

"I'm talking about the tip the FBI received about a rig full of trapped, terrified young girls and the heavily armed man driving them across state lines," he said. "They'll be rolling up on his ass with extreme prejudice soon enough, but knowing the reputation of hardened human smugglers, he's not going to give up a detail about the operation without a fantastic deal."

"It'll be days—weeks—before the name Verlice comes up." Arsenio picked up the pool cue. "Which gives us plenty of time."

"Whoa, no, no, no, no," he cried. "There's no need for that. Tell me what you want. Money?" Verlice rushed out. "I've got a safe full downstairs. It's yours."

I backed toward the door. Leaving was the last thing on my mind.

Paris said his good-boy routine was an act. Meeting the company he kept assured me of that. But watching this despicable human being, who accepted the risk of his brother's business, cower and plead before a twenty-one-year-old man who smiled charming in the press photos...

What did Verlice know that I didn't?

"I'm not here for money." Arsenio moved slow, rounding the bar. "They don't send me for collections."

"You're right, of c-course." Buckets ran down his face and soaked his collar. "I'll cut you and the Bedlam Boys in on the business. I'll— I'll— I'll get you a girl," he stammered. "As many as you want. Free."

"Got one of those." Arsenio winked at me. "I'm not here for negotiations, Verlice. The Bedlam Boys sent out a clear message. No side businesses. No crime rackets. No bringing in unwanted attention from federal agencies. Can you imagine what would've happened if someone else unraveled this ill-conceived operation as easily as we did?

"They would've swarmed this place. Picked apart your financials. Interviewed people who'd remember seeing Cairo roll through here every Friday. You put us at risk."

"I'm sorry. I wasn't thinking. I—"

"Are you sorry? Honestly?"

His head almost popped off he nodded so hard. "I am. I'll go straight. I'll pay on time. I'll pay double! Nothing like this will ever happen again, Mr. Creed, I swear. I didn't think of the risk to you, or Mr. Sharpe, or the Bedlam Boys."

Arsenio leaned back, resting the cue across his shoulders. "Don't know why we accepted that name. I never did like being called a boy."

"Men," Verlice corrected. "Bedlam Men."

Sighing, Arsenio shook his head, lips pushed up. "You know what? Okay. You sound sincere, and everyone deserves a second chance, right?"

What? A second chance? This man is a monster in human skin!

Verlice's face slackened. "Yes," he breathed. "Please, give me another chance."

"Come on." Arsenio held out his arms. "Let's shake like gentlemen."

He took a step and halted.

"What's the matter?" Arsenio asked. "I give you another shot, and you won't even shake my hand?"

"Of course, I will." He hurried out from the bar and shook roughly. "Thank you, sir. Thank you so much. You won't regret this."

"I don't believe I will, but what do you think?" Arsenio turned Verlice to face me. "We can trust him, can't we? He'd never do something like this again."

Looking into those blue, shining eyes, I said, "No. We can't trust him."

"Yes, you can—"

"Shh." Arsenio clamped on his hand, wrapping the other around his neck. "The lady is speaking. Why do you say that, de Souza?"

A thousand visions flashed through my mind.

Gran. Sheriff Sharpe. Cavendish. The letters. Jennifer. Bella. Frankie. Paris.

"What did you and your friends do to those women?"

Verlice said nothing.

"Answer the question," Arsenio hissed.

"We— We didn't do anything." His eyes rolled in their sockets, searching for an escape. "I'm a way station, like he said. I give them a place to eat and sleep for the night. That's it."

And then it came. That perfect, clear moment of calm as the path reveals. My heart slowed. My skin cooled.

"He's lying," I spoke, but the voice wasn't mine. "Someone who can't admit what he's done, can hardly say he's sorry for it. He wants us to walk out of here so he can go running to his brother. They'll pack up their money and the women they have left, and set up their operations elsewhere."

"No! I won't. You've got it wrong," he said. "I've been wanting out for a long time. This is my chance. With the FBI on the truck, my brother can't deny it's getting too hot. He'll let me out."

"You want out?" I repeated.

"Yes."

"Your brother's been forcing you to continue all this time?"

He bobbed his head. "Yes."

I closed the distance between us. My gaze moved down to the bulge I noticed in his pocket. Slowly, I reached inside and pulled it out. The condom roll unfurled, smacking the floor.

"I'd say that's telling," Arsenio rang in the silence. "What do you say, de Souza? Do we forgive him?"

I opened my mouth. "No."

"No, wait—"

Arsenio wrenched, yanking his arm up his back.

Snap.

"Ahhh!"

His shout blew me off my feet. I stumbled back—calm moment disappearing. I can't say I truly understood what Arsenio came here to do. Rough him up. Scare him shitless. Take the bribe and walk away. I could've pictured any of those possibilities from the man I was coming to know, even if I couldn't know which one.

Arsenio threw him over the bar. Verlice crashed into the shelves, toppling them, and bringing the last of his stock down on him.

Now I knew, without a doubt in my soul, what Arsenio would do. What he always planned to do since he told me to get in the car.

Arsenio snatched up the pool cue. He was ready as Verlice crawled his way up, clinging to the bar top. He smashed the cue across his face, snapping his neck to the side.

Backing up, I slammed into the wall. I was right next to the way out. To say those two were preoccupied was an understatement. All I had to do was run.

"P-please," Verlice sobbed. "Stop."

Arsenio jumped over the bar.

"No!"

He brought the cue down over, and over, and over again.

"Stop! Help! Help me, please."

The man's cries didn't slow him. If anything, Arsenio's savagery increased.

"Arah!" he roared. The cue snapped and he did not stop.

My feet lifted, carrying me away... from the wall.

I came up behind Arsenio, peering over the top. A bloody, unrecognizable mass lay at his feet. I couldn't tell what was face from blood or from teeth.

"Ah—" His screams cut off, hands flopping on the ground.

Arsenio kept hitting. Once. Twice. Four times.

The cue broke.

Throwing away a piece, he held the remains in both hands, lifting it overhead.

"Arsen—"

He brought it down, impaling Axel Verlice through the stomach.

Arsenio turned his back on the body, looking into my wide eyes. He picked up a rag, wiping off his bloody hands.

"Verlice mentioned something about a safe," he said. "You empty the register. I'll clean it out."

I said nothing. Did nothing as he brushed past me.

Arsenio killed him.

The sentence went through my mind and would not stick. This didn't happen. None of this was real.

Arsenio blew in here like a capo dei capi, the boss of all crime bosses, and beat and impaled a man while I watched. No hesitation. No remorse.

Did the Bedlam Boys know this is what he came here to do?

"*I don't go on collection runs.*"

Who were these guys? I tied myself to them in bonds I didn't know how to break, and I never truly knew them at all.

I couldn't tell how long I'd been standing there. Long enough that Arsenio returned holding a duffel bag.

"Where's the money?"

Shaking his head, he pried open the register himself, piling more bills in the bag beside a corpse.

"Why?" I rasped. "Why did you bring me here?"

"It was a gift. I assumed you'd enjoy it."

"What? Why?"

He came to me, backing me into the wall. My breath stopped in my chest as he ran a light, bloodstained finger down my cheek. "You loved killing Cavendish. Felt the most intense, orgasmic high when you let loose that arrow. You know what it's like, de Souza.

"You're like me."

"I... didn't—"

"Shh," he crooned. His lips were soft on mine, scorching me with the tenderest of kisses. "You don't have to hide. Not with us. Think about why we spared you. It wasn't for sex. It wasn't because I like you with a leash around your neck.

"It's because we see you, Rainey."

"See me?" My voice was small.

"The real you. The you that you've hidden. Buried so deep you forgot she was there." Arsenio tipped my chin. Spots of blood dotted his forehead. "We could've let the sheriff lock you up, but what would've been the point? The system would've destroyed you, and make no mistake, Rainey de Souza, you are perfect."

I was shaking—trembling in his hold. "I am?"

"Well." He smirked. "Almost. You haven't been given what we have. The sweet, happy childhood with the chickens and piggies. Your real self wasn't nurtured the way it needed to be. Whereas my boys and I have had no shortage of people in our lives, happy to fuck us up.

"Cavendish was the first step. Survival brought out the real you. Killing him broke the seal. And now we'll do the rest."

Spellbound, I hung on his every word.

"We'll break you. Tear you. Rip you apart," he whispered. "We'll be your monsters, baby. Surviving us..." He lifted a shoulder. "Little things like giving a rapist and trafficker what he deserves, doesn't compare."

He kissed me.

"Go in the car and wait for me." He handed me my phone and keys. "Call Cairo and let him know it's done. Verlice's friends won't be here until midnight. Chances are they'll run off and the first person to report the body will be the chef. I'll make sure there's no trace of us left behind, and that we've got all the money in this place."

"Okay."

Arsenio kissed me again, and I melted into him, whimpering like a bitch in heat.

He sent me off alone, with my phone and the keys to his car. It didn't cross his mind that I would take off and run from the man who savagely beat another human being to death, then promised me he'd bring the same vicious cruelty out of me. At any cost.

Or more likely it did occur to him I might run, and he dismissed the thought as immediately as I did.

It's too late for me to run. It was too late by the time they surrounded me in the barn.

I was theirs.

I climbed in Arsenio's car, tilting my head to the setting sun. When the calm came, I let go and gave myself willingly, eyes falling shut.

My phone lay unused on my lap.

I wouldn't be calling Paris, Frankie, or Bella that night. Frankie's children would go to school in the morning safe and sound.

Why would I need to warn them? Why should I call the police and drag anyone else into my battle with the Letter Man?

I knew exactly what to do next.

Chapter Twelve

Arsenio arrived clean-faced and seemingly normal, if not for the damp stains on his black shirt. He got in and reached for his keys.

"Arsenio," I began. "Will you let me stay? Paris can come pick me up."

"No."

"Please." I chanced stroking his arm. "It's important."

"If someone is threatening her, they won't live long enough to understand the mistake they made. Give me their name. We'll handle it."

He started the car.

"I lied," I told him. "I said it was about Paris, but it's about me."

"Meaning?"

"I was a virgin before Cairo decided I needed a change in status. I wasn't on birth control. Our relationship is between the six of us. I'm not ready for us to become seven. Are you?"

He flicked to my stomach, gazing at it with an expression I couldn't read.

"If you're pregnant, we'll do right by our kid."

My chest thumped at *our kid*.

"I appreciate that. I really do, but if I'm not pregnant, then it's past time to be responsible. I'm not far from the doctor's office, and I'd prefer to do this alone. Paris can drop me home after."

Arsenio gave me a long, studying look. He was a guy who wanted his yeses and nos obeyed without question. I also assumed he was a guy who wasn't looking to be fitted with a baby carrier in the next nine months.

He nodded.

Not wishing to test him, I hopped out and closed the door without another word. His car blew off, leaving me in the parking lot.

Naturally, everything I told him was more bullshit. I'd been on the pill since I was thirteen for acne and to regulate my periods. We were good on that particular front—except for the wild thoughts Arsenio put in my head at the mention of our kid. I called him a stunning collection of ethnicities in one handsome man. What would our baby look like? Would she or he do what I couldn't? Soften the beast.

I shook my head, chasing the pictures away. It was more than likely the Letter Man, or even the Bedlam Boys, would destroy me before I got to my picket-fence dreams. Time to do something about that.

I crossed the street, passing one bus stop and continuing seven more blocks to the right one. Frankie would drive up in about fifteen minutes. There was something I needed from home.

"THANKS, FRANKIE. ARE you sure you don't mind waiting?"

"Nah. You're fine. I don't pick up many people at this time, and those I do can wait."

Who could question why I'd do anything to protect this woman?

Even so, I didn't test her flexibility. I hopped the fence and ran all the way to the farmhouse. I didn't bother with Cruella's new lock. The Letter Man hadn't left a new one in the box. Just as well, because I had one for him.

Tearing a notepad and his last letter from my bag, I wrote two words on a blank piece of paper.

Axel Verlice

I couldn't believe that morning I mourned fate. The Bedlam Boys unwittingly gave me the perfect opportunity to kill Scott Cavendish and shift the blame away from me. I told myself another chance wouldn't be served up on a silver platter.

I'd never doubt them again. They were brought into my life to restore me. Fate had not let me down, neither would they.

I slipped the note in the black envelope and listened to the soft *ting* of the letter falling in the mailbox.

Crossing to the pen, I stuffed myself through the loose slats and breathed relief at the sight of my trunk waiting for me in the loft. Cruella removed everything that made the farm livable. But what was I going to do with a bunch of bows and arrows?

Nothing, I thought as I picked through my collection. I didn't need my bow, and a single arrow would do.

I held a small, tapered arrow in the light.

Perfect.

Frankie waited for me as promised. I stepped up, moving carefully due to the arrow secured by my bra.

"All set?" she asked.

"All set."

She dropped me off on the same street she picked me up. "Have fun with your friends. Girls' night out is exactly what you need."

"It is. Next time, it's you and me. We'll swing by your ex-husband and key 'cheating bastard' on his hood."

Frankie snorted. "Don't tempt me."

She honked off. Her bus disappeared around the corner, sending me in the opposite direction.

Highland Arms stood dark and empty for my arrival. No, for the arrival of the Tuesday Nighters. It made me sick to think of what those men did to helpless, terrified women week after week.

I went in through the back door—held open by the cinder block. Just as we found it.

Arsenio said this was my treat. The satisfaction I got from stopping Scott Cavendish hurting another person replicated in seeing another vile monster taken out.

It was a smoke screen, of course.

Fill my head with pretty, hypnotic words that he may mean, but ultimately had nothing to do with why he came.

Cairo got a call that morning at breakfast.

From who?

All the Bedlam Boys were sitting around the table, so who let them know there was a problem, and how many times has Arsenio gone out to deal with it?

I approached Axel's body, tiptoeing around congealing blood.

I didn't touch the broken pool cue stuck in his stomach. Arsenio stayed behind to wipe away our presence. Let me not make his work harder.

I wouldn't have come back at all if it wasn't for the Letter Man's request that I use an arrow again. I didn't know who they were, or how the information would get back to them, but when it did, there would be no doubt Rainey de Souza was here. He'd lose his excuse to put his filthy hands on my friends.

Breathing through my nose, I summoned the strength and plunged my arrow through his heart.

"You're a sad excuse for a human being, Axel Verlice. I genuinely hope there is a hell, so you will spend an eternity burning in it. But let this bring you some comfort during your millennia of torment, your death just saved three women and two sweet kids—which is better than you achieved in your entire miserable life."

Not sure where I got this habit of speaking to the dead, but my final words were the best place to leave it as I walked out and left Axel for someone's early morning surprise.

PARIS PICKED ME UP on a street corner miles away from the Highland Arms. Zara, Amy, Elise, and Presley claimed all the seats.

"Sorry, Rainey, you'll have to pick a lap," Paris said. "We were on our way to dinner when you called. How do you feel about tacos?"

"I'm having a love affair with tacos, and if they're cheating on me with you, I'll be so pissed."

They cracked up.

"I told you," Paris said. "I love this girl."

"Got your car back." I slid onto Amy's lap. It suddenly occurred to me my panties were still in Arsenio's pocket.

"Yep, and when I find the person who rear-ended me and took off, I'll kill them. They cost me six hundred dollars and a lecture about going to Ruckus Royale from my dad."

"Worse things happened that night than a ding in your ride," Elise said. "A man was murdered right in front of us."

"I know," Paris said. "I'm not trying to be insensitive. It's just Dad is using the whole thing as another excuse to warn me off Cairo. He won't say it, but I think he actually believes my brother could do this."

Axel lying dead on the floor crossed my mind. *I think your brother could do a lot of things. But this one was on me.*

"I'm sure he doesn't," Amy said. "Those two have never gotten along, but he knows Cairo isn't a killer." I felt her shiver. "It is scary that whoever did it is still out there. Can you imagine what a sick, twisted psycho you have to be to kill someone that way? A bullet to the head wouldn't do? How about smothering him or cutting his throat?"

"Ugh, Amy, please," Zara whined. "Can we not?"

"Sorry. I'm just saying. Burning him alive? I can't think of a more evil, cruel way to kill someone. They gave Scott Cavendish the worst death imaginable."

I leaned back, resting my head on her shoulder. Amy wrapped her arms around me—snuggling the cruel, evil, twisted psycho.

"Amy's right," Elise said. "I didn't sleep for a week. And don't get me started on Jennifer. She goes to Bedlam U too, and some guy snatched her right from the parking lot. I sent you all that link to buy pepper spray. I'm not kidding, get some."

"Guys, can we talk about something else?" Presley asked. "Like the photo Kingsley sent me this morning of our new friend Rainey riding Cairo's lap with a collar on her neck."

"What?" half the car squealed.

"Uh. Let's go back to the sicko stalking the streets," I said.

"Nope. Uh-uh." They hooted, hollered, and tickled me breathless.

"All right, all right," I cried. "Mercy."

"What's the deal with you guys?" Amy asked.

I shot a side look at Paris. If our conversation at the Highland was anything to go by, the Bedlam Boys weren't giving up their new pet anytime soon. I couldn't have Paris spending the whole time convinced I needed to be rescued.

"It started off rough," I admitted. "To be fair, it's still a bit rough. But I'm their girl now."

"Are you serious?"

"You are?"

The last came from Paris.

"Yeah, I am," I told her.

I caught the face she made in the rearview.

"Are you okay with this?"

"Are you?" she tossed back. "I've seen them and *their girls* over the last couple years. They're not exactly boyfriends of the year."

"They're different with me."

"Um," Zara drew out. "They put you on a leash and walked you around campus like a dog."

"I didn't say they were different in a sweet way."

"Guys, let's lay off her," Amy said. "I dated a guy for three months who liked giving me head during my period."

"Oh my gosh, Amy," Presley screamed over us acting up. "Did we need to know that?"

"I'm just saying," she replied, laughing. "Human sexuality is craaaaa-zy. Maybe the whole collar and leash thing is foreplay for them."

"Paris," I said. "Could you speed up? When I jump out of the car, I want to make sure I die."

They fell out.

"We're just messing with you," Elise said. "We'll share our kinks too. I love a good, manly armpit."

My brows blew up my forehead. "We talking the hair or the smell?"

The conversation devolved from there. I don't think I laughed that hard in years. Correction: I have *not* laughed that hard in over two years.

Growing up, my best friend was Ivy. We kept farmer's hours, so while everyone was in school, we were helping Gran, then all the kids got home, and our butts were at the kitchen table for our lessons. Other than the children of other farmers in the area, it was just us. Those farmers and their kids slowly packed up and moved out by the time the bank came for the last farm standing—mine.

The point was, I never had this. Just us girls laughing and goofing off over tacos. I didn't think it was a life I wanted, or could even have, until now.

"Seriously, Rainey. We want to know everything, and we want to know it now."

I gave her big eyes with a mouthful of taco. Paris brought us to a dive bar named Joe's and swore up, down, and sideways that we were about to have the best tacos we'd ever eaten. Damned if she didn't undersell it.

Presley held up her hands. "Stop me when I'm there. How big is Cairo's dick?"

"Yuck." Paris shoved her arm, nearly knocking the girl to the floor.

"I'll take Legend, Roan, Jacques, or Arsenio too."

I shook my head. "You ladies are a pack of stone-cold weirdos, and I love it."

"That's us," Zara agreed.

Joe's wasn't packed on a Tuesday night. A few guys lined the bar, watching a game and nursing mugs of beer. In the corner was a sweet couple feeding each other onion rings. Otherwise, it was us.

Elise dropped her voice. "Speaking of stone-cold hotties—"

"I said weirdos."

"But you meant hotties," she said. "Anyway, I didn't get a chance to tell you I hooked up with one of those Crow guys last weekend, Jonah. It was insane."

Paris nudged my arm. "Bathroom break. Come with me."

She wasn't asking, so I got up and followed her.

We squeezed in the two-stall ladies' room. I hopped up on the counter, bracing myself for the talk ahead.

"I don't want to hassle you," Paris said from the stall. "If you're happy with my brother and his friends, then I'm happy for you. You're supercool and Cairo's lucky to be with you."

"Thank you," I said. *Now for the but.*

"But what you said in the car isn't what you said to me. You told me they were holding something over you. If you guys worked it out, awesome. But if you're trapped and they're doing all that shit to humiliate you." The stall banged open. "Give them hell. I say this as his loving sister. Kick. Their. Fucking. Asses."

I smiled. "I hope your mom doesn't have more kids lurking around, 'cause I'm two for two crushing on the ones she's got."

"I know, sweets." She swaggered to the sink, winking like she had something in her eyes. "But it's not meant to be for us. I'm a health foods girl."

"What does that mean?"

"Bananas over donuts."

"Nice." We high-fived. "Your innuendos are both amazing and terrible. I have so much to learn from you."

We headed out, weaving around the tables for ours.

"—going this weekend? The Crows are renting a house on Bay Avenue," we heard Elise say. "Beer, weed, drugs, Jonah. They said the party's going to be bigger than Ruck—"

"Party?"

All eyes flew to Paris. They did not look innocent.

"What party?" Paris repeated.

"Jeremy and his friends are throwing a party this weekend," Amy said.

"Oh, it's Jeremy now, is it? The same guy who crashed Ruckus Royale and stabbed a man for no reason."

"Listen," Elise said, pulling her down. "Jonah explained everything. Rumors about the Bedlam Boys spread outside this town. The Crows knew when they transferred here, our guys would try to make them their bitches, so they came up with a plan to prove how big and bad they were at Ruckus in front of everyone. Show the Bedlam Boys they're not to be messed with.

"Jonah admits they went too far. Jeremy even sent Cavendish's girlfriend flowers and an apology before she... you know."

"Still," I spoke up. "They didn't prove they were tough by going after the Bedlam Boys directly. They went after people who were tied up and defenseless."

"And I heard they're the main suspects in Cavendish's murder," Amy added. "The Bedlam Boys can't make anyone their bitch from jail."

"No," Elise said. Her golden-brown bob danced with her head-shake. "They definitely didn't do it. Plus, look how hard it is for Paris and her mom dealing with the nasty rumors and suspicion toward Cairo. We shouldn't point the fingers at people until we know all the facts."

Flashing a polite smile, I nodded. *Damn, this girl is far gone.*

"You're right," I said. "We don't know them. Also, there's no proof they knew Cavendish. But, there is proof they're gunning hard for the Bedlam Boys. What's that about?"

She shrugged. "Nothing. I guess they were used to running things in Hunter's Crest. You're a farmer, you know what happens when alpha males get in the same pen."

"Yeah. Someone gets hurt."

That hung in the air, making everyone uncomfortable.

"That's reason enough for us to go," Zara tried. "Cairo is Paris's brother. If they're planning to *overthrow the kings*, we need to know."

"Infiltrating," Amy said. "I like it. Paris, what do you think?"

"The party's on my street. I have to go. If they are trying to fuck with the sons of the sheriff, mayor, judge, and dean, then I have to meet the stupidest guys on the planet."

"I'll second that," I said.

Elise put up her hands. "All I heard is you guys are going to come. Trust me, the Crows aren't what you think." She winked at me. "And if I tap Rainey's mojo, I'll get all of them riding my ass at the same time."

The conversation turned once again.

I laughed along with everyone, skating over details about me and the guys. In the back of my head, my conversation with Jeremy played on repeat.

Whatever these guys wanted, they weren't buying farms and sending flowers because they wanted to be the biggest boys in the sandbox.

Verlice. The Bedlam Boys. The New Boys. Cavendish. The Letter Man.

No one in this town was what they seemed.

ROAN

Me: I like it freaky. Dirtier the better. Hope that doesn't scare you.

CBP: Why would it? I like it freaky too.

Me: I don't think you can handle me.

CBP: Try me.

Me: You'll try me. Cover my cock in whipped cream and chocolate sauce, then lick every inch of me till I shoot that special topping in your whore mouth.

Half a dozen dick pics hit my phone.

CBP: What else are you going to do to me?

Me: You first. What are you going to do to me? And remember, dirty. Filthy. Nasty. You can't make me blush.

CBP: It's a bet.

"Roan."

I peeked over my phone. "Legend."

"What do you want to drink?"

"Lemonade."

I tucked my cell away. CBP was Cute, Butt, Plaything. What I thought of him and how I saw him in three easy words. I didn't put it in initials to save myself. If Legend saw these texts, he'd whip my ass raw.

I shifted on the grass, cock stiffening. *Probably why I'm not trying too hard to hide them.*

The lovely Rainey returned, loaded down with our drinks. That morning, we skipped bagels on the terrace and stretched out on Homer Green, enjoying the wide berth and private patch our presence afforded us.

It was Friday, the start of the weekend, and I had plenty of plans for it. Legend probably had plans too. Jeremy refused to get on his knees and beg for his brother, who ended up rolling into town ten hours later, as promised. Not the satisfying conclusion Legend wanted. I can only imagine what he'd think of next.

Rainey passed me my lemonade. "Anything else I can get you, lieges?"

"That sounded sarcastic," Cairo said.

Jacques confirmed it with a "Three."

"Pets fetch, Rain. Don't reject your natural function in life."

"Pets also sit," she said. "My feet are killing me in these heels."

"Take them off," Legend said.

She tugged them off and reached for Legend, making to sit on his lap. He held her back.

"Not yet, gorgeous. I like a show with my Americano. Last night, Nicki XXX introduced me to naked yoga. I think we'd all love to see you give it a go, wouldn't we, gentlemen?"

We nodded, murmuring agreement.

"You want me to get naked and stretch on the green?"

Legend gave her a long, smirking look.

"No," he finally said. "You can keep the clothes on. No one gets to have that picture in their spank bank but us. Turn around and give me downward facing dog. I like the sound of that one."

Rainey's fingers dug into her hips. I couldn't say for sure what she was picturing looking at that smirk, stormy eyes thundering, but I had a feeling if she acted on it, Jacques would hit the double digits.

She must've had the same feeling. Rainey turned in her short, velvet green dress with strings where the back should be. She complained about her clothes, but Legend didn't shortchange the woman.

Each outfit molded to her body. They accentuated her best features—her tits and that ass—and revealed what her endless collection of jeans tried to hide. A pair of perfect, tan legs that gripped as she bucked on top of me, spilling my blood.

Rainey bent at the waist, dropping her palms on the grass. I was inching for my phone and suddenly forgot why.

"Cobra pose," Legend said.

She dropped on the ground, lying flat on her stomach, then pushing up on her arms. Her hair cascaded down her shoulders—catching the sunlight and tossing it back. Rainey de Souza was an incredibly beautiful woman, and that she didn't know was evident by the fact she didn't stop and admire herself in every reflective surface she passed.

That's what happens when you spend your life in muddy overalls and the closest thing you have to a boyfriend is the goat that keeps headbutting you in the crotch.

Cairo's hatred of all things that reminded him of her farm days made a lot more sense.

"My turn," I said. "Happy baby."

She pinked. "At home."

"I say now."

"I say at home."

"Four," Jacques chimed in.

"I'm not doing that pose while wearing a napkin and a thong," Rainey said. "Ask me to again, and I'll give you a number."

The guys got quiet. Jacques didn't even say five.

"Is that right?" I sat up, draping my arm over my knee. "Don't leave me in suspense, baby. What happens if I get a number?"

"Thirteen."

My brows drew together.

"That's how many letters are in my name," she said, smile curling those sinful lips. "Where's your knife?"

My boy wasn't twitching anymore. He stood ramrod straight, pitching his flag smack on Homer Green.

"Just to be clear," I began. "Are you threatening to carve your name in my skin if I continue demanding you flash your ass to all of Bedlam University?"

She rose up, shifting into puppy dog stretch on her own. "Not much of a deterrent when it comes to you, Roan Banks," she purred. "But a girl's still got to let you know who's in charge."

I knocked my lemonade over getting up. "Come with me."

"I have class in twenty minutes."

"No, you don't."

"Ugh."

Quinn blocked my path as I turned to go, Rainey hanging under my arm like a saddlebag.

"You dumped me for that flat ass?" she scoffed. "Big mistake."

A comeback was on the tip of my lips. Something to do with the real order of events, and that included her panting moans while she jumped on my cock, they were so vomit-inducing we had to dump her before I got dangerously underweight.

I set Rainey on her feet, looking past Quinn to the guys two steps behind her.

"Unless you're into flat asses now." Quinn reinserted herself in my way. "To go with the blood fetish. And the cum fetish. And the sweat fetish. Did I ever tell anyone you got off on licking my armpits?" she half bellowed.

Quinn laughed. "Oops. Guess I did now."

"This," I said as the Crows fanned out around her, "is unwise."

"What's wrong?" Jeremy asked.

Their group wasn't six.

Students followed behind, broke off from their path, or dropped their footballs. Legend grasped Rainey's shoulder, guiding her behind us. That wasn't good.

It meant a fight was coming.

"Roan liked to let me put a saddle on and ride him around the living room," Quinn went on. "He's a freak, but that's nothing on Arsenio. He—"

"Junior year," Cairo said. "Dallas away game."

Quinn's grin melted away.

"Say another word. Open your mouth one more fucking time, and everyone learns that secret."

She didn't utter a sound.

"Hey." Jeremy pulled her close, kissing those pinched lips. "Back off my girlfriend. For fuck's sake, you guys can't take a joke. We get into a little argument, I don't fall for your prank with my brother, and now you are pouting out here, refusing to eat on the terrace. Would Bedlam Babies be a more fitting title?"

A few people snickered.

My eyes narrowed, searching them out. It was difficult. The crowd was getting thicker.

I lit on a vaguely familiar face. He forced through the crowd, hopping on a pair of crutches. Alphonso planted himself between Gael and Micah.

His bruises were in various stages of healing, and the colors did nothing to improve that once vaguely handsome face. His glare tried to burn a hole through me. I slid off him too fast for him to make an impact.

He should thank us for going easy on him.

"Our mistake," Arsenio said. "We came out here to get some fresh air, enjoy some peace and quiet, get a break from your constant chest pounding. If we'd known you'd get pouty and cry about it, we'd have been there first thing to give you attention."

I laughed out loud at Jeremy's snarl. Why? 'Cause it's what I do. What kind of idiot defuses a situation when it's just getting good?

"I was pouty 'cause we had to go all over tracking you down, just to tell you the good news." He clapped Micah on the back. "Why don't you do the honors?"

Micah squared up to Legend. "You're done. The people have spoken and Bedlam is no longer now or forever. So where does that leave the *Bedlam* Boys? Turns out most of the young voters in Bedlam tend to stick around since such a prestigious university offers them cheap tuition just for being a resident."

"Another little factoid," Jeremy picked up. "These young voters have gotten to know you and your methods very well, and they're not fans."

"Steals from my dad's business every week," someone shouted.

"Fucker beat my brother for being disrespectful!"

"The bitch boy deserved it," I called back.

"Roan," Rainey hissed. "Curb your natural instincts."

I chuckled. *She's starting to know me too well.*

Truth was, it didn't matter if this mob ended the way we were headed. Every single person in this crowd would regret this. Even if it wasn't us doling out the punishment. They had no idea the war they were about to start.

"They don't want you anymore," Gael said. "They don't want Bedlam, if this is what it means to live here. Getting rid of one group of tyrants only for another to take their place."

Jeremy grinned. "A wind's coming, baby, and it's sweeping your hick town away. Or at least the half that's reverting back to Crystal Canyon." He held out his hands. "We got the votes. We got the town. We've got you.

"Hey, Jonah," he stage-whispered. "How long did we bet we'd take over?"

"Gave it a month."

"I was being generous."

Cairo cast a look over his shoulder. "Rain, excuse yourself."

"Why?"

"Because I think he's going to keep talking."

Jeremy laughed, gesturing to us and yukking it up with his Crows. "So what if I do keep—"

Cairo punched him in the throat.

You'd have thought the guy would've learned to block that move by now.

Jeremy flew back and rebounded fast. Wheezing, he swung wildly, taking out a bystander to get to Cairo. Alphonso was already there, smashing Cairo over the shoulder with his crutch.

I ripped it from his hands and swept his bad leg. He went down under the mob surging at us.

They came from everywhere. Punching. Kicking. Fighting for our side and against. They trapped us in.

Quinn launched at Rainey. "Manure-stinkin' slut!" She tangled in her hair, wrenching a scream out of her.

Rainey seized the hand holding her, locking Quinn still, and smashed her fist in her nose. Blood spurted on her knuckles—the last thing I saw before five people were between us, pushing and shoving us apart.

A blow rocked my side, knocking me into Arsenio. I straightened for Gael's barreling charge, shoulder dropped to run me through.

I snapped to the side, shoving Arsenio back. Gael crashed into the guy coming after him. The crunch of bone on bone reverberated through my skeleton.

The crowd shifted. Bodies crushing. Shouts and screams banging in my ears. Arsenio was gone in the time it took to turn around.

I saw a punch headed my way and spun to meet it. Fist raised, the red mist cleared on Micah.

We jerked to a stop.

Micah dropped his arm and shoved through the bodies. I glanced around wondering if anyone noticed.

Movement shifted out of the corner of my eye.

I twisted, spotting the glint of metal. Time slowed.

Heart thumping in my ear, I moved between beats, throwing up a block. The blade glanced across my arm, slicing the skin, jolting the chest strike wide.

Bang!

A gunshot ripped through the noise.

"That's enough!"

Students scattered in every direction. The red sleeve covering the arm of my would-be killer flashed through the bodies.

"On the ground! Everybody, on the ground!"

Clutching my arm, I ran after them, forcing my way through. Someone shot in front of me. I collided into a hard chest.

"Mr. Banks," barked my mother's head of university security. "Inside, sir. Now."

There was no point fighting him or the three others who grabbed and ran me inside. No red sleeve. No glimpse of the hooked nose that stuck out from under their hood.

They were gone.

RAINEY

The earth rumbled beneath me.

Images blinked on and off. Swirling clouds. My bare feet skimming the grass. Polished shoes crunching in the gravel.

I peeled my eyes open, gazing into a sea of black. Pain flooded my senses. Giving over, I surrendered to the dark, falling far from pain's reach.

"... you're still..."

A voice floated through the haze.

"... goddess..."

Light pierced my lids. My vision cleared on the forest floor, watching my fingers sway to meet it.

My body was heavy—separate from me. I called my hands to move. My legs to carry me. My lips to open.

"... worship you."

The world spun and gentle arms set me down. Clouds came to blanket me, shielding the sun as a shadow passed over my eyes. Its soft presence drew on my lids, closing them.

Sending me back.

I JOLTED AWAKE.

What happened? How did I get here?

The last thing I remembered was the New Boys surrounding us.

Quinn came after me. She tried to rip my hair out of my head and got a broken nose for her trouble. People who didn't know farm girls, made fun of them. Those with sense, figured out a lifetime wrestling with stubborn goats, hammering posts, and working in the fields left you more than prepared for a fight.

She and I grappled on the ground and then... then...

Then someone fell on us. A jolt of pain pierced the memory, bringing it back in stark clarity.

Two guys were fighting and didn't see us. They tripped, coming down hard, and knocked the wind from me. A bloody Quinn was carried off by a friend who rescued her.

Then someone came for me.

Hands lifted me up. I made to shake free of them, and a tiny pinch pricked my arm.

I lifted my hand to see and something fluttered to the ground. Sitting up, my gaze fell on the single black letter lying on the grass. I wished that was the only thing beside me.

I swept around—a thick, sludgy horror crawled across my skin.

The sun was setting on Black Widow Hill, and its only two constant visitors. They had placed me on top of the unmarked grave, framed in a circle of white roses.

My stomach rebelled.

Pitching forward, I vomited in the grass—heaving and heaving past the point I had anything left.

He had me. He touched me! He took me!

The Letter Man took me with such terrifying ease. Under the eyes of dozens of people. Then he laid me on top of my closest-held secret.

I was stripped bare. Exposed. I felt his eyes on me through the trees, and for all I knew, that's where he was. Watching.

Waiting.

I scurried out of the flower ring. Getting to my feet, I scanned the tree line for a hint of movement—so much as the swaying branches.

If he wanted to hurt you, he had hours to do it. Sense cleared my hazy mind. *That's not why you were brought here.*

Looking down, I fell on the letter.

Slowly, I picked it up and broke the seal. A single white card lay inside.

Choosing Verlice was delicious irony, but then I never much liked the man.

I'm proud of you.

For a moment, I thought you were truly gone. That wonderful, wild creature destined to destroy Bedlam in her fire.

I believed guilt and conscience destroyed you. I should've had more faith. As you need to now.

One cannot understand the pure, righteous spirit of sacrifice until they are forced to make one. I have given you a gift. You have given me hope.

You're ready.

It is finally time for us. I will send the time and place of our first meeting.

Stay psycho,

Love you. XOXO

"THANKS FOR LETTING me stay."

"You didn't even have to ask." Paris skipped into the room. Both arms were loaded down with DVDs, a remote, a bag of popcorn, and two soda cans balancing dangerously on top of it all. "We've been planning this Doctor Who night for forever." She lost her smile. "I wish it didn't have to happen this way though."

I helped her lay out the stuff on the pink ottoman at the foot of her bed. I had to make room among the muffins, cookies, and chips. I pegged her as trying to cheer me up.

I needed it even though she didn't know the full reason why.

After leaving the hill, I waited for Frankie at my stop. I thought of going back to campus. Where he walked the grounds, waiting for the perfect time to steal me away.

I tried to get off at the stop and my feet wouldn't move. Frankie closed the doors and set off again. The next time they opened, I was a ten-minute walk from Bay Avenue.

The gate guy called Paris. Her voice sounded through the speakers and my ability to lie deserted me. I told her flat out someone grabbed me during the brawl and dumped me in the woods. I told Cairo the same thing.

"They're dead," he growled. "It was the Crows. They took you like Legend did that long-haired bastard. They wanted us going mad searching for you."

My pulse picked up at the thought me going missing would've driven them mad.

"Are you guys okay?"

"We're fine," he replied. "Roan was stabbed. He didn't see who did it."

"What?" I cried.

"Stay there. We'll get you in the morning."

Thus our conversation was over, but at least the guys didn't think I ran off and ditched them at the first sign of trouble.

"And this is trouble," I muttered. "Do you think it's true, Paris? Do the New Boys have enough support to chop our town into pieces?"

"I still don't understand what happened today." She bent next to the DVD player, flipping through discs. "I've been getting texts all day, telling me fifty different versions. All I know is from the last two years I've spent studying government, nothing is ever that easy. Jeremy and his buddies can whip those cowards into a mob. Doesn't mean he can get them all into the voting booth."

"That's true."

"The only thing he accomplished today," Paris said, "was pissing my brother and his friends off. They're going to regret that."

She dropped the statement as a fact of life.

"They will strike back, and when they do, they'll crush any resistance under their boot."

"Geez," I breathed. "Did you not scare yourself saying that?"

Paris's gaze grew out of focus. "They can't have Bedlam, Rainey. No one can."

"They won't. I'm sure it's like you said. Mob mentality is easy. Critical thinking about the future of this town, isn't as easy to control."

Paris shook herself. Her bright smile returned. "Bet your ass it's not. So, which Doctor are we feeling? Nine, ten, or eleven."

"Ninth for sure." I picked her phone off the nightstand. "Do you mind if I make one more call?"

She waved me on. "Go for it."

I went into the bathroom, locking the door behind me. I did have to make a call, but it was the letter I pulled out, not the phone.

I read it too many times to count since racing from the woods and climbing on the bus with Frankie. Backward and forward, it didn't make sense to me. If not for the standard sign-off, I'd have thought the letter was written by someone else.

The way they wrote to me, the message was almost... tender.

The Letter Man spoke like all of this had been a coming-of-age ritual and I'd finally proven myself to him. The trials were over, now for celebration.

It is finally time for us.

I hugged myself, rubbing my arms. Sitting on the hill among the roses that were my altar, a terrible feeling sunk into my bones and forced me to purge bile.

What if the Letter Man did not hate me at all? What if it was just the opposite?

But that was not the case for Cavendish. That man hated me only slightly more than he hated himself, and I'd have said the same about his friend before I received this letter.

I "killed" Verlice. I proved I was willing to sacrifice with the ultimate sin to protect my friends. Was this what they wanted all along? Is it over now?

I tossed my head, pacing the length of the bathroom. If that was it, why didn't it end with Cavendish? Why did Letter Man 2.0 come for me like I murdered his best friend, and then suddenly do a one-eighty? Why take the risk and snatch me off campus? Why bring me to Black Widow Hill and place me on the grave? How did they know about it?

Groaning, I slid down the wall. All those questions in my head, there was one rising above.

Would their next letter be a time and place to meet them, and would I go if it was?

He thought I was ignoring him and he sent me notes even more deranged than the last. Threatening me, my friends, and my secrets. If I didn't show up, what would stop him sending a tip to the police about the body? Why wouldn't he direct Sheriff Jack to Cavendish's killer?

Am I willing to die for my secrets? I could show up and be gifted an arrow in my heart.

Or you could show up and gift one in his.

I raised my head from my hands, gazing at the letter. My choices were simple, weren't they? They were what they had always been.

One: Involve the police and have them meet the Letter Man in my place.

Two: Ignore the request to meet and endure the wave of violence he'll swear to unleash on the few people I have left.

Three: End this menace over my life once and for all.

The police were never truly an option. At least not any officers that were Sheriff Jack or worked under him. For Paris, Frankie, and Bella, I could risk his involvement. Their safety was bigger than me. But for me, the last place I'd put my safety is in his hands.

To ignore the Letter Man was to continue in this endless cycle. He'd prey on all of Bedlam while I remained ten steps behind a phantom.

Doesn't that leave the only option I ever had?

I could confront him. I'd find out why they chose me, and I wouldn't arrive unarmed. I'd have my bow aimed at them the entire time. It was a certainty they couldn't strike before I did. There was only one problem with this option.

I couldn't kill again.

"Ahh," I cried, tears dripping down my face.

"Rainey? You okay?"

"I'm fine."

I tore off some toilet paper. My revenge fantasies were just that. The thought of actually making that decision again—of releasing that string and falling into the calm place. Righteous fury made me a victim.

Enjoyment made me a monster.

I picked up Paris's phone and dialed Ivy's number. Whenever I needed her, she was there. She had to sense I needed her more than ever.

The call rang and rang.

Giving up, I pulled the cell away.

"Rainey?"

"Ivy?" I straightened, banging my head on the wall and barely noticing. "Is that you?"

"It's me."

Of course, it was her. That smoky, mature voice and the slight lilt to the way she pronounced Rainey.

"I can't believe it's you," I sobbed. "Oh, Ivy, I've missed you so much. You don't know what it's been like here without you—"

"Rainey."

"I'm sorry for everything. I shouldn't have said those things. I didn't mean it."

"I know," she replied. "Your voice mails all said the same."

My lips trembled. "I meant it. You know that, don't you?"

"I know you're sorry. It just doesn't change anything."

"What do you mean?"

"It's time we both had our own life. You were happy to live on the farm till you were eighty years old, rocking your great-grandchildren to sleep on the porch. You were horrible for what you said to me," she said, voice shaking. "But I think a part of me was looking for a way out, and I found it. I have friends, a home, and a boyfriend here. I'm happy.

"You need to find your own happiness, Rainey, and that's something you have to do alone."

"But... why does that mean we can't talk? I've been calling you for months, Ivy."

"Why?" she repeated. Her tone changed in a snap. "Because you're a rancid bitch who said I didn't love the woman who raised me. We're done, Rainey. Stop calling me."

Click.

I lowered the phone, placing it on the bathroom mat. Unhurriedly, I moved to the sink, washed my face, picked up the letter.

I wasn't mad. Ivy said what I knew she must've felt all this time. Why else would my calls have gone unanswered?

An awful thing to hear during what she intended to be our last conversation. Even so, she left me with an older sister's wisdom one final time.

It was time to find my happiness.

I brushed my fingers over the card.

And discover why you're determined to take it.

In the end, there was only one option. I had to find my way out of the darkness, and cut down anyone who tried to stop me.

"Paris." I came out, grinning to crack my face in half. "Bring on that big-eared, leather-loving, alien from the north."

CAIRO

Rain hugged Paris, waved bye to Esteban, and came down the drive. She was making herself at home with my family, and she was welcome to them. She was either to be with us, or right where I could find her. Life was simple now that she understood that.

I shifted to the mirror and the hand-stitched gash above my eye. Alright, simple wasn't the word.

Rainey climbed in and reached for me. She was dressed in one of Paris's outfits. A blue dress that brought out light flecks in her eyes. Undoubtedly, she had an enjoyable time hanging out with the sibling who had all of a sudden become her best friend, in her mansion of eleven rooms for three people. She'd have eaten fresh muffins made by their housekeeper, Laurent, and possibly took a quick dip in the hot tub with those girls who were always hovering around Evie.

Compared to a leash, collar, and doghouse on the living room floor, it'd have crossed anyone's mind to trade up. Paris was the kind of bleeding heart to convince Nora to let the homeless farm girl stay with them.

Did Rain realize that if she chose to break free of me, this house was the only place in all of Bedlam she'd be safe. The one place I wouldn't enter.

I wouldn't be surprised if she did know. Paris wasn't one to keep shit that wasn't anyone's business to herself.

Still, she willingly climbs in my car like she waited on the hood for us after I claimed her.

I couldn't stop asking why. Something in her eyes said I wouldn't like the full reason.

Her touch skated my brow. "Are you okay?" Real concern laced her question.

"I'm upright, aren't I?"

She chuckled. "Yes, but your serfdom just rose up against you. Bet you're wishing now you used honey to attract more than mouths to your dicks. Could've paid to be nicer to people."

"I can tell you with certainty." I removed her hand. "People don't pay when you're nice."

"What's the deal with these payments?"

I started the car, rolling down Bay Avenue.

"I assume there's a reason you make everyone give you a cut. But when you're taking their money, and the New Boys are giving it to them, it kinda makes it easy to pick favorites."

"Nothing is given for free." My temper leeched out. "Once they find out the strings attached, they'll be hanging from them."

"What are you guys going to do? How can you stop this?"

I cut the engine off before a home six down. Grasping her hips, I tugged her toward me. Rain came willingly, settling on my lap.

"You ask a lot of questions." I skimmed up her thigh, finding the place those shapely legs met. "You also showed up, attached to my sister's arm, right as Jeremy and his crew blew into town."

Bright spots of color stained her cheeks—from the question or the finger I slid inside her, hard to tell.

"What are you getting at, Cairo? I did what I did to Cavendish just to get an in with you g-guys?"

Another finger joined the first, scissoring her open. Rain tripped over her word—a flash of discomfort crossing her features. Didn't stop her bracing against the steering wheel and easing me deeper.

"What a fantastically stupid plan that would've been."

I grinned. Amazing how she could be so obedient and so brash in the same breath.

"You could've just as easily handed me to your father. Lots of snooping I would've done in jail."

"Destiny brought us together, Rain, I've never denied it. Doesn't mean destiny didn't bring you other opportunities."

I worked her with the other hand, sinking four fingers in that deliciously tight pussy. Rain whimpered—squeezing her eyes shut—and took every digit. My cock strained painfully against my zipper.

I went up against guys twice my size who couldn't take half as much as her. They bitched and moaned over a few taps to the jaw, while I brought Rain past the limit multiple times and she refused to flinch.

Maybe that's why it was infinitely more satisfying hurting her.

All the things I've done—the people I've hurt. No one believes I see the judgment in their eyes. That I indulge the pain without remorse. In that, they are correct. I did not feel bad for a single broken bone, bloodied body, or destroyed life, but the former was not true.

I hear their screams and pleas for mercy. I see the betrayal etched on their face. How dare I hold them accountable when every other weak bitch lets them slide? How dare I prove they were one of them?

That judgement irritated me. It kept me going past the point they had enough. They brought this side out of me. They taunted the beast—dropped scraps of meat to lure it out. Then they got mad at what they found.

Not my Rain.

She met him. Smoothed her hand down his hackles. Traced his snarl. Exposed her throat.

I looked in those eyes and saw many things, but never judgement.

Never fear.

"I'd spend the rest of my life hurting you, Rain." I buried my face in her neck, inhaling her sweet, minty scent. "I'd keep you even if you betrayed me. Ran from me. Turned your arrow on me."

I felt her swallow. "Are you thinking any of those are a possibility?"

Humming, I continued down, tugging her dress off with my teeth. "Arsenio told us about your chat with Ellis."

"I told him."

"Smart move in case we found out from someone else. Can't say you were hiding it when you came clean on your own."

She rocked on my hands—little pants dropping from her lips. "What are you getting at, Sharpe?"

"You take his bribe and play for his side, while coming to us promising you'll feed him lies and play for us."

"You're a suspicious person, aren't you? Won't share your secrets in front of the family pet because you don't like how he stares."

I laughed. "You're angry."

"Yes, I'm angry," she snapped. "I wouldn't tell Jeremy or the New Boys shit. I trust him even less than you guys."

"You don't trust me?" My smile widened.

"Why would I? You haven't given me reason to trust you, whereas I have. What information could I give Ellis that's more damning than the trip Arsenio and I took to the Highland Arms?"

I shrugged, picking up the pace. Rain jerked and fell on the horn, blaring our fun to the entire street.

"Maybe you're waiting till you have that agreement in writing."

"Fuck you. You should know that—"

"That what?" I sliced in.

"That I wouldn't give anyone power over you while you have power over me. The only end to that story is we all end up the New Boys' bitches."

Rain tossed her head back, lifting her dress uncaring of anyone driving by. The sight of her overstuffed hole nearly undid me. I haven't come in my pants since my bout of wet dreams as a teenager. Fuck if she wasn't about to break my streak.

I freed myself, letting the guy breathe while I continued my work.

"That's your only reason?" I probed.

"What are you looking for, Cairo?"

Biting a curse, I drilled her, slapping a palm against her clit. What the hell was I looking for?

I didn't understand Rainey de Souza, and with every passing day, that fact needled me harder. She hated my father, but why? The guy spent his life shuffling papers around his desk or drinking himself to death. When did he have time to make an enemy out of a college girl?

I gave in and asked him about her the other night while I helped him upstairs to bed. Dad blathered on about his regrets, but didn't answer the question. I knew he heard me.

Now Jeremy Ellis is stalking my girl through libraries, and fuck knew the real reason why. He may have told her it was to spy on us.

Bullshit.

We kept Quinn around for months. Fucking her and letting her live in our house. Jeremy was quick to snatch her up. Five minutes into her scorned-woman ranting, he'd figure out she didn't know anything worth using. We never took her on collection runs. Arsenio didn't bring her on *outings*. We never let Quinn get an inside on what we do.

Ellis didn't have a reason to believe it'd be different with the girl we had for less than three weeks.

So what does he really want from her? Why did Cavendish choose her? Why does my father refuse to talk about her?

"I want to know what makes Rainey de Souza so special."

"Ask yourself that," she forced out, squeezing on my fingers. Her nails pierced my shoulders, breaking skin as her orgasm took her.

"You're the one who chose me."

RAINEY

Cairo shifted my boneless heap to the passenger seat. I had no idea what prompted his sudden desire to give me an orgasm. Maybe he thought it'd scramble my mind and make me easy to question. Either way, I was his to tease and torture once again.

Cairo hopped out of the car and casually strode up the drive. Dressing quickly, I chased after him, and curled around his arm.

"Where are we?"

"Legend's parents' place," he replied. "Ellis and his crew are staked out at ours."

"Goodness. A brawl is broken up by gunfire and campus police, and they're out looking for another fight?"

"They didn't get what they wanted the first time. Naturally they'll keep coming after us until they do."

"What do they want?" I asked.

"Surrender."

I traced the lines of his hard, handsome face. I didn't have to ask the question. I already knew.

The Bedlam Boys would never surrender. There was a single outcome acceptable in a situation like this, the total annihilation of the enemy.

The blood of revolutionaries runs in our veins.

Cairo retrieved a key and let himself inside the mansion. The home of the famous St. Jameses was what I expected of the larger-than-life man whose face took up every advertisement, and voice boomed through the factory floor during distillery tours.

A fountain two stories high claimed most of the driveway. It splashed little droplets on me as we made for the grand glass doors. Inside, Christopher St. James greeted me with a beaming smile, a gorgeous brunette, and his supernaturally handsome son.

Their portrait took over the front wall, standing taller than me. You could put it down to the things I've come to know about the man, but if you looked closely at that smile, you'd see the hard set to his jaw and the almost hidden sneer.

Gran hated working with Christopher St. James. He never missed a chance to undercut a deal, reject produce, or try to negotiate the bill even though it was the same as the delivery before, and the delivery before that.

The guys were waiting in the chef's paradise Legend called a kitchen. Jacques looked like he was in the middle of making another smoothie. The guys lined up along the island arguing back and forth.

Cairo slipped out of my grasp to join them. I hung back in the foyer.

"—this happen," Legend gruffed. His perfectly coiffed hair was a tousle of flyaways. As wild as the fire in his normally shining brown eyes. "They came for us in our town, in our home! The rumors they spread about the factory going under have spiraled.

"Workers are giving notice, looking for new jobs. We say we're doing fine and they think we're hiding something. Whispers are going around about a strike. If we're doing so well, we can afford to increase wages."

He brought his fists down on the countertop. "It's obvious what they're trying to do! The workers get riled up, go on strike, production shuts down, we lose money, and Foundry swoops in ready to buy us out."

"Foundry?" I whispered.

"Ellis admitted his father wants the distillery," Jacques said. "It employs half the town. If Steven Ellis becomes the boss, he'll have a hold on half the voters."

"He won't have shit," Legend snapped. "He's not getting the distillery. The return of Crystal Canyon will never make it on the ballot."

Legend riled up was a rare sight to see. He paced the length of the kitchen—a caged beast searching for its way to you.

"The Crows, and Steven Ellis, have been planning this for a long time," Arsenio said. "They came in too fast. Outsmarted us too quickly. They must've been watching us, taking note of our weakness-es. The collections were the perfect pain point to dig in."

"We're the evil tax collectors, and Jeremy and his Crows are the messiahs," Legend said, "come to save them and create their own promised land."

"Seems to be their plan."

He leaned over the counter, boring down on Arsenio. "How are we going to stop them? You going to pay them a visit?"

I tucked further in the corner. Was Legend serious? They'd kill the Crows for unseating their thrones and causing a little worker un-rest?

Arsenio didn't answer right away. My lungs failed me as the si-lence stretched.

"No," Roan spoke up. "That's not the right move. I don't need to tell you what'll happen if Foundry gets what they want. That cannot happen, but if Ellis knows, he knows. Getting rid of the Crows won't stop him. Getting rid of him won't either if he's got Foundry's board in on it. The mass murder of an entire board of directors right before they acquire property in a town with a bloody history, is bound to at-tract some notice. Plus, right now our own people are happy to offer us up as the main suspects," Roan said.

I found myself nodding along. Incredible that of all people, Roan was the one talking sense and calm.

He rubbed his bandaged arm. "If we strike back with violence, we're going to jail."

"Then what do you suggest? Huh? What?"

No one replied.

"Fuck!" Legend swiped a fruit bowl off the counter. It crashed at my feet in a shower of glass and oranges.

The guys looked up at my cry. Legend narrowed on me.

"The place is yours," he told them. "Do what you want. Stay as long as you fucking want. Folks don't come back for another week and a half."

He stalked toward me. I jumped—jerking back like I was going to run. Legend ended any thought of that by tossing me over his shoulder.

"I need a distraction. Don't wait up for us."

"Distraction?" I repeated. "What are we doing?"

"Yoga."

Legend carried me upstairs, bypassing the towering portrait. He brought me into a bedroom that had to be his.

A massive canopy bed dominated the middle of the room. That placement was odd for anyone else. The more I learned about Legend St. James, the more it made sense the activities that went down on that bed would take center stage.

"Wait for me." He set me on the couch. "Don't move."

And go where?

Legend walked out, leaving me to scope out his place in peace. It seemed the typical guy's room if obsessively clean. He didn't live here anymore, so it wouldn't be messy. That fact didn't tell me anything about him.

I got up despite my orders, searching for something that would.

Music posters covered every wall. Green Day, Papa Roach, Evanescence, Finger Eleven. If I hummed along to their songs while Ivy blasted them upstairs, they were on this wall.

Poking my head in the closet, I spotted mostly suits. These were left behind in favor of the normal college-student clothes. I moved on to the entertainment setup. A big-screen television was penned in by two shelves stacked with DVDs. I bent to look when I heard someone coming.

I hurried back to the couch. Legend carried something in his left hand.

"A balance ball?"

"Correct." Legend stepped down into the sunken living area, complete with my couch, two gamer chairs, and a coffee table. The coffee table was moved out of the way and the balance ball put in its place.

Legend looked at me, trapping my gaze as he unbuttoned his cuffs. Loosened his collar. I couldn't place the emotion in them. Couldn't name why it made me sink in my seat.

"What's the word you have with Cairo?" he asked.

"It's... fate."

He approached me, tipping my neck as he towered. "What's our word?"

"What's ours?" My mouth was suddenly dry.

"What's our word?"

"Um, it's—" Legend traced my trembling lips. "It's gentleman."

"Cute," he said, smirking. "I like it."

Legend went into the closet. I craned to see what he was doing, and saw nothing but his shadow moving about amid bangs and thumps.

"Get up," he called.

I did, getting to my feet as my more-than-a-rich-boy emerged. Something hung off his fingers.

"How good are you at yoga?" Legend came closer, giving me a proper look at the leather spanking paddles and whip.

My lips parted and nothing came out. How had I missed that hiding in his closet?

Squinting, I noticed something etched in the paddles. Legend kindly held them up for me to see.

SLUT.

BITCH.

SLAVE.

"How much do you know about yoga?"

"I did a few online videos," I rasped.

"Disappointing," he said, circling me.

The guys did that more than was normal. But then, they knew what I knew. I was their prey.

"This might not be as fun as I want it to be. Get on the ball."

I climbed on, wobbling and falling off twice. The third time I caught my balance and watched him place his tools on the coffee table.

"It's a simple game. You do your yoga without falling off or I"—he ran a finger down the whip—"help you try harder."

"But I can't do it without falling off." *Which is clearly the point.*

Legend winked. "That's quitter's talk, baby. Forward bend."

I didn't move.

"Legend, I know you're angry. The Crows are coming after your family business. They started a brawl and someone tried to stab Roan."

His expression hardened.

"Let's not do this while you're upset. We can just talk."

"That's a good idea. Let's talk," he said. "Let's talk about why I'm protecting you. You're the one who killed Cavendish, and because Cairo wanted a pet, I have to put up with the suspicion.

"The Crows are turning the town against us. They're whipping my employees into a strike, and how much do you want to bet they're using a certain murder investigation to make the lies go down sweeter?"

I raised my chin, chest rising and falling.

"Why shouldn't I do this while I'm *angry*? Did you think you were forgiven?" He ate the distance, knocking me off with his mere presence. "Don't tell me you thought your punishment was over? That we're your boyfriends now." Legend pouted. "Ah. How sweet."

"No," I said, hiding my balled fists behind my back. "I didn't think that."

"Didn't you?" Legend moved behind me. "You're a toy, de Souza. A pet. A distraction. A consolation prize at best." His breath was hot on my neck. "Cairo can fuck you. Roan can use you. Jacques can play with you. Arsenio can mold you. But that's all you'll ever be. Say you understand."

The words burned coming out. "I understand."

"Good 'cause right now, I'm playing with my toy. Forward bend."

I bent at the waist, reaching for my ankles, and pitched off the ball.

"The dress," Legend said. "Take it off."

Tugging the dress down, I glanced at him over my shoulder. It was hard to recognize the smiling, flirty man who teased my nipples and made me blush in public. Why was I surprised? Looking at the company he kept should've clued me in. I didn't know everything about Legend St. James.

"Grab the chair arms."

I did, knowing what was coming.

Pain erupted in my left cheek. I bit my lip, smothering a whimper. Legend did not hold back.

"Back on the ball."

I climbed on in nothing but my lace hipsters. Legend twirled the paddle around his finger. He opted for *slave*.

"Eagle pose."

My jaw clenched. For eagle, I had to twist my arms and legs around each other, then stand on one foot. The pose was impossible for me on solid ground.

"Waiting for something?"

I raised my foot an inch, and fell over. I couldn't catch myself and dropped face-first on the couch.

"Get on your knees."

"Legend!"

"Don't make me repeat myself." He selected *slut* from his collection.

I shakily got my knees under me, clutching the couch cushion. The paddle whistled cutting through the air.

"Ah!"

"On the ball."

I whipped around on him, glaring furiously. "This isn't going to make you feel better. It won't change a damn thing."

Legend was power, and fury, and sex contained in one mortal body. His thick thighs strained the fabric as he crouched. "Why not? It makes you feel better. We're not all so clueless, baby, I know why you got in our truck. I've always known."

"What?" I whispered.

"You want to be punished. You want us to make it hurt on the outside as much as it does on the inside. It's the only way you can live with yourself.

"It's the only way to breathe."

The words rapid-fired from his smirking, cruel mouth. There was no chance to take cover.

He laughed—a terrible, harsh sound. "I know a little something about that, and if you want to hurt, love, I have always been your man." Legend winked. "You didn't have to burn a guy to get my attention."

"Leg—"

"On the ball," he ordered.

I shoved up.

"Ah." Legend stopped me with the paddle. "Lose the panties."

I pulled them off and threw it at him. Legend laughed as they bounced off his face.

"Chair pose."

I fell off three times trying to get back on and find my balance.

Straightening, I raised my hand to do the pose I was meant to fail.

"*You're a pet. You're a toy.*"

I lowered slowly and the ball wobbled. It threw me off its back.

Landing smack on the carpet, I groaned at the jolt through my sore backside.

"Get up. Hands and knees."

"*That's all you'll ever be.*"

"No."

"Excuse me?"

"No," I cried.

"Get on your knees, toy."

"Screw you!" The torrent burst. Snatching up the ball, I flung it at him.

Legend ducked, cursing. I ran for the door.

Closing on the knob, I yanked it open. Legend was on me in three bounds. He slammed his hands on either side of my head—ripping it free of my grasp and banging the door shut.

"This is what you wanted," he growled.

"Not like this!" Sobbing, I slid to the floor, forehead pressed to the wood.

"What else is there?"

Legend pressed me in tighter—blotting out my light, sound, and my escape. "You did indulge your little fantasy that we were your boyfriends. Well, let me be the one to break it to you, this is all there is.

"We're not waiting for you at the end of it," he gritted in my ear. "There won't be grand confessions of love, or sweet speeches about wanting you all along, and now we can finally be together. You wanted this."

Legend punched the wood, stealing a cry from me.

"The pain. The choking. The begging for it to stop before it gets worse. We're sweat, blood, and agony. We're the last lost mile on blistered feet. I'll force you to go on, Rainey, because it's the only way to get to where you're going.

"Atonement."

My tears slowed. Hiccups softened.

"If it's too much for you, say the word, run out of here, and don't fucking come back. Otherwise, get on your fucking knees, pet. You chose your jailers, now take your punishment."

Rising up, I moved as he did—getting to my knees and Legend's weight disappearing.

"Face me."

Legend was an immense being blocking out the sun itself. He reached for his zipper, and my soul quieted.

"You're terrible at yoga, but maybe your talents lie elsewhere. Do a good job and I won't have to imprint another lesson into that lovely, unblemished skin."

Another game I'm meant to fail?

How could I do a good job? I'd never given a blow job.

Legend unveiled in all his thick, smooth, uncut glory. He pressed against my lips—demanding entrance.

I parted, accepting him. Legend drove home and filled me to the brim.

I gagged at first, but forced myself to relax, breathing through my natural reflex. Planting my hands on either side of him, I bobbed my head, sinking to swallow as much of him as I could. Pulling back to suck and lick the tip.

He grunted. "Shit."

Picking up the pace, the noise spurred me on. Maybe this was all there is and all there should be. I changed since I received that first letter. I'd done the unspeakable and dragged others down in my selfishness. The Letter Man said I didn't understand the meaning of sacrifice. That couldn't be farther from the truth.

I sacrificed my sister for vengeance. I sacrificed truth to live in peace. I sacrificed the Bedlam Boys to escape the consequences for both.

Any connection I felt with Cairo, admiration from Arsenio, or understanding with Jacques could not overshadow the simple truth that they are not my boyfriends.

They are my sacrifices, and they put me on an altar to burn.

I stroked Legend's balls, earning filthier curses and the flip of his on switch. He started pumping—fucking my mouth slow at first, and then faster as he lost control. I fought to accept him.

Choking and sputtering, Legend's mercy was to tangle in my hair, tugging my head back to open me wider. Tears streamed down my face. My gag reflex was out of control. But I gripped Legend tighter, nails piercing his hips, and determined to take all he had to give me.

He seized—muscles going rigid between my touch. Popping out, Legend exploded hot, dripping cum all over my face.

He propped against the door as I knelt there, blinking in wide-eyed shock.

"Terrible," he gruffed, voice ragged. "You don't have a fucking clue what you're doing, but damn if that hot little mouth isn't tasty. Let's split the difference, shall we?"

"No more spankings?"

He grinned, cutting a track through the mess on my cheek. "No more yoga."

Legend spanked me until "the message sunk in." Over and over again, not letting up after two screaming orgasms and another blow job to win my reprieve.

"That's enough." He dropped the paddle, leaving *bitch* to lie with *slut* and *slave*.

The good news was I didn't know any more pain. My ass fell numb half a dozen slaps ago.

Pushing myself up, I made for the door.

"Where are you going? I don't sleep alone."

Legend swept me up in his arms and carried me to bed. It didn't occur to me to fight him as he tucked me in the silk sheets. Why would it? It was the moment he slid in next to me, throwing his arm over my waist and pulled me close that gave me pause.

This was everything Legend said wouldn't happen. Closeness. Tenderness. Shouldn't he be carrying me to my new doghouse in the basement right now?

I relaxed, letting my eyes fall shut. It didn't matter if this wasn't real or the opening of what would be a cruel joke. All I knew was what I felt. This was not my jail.

This was home.

Chapter Thirteen

Friday morning, I walked the short distance to Paris's house. She was giving me a ride to school these days since the Bedlam Boys were sitting out classes at the command of their dean.

They shut down school for a day to collect witness statements and stem the flood of worried and irate parents who heard there was a shooting.

There was, and if you asked me, it was stupid crossing into insane that those guards fired guns and set off a panicking crowd. Did it work to stop the fight? Yes. Did four people end up in the hospital because of the stampede and now one is suing the school? Also yes.

To cool things down, Dean Banks removed the Bedlam Boys and the Crows from campus and allowed classes to resume for everyone else. I asked Roan why the guys were going along with this suspension, and he said, "You do not argue with Josephine Banks. Even I know the limit."

The Crows seemed to have gotten that message too, since I didn't see or hear a whisper of them.

The last few days at Bedlam University were the most uneventful since I started. Everyone pegged me as their captive, not their accomplice, so they didn't bother me now that I was set free.

That is everyone except for Quinn. She caught me and Paris rolling into school the day before, and had a lot to say to our backs as we walked away. Otherwise, it was life as my new normal.

Legend saw no reason to tuck the true side of himself back in the cage. If anything, over the last few days, the savagery our circumstances brought out in him, focused the man into a paddle-wielding beast.

The words *slut*, *bitch*, and *slave* were becoming permanent tattoos on my backside. Legend added *whore* the day before, so now I had it smack across both cheeks.

He was nothing like Jacques who waited till I gave him a reason. According to Legend, *I've already given him plenty*.

Sitting down was a constant challenge, even though after Legend tucked me in bed, I'd wake sometime in the night to find him smearing aloe on my cheeks. He'd let me stay in bed the next morning, air cooling my sticky butt, and watching TV while I waited for someone to bring me breakfast and Cairo to shower with me before school.

I cut through campus the back way, walking past Douglas Herbert's memorial. My thoughts turned to the Letter Man as they always did at some point, within every minute, during every hour.

Paris and I had different schedules. We came to school in time for whoever had their first class, and left after the last. Paris had evening classes every day of the week, which left me time to run off campus, ride with Frankie to the farm, and see if I had a new letter.

A time and date of our first meeting he promised me. So far, my letterbox was empty.

I stepped onto the sidewalk, taking it around to the square where I'd cut through to reach the bus station. Paris's classes didn't let out until five. It was one in the afternoon. I had plenty of time.

A horn blared.

"Hey, de Souza. Wait up."

Twisting around, I slowed as a Lexus pulled up to the curb next to me.

"Get in," Jeremy said. He rode alone. No brother or cronies in sight. "We're going to my place."

"Uh, no, thank you, stranger danger. Keep driving or I'll scream."

I set off, listening to Jeremy crack up. He inched along beside me.

"Don't be like that," he said. "I apologize for calling you a bitch. I was a bit upset over my brother going missing. I can be forgiven for that, can't I?"

"Sure," I replied. "It's siccing your new girlfriend on me that's putting you on my punch-him-in-the-face-next-time-I-see-him list. She ripped half the hair out of my head."

"That wasn't on me. The fight got out of hand. Besides, Quinn hates you because of the Bedlam Boys, not me. They threw her over like trash. Exactly how they treat you. If anything, you should be thanking me for knocking them off their pedestals, and doing it hard."

"Thanking you?"

He gestured to me. "You're leash-free. At least for now. I bought you a few days rid of the Bedlam Boys."

Not exactly.

"Come on," he pressed. "Get in."

"What do you want, Jeremy?"

"You told me to put our deal in writing. I did."

I stopped dead on the pavement. I couldn't have heard that right. "Excuse me?"

"I've got the contract for the farm buy back at my place. Don't tell me you're not interested anymore?"

I leaned on the car, sticking my head through the window. "Your father agreed to write up a contract stating he'll purchase and transfer ownership of my farm to me... if I spy on a couple college boys?"

"That's what I just said, isn't it?" He popped the lock. "Getting in or what?"

"What are the new terms?"

"What are you talking about?"

"You asked me to spy and tell you what they're planning," I said. "But you've taken them down. What's left for me to do?"

"Ah, de Souza. You've got your looks going for you. That'll get you far."

"What the fuck did you just say?"

"Don't get mad, darling. You don't have a head for these things." He leaned across the seat, oozing a charming smile though his words didn't match. "We won a battle, not the war. The Bedlam Boys will be holed up somewhere, planning how to stop us winning anymore.

"Get back in with them, and tell me everything they say. Even the shit they mumble in their sleep. Tell me when they leave the house. Follow them when they do. Get close to their families. Find out what they know about their sons and what they do."

"So you can use it to chop my home into pieces? Why would I want that, Ellis?"

"Your home is that farm. Admit it," he said. "How much did you have to do with the townies and their little lives before you started at this university? Your life was always fifteen miles that way." He pointed. "You never cared what happened on this side of the town line, don't pretend you care now.

"Make your choice, Rainey. Are you giving up everything your grandmother worked for over a change that's coming no matter what anyone does to stop it? Or are you going to accept what we all are at our core? Self-serving bastards."

It was a good speech. On anyone else, he would've had them the moment he honked on the horn. But Jeremy didn't hook me—until he brought up Gran.

Are you giving up everything your grandmother worked for?

No, I'm not.

I got in the car. "We have to make a stop first," I said. "De Souza Farm. I'm sure you know the way."

Jeremy drove me out to my empty farmhouse. I texted Paris on the way, telling her not to wait for me. Pulling up to the fence, I told

Jeremy I wouldn't be long and climbed over. A letter waited for me in the box.

I checked to make sure no one was watching, and peeled it open.

Saturday night in the place we always meet.

Midnight.

Come alone or you'll make me angry.

Don't make that mistake after all the progress we've made.

Till tomorrow.

Stay psycho.

Love ya. XOXO

I tucked the letter in my pocket and kept the words in my mind on the way down. He expected me to meet him tomorrow night at the farmhouse. No other place it could be. No other location that could be worse.

I'd be alone with him miles away from help or witnesses. There was nothing to stop him turning a discussion into a nightmare—except for me.

My mind was made up to go before I got back in Jeremy's car. It was made up before we drove here too.

I'd meet him alone but I wouldn't do it unarmed. He'd stand before me at arrow-point and tell me everything. Why he and Cavendish targeted me? Was I some random person they woke up one day and decided to torture, or was this something they'd been doing for years?

Both Letter Men spoke of sacrifice like it was a fact of life. They were doing something that must be done. How many of the missing people or unsolved murders in Bedlam's recent history could be laid at their feet?

I'll get there early. Have the bow trained on him the moment he comes through the door.

My head churned, turning over every inch of my plan and what I'd do if it went sour. Jeremy made no attempt to talk to me, and I didn't start a conversation either.

This is the part in the movie where the audience screams at the girl to call the police.

Let them know what's going on and have them on standby to arrest him. Even if I put my hatred of the sheriff aside, I don't know that I would've chosen that option. The Letter Man could be anyone. He was certainly someone who remained ahead of me and law enforcement. The cops in this town didn't know he existed.

What if he's on the force? What if he's Sheriff Fucking Jack?

Asking me to trust the very people who let me down to come through and save me this time, was too hard a sell.

I closed my eyes, resting my aching head on the cool glass. If I was honest with myself, none of that was the true reason I was going to walk onto that farm alone. The truth was the police wouldn't let me meet a serial killer in an abandoned barn armed with a bow. Frankie wouldn't just idle on the corner, hanging out with the promise I'd be back in thirty minutes.

No one would let me do this the way I knew it had to be done. I was going alone. That fact scared me in every place but one. A deep, calm island buoyed in my soul. That's where I'd hide until it was over.

Opening my eyes, I landed on the sign for Bay Avenue.

Jeremy drove us to the smallest house on the street, though that wasn't saying much.

It didn't have the two-story fountain or turrets breaking the sky. This one was two stories of stone and blackout windows. The lawn was mostly well-kept if not for the donut rings marring the grass.

Jeremy led me inside by the elbow. Did he think I was going to run? I made it this far.

We rounded a corner and I grimaced. Made it this far and it was a mistake.

The place was a dump.

Dirty clothes strewn all over the living room—not all of them men's clothes. Crumbs ground deep in what used to be a plush, white carpet. It was now a variety of colors.

Two of the Crows vegged out on the couch, clad in their boxers and rocking popcorn bowls on their stomach.

"Hey." Jeremy lobbed a stray shoe at Bentley's head. "Clean this place up. There's a party tonight."

I'd forgotten about the party. Half the student body was coming out to celebrate with their new masters.

We continued past Bentley and Gael, sensing their eyes on the back of my head.

I didn't care what Jeremy said, these guys would be no different from the Bedlam Boys. Judging by how easily they stabbed people and started brawls that resulted in hospitalization, they'd be worse in their own way.

We went up the stairs, going into a room at the end of the hall. The place clearly came furnished. I couldn't see a bunch of guys with neck tattoos and leather jackets choosing the floral wallpaper or the egg chair propped in the corner next to a tea nook.

"Sit."

I claimed the desk chair and scooted aside for Jeremy to come around and pull papers from the drawer.

"Here you are," he said. "Checked by our lawyers. Signed by Dad."

The next thing out of the drawer was a pen.

"Sign."

I took the pen and dropped it back where it came from.

"I'll need time to review this. Do you have your father's lawyer's number? It's easier if I tell him the changes I want to make directly instead of doing it through you."

Jeremy frowned, cutting a wrinkle down his smooth brow. "There won't be any changes. The deal is take it or leave it."

"Nevertheless, I'd like his number."

"Dammit, de Souza, stop—"

"Why is this a problem? Is there something in the contract you know I'm not going to like?" I tossed the papers across the room. "That saves me a lot of trouble. Bye now."

He snatched my arm, grabbing me in a painful grip. "Stop!"

"Hey! Get the fuck off me!"

Jeremy dropped my arm immediately. "Sorry," he said, smiling disarmingly. "I shouldn't have done that. Won't happen again."

I edged away from him, rubbing my arm.

"I am sorry," he repeated. "Look." Jeremy took out his phone, tapped a few buttons, and handed it to me. "Caleb Graham. He's my dad's lawyer. He'll walk you through the contract line by line. You can stay in here as long as it takes to see this is all on the up-and-up."

He tiptoed around me, hands held above his head comically. "Can I get you anything? Call out for lunch?"

"No," I said after a beat. "I'm fine."

"Great." Jeremy closed the door behind him.

It took me a minute to pick up the contract and dial the number. A deep voice picked up on the third ring.

"Hello, this is Caleb Graham with Graham and Associates. How can I help you?"

"Hi, this is Rainey de Souza. I don't know if you—"

"Miss de Souza, good to hear from you." His tone brightened. "I faxed the paperwork over this morning. Is everything in order?"

I eased into the seat. So far, so legit.

"That's what I'm calling you about. I'd like to go over the contract with you line by line. Is now a good time to talk?"

"Excellent time. What are your concerns?"

Caleb and I talked for hours. We were on the phone for so long, my stomach forced me to take Jeremy up on his offer of Chinese takeout, and the guys started blowing up my phone, demanding to know where I was.

I didn't reply with full knowledge I'd be punished later. This wasn't about me and the Bedlam Boys right now. It was about me and Gran. As much as they'd come to consume my life with their rare kisses and raw, dangerous power, this was one part no one got to touch. I had to do what my grandmother would've wanted me to do, and she wanted this farm in our family. I could not let anyone get in our way.

"As you can see," Caleb said, "it's standard boilerplate, Miss de Souza."

"Mostly," I agreed. "A lot of this is pretty standard, except for a few things. It says I have to give Jeremy or Micah Ellis weekly verifiable information about the Bedlam Boys, insert names here, up to and including their actions or their parents' actions against construction, mining, or the development of a new town."

"Yes?" Caleb prompted.

"What are we calling verifiable information? If I overhear a conversation that they want to beat the Crows into a bloody heap their own mothers won't recognize, how do I prove that's a credible threat before they... do it?"

"Ah, well, yes, I see your point. Stated threats are hard to verify before they're carried out. While of course the Ellises need to know if there is a threat against their lives, we're mostly focused on serious opposition to the creation of a new town. For example, if you overhear Mr. Creed say he's holding a secret town hall meeting to oppose the venture. That's something we can verify and take steps to address."

"Okay." I put that aside for now since the whole point of this was for me to spy. I couldn't ask for a lot of wiggle room on that one.

"There's also the part about ownership reverting to Steven Ellis in the event of my death."

"In the event you pass without heirs," he corrected. "Blood relations. Surely you don't object. He's investing a significant amount into this property. God forbid if something happened to you, why should that investment sit barren and empty?"

"What if I want to will it to another farmer? Someone who'll work the land and take care of the animals after I'm gone."

"You're more than free to do so, Miss de Souza, as long as that farmer is a blood relation."

I chewed the inside of my mouth, thinking. Downstairs, speaker feedback continually cut through my train of thought. The sun was setting. The New Boys were gearing up for their party.

This stipulation in the contract wasn't unreasonable. I just didn't like the idea of the farm not being mine to do what I want with.

If you die without heirs. Even willing it to Ivy would keep it in de Souza hands. She probably won't come back to live here, but she'd see that it was taken care of the way Gran wanted.

"Alright," I said. "Moving on."

We continued on through the rest, ending on a pleasant note.

"You have a bright future ahead of you, Miss de Souza," he said. "If you ever decide a small-town law firm is more your speed, join us at Graham and Associates."

I laughed. "Will do. Have a good evening."

"You as well."

It was five minutes after I hung up that Jeremy came into the room.

"What's it going to be?" He dropped down on the egg chair. "All good? Contract signed."

I handed him his phone, studying him. I'd been on many trains of thought since I got in his car. "Why did you come here?" I asked. "Do you know anything about a company called Foundry?"

"You've been talking to Creed."

"No, I overheard them talking—which is the point. To find out what they know, and they seem to know that you're more than you're saying. What is Foundry? What does it do?"

He shrugged. "My dad invests in many companies. I can't keep track of them all."

"Where does the distillery fit into all of this?"

Another shrug. "He wants it. St. James won't let him have it. Dad doesn't take well to no."

"But he doesn't need to establish his own town to buy out the distillery. Don't give me anymore bullshit answers," I said when he opened his mouth. "I've taken three classes dealing with land, property, and ownership. If he wanted to build his own distillery, this would make sense. He can't come in and do something like that without approval from town hall—which he wouldn't get.

"Bedlam has strict rules about commercial development. Lumber companies, grocery chains, golf courses, and all sorts have tried to claim the patches of land sitting empty. All have been shot down. In that case, I can almost see creating your own town where no one is going to tell you no.

"The effort you'll have to go through to get fifty-one percent of Bedlamites to turn their back on a town they're damn proud of, is overkill just to get your hands on one..." I trailed off, narrowing on my silent opponent. "Of course."

"Of course what?"

"I'm stupid. It's so perfectly obvious I should've seen it before."

Jeremy stood to face me. "You think you figured something out, share with the rest of the class."

"It's not about acquiring a business that's already there. Lumber, store chains, and golf courses. None of those companies were allowed to cut down or build here. Foundry wants to do both or either of those things, and they know it's going to be a flat-out no. That's why you need to create your own town."

Jeremy was expressionless.

"You guys in Hunter's Crest have already bought, sold, or developed every blade of grass within the city limits. While Bedlam is miles and miles of untapped potential and a huge youth market." I clapped. "Well done. Whatever business you want to start here must be insanely lucrative. No other reason you'd go through that much trouble."

"Interesting theory." A smile broke out on his lips. "But like I said, I don't think about what the old man gets up to, but while we're talking huge youth market, I should float the idea of a club. Definitely one or two smoke shops."

He flicked over my shoulder. "Hope your little revelation isn't going to stop you from signing. The land is still yours even if a new town pops up around it."

"I know." I tossed him the contract. "I signed ten minutes ago. I want the keys in my hand by the end of the month, and Cruella is to deliver them personally. Good luck with your diabolical plan. But just a warning, despite you calling us hicks every chance you get, Bedlamites aren't stupid. Other people will figure it out. We won't give our home up to developers as easily as you think."

Jeremy slung an arm around my shoulder. Apparently, we were buddies now. "Why are you telling me? All I know is Dad wants to bring back Crystal Canyon and the Crows are making a permanent move. We've got no interest in taking shit from the Bedlam Boys like everyone else around here is happy to do, so we put those puffed-up shits in their place. Again, you should be thanking me. But I'll show my thanks to you."

"How?"

"Stay for the party."

Jeremy led me out, sweeping his hand over the transformation below. The clothes were picked up and carpet vacuumed. That wasn't what impressed me.

Speakers stacked all along the back wall. Strobe lights attached to the ceiling waiting to be turned on. They copied the Bedlam Boys with the bowls of brightly colored pills and glow-in-the-dark paint waiting to shine under black light. Where they differed was the giant ball pit in the middle of the room, and an entire grand dining table's worth of alcohol. In the corner, the DJ prepped to blow our eardrums.

"Tonight will be bigger than Ruckus Royale ever was, and whoever misses out will set themselves on fire."

"That's not funny."

He laughed. "You're right. Too soon. But seriously, stay. Jonah says your entire crew is coming. Even Cairo's hot sister." He whistled. "Hard to believe they came from the same gene pool."

Are you implying the guy isn't hot? The man walks around with a warning label. Seriously, one of his tattoos says "caution."

"I don't know if I should. I have a paper due for Ethical Issues that I haven't started yet."

"That's what Saturday and Sunday are for. What's the problem?" He held out his arms, beaming away. "We're friends now, right?"

"We're business partners."

"Business partners can still party."

I blew out a breath. "Alright, I'll stay. But only because you got Chinese from the good place on Rose Street."

"That's almost the spirit." He shook me, riding high on a good mood. "I'll grab you a beer."

"Thanks," I said, tossing him a salute.

Why argue with the guy? I was literally a three-minute walk from Legend's house. I could leave whenever I wanted.

Fishing out my phone, I shot a text to Roan.

Me: You can call off the search dogs. I'm at the New Boys' place. They came through with the contract.

His reply came back in seconds.

Roan: Stay there.

Me: Why?

Roan: Why not? It's a party.

Me: For how long?

Roan: Till I come and get you.

I shot more texts at him but didn't get a reply. I gave up and put it away when I spotted Jeremy coming up with my beer.

"Cheers," he said, holding his up to clink.

Why not? It's a party.

"Cheers."

An hour and a half later, I was testing my *what the hell* resolve. This party was both the last days of Rome and the Mayan calendar rolled into one. Our town had the right name, because people were going insane.

"Rainey, try this!" Elise half fell on my lap. She tried to get a blue pill in my mouth and conked my forehead.

"No, thank you. I don't eat anything out of a shared bowl."

I gently peeled her off me, helping her sit properly on the couch. She turned on Zara and shoved the pill in her mouth instead.

"Whoo!"

Something, or someone, streaked out of the corner of my eye. I looked up as they hit the ball pit—launched from the second-floor balcony. A group of naked girls play wrestling in the pit, stopped their fun to see if the still mass sinking in the balls was alive.

Bentley popped up, pumping his fists. "Yeah! Who's next?"

Twelve people broke off and beat it upstairs.

I grew up on a farm. My idea of a wild night was racing to get the goats in the pen when a coyote was on the loose. This place was on another level. I wouldn't say it was bigger than Ruckus Royale, but it was close.

Almost the entire Bedlam University student body was stuffed in their suddenly too small mansion. The music blasted. People danced buck naked in glow-in-the-dark paint, and proved once again we've left all prudishness about public sex behind.

I pushed through the crush, searching out the water bottles for my high friends. I passed a group of ten—five guys standing and five girls on their knees. From the hooting and cheering of those watching, they were racing to see who could make their guy come first. Overhead, the big screen played a string of videos of other wild parties, some of it porn.

I made it to the drink table. *Come on. Come on, where are you?*

Vodka, beer, wine, cider, brandy, even sake. There wasn't a drop of water on the table.

Continuing on, I slipped outside on the patio. It was no less packed out there than it was inside. My classmates skinny-dipped in the pool. Further back, I spotted Gael's back of the shaved head setting off fireworks with a bunch of guys.

I was there to witness it and I still couldn't believe how easily they wrestled control from the Bedlam Boys. This crowd had changed allegiances.

"Fuck the Bedlam Boys," Jeremy roared.

"Yeah!"

That was the most telling evidence. About every fifteen minutes, Jeremy hopped on the speaker system rigged throughout the mansion and blared his feelings about my guys. All with enthusiastic support from the people who once dropped to their knees on Roan's order over the radio.

I saw a lot of things I couldn't unsee, but no water bottles in the coolers.

Tap water will have to do.

I turned to go back. Paris came up to me—dressed but dripping wet. "Some idiot threw me in the pool."

Putting my arm around her, I kissed her wet cheek. She didn't seem to be enjoying this party either. "We'll steal a towel and dry clothes from upstairs," I said. "First, I've got to get some water in your sloppy friends."

Paris howled. "They're your sloppy friends now too."

"Dammit."

The party was a fraction better now that Paris was melting by my side. We stopped off to get water, forced it on Elise and Zara, and then cut through the line of guys forming to get their blow job.

Yikes. I couldn't imagine giving them in an assembly line, and I had five guys who may one day get me on my knees and demand it. The blow jobs Legend got out of me every night to "improve my technique" were a full-time job. He said I wasn't good at them, but the grunts and filthy promises I extracted from him hardened my nipples and dampened my middle to the point a soft love tap with his paddle would set me off.

Upstairs, we burst into a random room. Paris went in search of a towel while I snooped to my heart's content.

Jeremy's room, I thought, picking up a photo of a young him and young Micah at the zoo. I knew it was his and not Micah's because of the second picture, about four feet tall and nailed to the wall. I assumed Micah did not put a portrait of his half-naked, green-haired smirking brother over his bed.

Otherwise, it was a nice place that benefited from the taste of the person who provided the furnishing. The king-sized bed was covered in a soft, blue bedspread. It matched the chevron border around the wall and the heavy blue drapes.

Pushing them aside, I gazed out across the lights, spotting Legend's house a few down.

"I don't know why I came." Paris came out of the bathroom with a towel slung on her shoulders. The tight, chiffon wrap dress was discarded in favor of a big T-shirt and sweatpants. "Elise went on and on, begging me to come and see the 'real' Crows. I think she's really into this Jonah guy, and she's convinced we're all bound to love him too."

"I don't know about Jonah but—"

"Bedlam is ours!" Jeremy's amplified shout cut in.

"—the Ellis brothers have ulterior motives and they're not hiding them anymore."

"They're not going to split our town apart."

Boos sounded from downstairs.

"Elise may be sex-high right now, but even... she supports— What is that?"

The booing was getting louder.

"Something is going on downstairs."

We came out, rushing to the banister. What was going on became clear immediately. Roan came to get me, and he didn't see the need to wait out on the curb.

The crowd parted for my red-haired devil imp. I called him that the day before when he sat in on my "yoga" time with Legend, and rooted for him to spank me harder, more, and with various whips and paddles he unearthed from their secret place in the closet. Roan found the nickname amusing.

"Booooo." They were in his face—shouting, spitting, and waving their fists at him.

Roan walked amid the hate unfazed. Dressed in a blue tee, brown pants, and a jacket, he was as casual as the expression on his face. That one-sided grin shone from all the way upstairs. Tousled strands flipped from his eyes as he looked up, saw me, and gave me a nod.

The music cut off with a screech.

"What the fuck do we have here?" Jeremy crowed. "I don't remember inviting the Bedwetter Boys."

His audience laughed as Jeremy emerged from the other side of the ball pit, claiming center stage in front of the TV.

Roan stopped before him and the path that made way sealed behind him, closed by the partiers who realized what was going on and rushed to spectate. Roan wasn't going anywhere.

"What are you doing here, Banks?" Gael, Bentley, and Jonah fell in beside him. "Have you come to admit defeat?"

"Yes."

Yes? Did he just say—?

"Yes, I am," Roan repeated louder. "Arsenio, Cairo, Jacques, and Legend aren't going to do this, so it has to be me. It's time for the war to end."

My mouth fell open. What the hell was he saying? Roan had been strange the last few days. He refused to join in on the guys' plans for vengeance, and when he thought no one was looking, I'd see him rubbing his bandage and glancing off into space.

I should've realized the grin he put on when he noticed me was fake. Someone tried to kill him. Run a knife through his heart, and the person is still out there. I knew what it was to have a shadow lurking over you. I'd want the fighting to end too.

"Mmmm." Jeremy's high-pitched hum grated on my nerves. "Just like that. You're ready to give in."

"Not to you." Roan wrenched the mic from his hands. "To them."

Roan turned to the crowd. "These shits don't matter. They're HC trash. Outsiders," he said. "But you're Bedlamites. This is our town. You're my people. If there's anything the Bedlam-born respect, it's a revolt."

The boos ceased. Jeering quieted. They were listening.

"If you don't want the Bedlam Boys running things anymore, we'll step aside, and I speak for all of us." Roan turned his head up to me—a brief glance, then he flicked away. "We were trying to help. It may not seem that way, but we didn't want to make you hate us or put you under another tyrant's rule. We for fuck sure didn't want to cause the destruction of Bedlam. Our town ripped in half for some company in Hunter's Crest to make a few bucks." He shook his head. "It makes me sick."

"It's not about money," Jeremy snapped. "This is our home now too. We want the best for it, and that's not living in fear of the consequences of pissing off your corrupt mommies and daddies. No one buys that the mayor, judge, sheriff, dean, and billionaire don't know what you guys do. They let you because if we're in your control, we're in theirs!"

Nods went through the crowd.

"The only way to be free of them is to build a new town. Put an end to their corruption."

"Yeah."

"Exactly."

"Bullshit," Roan said, blunt as a hammer. "*This is the only way. We don't have a choice.* You know which kind of fear-mongering thick-head uses phrases like that? You."

Jeremy launched at him and had to be held back.

"The only way isn't chopping our town in half and giving power to a bunch of guys we don't know," he said. "The only way is for you all to choose."

The half-drunk and high crowd exchanged looks.

"You choose who you'll trust with the future of this town. If it's Jeremy, his old man, and the Crows, the Bedlam Boys will back off. If it's us, we'll do what we always do and protect Bedlam from anyone who tries to fuck with us. It's your choice," he repeated, "but ask yourself this before you consider the Crows."

Roan pointed up. "Are these the people who'll lead you to the promised land free of corruption, violence, and extortion?"

Paris opened her mouth. "What's he—?"

The television screen went black mid-orgy. In a blink it came back on, picture whirling as the cameraperson righted themselves.

"Get 'em," a voice rang out of the speakers. "Fuck him up."

The shot cleared on a fight. Half a dozen guys stomped some mewling soul into the ground. They had crows on their necks.

"Shut that off," Jeremy cried. "Turn it off!"

He, Gael, and the others ran at the television cords. They found ten guys in their path.

I hardly paid attention to the unfolding fight below. The video was still going.

Photos of Gael passing baggies and collecting money in a drug deal. A video of Jonah at a party with a girl who was obviously barely conscious. They sloppily made out and then the video shifted. We watched him carry her passed out into a bedroom, and shut the door.

"I didn't do anything!" Jonah shouted. "I swear. I let her sleep it off. I didn't touch her!"

The video wasn't over. Bentley's handsome face filled the screen. The angle zoomed out, revealing a profile page on the website *Honeycomb*. I didn't know much about these things, but living on a farm wasn't living on the wrong side of a rock. Even I knew that site was for young men and women looking for sugar mamas. Sex for cash and gifts. Straight up.

Photos of them stealing things. Videos of them bullying people. Bentley making out with a woman old enough to be his mother in the back seat of a car.

"Turn it off!"

The Crows were throwing themselves at the barricade. Why? The damage was done.

"Ellis here wants to talk about corruption," Roan said. "He's got a lot to say about us and the shit we do. We grew up together. Y'all have known us for too long for me to pretend we're angels. We're not," he stated. "But we're also not this. And even the Bedlam Boys know there are lines you don't cross.

"Unlike Micah and Jeremy Ellis."

The picture faded out again and was replaced with a very naked Micah Ellis, winking seductively at the camera with his hand around his cock.

"I'm an open-minded person," Roan said. "Normally, I wouldn't judge a guy for what gets his blood flowing south. Unless we're talking about underaged kids... and his own brother. These were on Jeremy's phone."

"What?!"

I clapped my hand over my mouth, heaving as the photos got more explicit. Screenshots of their conversation appeared to drive the last of the Chinese food from my stomach.

Micah: No one can find out about us.

Me: It's too dangerous. What if we're caught?

Micah: I don't care. I want you inside me. There's nothing you can't do to me.

"That's not— I didn't—"

"Holy shit," someone said. Half the people watching looked as sickened as I felt. The other half hadn't picked their jaws off the floor. "He's your brother, man. That's not right."

"It's not true! That's fucking disgusting!" Spittle flew from Jeremy's mouth. "He didn't send those to me."

"Easy to prove," Roan said. "Make a liar out of me right now and show us your phone."

"Piece of shit!" Jeremy stopped trying to get at the television, and flew at Roan. I'd seen the Crow lose his temper. This was the first I saw him lose control.

Three half-naked guys got in his way. The tide was turning. I felt the shift. Undoubtedly the Crows did too.

"What the hell is that reaction?" Roan asked. "Just show us your phone."

"Yeah, show us."

"Give up the phone."

"Hand it over."

"Fine." Jeremy flung it at Roan's head. He caught it one-handed. "There's nothing on my phone. He did not send those texts to me. This is a trick," he barked at the crowd. "He got those pics from the same bitch faking profiles and doctoring vid—"

"Here it is," Roan said loud and clear. He handed the phone to someone next to him. "Tell everyone who those texts are between. Am I lying?"

The guy scrolled up, grimacing with each second looking at that screen. "Micah and Jeremy. It's true. He's fucking his own brother."

"It's not true! You're lying," Jeremy bellowed, eyes wild. "There's nothing on my— You! You did this, Banks."

"Me?" Roan repeated. "Yeah, it was me who did it. I exposed you all for what you are."

"You put those texts and nudes on my phone."

"So, you finally admit they're on the phone."

"Son of a—" The guys strained to hold him. He was fighting hard to get at Roan. "It's all lies!"

"All of it? The videos of you jumping guys five on one? Bentley's side business? Gael's coke-dealing? It's all made up?"

"No, the—"

"No," Roan said. "Exactly."

He turned his back in spite of Jeremy's hand breaking through the barricade, swiping desperately at his back.

"You know us," Roan broadcasted inside, outside, and to all of Bay Avenue. "And now you know the real Crows. It's your choice.

The Bedlam Boys won't stop you making it. But I'll tell you what I choose: Bedlam now."

"Bedlam forever!"

Roan flicked up to me again. "We're outta here, gorgeous. Come catch a ride."

My feet carried me down of their own power. Roan actually hoisted me up and carried me on his back. I secured my arms around his neck, resting my cheek on the back of his head as we left the struggling Crows behind. They had so many guys pinning them down, I was shocked they could breathe under there. But Jeremy was getting more than enough oxygen to say what he had to say.

"You're dead, Banks. I promise you, you'll pay for this. Do you hear me?! You're dead!"

Roan kicked the door shut, trotting down the drive. We were almost to Legend's when I found my voice.

"You faked those pictures, didn't you?"

"The cougars, drugs, beatdowns? Nah. Mom hired a private security team to patrol campus. I made the case the Crows were a problem waiting to happen, and they stopped denying it after the Homer Green brawl. All that stuff is just what they found on the surface. Who knows what they'll find with some more digging?

"As for Micah and Jeremy. Yeah, that shit's fake. Micah sent those texts and nudes to me. I made it look like they went to him. Not as hard as you're thinking."

My jaw worked. "You're sleeping with Micah?"

"That's what you got out of that?"

"Are you?" I repeated. Bitter, hot jealousy tightened the hold on his neck.

"Oooh," he rasped. "We can give autoerotic asphyxiation a try. I'd definitely be into that. But no." Roan smacked my ass. "He sent me nudes. We exchanged dirty texts. Hasn't gone farther than that.

"I've been working on Micah since I met him. I noticed him checking out my ass, and figured this could be used to my advantage at some point. Turning him and Jeremy into brother-fuckers was truly inspired. Some of my best work."

I leaned over him to catch his eye. "You've been flirting and sexting this guy for weeks, but you never planned to sleep with him?"

Roan heaved a sigh. "Still stuck on that. No, love. That guy isn't my type. He's submissive, and stupid. He came after my boys, my boyfriend, and my town, and thinks he'll get laid for it. While you, are perfection. You pegged those guys as double-talking shits from jump street. And you're still trying to choke me out."

I eased up on my hold, resting my chin on his shoulder. Roan said things like this so easily. But he also lied without remorse, stoked rage as entertainment, manipulated me for his masochistic pleasure, and made a target out of Micah Ellis before he gave him a reason.

I was beginning to understand the Bedlam Boys and what drove them. But not Roan Banks. Maybe not ever.

"I can prove it," he said. "Micah Ellis is currently blindfolded and chained to the bed at Hollow Grove Motel, waiting for me to deliver a ravishing that will never come. The maid will find him eventually," he dismissed.

"If you were planning this the whole time, why didn't you say something?" I asked. "Legend's stress has resulted in marks on my ass."

"And your cum on his sheets." Roan put me down in front of Legend's house. "I didn't say because I didn't know if I'd pull it off. My guards were dragging on going outside their job description. Micah was waffling on sneaking away from the party to meet me. And the whole thing hinged on Elise coming through with switching Jeremy's phone and switching it back at the right time."

"Elise? My Elise?"

He winked. "She was mine first. Oops." Roan unballed my fists. "There goes that jealousy."

"Why would Elise help you put his brother's nudes on Jeremy's phone?"

"She was crushing on that Jonah guy till I showed her the video. Jonah's lying about keeping his hands to himself. The girl he raped reported him to the police, but they never made it to trial. His family is loaded too. Elise was more than happy to help me take down the Crows after that."

"Wow." I dropped on the curb, stretching my legs over the pavement. Roan joined me—arm brushing against mine and staying there. "People underestimate you, don't they? And you make them regret it."

"That's the state of living, de Souza. People are always going to underestimate you. If you don't set out to prove them wrong, you accept the little they make of you. In which case you deserve it."

I hummed. "Some wisdom buried in there. I guess I have some people to prove wrong too."

"What other choice did you have?"

"What choice did you have?" I asked. "This war over Bedlam. Trust me, I don't want to see this town split up, but I don't understand why this is the Bedlam Boys' fight?"

Roan looked over his shoulder, glancing at the house. "What's Cairo told you?"

"Why does everyone assume he's told me anything?"

He inclined his head. "You're right. He's not about to give up information while you're still hiding things from us."

"I'm not..." The expression on his face silenced me.

"The therapists say I have a reckless disregard for authority and a penchant for making trouble that borders on pathological. I guess it was always going to be me who gave it up."

"What are you talking about?" I rested a hand on top of his.

"We all answer to someone, Rainey. Even the Bedlam Boys. The collections. Axel Verlice. Keeping the town in line," he said. "It's our job—along with keeping Ellis and Foundry out of Bedlam by any means necessary."

"Your job? Who gave it to you?"

"That's not nearly as important as why."

Roan turned his hand up, tickling my palm with stroking fingers. In the middle of a serious conversation and my skin was tingling.

He grasped my chin, trapping me in his light, burning pools. "Bedlam has a secret. One that's been protected for over a hundred years, and somehow Steven Ellis knows. His company, Foundry, is buying land and houses all over town.

"Other than Legend, we didn't have the money to stop them. That's why we started taking collections. Everyone pays—no excuses. They bitch and moan, but the money does go back into the town. We use it to counter Foundry's offers and stop people from selling. We put it into improving and protecting the place, so no one buys into their speeches that there's a better life waiting for them in Beckerburg or Hunter's Crest.

"Shits like Axel Verlice. The last thing we need are federal investigations and national news sites throwing a spotlight on this town. Can't have them looking into the lengths we've gone to keep Bedlam whole, or finding out why. If the world finds out the truth about us, Bedlam as we know it will disappear."

"So, you killed to protect it? Verlice wasn't the first, was he?"

"No, he wasn't," Roan said. "But every one of them was more soulless than the last. The first name was a pedophile who kidnapped little boys on their way home from school. The fifth was manufacturing bombs out on his farm. One of his targets was the university."

"Goodness," I breathed.

"I didn't shed any tears getting rid of them, and Arsenio's taken the job on solo without complaints. He enjoyed that part of our work more than the rest, and they say you should love what you do."

I shivered. We were having such a casual conversation about extortion and murder.

"Do we disgust you?" The question wasn't asked in anger. Roan sounded curious.

After a pause, I shook my head. "No, you don't."

"So, that's where we are. Foundry wants the town, but all the land they've bought doesn't make it happen. It's still subject to city code for as long as it's a part of Bedlam."

"So he sent his sons to handle part two," I finished. "Forming their own town, so they can do whatever the hell they want with it. I know. I figured it out when I was with Jeremy today. But what's the secret? What are they after?"

Roan smiled. "A hundred years, I'm not going to be the one who gives it up, even to a cute little spy like you."

"I would never—"

He kissed me, swallowing my heated protest. I moaned as he nibbled my bottom lip, stealing entrance and teasing my tongue to play with his.

"Again, we're having the wrong conversation. Obviously, they already know the only information worth hiding. It's too late for that. There's only stopping them now."

"Which you'll do," I whispered, "by any means necessary."

"Yes."

"But why? Is all of this worth it?"

"You tell me, Rainey. Home," he said. "The only place you know. Where you feel safe. Where you've made your memories and learned your history. Where your friends live with their parents, and your parents, and your parents' friends. The one that has the donut shop you love, next to the smoothie place you hate. Where you kissed your first boyfriend on the walk home from school. Is fighting for a place like that worth it?"

I didn't speak for a long time, and when I did, the calm had taken me.

"My grandmother was murdered."

Roan's brows snapped together. The only reaction he allowed himself. He didn't speak, waiting for me to go on.

"She had a heart problem and collapsed in the field one day. The doctor said it was natural causes, but I knew it wasn't true. For weeks—months—before her death, she was harassed by a company called AgriProspects. They were on her to sell, offering more and more money, but she refused. De Souza Farm had been in the family for generations. She wouldn't give it up for millions.

"When she suddenly died without a will, I knew— I *knew* they were behind it," I gritted. "Gran wanted to leave the farm to me and Ivy. She said as much to them a thousand times, so why wouldn't she have made a will?

"I pushed for the sheriff to investigate. He couldn't see past the old lady with a heart problem passing out in the sun. Open and shut. I harassed him every day for weeks to do a full autopsy, till he finally told his officers to throw me out if I walked into the station again. Desperate, I drained my first-year tuition money to pay for an independent autopsy."

"What did it say?" he asked when I didn't go on.

"Murder. My grandmother was poisoned with digitalis. It caused a fatal heart attack." I dropped my head, breathing hard. "With no will and the farm in debt, ownership reverted to the bank, and they sold to AgriProspects."

"Fucking bastards."

Perfect sentiment but I couldn't stop to acknowledge it. I started my story, I had to keep going.

"I forced into the station with the autopsy report, throwing my proof in his face, and ordering him to arrest Andrew Clein. The man who flew in and set up in town with the express instructions to get our farm.

"Sheriff Jack took the report and said he'd investigate—re-open the case."

"But he didn't."

"No." My voice shook, but not with grief. "He destroyed it. Buried it. I don't know. All I know is when I came back asking if he'd made an arrest, he pretended he didn't have a clue what I was talking about. I tried to call the medical examiner, and the phone rang and rang. No one has seen her since. He covered it up, Roan. My gran was murdered... and the sheriff covered it up."

"I see why you hate him. Actually, hate's too small a word, isn't it?"

"The word doesn't exist yet," I spat. "I was furious. Raging. I took it out on everything and everyone, and then one day, I snapped. I burst into AgriProspects' headquarters, found Andrew Clein, and beat him with his own phone. It took five people to pull me off him. After, I was sent *away* to a hospital. Doc Nash looked after me. He prescribed me pills when I got home that put me in a permanent fog.

"I can't remember exactly what happened during that time except for one clear memory." My tear dripped down my nose, painting my lips. "The night Ivy left."

"What happened?"

"Who knows what set it off. Something small that spiraled out of control too quickly. She said we'd done everything we could do, and now we had to forgive and move on. It was *what Gran would want*. She'd hate seeing me as I was, broken and consumed with revenge.

"I called her a traitor. Said she didn't love Gran or she would've been right there next to me, beating Clein's head in. I said she always wanted to get off the farm and leave Bedlam, and she was glad Gran's dead because nothing was holding her back. Then I told her to get the fuck out, and she did. It was a t-terrible thing to say." My chest heaved, rocking in sobs. "I wish I could blame the drugs, but that was all me, cutting down the only family I had left."

I swiped a rough hand across my face. "It was a while before I decided to get off the pills and work on getting my life back. In that time, AgriProspects ran out of money and never got their hands on the farm. I've been trying to get it, and Ivy, back ever since." I met his gaze. "Why did I tell you all of this? Because that's your answer, Roan. Anything. I'd do anything to protect my home and my family."

Roan laced our fingers together. "Are you in this with us, Rain?"

I thought of Jeremy. Foundry. Sheriff Jack. The Letter Man.

"Whatever it takes."

Chapter Fourteen

I held Roan's words in my ears on the ride to the farm the next day. I don't remember the excuse I gave the guys to get away. It was all a fog, and Cairo and the guys were distracted dissecting every word Roan said at the party the night before.

None of them were too pleased at Roan's promise to back off if they chose the Crows and Bedlam 2.0. He reminded them the best way to control the masses was to give them the illusion of choice and control. Look at the entire American government system.

Roan was an interesting guy with thought processes that I'd bet would dizzy me trying to figure out, but he struck the first serious strike against the Crows. I'd go so far to say he won the war. The Bedlam Boys were not good guys, and this experience would not reform them or make them nicer.

That said, they also weren't drug dealers, rapists, boy toys, or roving campus for random people to beat up just because. If someone was out there trying to make a case for the Crows, I wished I was there to see him sweat and stumble over his argument.

The sun had set by the time Frankie's fill-in dropped me off. It was her day off and she was entitled to a fun, relaxing night with her kids. It was me destined for nightmares.

I walked past the creaking farm sign, wishing I came earlier. It was eight o'clock. Four hours before the Letter Man was supposed to arrive. Plenty of time for me to set myself up to lie in wait.

I went inside the barn, set up a few hay bales, and picked up my bow. It was an odd feeling having it in my hands. I expected it to be tainted. That every time I closed on the wood, Scott Cavendish would pop in my mind.

No. All I saw was Gran and Ivy. Long summer days practicing while they cheered me on. Gran correcting my stance. Ivy tickling me so I'd miss and send it sailing through the trees.

I chose archery because it's about patience—and being badass. Finding your stance. Feeling your shot. Breathing, aiming, focusing, and letting nothing steal your center.

Archery was my calm place. With a bow in my hand, I was always strong enough to prove them wrong.

I stayed inside the barn, practicing my shot, reading on my phone, and eating handfuls of the snacks tucked in my bag.

Jeremy flashed on my screen forty-five minutes in.

"Hello?"

"Everything," he growled. "I want to know everything about them, where they're staying, and how to get to them now!"

I flinched, drawing the phone away. Not that I blamed him. Paris told me earlier that they shouted the guy out of his own house screaming *brother-fucker*. Coke-peddler, manwhore, and rapist were the words du jour gifted Gael, Jonah, and Bentley.

They locked themselves in their rooms and called the cops to bust up the party. She said the officers brought the Crows in too over the huge quantities of controlled substances sitting in bowls all over the place.

Jeremy Ellis was not having a good day.

"Is your brother okay?" I asked.

His tone sharpened. "Why are you asking about him? Everything Banks said was bullshit. He planted that stuff on my phone. I never—"

"Whoa, slow down. I promise it was an innocent question."

"He's fine," he snapped. "Roan was smart getting him out of the way, so he couldn't say who those texts were really for. Now we have to be smart."

We.

"Where are they staying? I see the lights on at St. James's place. Are they all there or just him?"

"I—"

"Doesn't matter, we need him too," Jeremy said mostly to himself. "Banks and St. James are fucking. Alright, tonight you'll get us into the mansion, de Souza. Once we have him, Roan will come running. Then—"

"I'm going to stop you there," I said, sitting against the hay bale. "I'm out of town tonight, so I won't be able to get you in anywhere. Even if I could, I won't be a part of this."

"We have a fucking deal!"

"For me to give you verifiable information in connection with construction or fighting your development in my town. That's it. I'm not obligated to become an accessory in the revenge plot I hear brewing in your head. Don't throw the contract at me again. I'm prelaw, Ellis. I know what it says."

"But Banks—"

"I know what he did and I know how I'd feel if it was me. That's why I won't help you. You should not make decisions right now. Cool down, and then call me."

I ended the call and silenced my phone to the others. This wasn't about Jeremy's vendetta.

It was about mine.

The clock ticked down to nine. Ten. Eleven.

Dusting off my hands, I checked outside one last time. No one had arrived or approached the house. Once you got to the trees, you had cover. Otherwise, it was clear sightlines on the twelve acres of farm.

I'll go inside and stand with my back facing the fireplace. I'll have them if they come through the front door or from the back. If they attack me, I defend myself.

A simple plan without holes—except when I considered the possibility all they wanted to do was talk.

The question invaded my mind on the walk across the green.

If the death of Axel Verlice changed things and now they were willing to tell me the truth, how would the night end? Do I hope to get him to the police station with a bow and arrow at his back? Do I entertain the thought of killing him, and ending his threat to my life once and for all?

I climbed the porch steps. *If I find out his name and who he is, I'll let him go. The police can mull over the dilemma of killing him in a shootout instead of—*

Pausing, I lit on a small, black envelope lying where the welcome mat used to be. When did he leave this? He couldn't have come while I was in the barn, so it must've been sometime before then and after Jeremy and I drove away from the farm.

I picked it off the porch.

Did you really think you could fool me, bitch?

I'll give it to you, you had me going for a second. That just makes the betrayal worse.

You're not who I thought you were.

You're a fake. A mistake. A waste.

Damaged garbage left in the discard bin, and you're too stupid to know it.

I bet you still don't know who's on the other side of this door.

I read the note once, twice, five times, palms slickening with each one.

Did I think I could fool him? What did that mean? Did he know about Verlice?

How?

Doesn't matter. I dropped the note, leveling my bow. I didn't know who was on the other side of this door, but I was going to find out.

"This ends tonight."

Grabbing the knob, I let the door swing open. It parted a crack and stopped.

"Hmm."

Planting my feet on the wood, I kicked it in, running inside.

"Hmmm!"

Bella screamed at me—eyes bulging and wetness soaking her gag. She thrashed in the chair she was tied to, banging the legs on the rotted living room floor.

"Hmm!"

Snap.

A tiny missile streaked across my vision. The arrow sunk in Bella's chest, and it wasn't mine.

"Bella!" I ran to her, dropping my bow and arrow at her feet. "Oh, Bella, no. No, I'm sorry. I'm so sorry."

Her head dropped to her chest, the light fading from her eyes.

"No!" I screamed. My lung ripped with sobs.

It was a trap. A trap that I sprung.

The Letter Man found out I didn't kill Axel, and my friend paid the price as promised.

"No, p-please. Bella, no. It's my fault. This is all my fault."

I scrabbled at her zip ties. She couldn't be dead. I'd get her to the hospital. I'd call—

Eeeee.

A door creaking open pierced my mania. The Letter Man was here. He came to watch the final moments with Jennifer, and now my destruction.

A polished black shoe stepped over the threshold.

Snatching up my bow, I whipped around, a keening wail breaking the silence, and released my arrow.

It stuck in the wood—centimeters from his face.

"Ouch." He stepped out of the shadows, and every beautiful inch of Cairo Sharpe revealed. "Not the welcome I was hoping for."

If you'd like to read the next book in the series, Riot Kings, click here.[1]

---

1. _http://mybook.to/RiotKings_

Keep In Touch

Join Ruby's mailing list for news, teasers, and more:
https://www.subscribepage.com/rubyvincentpage
Join Ruby's Facebook Reader Group:
https://bit.ly/3bNuCOq

ABOUT THE AUTHOR

Ruby Vincent is a published author with many novels under her belt but after taking a fun foray into contemporary romance, she found her love of saucy heroines, bold alpha males, and weaving a tale where both get their happy ever after.